THE MOUSEPROOF KITCHEN

Saira Shah

THE
MOUSEPROOF
KITCHEN

HARVILL SECKER
LONDON

Published by Harvill Secker 2013

4 6 8 10 9 7 5 3

First published in Great Britain in 2013 by
HARVILL SECKER
Random House
20 Vauxhall Bridge Road
London SW1V 2SA

www.vintage-books.co.uk

Addresses for companies within The Random House Group Limited
can be found at: www.randomhouse.co.uk/offices.htm

The Random House Group Limited Reg. No. 954009

A CIP catalogue record for this book is available from the British Library

ISBN 9781846556630

The Random House Group Limited supports the Forest Stewardship
Council® (FSC®), the leading international forest-certification organisation.
Our books carrying the FSC label are printed on FSC®-certified paper.
FSC is the only forest-certification scheme supported by the leading
environmental organisations, including Greenpeace.
Our paper procurement policy can be found at
www.randomhouse.co.uk/environment

Typeset in Fournier MT by Palimpsest Book Production Limited
Falkirk, Stirlingshire
Printed and bound in Great Britain by Clays Ltd, St Ives PLC

To my mother, for my life,
To Scott, for my happiness,
And to Ailsa, for my lesson in love,
I dedicate this book.

December

PAINS COME AND GO. I'm riding on waves of them. They're nothing like the orgasmic surges described by my New Age birthing teacher, but not nearly as bad as my mother's tales of pelvises split in two and of women losing their minds from the agony.

I suck on gas and air and long for the sight of Tobias's face, full of roguish charm, as if he's inviting the world to share a secret joke with him. When my mother first met him, she told him he looked like a friendly horse. It's a comparison he loathes, but I cherish it.

And finally here he is, his dark curls even more rumpled than usual, typically late for the birth of his first child. His haggard look is, I'm sure, simply due to an ill-timed night out on the town. Tobias is not one of nature's worriers.

I have a moment to be amazed that I knew, from the instant I first clapped eyes on him, lurching about on a dance floor, that he'd be the ideal mate and father of my child. Then the midwife gives a kind of cry: the baby's heartbeat is lost. Suddenly the room is full of lights. People in blue scrubs and masks rush in and Tobias, unshaven and sweaty, is weeping and saying, 'Yes, yes, anything, but please just make sure they're

3

all right,' and I'm being given an epidural and then I'm having an emergency Caesarean.

They put up a screen and there's a strange rummaging as if somebody is moving furniture around in my insides. I'm drifting in and out of consciousness. And the drugs – the natural ones of childbirth and the sock-off powerful ones of the doctors – must be great because, after nine months of obsessive fretting, I am calm and Zen.

More pulling.

Somebody shouts: 'It's a girl!'

There's a loud wail: my baby is here; she is behind the screen. They won't let me see her. Seconds seem like hours. I'm wild to see her.

Finally, finally, they bring her to me.

She has wide grey eyes, one a bit smaller than the other. I have a second of thinking: she's no beauty. Then a switch flips in my head and the nicest and best possible kind of face is a little lopsided with slightly uneven grey eyes. Tobias appears at my side, weeping uncontrollably with happiness, pride and love.

It's a perfect moment. One of those rare times when you wouldn't prefer to be anywhere else, doing anything else. Where past and future melt away and there's only now.

They're wheeling me out on a trolley with the baby tucked beside me and I'm thinking: this is just the beginning. She's mine now, forever, to have and to hold. We've got all our lives to get to know each other. I feel a flood of love like I've never felt before; it extends to the baby, to Tobias, and radiates out from there, enough of it to light up a whole world.

I've seen a couple of newborn babies before, and each of them was quivering, as if in awe at the splendour of this world and the immensity of the distance it had travelled. But not this one. My own little space traveller is perfectly serene.

Then she starts to twitch. I catch a glimpse of a clenched fist shaking. Tobias shouts: 'She's having a fit!'

I have a moment of primitive, instinctive dread: Oh no, it's over for this baby. Our normal lives are over.

Once again it looks like a scene from *ER* as doctors in scrubs rush in.

—

If you want things to happen, you have to plan them. I know this: I'm a chef. To make a béchamel sauce, for instance, you need the right ingredients in the right proportions, at the right time. Measuring, timing, taking care. These are all things I'm naturally good at. Tobias doesn't understand this. He's a musician who composes music for TV documentaries and for short films. He rarely gets up before noon and leaves papers, clothes and the debris of his life strewn everywhere. He is chronically, horrendously late. He says he likes to be open to fate and this he calls creativity. I'm creative too. But you can't be sloppy with a sauce. It just doesn't work.

Since we first started trying to have a baby, I've planned every last detail.

I know:

That our daughter will be called Freya (a nice old-fashioned name with a slightly New Age meaning: a Nordic goddess of love and birth) even though Tobias says I'll have to trample over his dead body first.

That our child will have broad shoulders and lovely long

legs like him and straight light brown hair and wide serious eyes like me.

That she will have his *joie de vivre* and my flair for organisation.

That as soon as we get out of this hospital we're going to sell up and move to the South of France.

So now, as I lie here in a morphine-induced haze, doctors in scrubs whisking Tobias and the baby away can't faze me. My plans are laid. All will be well.

In southern France, the sun will shine kindly on us. The people will be friendly. Our daughter will grow up bilingual, sophisticated, safe from paedophiles. She won't need the latest Nike trainers; she won't eat junk.

I can see the house we'll buy: a cottage in Provence with roses and hollyhocks around the door, a field of lavender dotted with olive trees, the deep blue of the sea merging into the azure sky.

I'm floating over that sea, that field and that house and somewhere, far below, Tobias, the baby and I are living our perfect lives.

———

I'm awake early.

I want to be with my baby.

It's hard to tell if the morphine's worn off. I'm still woozy and confused, but I'm also in terrible pain.

It's a huge effort to recall where I am: in the small private room the hospital keeps for what it calls special cases. Beside me somebody is snoring, reminding me that Tobias has been allowed to sleep here on a camp bed. On the table next to me my mobile phone starts ringing. I fumble and reject the call.

Seconds later a text bleeps: *neews?* My best friend, Martha. Architect. Single. Too busy to spell. I have no idea what to say to her. I push it away.

A nurse arrives to take out my catheter. I'd no idea I had one; I seem to have become divorced from my body at some forgotten point in the past eight hours or so. Pulling it out hurts like hell. I vomit, whether from the pain or the morphine I don't know.

'Are you all right?' asks the nurse and I've no idea of the answer but I need to get up so I lie that I'm fine and ask, 'Could I please go and see my baby now?'

Our daughter is in a darkened room full of machines going *tapocca tapocca tapocca* and babies the size of your fist in transparent incubators under strange coloured lights. I recognise her immediately: she's twice the size of any other baby in the room. She's in an open cot, curled foetally, with a tube coming out of her nose and a wire taped to her foot. Above her head there's a bank of monitors breaking her down into a series of vital signs: heartbeat, oxygen saturation, respiration.

A nurse explains that this is NICU, the neonatal intensive care unit, and shows us how to pick her up without disturbing all the tubes.

I hold my baby for the first time. She's perfect: rosebud mouth, elfin ears, eyes tight shut. I can count her eyelashes – four on her right eyelid, five on her left – and imagine them growing secretly in my womb like seeds under the earth.

'She's beautiful,' says a doctor. I feel a flood of pleasure and pride.

'If you don't mind, Mum, I'm going to use some special instruments to look at the back of baby's eyes.'

He takes her gently out of my arms and I watch her, utterly

7

absorbed in her, as they examine her. I listen to him discussing her with his registrar. It's very technical. They seem to be finding lots of things they're looking out for. I feel pleased for them, pleased with the baby.

After a long time he turns to me. 'She has a coloboma in her left eye. The retina of that eye hasn't formed properly and the iris of the same eye hasn't formed completely either.'

I look at him uncomprehendingly, because surely anybody can see that this little being is just as she should be.

'Your child will not be blind,' he says. 'She may be a bit long-sighted.'

The switch in my head flips and the lopsided face morphs again: a dear little kooky girl with outsize spectacles peering long-sightedly out of a school photo. And that in its turn becomes the sweetest and best of all possible faces.

'We'll have to have an MRI scan to be certain,' says the doctor, 'but it seems that her problems could be rooted in the brain.'

But I'm not paying attention because, as he hands my baby back to me, happy nurturing hormones are flooding into me, overwhelming me. They're at odds with all these awful words and far more powerful than any of them.

'It feels as if I'm falling through the floor,' says Tobias.

I wish he could share my certainty that everything is going to be fine. I smile at him. But he just snorts in exasperation and addresses himself to the doctor.

'I have quite a few questions.' He looks at me significantly. 'I wonder if we could have a chat outside.'

I watch the door close behind them, thinking how oddly they're all behaving. I only need to hold my baby in my arms to know that she's perfect.

The baby opens her eyes. The pupil in the left eye is elongated like a teardrop as if it's been painted in black ink that has smeared. I don't know any other babies with a pupil like that. It seems special. We look at each other solemnly for a moment then her eyelids close again.

I try to latch her onto my breast. She makes a puckering motion, delicately picking the very tip of my nipple between her lips. I feel a gentle pulling, a goldfish tug.

'She won't get any milk out like that, Mum,' says a brisk NHS nurse. 'She needs to open wide, like a little birdie.'

The baby and I have been working on it together. Now and again her mouth suddenly yawns, shark-like, and she makes a comical Benny Hill lunge at my breast. But something keeps going wrong; she snakes her body backwards away from me, her face contorts with fury and she flails with her fists. Then her warm body curls back into my chest and the morphine haze engulfs me again.

'Watch out, Mum, you're falling asleep,' says the nurse. 'You might drop baby.'

'I'm not tired.'

'You'd better go back to bed.'

But why would I want to be anywhere but here with her?

So here I am, clutching my baby in this room full of blinking lights and Perspex cots, thinking how strange it is that none of the babies ever seem to cry, as if the machines have taken their voices away.

—

'How was the labour, dear?' My mother's voice on the telephone sounds a long way away.

'Not too bad. The Caesarean was OK. The baby —'

'I was forty-eight hours with you. They wouldn't do a Caesarean in those days unless you were practically dead.'

'The baby —' I say.

'I don't know how I bore it. Still, in those days at least they let you smoke between contractions.'

I'm aware of a dim, familiar feeling of annoyance creeping through the haze. My mother has never once done or said a single thing the way she's supposed to, the way other mothers do.

Perhaps because she was an older mother for her day (I'm thirty-eight and she's sixty-nine) we've got nothing in common. She got married at twenty and has never worked in her life; I put off having a family for the sake of my career. While lesser mortals are forced to adapt to our changing world, my mother requires that everybody else adapts to hers. For years, she's got away with living in what she calls her ivory tower, a sort of idyllic 1950s landscape from which – glamorous and helpless – she issues orders. Any inconvenient truths are blotted out. During forty-eight years of marriage my late, saintly father helped maintain her on her pedestal, putting up with her capricious behaviour and actually trying to carry out her impossible commands. The smoking she stopped – abruptly and without comment – when he died of throat cancer nine months ago. In all other respects, she's worse than ever.

'Mother, I've got something important to tell you,' I say.

'I know, dear, I know. Tobias called me from the hospital when they were sewing you up. A little girl! Lovely! But exhausting. In my day, they put all the babies right away from the mothers, in a special room. It was much better. Nowadays they seem to insist on having them with you all the time.'

I try again. 'The baby —'

'Will you still be bringing her down here for Christmas?'

'Mother, I don't think so.'

'Perhaps I should come and stay with you over Christmas instead.'

'I'm not sure that's such a great idea. Mother, the thing about the baby is –'

'Actually, I need to stay here anyway.'

I can tell from her voice that something I've said has hurt her feelings, but my concentration is slipping away again.

'I can't possibly leave the bird table. Darling, I'm so sorry to mention it right now but could you call the RSPB and get them to take their starlings out of my garden? Since your father died there's nobody else I can ask and I'm afraid the poor tits will starve to death.'

Her voice rolls on and, as I drift off again, I wonder how much of what I consider my own personality is just a reaction to hers. Am I disciplined, tactful, conventional and in control simply because she's not?

'I'll come up tomorrow for the day,' I hear her say, 'just to take a peek at her, nothing more. Don't worry – I won't intrude. Stay in hospital as long as you can and get a nice rest. Don't lift a finger. Let the staff do everything.'

—

Time in the intensive care unit passes in a blur of gentle sounds and the soft coloured lights of flickering monitors. Everything is muted, as if we're in an aquarium. My baby and I wrap ourselves together and time flows by.

A nurse arrives to tell us that we're waiting. We're in the queue for an MRI scan.

The baby is still failing to suck properly. I've got no milk yet, just a minute quantity of colostrum. I manage to wrestle out a single, thick drop of the stuff. It looks like condensed milk.

I put a bit of it on my finger and press it to my baby's lips. Her face takes on an expression of epicurean ecstasy. This is her birthright, the food she should be getting, not glucose solution through a tube in her nose.

Tobias doesn't like the unit. He's absent more and more, slipping off to answer the voicemails and concerned text messages that are beginning to trickle in from the outside world. Our friends are starting to wonder why we haven't surfaced by now with a healthy baby.

'Martha keeps calling on my phone,' he says. 'Do you want to speak to her?'

'Tell her I'll call her later.'

I don't want to talk to anybody. Not even Tobias. But he's insisting we take a little time to ourselves, pushing me in a wheelchair down to the hospital lobby.

From her Perspex cot, three floors above, the baby calls to me.

'We should go up and see her now,' I say.

'OK. In a minute. Just let me buy a paper.' Tobias is a master of procrastination. He spends an age chatting to the woman at the cash desk in WH Smith.

The baby calls again. *Where are you?*

Tobias pushes me through the corridor at glacial speed. Every minute or so, he lets go of the wheelchair to gaze at the NHS posters on the walls. 'If you smoke, so does your baby.' 'Diabetes kills. Ask your doctor for a test today.' Flyblown and faded, they all fascinate him.

Come to me. I need you.

He spots a trestle table decorated with tinsel and covered with hand-knitted toys. A banner says: 'The Friends of St Ethel's Christmas Bazaar. Please give generously.' It's staffed by two old ladies. My heart sinks; Tobias loves old ladies and they love him.

Soon they're clucking over him. 'Your baby is in intensive care? Oh, don't worry, you poor dear. This is an excellent hospital. They say it has the best neonatal department in the country. They send babies here from all over England.'

'You've got some lovely things for sale here,' says Tobias.

'We do all the blankets for the babies on the special care ward too. And little bootees for the premature ones. And hats. They can't regulate their temperature, you know.'

'Do you think our baby would prefer a bunny or a tiger?'

The baby calls again, more urgently.

I don't want either of them. I want you.

'Tobias, please let's go now.'

His face, usually so open, is clenched and tight. 'I need a coffee. Won't you come too? We could have a little more time together.'

But my baby has a gravitational field. It draws me to her. 'I don't feel like coffee,' I say. 'I think I should go to her. I'm sure I can walk if I take it slowly.'

Tobias looks at me as if he wants to say something more. He thrusts a knitted bunny rabbit into my hand. 'Take this up to her. I'll join you later.'

I hobble down the corridor. Standing for the lift is an aching agony.

The doors creak open. The lift is jammed. I edge myself into a tiny space, trying to guard my stitches from the crowd. The door swings shut. I feel my baby pull me safely up the shaft towards her.

—

'The MRI people have had a cancellation,' says a nurse. 'You can go for a scan, as long as you arrive within forty minutes.'

'Hurry up, Anna,' says Tobias. 'If we miss our slot we'll never find out what's wrong with her.'

But first the baby has to be changed into clothes without metal studs because the MRI is a gigantic magnetic field. Then there are fifteen pages of forms to be filled in. Finally all the tubes and monitors have to be transferred to an industrial-looking hospital pram.

A junior nurse on her first day at the hospital pushes the baby and Tobias pushes my wheelchair. At high speed. Every time we hit a bump I yelp in pain, a reminder that less than twenty-four hours ago I had major abdominal surgery.

Somewhere, rushing down endless corridors, getting lost and being misdirected, Tobias says: 'I've been thinking. Freya might be a good name after all. She *is* like a little goddess, and I suppose she's a triumph of birth against the odds.'

And from that I finally understand that he's really, really worried. That he hopes giving her the name I want and he detests might appease the gods and somehow make it all right after all.

We've already overcome enough obstacles to have this baby.

I wanted her last March. That meant conceiving in June, so I booked leave on the right date (I worked at the Michelin-starred Cri de la Fourchette in the West End six nights a week), planned a menu for an idyllic evening in (lobster bisque with a bottle of Meursault) and awaited results.

Nothing.

I'm not the type of person to be daunted by a minor setback, so I simply rescheduled. But before I knew it, the months were rolling by. Until finally I broke down and sobbed on Tobias's shoulder. 'I don't want to die childless and of course it's all your fault because you dithered about having children for so long and perhaps my mother's right and I've stretched my womb by having a career.' And Tobias hugged me and said all the right things and we made love and, just as I was about to despair, the miracle happened.

Life didn't get any easier. My boss, Nicolas Chevalier, the celebrity chef, made it clear he doesn't believe pregnancy and motherhood are compatible with the fourteen-hour day, six-day week he requires from his subordinates. Luckily Tobias was having a good run of composing so I handed in my notice, kicked out my tenants and sold the bachelor flat I bought years ago. Which means that, after paying off the mortgage, there's now a nice lump sum in the bank for a deposit on a place in France.

It's taken months to persuade Tobias to give up his comfortable London life and move to Provence. The less said about the whole traumatic process the better. But the good thing about composing is that, really, you can do it anywhere. As for me, I trained at the Lecomte Institute of the Culinary Arts in Aix-en-Provence, where I was something of a star pupil. I'm pretty confident I can persuade René Lecomte to take me onto his staff. I'm working on him.

Meanwhile, I've been scouring property websites and watching episodes of *A Place in the Sun* until I've driven Tobias nearly mad. I've even managed to hire a property scout. She's called Sandrine and is quietly efficient. So far everything she's suggested has been impossibly expensive, but one day soon, I know, she'll find us the perfect house on a pauper's budget.

While Freya is being scanned, we go to the cafe for some soup. I still have no sense that this is really happening to us. It's like being in a film, watching ourselves running around on the screen.

15

Surely, in a few hours we'll be given the all-clear. We'll breathe a huge sigh of relief, pick up the phone and notify the world that our first baby has been born. Later we'll laugh and tell our friends about the ridiculous fuss that was made about her in the first few days of her life. 'It gave us a hell of a shock, I can tell you.' And we'll take time to remember all the poor children and their parents who haven't been so lucky.

At the table next to us is a little girl with cerebral palsy. She's pretty but thin and strange, wearing a neck brace. Her movements are jerky and stiff-backed. She's playing a game with her father: she keeps lunging towards him; each time she lunges he reaches out his arms for her and kisses her on the forehead.

What would it be like to care for a child like that? Neither of them seems particularly unhappy. They're just getting on with a normal day, which happens to be taking place in a hospital cafe.

Tobias sees me looking. 'I signed up for a child but I don't think I signed up for that,' he says.

'Oh no,' I agree. 'But Freya is so lovely. I have a good feeling about everything. I can't believe there's anything wrong with her. I'm sure the MRI will show that there's just been a mistake.'

—

'Your daughter is suffering from . . . well, she has a lot of things wrong in her brain but the main one is called polymicrogyria.' The consultant who's brought us the MRI results has arrived at the unit flanked by two nurses. A bad sign. 'The gyria are the grooves on the brain. Poly means many. You'd think having too many grooves on the brain is a good thing but in your baby's case the grooves are very shallow.'

He's hurrying on as if he hopes this will be enough for us and he'll be able to get the hell out of here. 'As a baby, she isn't required to do much. Her motor coordination and so on aren't expected to be very good. But as she grows older, there will be more demands on her. She's likely to suffer from some degree of mental and physical disability.'

The last dregs of morphine and my childbirth happy hormones vanish down an invisible plughole and are replaced by a surge of adrenalin.

'Mental and physical disability, what does that mean?' I ask.

'It's impossible to say at this stage. Some children with very bad MRI results do quite well, while others not so bad on paper actually do worse.'

'What does quite well mean, actually?'

'There's a spectrum.'

'Well, all right, where does this spectrum begin and where does it end?'

'It's very hard to predict.'

'What caused it?' asks Tobias.

'We'll do some genetic tests – we may find a faulty gene. Either a spontaneous mutation or a recessive gene that both of you happen to carry. Or it could have been an infection in early pregnancy that wasn't picked up.'

'But I had every scan going,' I say.

'This sort of thing is difficult to spot on ultrasound. Look, this doesn't mean she can't have a long life, or a happy one. She can be very contented. Don't try to look ahead.'

One of the nurses squeezes my arm.

'There's a quiet room next door. Would you like us to wheel her there, so you can spend a bit of time alone with your baby?'

They show us into a little room done up in a parody of a living room – it has two armchairs and a table with a prominent box of Kleenex. In the corner is a tinsel Christmas tree that's starting to sag.

Tobias and I sit with the baby, crying. When I look at her battered, lopsided face I wonder what long, terrible journey she's had, to arrive so damaged, so incomplete. She gets her wide-spaced eyes from me but unlike mine they slope down. She looks like a Tibetan monk.

Perhaps, as a very old monk, she was watching a sunset spread out against the Tibetan mountains when she was called to Nirvana. But she begged for one more life here on earth, so most of her soul came rushing to me while a part of her brain was left behind, as shattered and fragmented as the sunset on the clouds.

                                   —

Tobias wants me to eat some supper. 'I know you're looking after the baby, but I'm going to look after you.' He looks fierce and protective in a way I'm not used to. But what's he protecting me against? Against myself? Against her?

We sit in the hospital canteen and toy with unidentifiable brown stew. The adrenalin has disappeared and we feel shaky and weak. There's a ringing in my ears as if I've been living in the hammering of a building site for hours and days and the echo of it is still with me.

We sit for a while, letting our stew get cold, holding hands and looking into each other's eyes. We used to do this when we first fell in love.

My mobile phone vibrates against the plastic tabletop. I've

turned the ringer off. There are six missed calls from Martha and another text: *NEWWS???* I can't face trying to reply.

We struggle back to our room.

'I can offer you a luxury NHS camp bed if you'd like,' says Tobias.

We both climb onto his camp bed. For a few minutes we hold onto each other as if we're about to burst apart and fly away. I sob on his shoulder and let his strength seep into me. Little by little, some of the hammering in my head quietens down.

'We mustn't let this break us,' I whisper.

I feel his arms tighten around me. 'You've got to understand something,' says Tobias. 'I'm not going to be able to love this baby.'

'For God's sake, that's an awful thing to say!' Even as I rebuke him, some part of me is guiltily grateful to him for voicing fears I don't dare to admit to, even to myself.

'We don't know how bad it is yet,' I say. 'It might be very . . . mild. Do you remember the woman who used to live opposite? Her boy had Down's syndrome. She had a bit of a struggle but he did brilliantly. He even managed to get a job in Tesco's.'

'I don't want to sacrifice my life so my daughter can get a job in Tesco's.'

'But she's so lovely.'

'She's lovely,' says Tobias firmly. 'But she's a life sentence.'

In the early hours, there's a hammering and the door bursts open. Two or three people in scrubs turn on the light, with a cry: 'Your baby has had another seizure.'

19

I have an instant of fear – or is it hope? – that she's dead.

'Do we have your permission to give her baby medicine?'

Blearily, we say yes and I ask if I should come along. I'm relieved when they say no.

We sink back into sleep. I dream I'm shouting at the top of my lungs: 'I do not want to be the mother of a disabled child!' But nobody can hear.

—

Freya's very sleepy this morning. I'm sitting holding her, feeling her curl into my body, enjoying the goldfish pull of her lips against my breast. It's as if our two bodies are still joined, as if they can't yet break the habit of being of one flesh. My own body responds to hers: my breathing changes, my happy hormones return, the hospital unit fades away. This becomes the nicest place in the world because we're in it together.

The baby and I have been drifting away to France.

Our cheerful cottage is pretty and neat. She's learning to crawl on clean stone flags with the sun piercing through the doorway while I toss a salad of fresh crisp lettuce and our own tomatoes. Tobias comes in from the garden and she crawls towards him. He scoops her up and kisses her. She stares into our laughing faces and crows with delight. I pop her into her high chair, put on her bib and deftly feed her a vegetable purée I've concocted. One day she starts to walk on her chubby legs and before we know it she's getting into everything. Tobias and I sip crisp white wine and have lunch parties for our friends and chuckle over the funny things she says, until suddenly we're sending her off for her first day at school and it's only then we finally understand that the doom-mongering doctors have got it all spectacularly wrong.

'Are you all right?'

A plump motherly woman is gazing at me.

'Mum — are you all right?'

'I'm not sure I am all right,' I say. 'I've been told that my daughter will be disabled — but nobody will tell me how badly and none of the doctors talk English, only gobbledegook, and nobody calls me anything but Mum.'

The woman smiles. 'Well, I'm one of the doctors. My name is Dr Fernandez. I won't call you Mum any more. And I'll try not to talk gobbledegook.'

I nod. She looks kind and sensible, somebody you'd be able to safely confide in. Like the mother I'd like to have rather than the flaky, attention-grabbing one I've got.

'As you know, Freya had another seizure early this morning. We've given her a large dose of a drug called phenobarbitone. A seizure is a bit like an electrical storm in the brain and what we do is put the patient to sleep. To allow the system to reboot, if you like.'

'I think I've heard of phenobarbitone,' says Tobias, drifting in. 'Wasn't it the drug that Marilyn Monroe over-dosed on?'

'Well, yes. Pheno is a 1950s barbiturate. I'm afraid that we don't have very good drugs for young babies. Drugs companies don't want to run trials on newborns for ethical reasons. But pheno works and we've been using it safely for years. It's made Freya very sleepy.'

'We're planning to move to France,' I blurt. Tobias looks at me in surprise; we haven't discussed France since Freya was born.

If Dr Fernandez, too, is surprised, she doesn't show it. 'I'll look into it. We should be able to coordinate with the French system if that's what you want to do,' she says as if this is the most reasonable request in the world. There's a brief pause. 'We can also arrange for you to see a counsellor if you need to.'

'No thanks,' says Tobias quickly and I too shake my head. The thought of raking over how we feel right now is too horrible to contemplate. 'If only we knew how bad she's going to be,' I say. 'Nobody seems to want to commit.'

'You're going to have a lot of visits from a lot of specialists, who'll talk a lot of jargon,' she says. 'They'll all want to cover their backs. I'll promise you this: I'll find out what they really think, and I'll give you an absolutely honest report.'

'Thank you.'

'Is there anything else for now?'

'We're not sure we'll be able to cope with her,' says Tobias boldly, looking sidelong at me.

'That's perfectly normal. There's no law that says you have to cope.'

I'm not a needy person, but I find myself latching on to Dr Fernandez the way a drowning person in a turbulent sea might cling to a reassuringly solid log.

Up until now I've assumed that we're required to cope.

———

'Tell you what,' says Tobias, 'let's head for the airport, take a flight to Brazil and not leave a forwarding address.' The sheer relief of the image makes us both laugh.

'But if we did that,' I say, 'we'd end up like Graham Greene characters, propping up a bar in Tahiti or somewhere.'

'That sounds like a pretty good option to me,' says Tobias.

'We can't though. My mother's arriving any minute.'

'That's all I need, your mother.'

'The trouble is, I want this meeting to go well but I know she'll end up saying something so crass that I'll rise to it.'

'Anna,' says Tobias. 'I'm no fan of your mother, God knows, but you two are like a couple of cats in a sack. You've got to understand that she's so overexcited about her first grandchild, she'll be saying or doing anything she can think of to get your attention.'

I snort. 'Overexcited? She couldn't care less about Freya. She keeps ranting on about her bird table.'

'Don't ever listen to a single word your mother *says*,' advises Tobias, 'think about what she *means*.'

———

My mother shows up at the hospital wearing a long green cloak with a tippet biting its own tail at the neck and a fox-fur hat. She knows I oppose killing for fur. Sometimes I think she does it just to embarrass me.

'For goodness' sake, you just can't wear that kind of thing in London nowadays.'

'Nonsense. What's wrong with a fur hat? I'll have you know this was a present from your precious father, whom you always preferred to me.'

And there we are, at daggers drawn again, as easy as that.

I make an immense effort. 'I'm glad you came.'

'Well, of course I came. What makes you think I wouldn't come? This is my first grandchild after all. Look, I brought her a present.' Wafts of Chanel No. 19 drift down the corridor

as she scrabbles in a Harrods bag and produces a battered teddy.
'Do you recognise it?'

'It's my teddy.'

'Yes, dear, I've been keeping it all these years for when you have a daughter of your own.'

'Mother, I have something I need to tell you.'

'What is it, dear? When can I see the little pet?'

'Mother, just once in your life, *listen* to me. Her brain didn't develop properly. It's very rare, apparently. Nobody knows why it happened. They didn't pick it up on any of the scans. She'll be physically and mentally handicapped.'

Just for a moment, her face falls. Then her expression snaps into the implacable rejecting-all-bad-news mask I know so well.

'Doctors always exaggerate, dear,' she says. 'I'm sure they'll find out there's just been some silly mistake.'

Why am I so angry with her and her Chanel and her Harrods bag and her comfortable life that's never been challenged?

'There's been no mistake. They've run a lot of tests.' My voice is more brutal than I meant it to be.

And then the impossible happens; my tough, indomitable mother starts to weep. I'm used to her using tears as a weapon but never – not even when my father died – have I seen her give way to genuine, uncontrolled grief. Somehow the sight of her sadness shocks me more than anything so far, as if here is external proof that we've genuinely been struck by tragedy. I try to give her a hug but she pulls away. She hates me to think she's vulnerable.

I have a glimmer of understanding that Tobias may be right. That the make-up, the Chanel No. 19, the fox hat, the tippet, might not be for the hospital, or even for me, but for her granddaughter. And who knows, maybe all the talk about her bird table might have been sheer nerves because, while her relationship with me might have irrevocably broken down, she now has a chance to begin a new one with Freya.

I say gently: 'I'll take you to see her.'

My mother sniffs. 'Well, all right. I don't mind going to see her, certainly not.' She dries her eyes and tucks the teddy bear hastily back into the Harrods bag.

—

Freya curls her hands like baby ferns against her face and makes adorable squeaking noises of protest as I pick her up. She moulds herself into my shoulder without waking.

'Here, take her.' Trying to pull her off my shoulder is like pulling away moss.

My mother is staring, fascinated, at an invisible point just above my shoulder. I can't tell if she's avoiding looking at the baby or if she simply doesn't know where or how she should look.

'I wanted you to be here with me when I give Freya her first bath,' I say.

'Well, well,' says my mother, darting a quick, almost hungry look at her granddaughter and instantly averting her gaze. 'This is a very modern ward. Very up to date.'

Bathing at the unit, it turns out, involves a complex NHS ritual, full of rules. A care assistant must bring you the bath. She also provides two buckets, a yellow one for waste water and a white one for clean water. We're allowed to fill the bath ourselves. My mother stands immobile, watching me as I do so.

'I haven't bathed a baby before,' I coax. 'Could you please show me how?'

My mother begins to move, infinitesimally slowly, towards Freya. Just as she reaches her, a nurse appears.

'Not like that, Mum,' she says to me, ignoring my mother. 'This is how we bath baby.'

I might have known the NHS would have a drill for this bit too. But by now I'm just watching, entranced. It's quite obvious that Freya is interested and delighted with this new sensation. She stretches out her froggy legs, cocks her head and goes quite calm. I splash warm water over her and she gives a couple of solemn kicks.

'That's enough now, Mum, you don't want to leave baby in a cold bath,' says the nurse.

I wrap her in a towel and ask my mother if she'd like to hold Freya.

'Yes. I don't mind holding her,' says my mother, adding in a penetrating voice: 'Even though she's the way she is.'

I hand Freya to her. 'She's a pretty little thing, don't you think?' I say.

My mother isn't prepared to go that far. 'So,' she asks, 'is she brain-dead then?'

'She's not brain-dead. In fact, we don't really know yet how her brain abnormalities will affect her. All sorts of specialists will have to look at her and then we're going to get another briefing to try to put the whole picture together.'

'But she'll be handicapped?'

'They seem certain that she will be.'

'And do you plan to look after her yourself?'

'I'm not sure we have any other choice.'

'And Tobias?'

'He says he doesn't want to take her home.'

There's a long pause.

'I read in the papers the other day about a single mother throwing herself off Vauxhall Bridge with her handicapped child,' says my mother slowly. 'She couldn't stand the strain.'

'Well, we're a long way from that.'

She looks narrowly at Freya and her lips purse. 'This baby had better realise that she can't have everything her own way,' she says.

———

A parade of doctors has taken turns to visit us to examine Freya. It's as if word's got out that there's an interesting case on the ward and every imaginable discipline wants to get in on the act.

They've put electrodes on her scalp and measured her brain waves. They've looked into her eyes. They've listened to her heart. They've taken blood from her feet and, when they've exhausted the veins there, from her legs as well.

'. . . Your daughter has what we call a shopping list of brain malformations. In addition to polymicrogyria, the corpus callosum, which connects the two halves of her brain, is entirely absent and the cerebellum is extremely small . . .'

'. . . These sorts of cases are usually associated with a genetic disorder or a first-trimester insult. Have either of your families any history of babies dying?'

'. . . The left sylvian fissure is abnormally deep and there is a pronounced lack of grey and white matter . . .'

'. . . Her symptoms don't match any known genetic disorder. But there's always the possibility of a recessive gene – some faulty coding that both of you carry . . .'

'. . . I have made a special study of these cases for seventeen years. This is the most extensive example of a neuronal migration disorder that I have yet seen . . .'

It's not as if we revel in each piece of bad news, just that we've stopped being horrified. As if some deep, primitive part of us concerned with survival is saying: 'This baby is fucked anyway. Let her be so utterly completely fucked that nobody, but nobody, will blame us for bailing out on her.'

'She's gone from being a precious baby to being a special baby,' Tobias jokes bitterly, and we share a guilty laugh together when the doctors can't hear.

———

Days and nights roll into each other. I've lost all sense of how long we've been here. I haven't been off the hospital grounds since Freya was born. Although I've been discharged we've been allowed to carry on staying in a parents' room next to the unit. I'm aware that Christmas comes and goes but it means nothing to me. It feels as if my world has shrunk, and family, friends, my home, my job, even Tobias have been sucked away from me in a giant vacuum cleaner. All that's left is this.

In the middle of it all, Martha arrives uninvited. She's frightened, and furious. 'Why the hell didn't you answer my calls? Why didn't you want me to come and see you? You can't do this kind of thing alone.'

'I didn't know what to tell you. We still don't know how bad it's going to be.'

Martha and I have been inseparable since primary school. She's always looked out for me; she always speaks her mind. 'You look a wreck,' she says. 'How's the Caesarean?'

'Fine, actually,' I say, surprised to be reminded of it.

'Really? Doesn't hurt at all?'

'It hurt like hell at first. But now it's completely numb. Or maybe that's just how I am right now.'

'Hmm.'

I attempt a feeble joke: 'All those women who complain about surgery should try the my-baby-has-no-brain recovery programme.' But Martha doesn't seem to think it's funny; she gives me a sharp look.

She's brought practical presents – a five-pack of sleepsuits and an acrylic, easy-wash blanket – which I immediately put to use. Tobias cracks open the half-bottle of champagne I've got hidden in my baby bag. I'd imagined the pair of us drinking this bottle together secretly straight after the birth, overflowing with happiness and love. He pours it into three plastic cups from the water cooler.

'Let me have a cuddle,' says Martha.

I take Freya, soggy with sleep, out of her cot. As she snuggles up against Martha's chest, I feel a stab of ridiculous jealousy; my child is in another woman's arms.

My mobile phone rings. I've still not been picking up calls. I don't want to have to tell people about Freya; I have no idea what to say to them. But this is Sandrine, who can't possibly be calling to find out how we are. On impulse, I take it, make a significant gesture to Tobias and put her on speakerphone.

'Have you found something? A property?' I ask quickly, to forestall any questions from her.

'Well, yes . . . bigger than you asked for but I think it might be worth considering . . . a farmhouse, on top of a hill. And it's in your budget.'

It's so good to be talking about normal things again. About anything that isn't to do with the baby.

'It's not quite where you wanted,' she says.

'Not too far outside Aix though?'

She sounds flustered. 'Er . . . not in Provence. In the Languedoc. The part near Spain. Look, Anna, what you want in Provence for the budget you have, it's not realistic. Languedoc is much better value. I think it might be worth a visit. You could go there in the new year.'

'We've got to be close to Aix-en-Provence. I'm hoping to get a teaching job there. Besides, I'm not sure we can go anywhere at the moment.'

'The baby?' asks Sandrine.

'Yes.'

'It's arrived! Oh, the little precious one!' I've known her for six months now, but I've only ever seen Sandrine in a business jacket, armed with a clipboard. I don't recognise this soft, cooing person. Babies are the gatekeepers to a secret club. They open up aspects of people they usually keep hidden.

'We're still in hospital,' I say.

'Is everything all right?'

'Sandrine, she isn't . . . very well. The truth is, she's going to be handicapped.'

There's a long, long pause at the end of the line. When she speaks again, the cooing person has vanished and Sandrine is her old efficient self. 'Of course you can't visit France right now. And this property would not be suitable.'

I'm not listening. I'm thinking that I'm going to have to find a glib form of words to explain Freya because this is a conversation that's going to crop up a lot. I put down the phone.

'Never mind,' says Martha. She's been campaigning hard against my plans to move to France.

She takes me down to the canteen where she insists on paying for the sandwiches and coffee. I can sense her feeling of helplessness, the impossibility of making a gesture to match the horror of the situation. In spite of our long friendship, we don't have a template for this. It opens us up. We have to start writing the rules of engagement all over again.

'What are you planning to do?' she asks.

'Oh, Martha, what can I do? Mother love is supposed to be unconditional, but how many parents have to test that out? Three weeks ago I had all sorts of things in my life. Now . . . I could lose everything for her. I could lose Tobias. And if I give it all up for her and then she goes and dies on me . . . where will it leave me? Look, I know this sounds horribly selfish –'

'Not at all,' says Martha. But in the way she says it, I can tell I've gone too far. I've crossed some kind of forbidden line. Suddenly there's an undisclosed row, or struggle, taking place between us, as if I'm letting her down in some unspecified way.

'Martha, I don't even know if I can love this baby. I seem to be half joined to her physically at the moment, but will I be able to *love* her? And can I even afford to love her if I might have to give her up?'

'It's not my place to interfere,' she says. This is not a view she's ever taken before. Starting with the time Tommy McMahon tried to kiss me in year five, she's offered guidance on every boyfriend, every career move and every major decision in my life – and has got me out of the resultant scrapes when I've ignored her advice. But this is way out of her league.

'I have to go now,' she says, a shade too abruptly, and in her slight stiffness I can feel my best friend starting to slip away.

Dr Fernandez is late for our big meeting. The one where we're finally going to find out how bad Freya's condition really is.

My mind has been going back again and again to her telling me that doctors are apt to cover their backs. Like my mother, this part of me is still inclined to hope there's been some sort of mistake – or at least an exaggeration. I can't help deferring a final judgement until she gives us the honest verdict she's promised.

As Tobias and I wait in stilted silence, my head fills with a memory: I'm waiting tearfully after school in the hospital where our dear, ninety-three-year-old neighbour Fred has been admitted. When they finally let me see him, he tells me a rambling tale of a daughter he's never mentioned before. She went missing on a school canoe trip. Her body was never found. He starts to cry and I'm childishly stunned that there could exist in the world any sadness that still has the power to make a man cry at the age of ninety-three.

When Dr Fernandez and a nurse finally appear, she leads us back to the little fake living room and settles us in the comfortable chairs. She perches on the edge of the table and the nurse sits on a hard chair beside her. The box of Kleenex is still in its place.

'There is still a lot we don't know about the brain,' she begins. 'The temptation as medical professionals is to hedge our bets.'

She pauses, puts on the glasses that hang from a chain around her neck, and carries on slowly.

'However, you need an honest idea of what to expect. So I've gone to all the specialists and I've asked them their personal rather than their professional opinions. A picture has emerged with which I also agree.

32

'We believe that Freya will have grave difficulties with simple things. For instance, sitting, walking and speaking.'

There's silence for a moment. Her words hang in the air.

'She's floppy and that's a reflection of her brain function. In the future she could remain floppy but probably she'll stiffen up. That may bring physical problems. There's a risk of the lungs not being well expanded, which may result in complications like chest infections and pneumonia. She may have severe muscle contractions, although physiotherapy can help this. She could also have surgery to release her tendons at between five and ten years if she gets there.'

'How long is she likely to live?' asks Tobias.

'Difficult to say. The first thing you need to know is that, when the brain's wiring is as wrong as this, sometimes it just fizzes and goes out. Then, in the first two or three years, many kids like her get chest infections that may be fatal. However, Freya has a good gag reflex and currently no problems breathing. If she gets past infancy, she could outlive you.'

'Will she get worse?'

'In theory no: she has a static condition due to the structure of the brain. But, as she won't be very active, she could suffer from muscle wastage.'

'Do you think she'll have more fits?'

'The consultant neurologist thought it likely she would seize again.'

'Can we do anything to make her better?'

'My personal feeling is that probably nothing will help.'

'Will she have any level of interaction or awareness of her surroundings?'

'It's difficult to say. She feels comfort and pain.'

'Will she know us?' I blurt.

33

'Probably not,' she says. 'She needs somebody to meet her needs but it wouldn't really matter whether or not it was you.'

And I suddenly know that this is it – this is the thing that will always have the power to make me cry, even if I live to be ninety-three.

Then a shutter slams down and my mind sort of stalls, as if there's no space left in my brain to process emotions. I hear myself asking practical questions and Dr Fernandez answering them, her voice compassionate, but quite certain and firm.

'Will she need equipment?'

'Well, she might make it into a wheelchair but more likely she'll have to stay in bed. As she gets heavier you'll need a hoist to lift her. She may need artificial ventilation and feeding. She'll need twenty-four-hour care for the rest of her life.'

'What are our care options?'

'The system will provide some support for you to look after her in your own home.'

'Carers?'

'Well, no, I don't think so – resources are tight – but things like respite help and physiotherapy.'

'What about France?' I ask.

'People are always saying to me that they want to take their profoundly disabled child to Bolivia or somewhere,' Dr Fernandez says slowly. 'As a clinician, naturally I'm horrified. But as a human being . . . I think about it, and it makes very little difference really. If you want to go to France you should go. I can give you a stock of phenobarbitone to take with you in case she has another fit. You mustn't throw your lives away. She'll never be more portable than she is now. If she has a shorter life but a happier one, that's OK. If she gets a chest infection and you can't take her to hospital quickly enough, well . . .'

Another pause.

Tobias says: 'We've been wondering what would happen if we didn't take her home.'

'If you don't collect her from the hospital, social services will be obliged to arrange foster care.'

I begin to cry, in big, childish gulps.

Dr Fernandez puts an arm round me. 'Don't do anything drastic right now. Look, you need some time to get your heads clear. Freya needs to stay with us for a couple more weeks. Think of it as free childcare. Take a few days out. Go away somewhere and think it over. Stay well away from the hospital.'

As we're leaving Dr Fernandez says: 'I know this is a lot for you to take in. But we really need to discuss resuscitation policy. The law is very clear about what we can and can't do. There are some areas where we have leeway. What to do, for example, if she had a medical crisis. To what extent would you allow resuscitation?'

The nurse breaks in: 'It sounds silly, but those kinds of deaths can be quite nice. Calm and dignified and peaceful.'

The switch has flipped again in my head and this time I see a wasted body lying on a bed. Her eyes are fixed unseeingly on the ceiling. There's a tube in her stomach and a cylinder of oxygen by her side. She's breathing with the aid of a ventilator, in heavy mechanical breaths.

Tobias and I are lying together in our hospital bed. I can feel his tears, wet against my face.

'You've got to understand,' he says. 'If we kept this baby I couldn't afford to be a freelancer any more. I'd have to find a job somewhere. And we'd have to give up that idea about us moving to France, whatever Dr Fernandez might say. All our dreams. The whole of our lives. Everything we've worked for.'

I explore his face with my hand. 'You won't give up your freedom,' I say. 'We'll have our life in France, the recording studio, everything we dreamed about. We're a team. A small team. I won't let one part of that team take all the resources from the other two. I won't let her destroy us.' 'When Sandrine called today,' I carry on, 'it was so good to be treated like normal people again. I don't want us just to be about disability and illness and . . . compromise. And I'm not going to let it happen. Don't you remember me telling you about when I was sixteen?'

Tobias's face is buried in my hair. 'Mm, I think so. Tell me again.'

'Martha and I went on a school exchange. We'd hardly been out of Sevenoaks in our lives, and here we were in Paris. We couldn't afford to eat anywhere, so we drank a cup of coffee between us in a posh café in the sixth arrondissement and scoffed chocolate éclairs from paper bags hidden on our laps. A young man smiled at me, and he seemed so impossibly sophisticated. I said to Martha: "One day I'll live here, one day I'll speak French, one day I'll be sophisticated too."'

'Well, you did all that,' says Tobias. 'After all, you did get to study in Aix-en-Provence, remember?'

'I want to take you back there,' I say. 'You and Freya, both of you.' I feel him stiffen in my arms and add quickly: 'We don't have to decide right now. Freya can stay in hospital for the time being. Dr Fernandez said we should get away for a few days. I've been thinking about that property Sandrine's found in the Languedoc. I know it's not the right place but let's go and look at it. It's a good excuse for a trip. Just to clear our heads. I can pack a breast pump.'

'I may not love this baby but I do love you,' whispers Tobias. 'I don't want to lose you.'

'I promise you that I'll always choose you over her. I have to.' The words sound like a betrayal. I repeat: 'I have to.'

——

I can't get to sleep. I lie and listen to Tobias snoring. At 3 a.m. I give up and get out of bed. The neonatal intensive care unit is as warm and comforting as a womb.

I make straight for Freya's cot. Without being able to roll over or apparently to move, she's managed to snuggle her cheek up to her knitted bunny's soft feet. It floors me. Utterly, utterly. I sit by her bed and weep and I can't stop.

I must rescue this child. I must take her home. If she can find comfort in bunny's feet, isn't she worth my effort? Shouldn't she be getting her comfort from me? Haven't I failed her already, weeks into her life?

I bend down, slyly, guiltily, and kiss her on the top of her head. It feels wonderful.

I inhale the new baby smell, feel the softness of her hair. I begin to kiss her again and again, in deep refreshing draughts, as if I could drink her. Like a drug addict, I bend over for just one more kiss, and another.

January

L ES RAJONS SITS ON top of a hill, exposed to the winds on all sides. We're approaching on a road that winds up to it from the valley in a series of hairpin bends and through a narrow corridor of rock. The road passes the hamlet of Rieu, clinging for dear life to the side of the hill, and then seems to lose heart, turning into a mere piste of stone and dust.

It's hard to believe that twenty-four hours ago we were in the hospital. During the flight to Montpellier it was possible, even easy, to watch the clouds pass by and to pretend that we'd nothing better to do than take a trip to France. But the further we've got from London, the more I've begun to miss Freya: her little battered face, her wonky eyes, the odd little craning motion she makes with her head.

Our hire car turns one final bend of this impossible track and, suddenly, spectacularly, the house is before us. Now we can see that the property itself is a collection of farm buildings. Part of it is in ruins and the mottled grey stones have been pillaged to build other parts. The whole place seems to be springing out of and falling back into the rock in a perpetual state of growth and decay. There's a feeling of being open to the sky and quite close to it.

'It's wild,' says Tobias.

'It's creepy,' I say. 'And it's huge.'

'What a gateway!' says Tobias. 'Look at that stone pediment.'

'There's no wall,' I point out. 'The gateway's standing in the middle of nowhere.'

'The wall must have fallen down. It's like a Roman ruin.'

We're standing just inside the gateway in a courtyard formed by a horseshoe of stone buildings. Directly in front of us, the house stares back.

'Oh, I don't think so,' I say.

'Wow!' says Tobias.

'The door's half off its hinges. And the windows are broken.'

'Imagine owning all that!'

'There's something weird about this place. I can't keep track of it. As if the buildings are shifting about when I'm not looking.'

'Oh, now you're being fanciful,' says Tobias. 'It's perfectly simple. The house is straight in front of us. Quite standard French farmhouse, door in the middle. The two wings are outbuildings. Look, the whole of the wing on our right is one huge barn, attached to the house by that wooden bridge. The other wing's made up of a series of smaller buildings and another courtyard . . . no, hold on, that's not a courtyard, that's a ruin. The grass has grown over it so it looks like a walled garden . . .' He pauses, frowning. 'Or perhaps I'm wrong and it's a . . .'

We both stare, unable to process this place, grappling with it.

At one edge of the vast courtyard, unevenly supported on blocks, we make out a rusted shipping container. As we watch, a petite figure emerges from it. She waves and begins to walk towards us, her hair – straight and jet black – swinging jauntily behind her. In surprise, I think: she's a child. She can't be more than nineteen or twenty.

As she gets nearer, I see that her face is already roughened as if she's spent all her life being blown about by the elements. But the main thing I register is the intense greenness of her eyes in her nut-brown face.

'Hi, I'm Lizzy. The *gardienne*. Sandrine said you'd be coming. I'm supposed to show you around.' Her fluent French is laced with a thick drawl.

'You're American?'

'From California,' she says, lapsing into English.

'You live in the shipping container?'

'Yes.'

'Not in the house?'

She shudders. 'No way. Absolutely not in the house.'

'Have you been here for long?'

'I've been here nearly a year. In summer the container's too hot, so I sleep in a hammock under a tree.'

'How on earth did you wind up here?' asks Tobias.

'I managed to mooch enough for a plane ticket to Paris.'

'And from Paris?'

'I walked.'

'Walked? From Paris?'

'Yes. I didn't have the train fare. It took a few months. I was pretty skinny when I arrived.'

'But what did you eat?'

'Oh, sometimes people gave me food. Sometimes I found berries. And some lovely leaves.'

'But . . . weren't your family worried about you?'

'I have no family. Only a couple of foster ones. They won't miss me.'

43

'That's absolutely amazing,' says Tobias.

'I like to be free.'

'You're obviously an amazing woman.'

She reminds me of some creature but I can't put my finger on which one. A seal? The same fluid energy, but too slim. A cat? More vivacious than feline.

'We'll start in the barn,' says Lizzy. 'It's my favourite part.'

'What a wonderful roof.'

'It has the traditional round tiles of the Languedoc. Apparently, in the old days, they moulded them on the thighs of young girls.'

We enter via some sort of workshop and climb a rickety ladder that takes us up into a small room with straw on the floor. As I arrive I feel a rush of wings and just have time to see a barn owl, white and majestic, sweeping out of an open window.

Tobias gasps. 'That was incredible! He just sat trying to stare us out for a minute. Did you see him? Like an angry ghost.'

'They're a pair. They nest here,' says Lizzy. 'I try not to disturb them. Look through there.' She points to an opening the size of a small window and we take turns to peer through at the barn.

'It's enormous,' says Tobias.

'The floor needs mending,' I say.

'This would be a great recording studio,' says Tobias, adding cunningly: 'Anna, you could have your own restaurant here.'

'Don't be silly. It's miles from anywhere. How could I have a restaurant out here? Besides, it's got no door.'

'It's for storing hay,' says Lizzy. 'You can climb up into it through a trapdoor in the ceiling of the stables below.'

She leads us through a doorway onto the covered wooden bridge. There's a gully below us. 'It looks like a dry riverbed,' I say.

'Oh, it becomes quite a big river during the rain,' says Lizzy casually. 'We have plenty of storms. It's awesome to stand on this bridge and watch the lightning – balls of it flying over the house, daggers in the hills.'

'Cool,' says Tobias.

I look down from the bridge and wonder how it would feel up here in a raging storm with water hurtling below. The bridge itself is solid and pretty. It has the added attraction of being a reasonable size in this place where the enormous buildings seem to be trying to compete with the grandeur of elemental forces.

'It might be nice with a few geraniums in pots,' I say. Neither Tobias nor Lizzy is listening.

'I'll take you into the main house from here,' says Lizzy.

We cross the bridge and find ourselves in a large upstairs room with first-floor French windows secured by a cast-iron Juliet balcony.

'The master bedroom,' gloats Tobias. 'What a view!'

On the same floor are two other bedrooms, one with its floor almost rotted away, and a rudimentary bathroom.

'And now the attic,' says Lizzy. 'Be careful – some of the roof has fallen in.'

We take turns to climb a ladder on the first-floor landing. I perch on the top rung and find myself peering up at an expanse of sky through broken tiles. A collection of receptacles on the attic floor hints that the roof must have leaked for years before its final collapse.

When it's his turn, Tobias stays up on the ladder for a long time. His enthusiastic voice floats down to me.

'A cast-iron hip bath! That's a genuine antique! And look – are those bats up there?'

We go down a flight of oak stairs ('Quite grand ones,' says Tobias), through a hallway into the living room. I find myself staring at oak beams, ornamental plasterwork including a niche with a painted madonna, uneven flagstones, a fireplace and a crumpled art-deco stove.

'This was once a convent,' says Lizzy. 'The nuns did the plasterwork.'

Tobias disappears into the back of the house.

'Here's the kitchen! There's a bread oven! And a butler's sink!' he shouts from deep in the interior. 'There are quarry tiles on the floor. And wow – it's huge. There's a stone arch in the middle. You know, I don't think it would take too much work to turn this back into a liveable house.'

I feel tired and snappish. The beginnings of fear grip me. 'Are you crazy? It hasn't even got a roof.'

'The owner will repair the roof when the *compromis de vente* is signed,' says Lizzy. 'Also the windows and the front door.'

'Imagine growing up here,' says Tobias. 'What an adventure!'

'Nonsense. It's far too dangerous a place for a child –' I bite back the remains of my sentence. Two days ago I signed a document authorising the hospital to mark my baby's notes 'Do not resuscitate'. What worse danger could possibly lurk in this place than me?

Lizzy leads us out of the house into the series of buildings on the other side of the horseshoe. We inspect a wine press, flanked by two oak wine containers, each one the size of most people's living rooms.

Tobias climbs a set of rudimentary steps and peers into a container. 'It smells of grapes. And it's still covered in dried juice and bits of fruit.'

'There was a winery here once. It fell down but they saved the wine press and the barrels. There are vineyards lower down on the south slope of this hill. They once belonged to Les Rajons. But not now. There are a few grape vines here but the remaining land is really too high for wine.'

'How much land does it have now?'

'About ten hectares. Not so much. Most of it is *maquis*, scrubland.'

'I can't believe,' says Tobias, 'that you get so much for the money. We could organise a music festival.'

Lizzy leads us along a rocky track past a group of ruins, an orchard of stunted trees and a neat vegetable garden, ploughed up and bare. 'The potager,' she says. 'There's a tenant who has the right to cultivate one half of it until the end of the year. You can plant your vegetables in the other half.'

'Vegetables,' says Tobias. 'Of course, vegetables.'

'Would you like to see the best view?'

Even at this time of year, the hillside smells of thyme and lavender. You climb until the track dwindles and you're forced to scramble up a rocky slope. Finally you reach the top of a boulder with a panoramic view of the hills. You might as well be on the top of the world.

'You can see the Pyrenees on one side and all the way to the Mediterranean on the other,' says Lizzy. 'Isn't it beautiful? Wild and beautiful and free. I'd like to die here.'

Freya will never be able to see all this. When she gets older we won't even be able to get her wheelchair up here. If she makes it into a wheelchair.

'It's great,' says Tobias. 'Absolutely magical. The Pyrenees! The Mediterranean! You're a lucky woman, living here.'

'This is known as the *col* of the thirteen winds. Sometimes they come from one side, sometimes from another. It's very hard to predict. The locals say that when they blow just right they hit those rocks and make music, but I've never heard it.'

Lizzy turns her face into the wind and leans forward into it, her arms outstretched. 'Can you feel it? Can you feel the spiritual vibrations here? They're very strong.'

Tobias laughs good-naturedly and copies her. The wind is picking up enough for him to lean quite far forward. He and Lizzy begin to giggle, competing to see who dares lean the furthest. A wild look comes into her green eyes and her black hair flies out behind her.

An otter. That's the animal she reminds me of. Physical power in a lithe, mischievous form.

Lizzy gives a final wriggle to try to balance herself and collapses. Tobias is the victor. He's obviously pleased.

'Perhaps I do see what you mean about spiritual vibrations,' he says.

'So – are you going to buy this property? It's going cheap.'

'Yes, why is it so cheap?' I ask.

Lizzy shrugs. 'The *propriétaire* has spent years trying to do it up. Now he's growing old. He's losing hope and he needs some cash for his retirement. It's time for somebody younger to take over. So, will it be you?'

'Well,' I say, 'we have to discuss it of course but I'm not quite sure it's for us.'

Lizzy looks pleased. 'Plenty of couples take a look around and that's what they all say. Too big, too scary. But one day a man will come. He'll be alone. He'll fall in love with the property. And he'll marry me.'

She's priceless; I roll my eyes at Tobias. But he looks away. I swallow my amusement and take a deep breath of lavender and thyme. It feels like the last free breath I'll ever take.

'Anna, just look, really *look*, at the view,' pleads Tobias.

And truly, the view is spectacular. Purple hills rolling away from us in every direction. On the left, a line of snow-capped Pyrenees so distant that they seem to float on the horizon, softening and merging into the clouds. On the right, the far glint of the Mediterranean Sea.

We could give up the baby. We could walk away from it all and slip back into our old lives. In a few years I could become head chef at a London restaurant. Tobias might write an advertising jingle. We'd have comfortable lives. The pain won't burn forever at this intensity. All that will be left of Freya will be a dull ache.

But over here lies the glimmering of another way: a house in France, a baby with mental and physical disabilities to bring up, a future that slips into a haze of uncertainty as the mountains slip into the sky.

———

'I wanted to move to Provence.' Even to me, my voice sounds petulant.

'But Provence is too expensive,' says Tobias. 'We can't afford a broom cupboard in Provence. This is enormous, it's full of potential and it's really cheap.'

We're back in the hire car, trundling down the motorway towards Aix-en-Provence, the France I know – the France of

49

the azure sea and the beautiful people and the gentle olive groves.

Back in London, it seemed like a good idea to tag a visit to René onto this trip. But right now I'm just full of desperation to be with my little baby. I'm only surviving this day away because tomorrow night I'll be able to see her.

'What's the matter?' Tobias asks. 'Nervous about seeing René again?'

'Well, a bit,' I say. It seems easier.

'That's natural. You've got a lot riding on this.' There's another pause. 'He hasn't actually offered you a teaching job yet, has he?' probes Tobias.

'Well, he won't if we buy a place that's over three hours away.'

Tobias looks sulky. 'I'm just saying that you could consider other options. You're basing a lot of plans on something that might not happen . . .'

'It'll happen. René's like family. OK, for three years he hectored me mercilessly in the student kitchen, but he's always looked out for me. Nicolas might be successful, but he's just a machine; his life is completely empty apart from his work. René's managed to find a way to be a world-class chef *and* a fully rounded human being. He'll sort me out with something.'

⁓

Returning to the Lecomte Institute is like going back in time. I feel like my quaking seventeen-year-old self, walking up the immaculate stone steps to the imposing doorway for the first time.

Today, I don't need to ring the bell. The door swings open

and René is waiting to meet me. He's aged since I saw him last; the encroaching bald patch now covers most of his head. His skin is paler and he wheezes slightly as he kisses me three times.

'Where's Freya?' he demands.

'Still in the hospital. You know, I said in my email –'

'Well, doctors don't know everything.' He looks discountenanced for a moment; I'm not used to larger-than-life René being at a loss for words. 'Give me another kiss. Anna, it's good to see you.'

'René, you've put on weight again,' I say severely. 'Are you following that diet? You know what the doctors said, even if they *don't* know everything.'

'My father died of heart failure and so did my grandfather. Why should I break with family tradition? It's how you live *before* that counts.' He makes to kiss Tobias, then changes his mind and shakes hands in an elaborate parody of English manners. 'Come in – I have something special for dinner. But first I'll show you to your room.'

As we walk down the corridor he says: 'Anna, you look just the same as the day I met you.'

'René, how can you tell such lies? When I first met you I was seventeen.'

'That's right.' He turns to Tobias. 'Would you believe that this English schoolgirl writes me a letter demanding a scholarship at my institute? I thought I'd better take a look at her.'

Later, as we sit down to René's legendary bouillabaisse, he launches into a lecture, mainly for Tobias's benefit. I've heard it all before in the student kitchen.

'You need patience to make bouillabaisse. Above all, you mustn't boil the stock – the collagen from the fish bones and crab shells needs time to dissolve gently. You should start simmering them in the morning to achieve a perfect stock for dinner that night.' René savours his plateful for a moment. 'You should sweat a little when you eat this dish,' he says. 'You should be able to imagine the Marseilles fishermen's wives in olden times heating up huge vats of fish heads and crab shells on the shore while they waited for their husbands to come home. When they arrived, the men poured their catch straight into the broth. In those days the sea was permitted responsibility for the direction of the dish –'

'It's . . . quite something,' mumbles Tobias, but René waves his hand to signal that he isn't finished.

'Of course, nowadays, to make a proper *bouillabaisse de qualité*, we have imposed some rules on nature. To be correct, a bouillabaisse must contain at least four out of a list of six types of fish: scorpion fish, white scorpion fish, red mullet, skate, conger eel and John Dory. The *cigale de mer* and spiny lobster are tolerated, but only as extra ingredients. The fish must be added one by one, in order of thickness, so each is perfectly cooked.'

He points to a groaning platter of Mediterranean fish. 'And here, you see, is the result. It's the perfect example of a peasant dish that has been refined to haute cuisine status. Can you imagine that a dish so sublime could have had such humble beginnings?'

He puts down his cutlery, takes a satisfied sip of wine and I realise that this is the perfect moment to make my pitch.

'So – have you had time to think about the idea of my coming and teaching here?'

'I'm not saying it's impossible,' says René slowly, 'if you really need to.'

'I could teach the Brits who don't speak French,' I pursue.

'The Brits . . . I am sorry to say it, Anna, but your compatriots don't really want what I'm offering. They want a holiday with cooking thrown in, not to sweat for hours in a commercial kitchen. Besides, is this really what you want to do now that you're a mother?'

'Motherhood won't interfere with my work of course,' I say.

'Anna, I very much hope it *will*,' says René. 'Becoming a mother is an important thing, you must give it the time it deserves.'

'We've found a property we're interested in,' jumps in Tobias. 'But it's in the Languedoc. I've been trying to interest Anna in starting a restaurant there.'

I think I see René brightening.

'The whole idea's crazy,' I say quickly. 'The place is completely wild, on top of a mountain. There's nothing up there. It's not even near the sea.'

'Consider it, Anna. For what it's worth, I agree with Tobias. You need some space, a proper change.' I feel a paternal hand on my shoulder. 'When you wrote me that letter, all those years ago, I was impressed by your determination. That's why I gave you that scholarship. Anna, you can do anything you set your mind to.'

———

It's late when we get back to London. Far too late, insists Tobias, to call in at the hospital. I'm so tired and sore by now that I let myself be persuaded. It's nearly three weeks since Freya was born and we haven't spent a night at home since then – we've merely popped in once or twice to grab clean clothes and to pack a bag for France.

We feel like astronauts returning from a trip to space. It's weird that there's traffic on our street, people shopping in the late-night corner shop, that life has carried on as usual while we've been on some other planet. We pick up some fresh vegetables, bread and cheese and head home.

Our doormat is piled with presents and cards, in sedimentary layers. At the bottom are the early birds, the people who acted on the first news of a birth. Their cards are virulent pink, with cartoons of storks and cheery messages. 'Congratulations – a baby girl!' A bit higher up the pile, as our silence must have suggested that something was wrong, the tone is a bit less certain, but optimistic still: 'We trust that all is well at this joyful time . . .' At the top of the heap, the congratulations merge into confused condolence. 'Thinking of you.' 'I am so happy that . . .' 'I am so sorry that . . .' 'Your special gift . . .'

The task of answering them is too much. How can I write those notes?

'Thank you so much for your thoughtful gift. Unfortunately our daughter, Freya, will never even know who we are. I am therefore returning your item . . .'

Our flat is as we left it, clean and spruce. Apart from the empty Moses basket beside our bed and the changing station in the bathroom, it would be possible to pretend that we never dreamed of having a baby. Our old life is still here, for the taking.

'I'll go and see what I can sling together to eat,' I say. It's an excuse, of course. Squirrelled away in the freezer are neat Tupperware containers of the home-made nourishing meals I spent weeks preparing during my final nesting phase of pregnancy, when I feared that having a baby might leave me unable to carry out the slightest task.

But just now I need the familiar, reassuring ritual of cooking more than I need to rest my tired body. I'm not up to making anything fancy – just something simple, from fresh ingredients.

My kitchen is a self-contained world where everything runs exactly as it should. Its beating heart is a resplendent Lacanche Range cooker, the Aga of France, lovingly made by artisans in Burgundy. I saved up for two years to buy it. On butcher's hooks around it hangs my *batterie de cuisine*. Each pan and utensil has its own precise place. On the worktop next to the cooker are my chopping boards and knife blocks. My spices are on their rack in rows. If you blindfolded me, I could still pick out any one I wanted.

I pick up the soft steel kitchen knife my father gave me when I started training as a chef. Its boxwood handle fits reassuringly into my hand. Years of sharpening have worn its blade to a crescent, perfectly shaped to my own chopping style.

I begin to dice beetroot, enjoying the precise way my knife slices through the vegetable flesh, the quick glint of silver, the earthy smell of juices seeping into the wooden chopping board. I love watching a meal taking shape, assuming a personality of its own. This is my meditation.

I rub the beetroot in Ligurian olive oil, fresh rosemary and coarse sea salt and put it into the oven to roast. Next I begin on a sweet potato, treating it the same way but roasting it in a separate pan to keep the colours from mixing.

When a delicate smell begins to suffuse the kitchen, I prepare a platter of watercress. Its peppery flavour will pair well with the earthy sweetness of the beetroot and sweet potato. To top off, I add a sturdy Camembert. I've been craving this; I haven't eaten soft cheese in months.

I arrange the dice of beetroot, sweet potato and Camembert

attractively on the watercress, enjoying the contrast of colours. Then I slice a wholemeal loaf roughly, put everything on a hostess trolley and wheel it through to the living room. Who says TV dinners are difficult? I can't imagine why people buy them ready-made.

I find Tobias sitting on the sofa googling social services and babies with disabilities, looking frightened and grey.

'The social services websites are all about how they'll help you cope at home,' he says. 'I don't even want to *bring* her home.'

'There must be some websites by carers. Or support groups.'

'Take a look.'

The Internet, it seems, is full of scary sites by people who've given up their jobs to get to the head of the queue for a wheelchair. Parents who have to ventilate their kids every twenty minutes, working in shifts, day and night. People for whom the punishing schedule of caring leaves no time or energy for any other activity. For whom the rest of the family, other children, any form of pleasure, must take a back seat.

Whatever we do now, our old life has gone forever.

'Don't give up hope yet,' says Tobias. 'I'm still looking for the site that tells you how to leave your baby on the doorstep of the Sisters of the Annunciation at midnight.'

We both laugh. Our jokes have become like shared secrets. Nobody else will ever understand how we need black humour. The few people we've told about Freya have been stilted and uncomfortable with us, the way people are with the recently bereaved.

'We need to leave her at the hospital. Then social services will have to step in. They'll find a foster family. One who can really give her the care she needs. They pay them to do it.'

'What if they're mean to her?'

'They won't be mean to her. People who foster disabled children are, without exception, wonderful human beings.'

I sit on the sofa with the breast pump the hospital has lent me. Its suction is like an artificial mouth, hungry and regular, never satisfied.

'Look at this website, Anna. A residential home for babies and children. It looks fantastic.'

The home has a hydrotherapy pool and a sensory garden, full of smells and textures. The rooms are kitted out with the latest equipment. In the photographs, the residents sit by the pool in electric wheelchairs with high headrests to support their drooping necks.

'Tobias, that's a private home.' It costs over a hundred thousand pounds a year to keep a child in this place.

I look down at the breast pump. In the bottle there's a huge surprise. Instead of the tiny quantity I'm used to, it's filled to the brim with milk.

I feel happy and proud and grateful and terrified. Another proof that I'm a mother; another fetter to this baby.

⁓

When we get to the hospital, Freya's cot in NICU is empty. We panic. Has something terrible happened to her while we've been away?

It turns out she's just been moved down the corridor, to SCBU, the special care baby unit. It means she's getting stronger, further from danger. It's a step down in terms of care, a step closer to the time when she'll be ready for discharge.

Linda, one of the nurses, says they tried cup-feeding her and she 'ate and ate' last night, a whole cupful in one minute flat.

Alice, the physiotherapist, shows me some exercises I can do to help Freya's muscle tone. 'These cerebral palsy babies often have very slack muscles,' she says. Hairs prick on the back of my neck; it's the first time anybody's mentioned cerebral palsy.

'We don't like the term cerebral palsy,' says Dr Fernandez when I tackle her later. 'It isn't a proper medical condition, it's just an umbrella term for a collection of symptoms.' But it is a term we can understand and project a future into. Perhaps that's why the doctors don't like it. I think of a whole lifetime of doing pointless exercises that will never give back voluntary movement to my poor little child.

Martha's been phoning every day, trying to offer love and support. Sometimes I feel up to taking her calls, sometimes I don't.

I hold Freya's floppy, snuggly, drugged-up little body. The more I think about abandoning her, the harder and sadder it is to see her, to spend time with her. And the more precious every moment with her is.

Tobias and I have been taking photos of her – neither of us says anything, but we both know it's so we'll have a memento if we have to say goodbye. We've scooped up her little wristbands, every scrap of paper concerning her, and have put them in a file.

Dr Fernandez tells us that Freya will be ready for discharge in a week. 'We can hold onto her for an extra fortnight or so if you need more time to make a decision. But why not take her home and enjoy her? She's the most normal now she'll ever be. If you hadn't had a diagnosis at this point, you wouldn't have known anything was wrong with her.'

And that, in a nutshell, is the problem. It's easy to talk of abandoning her when she's not in front of us. Then she becomes the Freya of the doctors' reports – a bad bet by any yardstick. Loving her, investing in her, is a sure-fire route to pain and anguish.

Then we go – fresh from yet another awful medical meeting – and there is our beautiful, perfect daughter, smelling of new baby, her skin clear, her cheeks flushed, lying in her Perspex cot in SCBU. Reconciling the cataclysmic prognoses, the talk of a no-resuscitation policy with this vision of normality is not emotionally possible.

When I'm with her I feel the gravitational tug of motherhood. My breasts spurt milk, my stomach churns. I love this little person with a love that is purely physical. I want to scoop her up, rip her from her Perspex bassinet. Feed her and care for her, indulge her in all things and forget the doctors with their prognoses. Live life in the moment and pretend.

This is what terrifies Tobias: will I lose my marbles and insist on a life of martyrdom for both of us, tending a daughter who will never develop? Because it's growing increasingly clear to both of us that one day we'll have to let her go – either she'll die, or her physical needs will become so great that we'll not be able to care for her without sacrificing the rest of our existence, any hope of other children, happiness, rewarding work. There may never be a clear-cut moment when we fail to cope – but gradually she'll chisel away the bedrock of our lives.

I try to explain some of this to Dr Fernandez and she looks horrified. 'Of course, if you take Freya it should be because you love her, not because she's some sort of huge burden.'

It seems incredible to me that she believes there's a world in which Freya might *not* be a huge burden.

'But what if she dies? How will I bear it?'

'This is not me speaking as a professional, but can't you just have your baby time with her?' wheedles Dr Fernandez. 'Love her but keep a little bit back, so you can let her go if the time comes?'

———

Tobias and I are lying in our own bed. Neither of us can even imagine having sex at the moment but we need physical closeness. Despite our differences, we both feel as if we're falling in love with each other all over again. Perhaps it's all that love for our baby sloshing about with nowhere to go.

He's returning, inevitably, to the subject of Les Rajons.

'There's something . . . magical about the place. I can't get it out of my head. It's the kind of place you could invest your whole life in.'

'The owner grew old trying to do it up,' I say. 'Doesn't that tell you something? And you can't even hammer a nail in straight.'

But Tobias is carrying on as if he hasn't even heard me. 'If we sell this place as well as using your savings from your flat sale, then our mortgage on Les Rajons will be minuscule. It's a steal.'

'But how will we pay even a small mortgage if René doesn't give me a job?'

'Hey, my composing is doing brilliantly at the moment. My agent says directors are starting to ask for me by name. Think how much more work I'll be able to do in the peace and quiet out there. With no distractions. And anyway, it will only be until you can get your restaurant up and running. You're such a fantastic cook – I know it will be a success.'

For the first time since Freya was born, I see his youthful self, the man I fell in love with. Full of enthusiasm and ideas. The only man who can sweep my cautious nature aside and make me feel as wild and free as him.

'I still don't know,' I say. 'The baby —'

'We've got to face up to it, this baby is a bust. Make no mistake — she's not going anywhere. You might enjoy changing nappies now, but how about in five years' time? Or in ten? At least living over there I won't feel that changing nappies is all we've got to look forward to for the rest of our lives.'

I don't say anything. I'm thinking: I *must* have her home. I need it. Although I know that taking her home is fraught with peril and I'm afraid that, even if Tobias manages to cut himself off from her, I will be lost, swimming in love, and how will I ever manage to let her go?

He's still talking. 'If I go for this baby thing — just for now, mind, I'm not making any promises for the future — will you do me a deal and let us do it at Les Rajons? With some other things in our lives as well? You've always wanted to be your own boss. I've always wanted to expand my creative horizons as a composer. How about it? Shall we go for maximum madness and see where it takes us?'

Freya can hear. That posh residential home we can't afford makes a big deal about having a sensory garden, full of smells and sounds. What is the whole of Les Rajons other than a gigantic sensory garden?

'All right,' I say slowly. 'I've got a deal for you — I get to take her home and you get to move us all to that insane house.'

'Anna! You're a star! This is absolutely the right decision, you'll see!'

I'm still in mourning for the neat house in Provence, the

fields of lavender, the azure sea. This is an altogether rougher proposition: wilderness, winds, scrubby rocks and stony earth. But a few days ago Tobias was refusing to bring Freya home from the hospital at all. Somehow that place has already begun to change him.

———

My morning ritual: pack hospital bag – hand pump, muesli bars, prescription painkillers, breast pads. Put breast milk on ice. Take baby sleepsuits out of wash and hang them up to dry. Do one or two extra chores – stack dishwasher, put in laundry, tidy living room, prep something for supper – just to give me a sense of getting on top of things. Then rush to the hospital to be with my child.

To make things even more stressful, our friends and family can no longer be kept away. Every day brings a new visit to the hospital.

There are two standard reactions to Freya. The first is: 'She won't be as bad as the doctors say.' The second: 'She's lovely as she is.' I'm in no mood for either.

Sometimes they ask me how I feel, and this is what I dread most of all.

I'd love to be able to explain to them: 'At this very moment, I don't feel anything at all, because if I did, I wouldn't be here talking to you, I'd be prostrate with misery.'

In company, I'm a liability. 'We don't think Freya will live very long and we think it's better if she doesn't anyway, so we're quite philosophical about it,' I say breezily, as I give my child a bottle. Occasionally I catch a glimpse of other people's aghast faces and I feel utterly alone.

Tobias's mother lives in South Africa with his stepfather and a tribe of his half-siblings. They arrive on a plane, install themselves in a nearby hotel, and insist on dragging us out with them all to dinner.

I barely know them anyway, and now isn't the ideal time to bond. Their tanned faces are jet-lagged and full of concern. Before I know it, the subject of Freya has come up and I've lost my way again.

'Perhaps the best thing that could happen is for us to have a good six months loving her and then for her to slip peacefully away,' I hear myself saying. There are sage nods from everybody just as I realise that, for me, this would be the most devastatingly awful scenario of all.

My emotions are like some delicately calibrated measuring device that's been ramped up so far beyond its capacity that a vital fuse has blown. I've no way left of navigating so I'm flying blind, without instruments. It's left me open to all manner of things I'd normally be proof against – this move to a wholly inappropriate house in France for instance.

I'm secretly hoping that either the sale of our flat or the purchase of Les Rajons will collapse. But Tobias has become a human dynamo, keeping the wheels turning smoothly and at breathtaking speed. He's put our flat on the market and has succeeded in getting the already laughably low Les Rajons price reduced still further. In one of those quirks of the London housing market, Newington Green, which was a marginal area when we bought here ten years ago, is now positively desirable.

My mother's started phoning me every day. Never ostensibly about the move, but her conversation always heads back there in the end.

'Darling, is Tobias quite happy, do you think?'

'Well, both of us have been better. He's as well as possible. Under the circumstances.'

'It's just – you say that it's he who wants to go to this strange place in France . . . well, I've been thinking, men have certain *needs*, and after a birth, the woman doesn't necessarily want –'

'Honestly, Mother, I can absolutely promise you that moving to France is nothing to do with my sexual failures as a wife.'

'Darling, if he was more *fulfilled*, I'm sure he'd stay at home. I remember your father used to come up with some very strange ideas when he was feeling a bit neglected. Men need their egos smoothed.'

~

'Let's go to the pub,' says Tobias.

'God, no, I'm too knackered.'

'Oh, go on, it's been so long since we've had a drink with our friends.'

Without quite knowing why, I force myself along to the pub with him. As we walk in there's a stunned silence among our friends, then inconsequential small talk. Of the kind you get when everybody else is desperate for you to leave so they can discuss you behind your back.

Tobias seems unconcerned; he's chatting to Sally, a director friend of his who is enthusiastic about his work and whom I've always suspected of having a bit of a thing for him. He's done music for some of her shorts. Now she's working on a major film dramatisation of *Madame Bovary*.

Sally is enchanted that we're moving to what she calls '*la France profonde*'. Soon she's promising that if Tobias gets his agent to put him forward for the job, she'll make a big fuss to her bosses about using him to write the soundtrack. At which point, Emma Bovary's travails in nineteenth-century France become so fascinating to him that I wonder whether we'll ever get to bed.

'I have a good feeling about this one,' Tobias says afterwards. 'A proper feature-length film. I won't get paid for months, of course – but eventually it should be seriously good dosh. And what's really important is that this could be my artistic breakthrough.' He grins. 'It goes to show that living at Les Rajons isn't bad for my career.'

'Not so sure about mine,' I say gracelessly.

'It will be great too, you'll see. It's all slipping into place. As if it's meant to be.'

─

The estate agent calls: there's been an excellent offer on our flat. Cash buyer, no chain. Only catch, they want to move in by next month.

'Which means moving to France in February. Oh, Tobias, we'll have to turn that offer down. We just can't manage that.'

'It's OK – I've just spoken to the vendor of Les Rajons. He says there's no problem. He's already begun the repairs. We can sign the final contract and move in a couple of weeks after we've paid the deposit. I'll nip back to France this week to sign the *compromis de vente* and hand over our ten per cent. Easy as pie.'

I can't even argue. Going to France was my idea in the first place, and now it seems as if fate is trying to push us there.

─

Tobias has been putting off getting an MOT for the car. I think I know why: the MOT has become associated in his mind with taking Freya home.

I take matters into my own hands and phone our friend Ed, who owns a garage. I can tell he's heard the news. He doesn't ask about the baby and nothing is too much trouble for him. 'Of course,' he says. 'I'll make a booking for tomorrow.'

'I don't know whether I can go through with this,' says Tobias as he leaves. He means Freya.

'We don't have to make the decision until we're out of the hospital door,' I say. 'We can change our minds at any time before then.'

A couple of hours later, my mobile rings.

'I've got good news and bad news,' says Tobias.

I wait. At the moment, good and bad seem like relative terms.

'The car is a wipeout. At least, it would cost eight hundred quid to get through the MOT.'

'Oh no.'

'But the good news is that for eight hundred quid I've just bought a convertible.'

'Oh my God. What kind of a convertible can you buy for eight hundred quid?'

'Well, look out of the window and you'll see.'

Tobias, looking pleased with himself, is posing on the bonnet of a bottle-green Vauxhall Astra of uncertain vintage and many dents.

'Ed tried to make me buy a Golf, one careful owner, very straight. But it was so dull. It felt like I'd given up and died. He kept saying: "The Astra *might* be a good car but I don't

66

know its history. I'd prefer to sell it to somebody I don't know quite so well."'

It's so typical of Tobias. I laugh, a deep happy laugh that begins in my belly and bubbles up to my throat. 'You're a prize loon.'

'Get your coat on, I'll take you for a spin.'

We drive around with the top down. The cold air is as painful and invigorating as plunging into icy water.

'Maximum madness?' says Tobias as if he's putting a proposition. His voice is serious but the old twinkle is back in his eye.

'Maximum madness,' I agree.

———

At the hospital, we wait for a discharge letter setting out everything that's wrong with Freya's brain.

'This is the longest letter I've typed up for quite a while,' says the secretary.

Touchingly, the nurses queue to say goodbye. They all say some version of: 'We hope you have a lovely life in France.'

'Freya is much loved here,' says Dr Fernandez. 'Sometimes it's the more . . . complex babies that catch our hearts the most.' She smiles at me. 'You mustn't underestimate her achievements here, you know.'

What achievements? Freya is already falling behind a normal baby. Her eyes aren't following as well as they should, her neck is too slack, she doesn't react to faces. But Dr Fernandez means the simple things: sucking from a bottle and breathing without a ventilator.

We carry Freya in her car seat out into the battered convertible. Tobias insists on having the top down.

'It's freezing. She'll catch a cold.'

'Nonsense, it's perfectly sunny.'

I wrap Freya up like an Eskimo baby in a pram suit and woollen hat and layers of blankets and off we go. The icy wind cuts through my hair but the weak sunshine is like liquid life pouring into me.

February

WHEN I WAS A young girl, I used to pretend that my bed was a ship and I was on a voyage. Now, as a new mother, I'm playing the game again. Every morning, after Tobias has leapt hastily out of bed, I take Freya out of her Moses basket, tuck her under the duvet beside me, and we set off. We cross to different continents and over wine-dark seas. She is my world; our journey is one of discovery.

She makes exquisite little hand movements, delicate as rare orchids in high cloud forests. Her expressions change like weather fronts. I love the serious way she takes her milk from a bottle, a thousand-mile gaze of concentration in her slate-coloured eyes. Afterwards she's sated, drunken, collapsed. When I tilt her forwards to burp her, her arms swing forwards reflexively, a baby monkey clinging to its mother. As we drift off to sleep, she swims towards me. I never see or feel her move but when I wake she's snuggled under my armpit, the sheet soaked where my breasts have rained down on her.

She's my own, my baby, and she's perfect. I'm entirely content.

Then the switch flicks in my head and the doctors' diagnoses become abruptly real. I hang on to her and cry, for minutes, for hours.

71

The switch is either on or off. When I'm content, I can't imagine why I'd possibly be anything else. When I'm distraught, there's no way out of this misery.

After a bout of weeping, I'm calm for a while. At these times, I try to get inside Freya's mind, to imagine her internal world. But it's too difficult. What's it like to have no connection between the two halves of your brain? She doesn't make eye contact, her eyes are unfathomable pools.

I listen to the rough rasp of her breathing, wondering what I'll do if the breathing stops. In some ways, it would be the easiest thing. In other ways, unbearable. We lie, the baby and I, in this womb of a bed and hide from the world outside.

———

Tobias keeps popping back to France. He never complains about going alone; he seems to enjoy escaping from us. He's signed the final contract, supervised the work the owner's been doing and has assured me that all is proceeding smoothly. I'm barely interested in any of this, except as a vehicle for holding onto my baby.

The removal men come and go, taking virtually all our possessions out of our flat. We've given them the keys to Les Rajons. They'll deliver everything the day before we arrive.

Tobias wants to take his music equipment down in the Astra with us, but there's not enough room in its boot. He fusses like a mother hen as they pack up his iMac, MIDI keyboard, his precious speakers and an inconceivably large quantity of cables and computer boxes.

'Nice kit,' says one of them.

'Hey, careful, that's an RME Fireface you're holding,' moans

Tobias. 'It's worth about a grand. And those drives have got everything on them. My whole livelihood.'

I watch as my old life is stripped away in front of me, but I can't make it mean anything. My *Larousse Gastronomique* and Maguelonne Toussaint-Samat's *A History of Food*, both gifts from Tobias, end up in different, unmarked boxes. The Lacanche Range, my pride and joy, isn't coming with us at all: we've had to leave it for the buyer. In any other world, this would have been a major trauma. Now I hardly notice it.

I should be making a list of things to take with us. I should be making plans for a new life and a new career. At the very least, I should be preparing for a long journey with a fragile baby – anticipating her needs, collating emergency numbers and hospital addresses along our route. Instead I give in to an overwhelming fatigue. I begrudge every minute spent away from Freya, anything unconnected to the immediate physicality of her. My emotions are muffled, as if my inner world has also been packed away. This move doesn't worry me because I can't believe it can happen, any more than I can, emotionally, believe there is anything wrong with my child.

Tomorrow at crack of dawn we're leaving for France. I'm nodding off with Freya rooting for my breast when I feel the tiniest tug. I open my eyes and find she's managed to latch on and is sucking contentedly.

It's a wonderful feeling. When our dog had puppies, she used to lie back and let them suckle and you could see there was nowhere she'd rather be. It feels like that now: nothing matters except her pulsing mouth. Her eyes close in satisfaction as she draws milk from my breast in a series of greedy gulps.

Tobias finds us in this blissful state and becomes inexplicably furious.

'I don't want to end up like Mr and Mrs Sparrow looking after a cuckoo's chick,' he rages. 'We've got to hand her back.'

'Hand her back? Hand her *back*? Who to?'

—

We wake early and pack the few things the removal men have left in the flat. We can't fit much in the Astra: Freya's Moses basket, her sleepsuits, nappies, breast pump and bottle-sterilising equipment, one suitcase of clothes between Tobias and me. All that remains of my kitchen equipment are two plates, two cups, two glasses, some cutlery, the knife my father gave me and a couple of pans. I wrap them up in a tablecloth like a picnic. It's only now I realise I've forgotten to empty the freezer. I stack my home-made frozen Tupperware-packed ready meals in the footwell beneath Freya's car seat. At Dover, we panic and load up on reassuringly familiar British groceries – tea bags, bacon, fresh milk, Cheddar cheese, Marmite, Nutella and wholemeal bread. Then we're off, across the Channel, heading for the life I've always said I wanted.

—

We arrive at Les Rajons very late. A storm is raging; a Greek chorus of green oaks whips leaves and lashes branches at us and the roars of the wind are like dragons passing over our heads.

We keep the car engine and heating running and leave Freya, fast asleep, in the back seat. She seems safer there.

The front door has been roughly mended and secured with a large padlock. Our worldly possessions are piled in the living room in boxes. The rain thunders a tattoo on the corrugated iron the previous owner has used to patch up the roof. The house is cold as only a building with three-foot-thick walls of stone can be. As you cross the threshold the chill seems to grasp you by the throat, to embrace you in icy arms, to breathe dampness into your bones. It's like being buried alive in a cold grave.

'The vendor hasn't even mended the roof properly,' I moan at Tobias. 'I thought you were supposed to be checking up on him. And it's freezing.'

'It's only cold because it hasn't been lived in,' says Tobias. 'It'll soon warm up with a good fire.'

We try to light the charming art-deco range ('An original,' says Tobias). But it sulks and broods for a while over the damp wood and finally goes out. We try to light the baronial-sized open fireplace at the other end of the living room but the chimney produces only clouds of black smoke, a fall of soot and something that looks like a bird's nest.

'We can't leave Freya in the car any longer,' I say. 'I'm going to bring her in.'

I carry her, still in her car seat, into the living room, looking around for somewhere to set her down. Between the filth and the boxes, I can't find anywhere. Defeated, I leave her in her car seat next to the cold stove. She sits there, head lolling to one side like a sparrow mauled by a cat. Soon she begins to sneeze in sets of four, very regularly and neatly, every two minutes. I lay her in her Moses basket and cover her in blankets but the sneezing continues. The plaster madonna in her niche watches over her with sad, downcast eyes.

'Look, this bloody house has given her a cold.'

'Oh, what nonsense, there hasn't been time. She must have caught it in the car.'

75

'All right then, in that awful car you stupidly bought, which has dripped rainwater on us for fourteen hours all the way along the autoroute. Thank God it didn't break down, at least.'

Tobias and I square up to each other like boxers.

'I'm sorry,' I make myself say. I don't feel sorry. 'I'll get us something to eat.'

All I need to do is to warm up a couple of my ready meals and we can eat a civilised hot dinner together in our new home.

I step into the kitchen.

It has a dank, greasy feel. The bare low-wattage electric bulb is suggestive of creatures hiding in the shadows. Unplugged against the back wall is a rusted refrigerator. When I open its ill-fitting metal door, the smell of bats and gradual decay wafts out to me. There's a green and nasty butler's sink beneath a cracked window, a greasy bread oven, a rickety wooden table and some primitive shelving. There's no electric ring or cooker, nor a single surface on which I'd trust myself to put food. The tabletop, the shelving, the sink, are all covered in small black pellets.

'Tobias! This is disgusting! There are mice in here! Look – they've shat everywhere.'

Tobias looks at the pellets and frowns. 'I'm not sure it's mice. It's probably just little bits of dirt. We'll clear it up in the morning.'

Along one wall, the shadows converge into blackness.

'There's some kind of an opening,' I say.

'I told you,' says Tobias, 'there's an archway through to this other really cool bit. I'll show you – there must be a light switch somewhere.' He fumbles in the gloom while I try not to feel threatened by this room with no defined limits, no clear beginning or end, tapering on into the shadows.

76

Then another low-wattage bulb flickers to life. We're looking at a narrow triangular space ending in a four-paned stone window with an ugly butcher's hook hanging in front of a stone sink.

'I think this part must be a game kitchen,' I say. 'For hanging game.'

Tobias is examining the archway. 'There are hooks for hinges on the sides – this bit had a door once.'

'The floor is covered in snow.'

'Don't be silly. Cold as it is that can't be right.'

I look again. 'No, it's small white balls. Polystyrene. The ceiling and walls are lined with it. What could cause it to fall like that?' As I stare in the dim light, trying to work it out, the shadows resolve into a distended shape.

'Gaaa! Tobias! Come quickly!'

'What?'

'Look – up there. Poking through a hole in the ceiling. A dead mouse.'

'Its mouth is full of polystyrene,' says Tobias interestedly. 'It must have tried to eat its way through – and got too fat to wriggle out.'

'I don't care what it did. Tomorrow morning, first thing, we're giving this filthy house a damn good clean.'

'OK, OK, just so long as you let me get some sleep first. Come on, I don't want food. Let's go straight to bed.'

I carry Freya, fast asleep in her Moses basket, upstairs to our bedroom. We lie on an airbed next to her, listening to creaks and a sort of scraping thump as if prisoners in chains are dragging iron trunks across the floor above us.

'It's just an old house. It's settling in,' says Tobias.

The house groans all through the night like a galleon under

sail. An ear-piercing hissing noise wakes us three or four times. 'Go and see what it is,' I order Tobias in a whisper.

'Not bloody likely,' he whispers back. 'It's obviously a hissing ghost. You go and look if you want to see it.'

—

Freya wakes us long before dawn. Tobias goes downstairs to begin unpacking the crates in the living room. I lie in bed with Freya tugging at my breast, watching her breathing, counting her eyelashes, gazing at the downy curve of her cheek. As the house comes awake we drift off into a delicious stolen sleep together.

At ten o'clock I'm woken by the smell of coffee. I open the door onto the covered wooden bridge. A shaft of sunlight insinuates itself into the musty bedroom, and the sound of birdsong.

It's a beautiful day, sparklingly clear, without a breath of wind. There are snowdrops and winter crocuses in the court-yard. I step through the door onto the bridge. It gives onto a view of blue and purple hills; nature has never seemed more tender and loving. We'll come out here often, I tell myself, Tobias and I, to share breakfast on this bridge-balcony, looking at this view.

I run my hand along the smooth wooden handrail and feel a rough patch beneath my fingers. There's a name carved in the rail: Rose. It's an oddly intimate thing to have found. A sign that another person has enjoyed the prettiness of this spot; has come here, perhaps, on a morning like this, wrapped up in their own thoughts and preoccupations.

When I take Freya downstairs in her Moses basket I find

one corner of the living room already cleared of packing cases and the art-deco stove polished to a shine, a blue tin coffee pot steaming cheerfully on its hotplate.

'Tobias. You're wonderful! How did you manage to light the stove?'

Tobias is assuming an expression of modest smugness when Lizzy walks in with an armful of wood. I'm so amazed to see her that a moment passes before I can speak.

'Oh, welcome. I'm sorry I wasn't here to greet you last night,' she says. 'I'd given up on you – it was so late. I've cleaned the stove. The chimney was blocked with *so* many things.'

'Lizzy. I . . . I didn't expect. At least, I assumed . . .'

Tobias is manoeuvring me a little to one side. 'Lizzy's still looking for another place to stay,' he half hisses.

I glare at him.

'It's OK,' says Lizzy. 'I can go now if you want. There are some people down in the valley who want me to move in with them. But Tobias seemed to think it might be useful for me to stay for a week or two to help you guys move in. He *asked* me.'

Now it's Tobias's turn to glare at me. '*Please* don't hurry away, Lizzy,' he says. 'You've been such a star – I can't imagine how I'd have managed to sort so much out so quickly without your help. After all, Anna *did* leave most of it to me.'

There's a beat of silence during which I get as far as opening my mouth. Tobias points quickly at a collection of wine bottles, unlabelled and dusty, on the living-room table. 'Look. The neighbours have been arriving all morning from farms all around. They've each put a couple of bottles of their own home brew on the table. They wouldn't stay. How they knew we were here, I can't say.'

'Everybody knows you're here,' says Lizzy. 'Besides, it's the day of the *chasse*. All the locals are hunters. They're parked just outside in their *quatre-quatres*.' When Tobias looks enquiring, she adds: 'Their four-wheel drives.'

There's a hammering on the door.

'Another one,' says Tobias.

Freya wakes with a start and begins to howl.

'I'll get it,' I say, 'and for God's sake pick your daughter up occasionally.'

A small man is standing at the door. His large leather hunting hat makes him look foreshortened, as if he's wearing a cooking pot on his head.

'Hello, I am your neighbour.' As he says this, he straightens his back and shoulders like a soldier on parade. His hand in mine feels like carved walnut wood but there's a definite twinkle in his eye. 'I am also your tenant,' he adds. 'I have the right to plant in the vegetable plot. My name is Ludovic Donnadieu.'

He takes off his hat with a flourish and produces two dusty bottles of wine with no labels.

'Please do come in,' I say.

He steps inside and stares at Freya, precariously balanced on Tobias's knee. His look has the darting brightness of a woodland animal. 'Your first? I remember holding a baby the same way; I didn't know how to do it, so I rested him on my lap just like that – so secure, no chance he'd fall – and I felt so proud.'

'Would you like a coffee?' I ask.

'A coffee? Ah . . .'

'Perhaps a *petit apéro*?' suggests Tobias in franglais.

'*Mais oui, un apéro, volontiers!*'

I pour us glasses from one of his bottles. He settles at the table, sipping his familiar tipple. His wine is gluey with sweetness.

'Where do you live?' I ask, making conversation.

'In Rieu, the village halfway up the hill. The last bungalow. Anything you need, you must come by. Don't hesitate.' I can hardly make out what he's saying through the thickness of his accent.

'That's very kind.'

'You speak good French,' he says. But then he adds: 'Like a northerner,' and makes a sort of shrug with his mouth and eyebrows.

'Well, it's all the same country, I suppose.'

'This is the Pays d'Oc. Our own language is Occitan, not French. We have our own customs.'

'Are you a builder? Or a farmer?'

'I am a *paysan*, I work the land. Your husband does not understand French? You must translate for him.'

'All right,' I say. 'I'll try. Tobias – he wants me to translate as we go along. He's saying: *My uncle owns Les Rajons, it is in our family for centuries. We have all the vines on the slopes and we make wine in the press* . . . Surely that can't be right, can it? Nobody mentioned that . . . oh . . . *until the eighties* . . . he seems to have slipped in time. God, his patois is hard to understand. *But the EU it pays to* . . . *dig up the vines. The wine here is not high enough quality; the soil she is too* . . . I'm not sure, too something – hard? heavy? *The soil, she is a cruel mistress. You must learn to manage her. Otherwise she will break you as she has broken us for countless generations.*'

'Do people really talk like that?' asks Tobias. 'Outside agricultural novels, I mean?'

'*Nobody wants to buy this house. She has a dark energy, due*

81

to her history. *This wine is good – I make it from my own grapes,
I have kept some vineyards lower down the slopes. They are good
vines, over a hundred years old. They served my grandfather. They
are red grapes. I peel them by hand to make white wine. I put in
plenty of sugar. I recommend drinking it with a . . . sirop de fraise*
– that's raspberry, no, strawberry syrup. Must be disgusting.
It gives a beautiful colour. Tobias – I don't think I'm terribly
good at spot translation. Can I stop now?'

'No, no – you're doing great. This is really important stuff.
Ask him about the history of the house.'

But I decide I would prefer not to know about the house's
dark history.

'Oh, he's off again. *What will you do about the water?*'

'The water?' says Tobias. 'It just sort of comes out of the
tap. Is there a problem?'

'*You have not the mains water. You have but the water of rain.
How will you irrigate your land?* I don't suppose we'll really
need to irrigate the land, will we, darling? Shall I tell him that?'

When I do so Ludovic chokes on his glass.

'He's off on a bit of a rant. *Outsiders are buying all the
property around here. All our young people are leaving. Now it is
only the old who know how to work the land. And the young cannot
afford to come back and live here any more.*'

'Tell him that's very sad,' says Tobias. 'But presumably it's
the locals who sold the property in the first place.'

'Oh dear, he's getting a bit stroppy. *The previous owner of
Les Rajons refused to sell to a local, at a reasonable price. Of
course, he knew he could sell it to foreigners who don't know the
prices of things and who wouldn't look after the land. I do not, of
course, refer to you. So what are your plans?*'

'Well, we're going to try to do up the house slowly.'

'*I don't mean the house.* He means the land! *You have ten hectares here. What are you going to do with those fields below the house?*'

'Fields? Those pieces of scrubland? I didn't know they were fields.'

Ludovic Donnadieu finishes his glass in a single, angry gulp. 'Our ancestors spent generations building terraces with their bare hands. They knew every stone of their own property. Now nobody maintains the land. In another twenty years all their work will have disappeared.'

—

Tobias and I spend the rest of the morning working on the kitchen. We tear down the polystyrene on the ceiling. ('There's a perfectly good wooden one above,' Tobias says of the bare floorboards with light glinting through that this reveals.) Together we haul the old fridge outside. ('We'll buy a new one,' says Tobias, 'and a gas ring to tide us over until we get a proper range.') Tobias makes a bonfire and burns piles of debris while I scrub every kitchen surface with soap and bleach.

—

Under the grime in our kitchen, we've uncovered a primitive but acceptable room. The walls are still rough with saltpetre but at least the sink is clean and the shelves have turned out to be oak. I've rummaged in our packing cases for my essential store-cupboard ingredients: paper packets of cornflour and gelatine, arborio rice, muscovado sugar, flaked and blanched almonds, puy lentils, Valrhona chocolate, Italian 00 flour. I've placed them neatly on display.

The space that lies beyond the archway is more challenging. Here the saltpetre is much worse and the polystyrene has been stuck down with some irremovable resin. There's a tangle of loose wiring, presumably belonging to some long-defunct farm machinery, that we're too frightened to touch.

'I'll gaffer-tape a piece of cardboard over the archway and we'll leave that part for now,' Tobias tells me firmly.

During the whole cleaning operation, Freya's been lying in her Moses basket next to the stove in the living room, apparently content. I keep breaking off my work to look at her, sleeping sweetly, her chubby arms stretched out, her little froggy legs sprawled. She rarely cries, even for feeds; instead she hiccups when she's hungry.

Now that she's begun to take the breast, I have to feed her more often. These moments punctuate my day, form oases of intimacy between us. At one point this morning after she drank her fill, she plunged her head towards my chest. She's done it after every feed since. This new action has touched me deeply. I'm quite certain it means that she wants a cuddle.

When she was born, I had no doubt whatsoever in my mind that I wanted no resuscitation in the event, say, of a chest infection. It made it easy to make bold decisions, like risking her life by coming here. Now, the thought of being without her is too horrible. I tell myself that these feelings are just as selfish as my initial reaction – I want her with me for longer.

What was I thinking, bringing her to this freezing, filthy house? What if she catches cold, or some dirt-borne illness?

But now that we've sold our flat, this is our only home. We have nowhere else to go.

We're slipping into a routine. In the mornings, Lizzy helps us to clean the house and unpack our belongings. She seems determined to make herself as useful as possible. Despite myself, I'm growing fond of her. She's so terribly young, so completely alone. She never mentions what must have been a grim childhood, but there's something heroic in her refusal to be knocked down by it. I often picture her small figure putting one foot in front of another as she sets off to walk the length of France with nothing to sustain her except hedgerow plants and the kindness of strangers.

At lunchtime, Tobias, Freya and I drive into Aigues and eat at the cafe in the square – an expensive habit, but we still don't have a proper cooker. There seems no point in buying a range until the kitchen is done up.

Try as I might, I can't crack the kitchen. Nature keeps creeping back. Geckos peek from behind shelves. Spiders lurk in corners. Hairy millipedes crawl up and down. The bread oven weeps yet more soot onto the quarry tiles, fresh saltpetre glistens on the walls. A strange black mould is growing over the rickety table and worktop. The cardboard Tobias has taped over the archway into the game kitchen sags like old Elastoplast over a gaping wound. And everywhere are those sinister pellets of mouse shit and the sweet, rank smell of their urine.

In the afternoons, Tobias and I put Freya into her sling and go for walks. Armed with the map that came with the title deeds, we revel in the discovery of our terrain.

The weather is glorious. It's only February but it might as well be May, except that the leaves aren't yet out on the trees. All this week the sun has shone, coaxing the plants to come alive and the birds to sing. During our walks, Freya sleeps in her sling against my chest, the magic of the place drips into us and we become happy and excited and explore like children.

Ten hectares turns out to be rather a lot. There's the orchard of little fruit trees, still in their winter sleep. There's the vegetable plot, bare and neatly turned. Down the hill, past the fields we thought were scrubland, we discover we also own a stretch of river and a strange stone channel that we've eventually worked out must be for irrigation.

Day by day, we've become more adventurous, leaving our own land, walking further afield, mapping and naming this new world. We've found a narrow ridge of rock that leads like a bridge over the valley to the next hillside, a stark jumble of boulders falling away from it on both sides. On the next hill, which is much higher than our own, we've discovered a river cascading down the mountain and a secret pool, fed by a water-fall, whose lip causes a *trompe l'oeil*, making it appear to flow endlessly into nowhere. We've crossed deserts of neglected chestnut trees, once coppiced and now grown back in tortured, shattered shapes that make me think of the no-man's-land between the First World War trenches.

Scrabbling through the chestnut woods, Tobias says: 'Look at this, Anna. It's a vanished civilisation.'

He's found stone terraces and little stone houses with fallen roofs, an entire village lost in the undergrowth.

'This village must have been full of people,' he says. 'I wonder what happened to them?'

We peer across the stone thresholds into the collapsed houses. 'They were burned,' I say. 'All of them. There must have been a huge fire. I wonder when. Oh, Tobias, please don't do that – it's terribly dangerous.'

Tobias has jumped down into one of the houses and is poking around in a mass of broken stone tiles and charred beams.

I have a vivid image of the wall collapsing. Of me trying and failing to pull him out from under the rubble. Of my mobile not working. Of having to leave him, trapped, while I run for help. Of him dying there, alone.

I'm amazed at myself. My heart is pounding, my breath ragged, my palms sweating. It's not in my character to panic this way. It comes down to this: I can't afford to lose him too.

'Look,' Tobias is saying, oblivious. 'An iron stove. Stamped 1940. These houses aren't as old as they seem.'

'Come on, Tobias.' I'm scared to let him know how frightened I am. 'I don't like it here. Let's go back to the main track.'

The piste winds past a patch of pine forest with a stone hut in it and a memorial to the Second World War dead. We see a column of 4x4 vehicles on it. A line of men in an odd combination of camouflage clothing and fluorescent jackets are staring into the forest, guns at the ready.

'It must be the hunt,' I say. 'Shall we go and talk to them?'

A figure detaches itself from the group. Ludovic, glowering beneath his oversized hunter's hat, is making towards us.

'What are you thinking walking so close to the guns? It's very dangerous. The hunt is all around you. You're not even wearing fluorescent jackets. Our men could easily have fired on you.'

Tobias, always the peacemaker, catches the expression in his voice, though not the meaning. 'No problem,' he says. 'It's all cool.'

Ludovic takes a breath as if he's going to say more. Then he looks at Freya, asleep in her sling, and says: 'I had better take you home. I know where the hides are.'

We retrace our footsteps at a rapid pace, Ludovic walking one or two steps ahead of us, Freya bobbing up and down in her sling.

'What are you hunting?' I ask.

'Wild boar. The forests are full of them. And deer too. They're a menace. They need keeping down.'

'Of course,' I say soothingly.

He looks at me with suspicion. 'Foreigners detest the hunt.'

'Not me,' I lie. It seems I'm going to have to compromise my humane principles somewhat. 'I'm a chef. I like to cook game.'

He looks interested for the first time. 'A chef? You have a restaurant in England?'

'I worked in somebody else's restaurant. My husband thinks I should start a restaurant at Les Rajons one day. Perhaps the hunters could supply me with game.'

'Humph. Perhaps. I am fond of wild boar stew . . .'

'Well then, I'll have to cook it for you one day.'

'Humph.'

Ludovic is warming a little. His body as he leads us down the path is less rigid.

He even suggests a pause to look out over the valley. 'If I tell you what this once looked like, you wouldn't believe me. Terraces down to the river – olive trees, vines, cherry orchards. Irrigation channels. Chestnut woods. All the land clean. The war disrupted things. People were obliged to leave to find jobs. They never came back. We who are left can't fight against the tree heather and the brambles. Now most of the land is just *maquis*, scrubland – good for nothing but the wild boar.'

He stares over the hills and valleys with eyes that see something quite different to the unspoilt loveliness it seems to me. 'Nature came back,' he says, at last. 'Nature is strong. She needs to be controlled. But we – we are grown old and weak.'

When the wind blows here, it blows out of a blue sky. It kicks sand in your eyes. It punches you in the face. It's like nothing I've ever experienced before.

We're heading into Aigues to introduce ourselves to the mayor. During our drive, the wind slams into the side of the car like a fist and blows grit at us. It's impossible to tell which direction it's coming from: often it seems to be going round in circles.

We veer down the hairpin bends. Beyond Rieu the view opens up and you can look right down into the valley at the broad silver thread of the River Aigues and the fertile corridor along its banks. This land is still lovingly cultivated. After the wilderness in which we live it's a paradise of order.

Again and again the road returns to the same view of fields, vineyards, orchards and allotments, a little closer with every turn. I think of Ludovic and his vanished world. Here, the slope of your land, how sheltered it is from the wind, its depth of soil, determine your ability to survive. The farmers have already been driven off the hillside. This valley has become, in turn, the marginal land.

I have good days and bad days. Today is a bad day.

Down in the village I see children everywhere as if the wind's blown them there. Toddlers dragging along on stubby legs, babies buffeted in prams, kids throwing tantrums in the streets. Their mothers harassed, scolding, worn down. Taking it for granted that their offspring are normal.

'The town hall will be in the square,' says Tobias. Next to it we see a school with windswept children playing outside.

I think: she will never go to that school, she will never play in that courtyard, she will never learn French.

Mothers are arriving to collect their kids. A little girl runs into her mother's arms and starts prattling about her day. I cancel the expectation that Freya will ever do the same.

When she sees Freya in her sling the mother catches my eye and smiles, the way women with children do. Freya's disabilities aren't yet obvious. I find volunteering the information to people exquisitely embarrassing. If I can help it, I don't tell, even though I know I won't be able to get away with this for long.

'Was she premature?' the woman asks me, already sensing something not quite right. I nod; it seems better than a lie, easier than an explanation.

'Enjoy her now. It passes so quickly; she'll pass onto another stage.' I nod again, with a pang of exquisite sadness because this is not a stage but how she will be forever.

The mayor is in his office. As we walk in, he shakes our hands and says: 'Les Rajons, you have bought Les Rajons. That is superb. I cannot give you mains water. You must dig a well. That is the best thing. Water from the village, that is impossible!'

'Well, really we just came to say hello.'

'I am enchanted to meet you. I advise you to dig a well without delay.'

Ten minutes later we're back out on the windy square. We look at each other, at a loss.

'Well, that was a bit *Jean de Florette*,' says Tobias.

We linger by the war memorial with its impressive list of the dead in two world wars. Then a particularly violent gust of wind catches us. Tobias grabs my hand and pulls me into the cafe.

'Hello, Yvonne,' he says to the owner. He's got a thing about finding out everybody's name; it's part of his charm. He's already discovered that Yvonne is twenty-two and that her father, the butcher, has helped her set up this cafe. Yvonne's plump face dimples into smiles at the sight of him.

Over the past week, I've had time to grow used to her extraordinary taste in interior decoration: the vaulted stone ceiling, the forest of monumental sandstone pillars, the French lace drooping at arrow slit windows, the pewter jugs and plastic doilies lying on waxed oak tables, the massive walnut bar, every inch of which is covered with a vast collection of laughing porcelain pigs. On our first visit, Yvonne invited us to tap the vaulted ceiling and sandstone pillars, revealing that they're all made of plaster.

There's something engaging about Yvonne. She's exceptionally pretty, in a way that transcends both her fashion sense and her curvaceous form. Her eyes and skin have a certain transparency and her personality too, I feel, is transparent: everything she feels shines forth to the world. With her flaxen hair and cherub's mouth she looks like a Renaissance madonna; a goddess in a size sixteen polyester shell suit.

'It's windy today,' says Tobias.

'This is the *tramontane*,' says Yvonne. 'The wind that blows for three, six or nine days.'

'Er . . . what?'

'If it blows for one day, it will blow for three – and if it goes on for a fourth day, it means it will blow for six and so on.'

Tobias and I exchange looks.

'That's a lot of wind.'

'Oh yes, Languedoc is the windiest region of France. The *tramontane* is just one wind. We also have *le mistral*, which is hot, *le vent marin*, which blows from the sea and brings wet weather – and many more. Living up at Les Rajons you'll soon get to know them all.'

I glare at Tobias. Yvonne rescues him. 'I have something special today. Do you want to try it?' She pulls a large dried sausage from under the counter and begins to cut thick slices from it. 'I made it myself from the black mountain pigs. They eat acorns and chestnuts in the forest.'

The sausage is superb, not too salty or fatty, and full of the flavour of mountain herbs.

'I didn't know you were a *charcutière*,' I say.

'Oh yes, I've won many prizes for my sausages. This year I've entered the Concours National du Jeune Espoir.'

'You deserve to win,' I say. 'This is the best *saucisse* I've ever tasted. Could you supply my restaurant, do you think?' That is, I add mentally, if I ever manage to open it.

'It would be a pleasure. And I've been meaning to ask you – I know you have a game kitchen at Les Rajons. Do you think I might be able to rent it from you to work in? I've been using the back of Papa's butcher's shop. It's not really suitable.'

'That's a great idea,' says Tobias. 'Actually, it would be a really useful bit of income for us. I'm hoping to get a big film job, but it won't pay for ages. Of course the game kitchen needs a tiny bit of doing up. Come and look at it and make up your mind.'

But Yvonne has stopped listening. 'Oh – I think I see Julien walking across the square. I wonder if he'll come in.' She dives out from behind the counter and waves a white arm out of the door.

'Julien! Come and meet some people!'

There's a figure walking purposefully across the square. At the sound of Yvonne's voice, it turns without pausing and strides with equal determination in our direction. I'm reminded of the time at school when the teacher showed us bobbing particles through a microscope, explaining that the impression they gave of conscious movement was an illusion; in reality they were being buffeted by forces imperceptible to our eyes.

'Yvonne,' he says, 'who are your new friends?' His French is thick with the local accent.

He isn't good-looking – his face is too thin for that. His features are all wrong too – his nose too long, his cheekbones too high, his eyes too large, his mouth too wide – making him look somehow elfin, not quite of our world. I try to guess his age: maybe twenty-nine or thirty.

'Julien, meet the new *propriétaires* of Les Rajons,' says Yvonne. 'They are English.'

Julien regards us with calm grey eyes and shakes our hands in turn. His touch is firm and sure. 'Pleased to meet you,' he says in English. I like his measured tone. He speaks fluently but carefully, as if he isn't used to the feel of the language in his mouth. 'You're brave people to take on Les Rajons.'

'Julien, won't you join us for a drink?' asks Yvonne.

Julien looks at her and smiles. 'What do you suggest?'

'I have some peach syrup. It's very nice in muscat. I could make us each a cocktail. Like in a New York bar.' She pours thick sugary syrup into four glasses. 'I'd love to see New York. One day I'll win the *médaille d'or* at the Concours National du Meilleur Saucisson. Then I'll go to the United States and see Las Vegas, New York, Hollywood and Dallas, Texas. And I'll win all the great charcuterie competitions of America. This valley will be proud of me.'

Julien and Yvonne begin speaking together in rapid French, laced with patois that I can barely follow.

'You're a party girl,' teases Julien.

Yvonne tosses her hair. 'It's so boring here in the valley in the winter. It's good to have new people. Perhaps they'll make things happen.'

'Get out of the valley, then. Come up to the hills with me.'

'You know I can't. You're not . . . proper.'

'Oh, proper. Not that again!'

'Hey,' says Tobias in English. 'What's the issue about water at Les Rajons? We went to say hello to the mayor just now and all he could talk about was how he couldn't give us water.'

Yvonne and Julien look at each other. 'Everybody knows there's no water at Les Rajons,' says Yvonne.

'That's not true,' says Julien.

'But that's what people here say. That's why nobody would buy the house.'

I glare again at Tobias. 'That's why we got it so cheap,' I say.

Tobias glares back at me. 'It was a joint decision to buy that house. I'm sick of being blamed for it,' he says.

Julien holds up a hand. 'It's not so bad. You have a rainwater cistern. It's just that the mayor doesn't want to approve *l'eau communale*. It's too remote. So you depend on nature for your water, rather than the town council.'

'He says we should dig a well.'

'I can save you the trouble,' says Julien. 'Your land's on *schiste* – for well water you should be on *calcaire*.' He catches my puzzled look. 'They're different types of rock – *schiste* is an impermeable rock and *calcaire* is limestone.'

'Well, that's just great,' I say. 'Thanks, Tobias, for not checking *that*.'

Tobias flushes and I have a second to see the pain in his face,

94

the pain of somebody who has gritted his teeth and tried to do the right thing, who feels lost and humiliated. Then the door of the cafe has slammed and he's gone.

'Oh,' says Yvonne. 'But we haven't had the peach cocktails. I'll follow him and try to get him back.'

The door slams again. Julien, Freya and I are left alone. I feel suddenly shy. He bends down and looks at Freya. 'She's lovely,' he says. 'Peaceful.'

There's no need to tell him about Freya. I open my mouth meaning to say something non-committal and measured but crazy words come tumbling out instead.

'She looks peaceful, but her brain's like scrambled eggs. I wanted a baby so much and now I'm sometimes not even sure that she's a real baby. Have you heard of changelings? Was that how they started? With babies where something wasn't quite right, so in the end people wanted an excuse to get rid of them? And the sad thing is that after it first happened, Tobias and I felt as if we were falling in love all over again, but now we fight all the time about stupid things. And the house is so awful – at least, he loves it but I feel threatened by it. As though it has a personality of its own. We don't really know why we've come here. We were just running away, I think – but when you run away, of course, you arrive somewhere, and then you have to deal with that.'

I stop, horrified. 'I'm sorry. I hardly know you and I've said more than is . . . polite.'

'I don't like polite. Too many people around here are too concerned with what's polite, what's done and not done. Please – carry on.'

'Well – nature's so unpredictable around here. The wind howls for days on end, the kitchen's infested with mice. Frankly, it scares me. There's just . . . so much of it. Everywhere. Even in the house. Especially in the house. Our neighbour Ludovic thinks nature needs to be controlled.'

Julien laughs. 'Around here, you need to make peace with nature. Live in harmony with it. If you try to fight, it'll break you.'

'Well, you and Ludovic agree about that, anyway.'

The cafe's doorbell tinkles and Yvonne and Tobias return. Tobias is rarely angry for long and Yvonne seems to have smoothed him over.

'Let's drink the peach cocktails and welcome you to the valley,' says Yvonne. 'I made a gaffe. Les Rajons is a wonderful place. The lack of water wasn't what put off the locals.'

'No,' says Julien. 'That will be the ghosts.'

As we leave, Julien puts his hand on my shoulder. 'Come to my place one day. I live in the forest on the mountain next to yours. Over the stone ridge, by the infinity pool – you know, the one with the waterfall. Just past the burned-out village in the chestnut woods.'

―

I go to sit upstairs with Freya in the bedroom, feeling her gentle tugging at my breast, enjoying the peace of it. We breathe together, her little body curled against mine. She gazes raptly just above my head. Then her eyes roll up and her lips smack. Her left arm jackknifes up into the air, her fist clenches and she begins to shudder and turn blue. In seconds, she's stiffened into a corpse; I can't reach her; she's no longer my child. Slowly, stupidly, I realise that she's having a fit.

It seems to go on forever although I see from my watch that it's only a couple of minutes. Then she draws a gasping breath, her colour returns as abruptly as it went and she's my own little baby back again.

I call Dr Fernandez. 'Two or three minutes? Put her on five mil a day of phenobarbitone and we'll see how it goes. If a fit lasts for more than five minutes, give her the rectal Valium we gave you. Anything very major, take her into A&E.'

The nearest hospital is two hours away. *If you don't manage to get to the hospital on time* . . . I push the thought out.

Why did I speak to Julien about changelings, about people trying to get rid of unwanted babies? I've jinxed us. Or maybe this house has cast a malign spell.

As I go into the kitchen to fetch her medicine, I have a subliminal impression of a dark shape exiting via the bottom of the wall. There's a hole I haven't noticed about the size of a golf ball in the skirting board and a trail of mouse droppings on my newly scrubbed worktop. My box of cornflour has been knocked onto the floor and when I pick it up, a fine stream of flour pours from a nibbled corner.

I wash a medicine syringe with boiled water from the kettle and measure out the phenobarbitone.

Freya looks calm and normal again. She laps up the sticky dose I squirt into her mouth; it's laced with sugar. I hold her tightly to me and stroke her head until she falls asleep.

Later I stand looking at her as she lies in her Moses basket. She's in her favourite position, on her back with one arm thrown up against her face. Her breathing is soft and even, her colour pink. So poised and so fragile.

I already love her more than when she was born, but I can't protect her.

—

Without warning, the weather has turned cold. Tonight, I'm sure, it'll freeze solid and the crocuses will die.

I'm going to fix the kitchen once and for all.

I go on the attack, sluicing out the bread oven, chipping at the saltpetre with a chisel, setting about the walls and corners with a broom, sweeping away spiders' webs, showering flakes of plaster on the floor. Then I put on a face mask and yet again I scrub the mouse shit off every surface with bleach and detergent.

The surrender is total and unequivocal. Spiders scurry before my broom. Plaster dust disappears into the vacuum cleaner's jaws. The pellets of mouse shit dissolve in bleach.

Then I leave Freya with Tobias and drive down to Ludovic's house. It's an orange breeze-block bungalow with a neat concrete balustrade and an imposing metal gate. Every inch of ground in his front yard has been cemented over.

Ludovic seems pleased to see me. 'I built this house myself,' he says with some pride. 'I may be retired but I like to keep active.' He gives me a penetrating look. 'Guess how old I am.'

'I'm not sure,' I say, but he won't let me get away with this. He stares at me expectantly until I add with only a touch of flattery: 'About sixty-five perhaps.'

'I'm seventy-nine,' he announces, clearly delighted.

'You can't be,' I say.

'Oh yes,' he says with great complacency. 'The facade is smart, but the building is collapsing.'

A masculine-looking woman who appears to be in her late sixties is hanging washing out on a nylon line. 'That is Thérèse, she is my concubine,' says Ludovic. He makes no move to invite me into the house nor does he interrupt Thérèse's labour with an introduction.

'We've got mice running around in the kitchen,' I say. 'I'm afraid they're a health hazard. For the baby. I need to know what to do.'

'You must use poison,' he advises.

'Oh, I'm not sure about that. I don't like poison.'

He shrugs and disappears into his house, leaving me standing in the concrete garden, watching Thérèse at work. Five minutes later, he comes back with four little wooden traps.

'Take these for as long as you need.'

'Thank you, that's very kind.'

'That's OK. We are neighbours.'

I drive back up the hill. The winter palette is all blacks and greys: dark soil, dead wood, cold stone. The bare vines look like the shrivelled hands of corpses poking out of the earth. I'm in a bleak enough mood to appreciate this landscape. It's orderly and contained.

Before I go to bed I bait the traps succulently with cheese and bacon and lay them at strategic points around the kitchen.

The first thing I see in the morning is a gecko peering at me from behind the kitchen shelves. The spiders have been busy in the night rebuilding their webs. There's a new film of plaster dust and trails of mouse shit on every surface. Even the black mould's already begun creeping back.

All four of my traps have been sprung and the bait's gone. But the culprits have escaped.

March

S PRING IS COMING TO the valley. In the peach orchards beside the River Aigues I've spotted tight buds bulging from the dark twigs. They look like tears, squeezed reluctantly through closed eyelashes.

'Now just listen to me for a moment, dear. I want you to get me one of those orphans.'

'Mother, what are you talking about?'

'Oh, you know, one of those Chinese orphans. I saw a documentary about them. I think you ought to adopt one for me and I'll give it a good start.'

I stop myself wondering if my mother is lonely; I simply don't have time to worry about her too.

'Why don't you get your own orphan?' I say instead.

'Oh, don't be silly, dear, nobody would let me adopt – I'm a widow now, you know, and I'm the wrong side of sixty. But you and Tobias could do it easily. Or a Vietnamese one. But I think the Chinese need it more.'

'Mother, you're being ridiculous! I can't get you an orphan.'

'You could adopt one yourself then and give that other baby away.'

'An orphan is a human being,' I say. 'A child. It's not one of your cats.'

There's a huffy pause on the other end of the line.

'If that's what you think,' says my mother finally, 'then I'm not going to let you look after *my* cats.'

Suddenly, the world is full of every kind of baby thing. And my mother's infuriating idiot-savant knowledge of me holds true. Deep in my chest there's a growing ache for a baby creature of my own: a puppy, a kitten, anything.

As dusk falls, a huge female wild boar lumbers past our house, her preposterously long and hairy nose snuffling the ground. Around her are her young, six of them in all. They're reddish, streaked with beige, as playful and wrapped up in their own world as children anywhere. It's all I can do to stop myself scooping them up to take them back inside.

When Yvonne calls round to look at the game kitchen, she picks Freya up from her Moses basket by the stove and carries her around like a doll.

'This is an excellent *laboratoire*,' she pronounces. 'The stone is so thick it stays cool all year round. It's very good for the *saucissons*. But at the moment it's not suitable. It's too dirty, I'll need running water, and the wiring doesn't conform to the norms.'

'Don't worry,' says Tobias cheerfully. 'Anna is looking into getting the kitchen rated for her restaurant. She'll get this bit done too. I can't imagine it will take long.'

I give him a panicked look. The truth is that – now the hunting season has ended – a parade of men in vans have already beaten a path to our door.

They've gazed in horror at the antiquated wiring, the crumbling plaster, the leaking roof, the non-existent plumbing.

One of them has taken me pityingly to the back of the house and shown me where the waste from the loo runs untreated down the mountainside.

When I've mentioned doing up the game kitchen for a professional *charcutière* they've shrugged their shoulders and made Gallic noises of derision. Everything at Les Rajons, they say, has been '*mal fait*'. Badly done, I've discovered, is the ultimate insult, the French equivalent of the British builder's 'that'll cost you'.

They've quoted us prices we can't afford and then told us they don't want the work anyway.

———

Early morning, just after dawn, is my favourite time of day. I slip out of bed and retrieve Freya from her cot. As I lift her, she squeaks like a gerbil, protesting at being taken out of the warmth. Then her spine bends forward, her fists curl in front of her face and, without waking, she moulds herself into the cavity of my chest.

I lay her down on her baby gym beside a music box and watch her kick her legs. She doesn't smile but I can tell she's pleased. All this, I know, is dangerous. She likes cuddles, she appreciates music. I'm beginning to get to know her.

The telephone rings long before breakfast time.

'Hello, dear, how are you managing in that terrible place? And how is . . . that baby?'

'Not too bad, Mother. She sleeps a lot.'

'Oh, darling, I wish I could help. I've been trying to think what *my* father would have done. I think I know, of course.

But you *could*, in those days, without being thrown into prison and, after all, he *was* a doctor.'

⁓

The more time I spend with Freya, the more wrapped up Tobias gets with his demo for the *Madame Bovary* job. Because he hasn't done a feature-length film before, Sally's executives have insisted that he first pass a test. He has to score the end scene of the movie, in which Emma Bovary commits suicide. This involves replacing the temp music, which is Mahler's Fifth Symphony.

'It's a tall order, Anna,' he keeps saying. 'I've never written anything classical or orchestral in my life before.'

I'm used to him composing effortlessly. Sometimes, in the past, I've even suspected him of indulging his idle nature, limiting his gifts and composing by numbers. But not this time. He's set his kit up in the living room and he sits for hours in front of his iMac, headphones clamped to his ears, trying out ideas on his MIDI keyboard. Across the screen flow soundless images of Madame Bovary's despair at being in debt and in provincial France. Tobias plays them over and over again, frowning to himself.

I can sense him disengaging from Freya and – when I remain wrapped up with her – from me as well. I stand in the living room, trying to connect with him, while he sits twiddling with his computer and keyboard. Looking out of the window, I see Lizzy's petite figure processing in a clockwise direction around the courtyard.

'Do you think Lizzy is a bit strange?' I ask. 'I mean, she always was a bit fey, but spring seems to have turned her head completely.'

'Mmm.'

'Tobias, did you hear a word I just said? She's bowing in front of every tree.'

'Hmm. Who?'

'Lizzy.'

Tobias takes off his headphones and comes to the window.

'She's a pretty thing, poor soul,' he says.

'But what is she *doing*?'

'She told me the other day it was part of her ritual for spring,' he says. 'She has to greet the spirits of all the trees and remind them to wake up.'

'But they're going to wake up whether she does that or not.'

'We must persuade that kid to stay with us,' muses Tobias. 'We'll give her some work. She can do childcare and housework or something. She has no money.'

'Tobias, we don't know whether it's even *allowed* to leave a child with convulsions in the care of an unqualified adult.'

'Don't be silly,' says Tobias. '*We're* not qualified either. Leave it to me. I'll speak to her about it.'

~

Down in the valley, the fruit trees have been flowering in relays: almond, peach, plum. Clouds of blossom hang over the valley like smoke in a slow-motion artillery battle.

Like an old gunner, Tobias has developed selective deafness. He can only hear frequencies he likes. This doesn't include Freya crying. Nor, I'm beginning to accept, the sound of my voice.

I'm trying to get us on to a schedule. Tobias and Freya thwart me. Freya dozes through her carefully planned feed times. When she does wake up I have to drop everything, otherwise she slips back into sleep.

When I feed her, she arches backwards, stiffening her whole body. More often than not, she vomits and I have to start again. All my clothes are stained with baby sick. I empathise with the frantic parent birds dashing about outside. Like theirs, my whole life is one long feeding programme.

I've been trying to teach Lizzy housework and babysitting. It seems to panic her. All trace of her self-reliance vanishes as I lecture her about the correct way to sterilise bottles and how to warm milk in a bain-marie. She tries her best, but her fingers fumble, spilling precious containers of my expressed breast milk onto the floor. Reflected in her frightened eyes, I see an image of myself as a chiding older woman, obsessing about unimportant details. After these sessions Lizzy, as often as not, creeps off filled with confusion to hide in her shipping container.

'Tobias,' I say when we're alone, 'please give Lizzy a lesson in looking after Freya. I think she's intimidated by me; she can't take in my instructions.'

'Lizzy's *great* with Freya,' he says. 'Always ready to help.'

'She's always ready when *you* ask her – it just shows how much I need you to get involved in practical aspects of our lives.'

But Tobias has stopped listening. He's found a corner he likes next to the stove in the living room. When he's not composing music, he's busy consulting Sally on email or Skype. To my chagrin, high-speed broadband is the one trapping of modern life we've successfully installed.

'Will you call the DVLA, dear, and tell them they absolutely must give me my driving licence back?'

'Driving licence? You've lost your driving licence?'

'Yes, it is really most inconvenient. It was bad enough of your father to die and leave me to do the driving myself. I need it back right away.'

'How on earth did you lose it?'

My mother's voice on the phone sounds shifty. 'Never you mind, dear. Such a rude letter. They claim I can't see well enough to drive. But that's utter nonsense. I may not be able to see a *mouse* in the road. But I could certainly see a *child*.'

～

Life is marching up the mountainside towards us. In our orchard, the twigs of the apple trees are rupturing into leaf. The browns are turning gaudy green. The courtyard is messy with daffodils. The rosemary bushes have flung into purple flower and bees are everywhere.

Along with spring, I feel, comes the chance of a new beginning. I need Tobias to engage. Nobody but he can possibly understand what it's like for me living here, dealing with Freya. I can't bring myself to email my friends. Even my exchanges with Martha seem forced and artificial; any real intimacy with her will have to wait until she visits us in August. And it's not as if I can talk to my mother.

I have to get through to him.

'Tobias.'

'Mmm.'

'It's a beautiful day. I love you. How about dropping everything and going for a walk?'

'Love,' says Tobias, deep in his silent music. 'Love – that's great.'

I wait a few minutes, watching his face dyed a flickering blue by the screen. 'Do you think you'll be finished soon and able to come for a walk? I think it would be a lovely thing to do.'

'Oh yes, a lovely thing. I just have to email Sally an MP3. How about in ten minutes?'

'I'll go back upstairs and hope it works out then.'

He's already intent on his keyboard and acting as if I'm not in the room.

So I wait. And wait. An hour later I have a surge of blood to the head. I picture myself rushing back and beginning to scream: 'Just pay me some attention – at least answer me when I talk to you!' and not being able to stop. And Tobias doesn't pay me any attention at all so I pull the linen out of the sideboard cupboards onto the floor. And he still taps on his keyboard so I pull out all the drawers and this is more satisfying because there are hard things in there that rattle onto the ground. But I haven't yet broken anything so I smash the living-room windows and he still doesn't notice me. I begin to slash my wrists with the glass and to scrawl in my own blood 'Just answer me, you fucker!' on all the walls and eventually he has to section me, and that is that.

—

Overnight, total victory has been declared. The full moon rises to a southern warmness and the cloying perfume of mimosa. I find a moth the size of a handbag resting on the barn door, the strange false eyes on its wings gazing blindly at me.

Early the next morning Ludovic is out digging in his half of the potager.

When he sees me with Freya in her sling against my chest, he leans on his spade and lifts his hat.

'How is *la petite*?'

'Very well thank you. You're out early.'

'Of course,' he says. 'Gardening is my métier.'

I smile at his quaint turn of phrase in referring to gardening as a job or trade. But he adds seriously: 'My father's too. During the war he grafted tomatoes onto potato plants. The Germans requisitioned his tomatoes – but they didn't look beneath the ground. Thanks to him, we were never hungry.'

Deciphering this sentence requires a bit of a struggle with his patois, but I'm beginning to get used to his way of talking.

'What did your mother do?'

'Rose? Schoolteacher.'

'Rose?' I say. 'There's a name Rose carved on my balcony.'

'That's her. Rose Donnadieu. We used to live here when her brother, my uncle, owned Les Rajons.'

'I've been wondering who she was. Trying to imagine what she was like.'

He gives me a shrewd look. 'Beautiful. Tiny as a sparrow. But fiery with it. Rose, she is a tyrant. She shouts: "I am a schoolteacher and the sister of a schoolteacher but you are nothing but a dirty-handed *paysan*!" And my father, he just stands there, gazing at her. He's thinking: how lucky I am that she agreed to marry me.'

I look at Ludovic's crumpled figure, trying to discern

the romance of his father and his beautiful, fiery mother. But I can't see past his battered hat and his dusty work clothes.

'If you ever need somebody to look after *la petite*,' he says gruffly, 'I can watch her while I'm digging. I am experienced.'

'Do you have children?' I ask to cover my surprise at this offer. He shrugs. 'Not any more,' he says in a voice that silences all further questions.

———

Julien calls round. 'It's the waning moon of March, Anna,' he says. 'Make sure you plant your seeds today.'

'Do you always have to plant on a waning moon?'

'Oh yes. Absolutely.'

There's often a teasing expression in his eyes. I can't tell whether or not he's serious.

Julien has taken to dropping by. Or rather, he's put us into his morning round. He walks past our door on his way down into the village for his daily pilgrimage to Yvonne's cafe in Aigues.

'Do you think it's a crazy idea, trying to turn this place into a restaurant?'

'For eight weeks in the summer the valley is full of tourists,' says Julien. 'There's no reason they shouldn't come up the hill to eat here. It's a beautiful spot.'

'I don't know whether an eight-week season will ever make enough money to live on.'

Julien shrugs. 'That depends what you need. Look at me. I'm not in the tax or welfare system. I'm not on anybody's books. I don't earn and I don't exist. And yet somehow, here I am.'

'It's just that setting up a restaurant is such a big investment.'

'Use local ingredients then. You can get them for free. Here, leave Freya with Tobias for a moment – I'll give you a lesson in foraging.'

'Really? Do you have time?'

'Anna, the only thing we truly possess is time. We just have to learn what to do with it. Bring a basket.'

I try to give Freya to Tobias, but he absently shakes his head and motions to Lizzy. I have a pang of nervousness to see my child in such inattentive company. But Tobias is her father. He's got to take some responsibility, or he might as well be in London.

In five minutes we're out in the sunshine. Julien leads me to the edge of the woods.

'This is a good time to look for mushrooms. It's warm and the ground is still wet. *Morilles, cèpes, girolles*. You can even find truffles if you know where to look.' He begins tossing fungi into the basket. 'Watch out though. You need to be able to spot the poisonous ones. There's the *fausse girolle* and the *fausse cèpe* – both of those can make you sick. And the death cap or Satan's boletus can kill you.'

'Julien – maybe mushrooms are too advanced for me.'

'No, you'll learn. Just take one or two at a time, get to know them really well. You can branch out later. Or, what about this?' He rummages in a hedgerow and uncovers a low bristly plant. 'What does this remind you of?'

I look at it doubtfully. 'I can't imagine eating that. It looks prickly.'

'Look again. At the shoots.'

113

I stare and suddenly I see it. 'It's a miniature asparagus!'

'Yes – wild asparagus. There's plenty of it at this time of year. Absolutely delicious. You couldn't possibly afford to buy it.'

'It would be perfect for my restaurant. So exotic! I could serve it with a *sauce mousseline*.'

He pulls handfuls of greenery out of the hedgerow, apparently at random. 'With wild leeks and garlic – here. Or on a bed of dandelion.'

'This is fantastic! It can be a theme of my cuisine.'

'How about some nettles? They make delicious soup.'

My basket is almost full.

'Well, I suppose I'd better be going,' he says.

'Julien – how can I thank you? This has been wonderful.'

He smiles. 'Don't mention it. Being outside the money economy means I'm free to spend my life doing things I enjoy. Which, as far as I can see, makes me richer than any millionaire.'

'Well, actually . . . I was wondering if we could hire you to help with the land,' I say. 'Now spring is here it's beginning to get out of control.'

'Hmm.' Julien looks at me as if I've made some kind of faux pas. Then the grey eyes twinkle. 'Of course, if Tobias wants a hand when he goes out to cut down the undergrowth, I'd be happy to help, as a friend.'

'Not for money?'

'If you wanted to make me your wage slave, to work for you regularly for money, then . . . well, you'd also have to have something that I *really* wanted.'

He smiles, to mitigate what might, from anybody else, have been a put-down. I watch his straight, wiry back disappear down the hillside and think: what he's trying to say is that he is free, that's what's important to him.

～

It's begun to rain. Implacable warm spring rain. I should have listened to Julien – I didn't plant any seeds yesterday and now it may be weeks before it's possible to get outside. The weeds are busy growing instead.

When Julien comes by I invite him to join us for lunch and throw together grilled wild asparagus, *omelette aux cèpes* and *salade d'orties*. We sit on the covered veranda outside the house and watch the rain falling in vertical sheets against the greenery like a tropical monsoon.

'Delicious,' says Julien.

'Anna,' says Tobias with a look of rebuke in his blue eyes, 'the salad has stung my tongue.'

There's a clap of thunder and the rain redoubles.

'Make sure your water cistern is watertight,' says Julien. 'You need this rain. You're going to have to store all your drinking water over the dry season.'

The idea that it will ever be too dry is inconceivable.

～

It's still raining. The river's filled with newts and tadpoles. Wherever I look there's new life, untidy and uncontrollable, sprawling into every available space. I pop down onto the land and find roquette in the vegetable patch, and white radishes, and I think: we really should start to cut the brambles and collect brushwood and plough up the soil and buy manure and dig it in and prune the fruit trees and plant our first seeds and set up a watering system and buy a cold frame and grow indoor seedlings and cut back and cut back and cut back – and in twenty minutes I'm so exhausted I have to go back to the house to lie down.

The kitchen's danker than ever. The black mould has given way to virulent green lichen. I find Tobias gazing at a pair of sleek black-spotted slugs swinging from the ceiling, entwined together.

'Look at this,' he says, enraptured. 'They look like they're kissing.' A pale blue cloud of mucous envelops the slugs like a veil. They're clearly in the throes of passion.

In a sudden fury, I snatch them up in the dustpan and throw them out of the window. I expect Tobias to protest, but he just makes a tiny tut with his tongue like a disappointed child. Somehow it puts me on the back foot.

'I haven't time to keep cleaning this place,' I say. 'I'm knee-deep in bureaucracy. I've asked for twenty quotes for turning the barn into a restaurant and twenty men have sucked their teeth and told me "*C'est impossible*". The bottom line is that we can't have a restaurant if we don't have mains water. It doesn't conform to the norms, whatever those may be. In fact, nothing, absolutely nothing in this place conforms to any kinds of norms at all, let alone the norms of France.'

'Oh dear,' says Tobias, sounding unworried. 'I've got a couple of documentaries I can do that will cover the mortgage this month. But it's harder to keep those coming if I'm not in London.' He fixes himself a coffee.

'We can't keep going on the odd documentary. It's not just the mortgage; this is a huge place. What you're bringing in now doesn't cover living expenses. I think I'm eligible for a business loan of seven thousand euros – there's this thing called a *prêt à la création d'entreprise* – although God knows how we'll pay it off. With that and your documentary income, we'll be able to stagger on for precisely nine months by my reckoning. If I don't start earning by then, we'll have to sell up and go home.'

'Well, I'm not sure we'll be able to sell. Remember we got this place cheap because nobody wanted to buy it.'

'You're missing the point. The point is that I'm working all hours trying to make a go of this and the place is falling down round our ears. We're paying Lizzy to do housework. Why's it such a mess?'

'Well, housework in this place is a bit . . . overwhelming,' says Tobias, wandering into the living room with his coffee. 'Where would she start?'

'I'm going right now to ask Lizzy to come and clean up this mess.'

I step out into the rain. Lizzy isn't in her shipping container. At the edge of the courtyard, I spot her slight figure gyrating under a walnut tree. She's soaking wet, her black hair sleeker and more otter-like than ever with the water dripping off it in sheets. She looks as if she's doing some sort of dance. With an enormous effort, I restrain myself from asking her what on earth she's up to.

'Lizzy,' I say, 'please could you do a bit of housework?'

Lizzy gives me a hurt look. 'I'll come in a moment,' she says. 'The spiritual impulse is very strong right now and I don't want to miss it.'

⌣

I've written a list.

To do – the House:
Roof
Wiring
Drains
Plumbing
Water! (connection/filtration/storage)
Septic tank
Plastering (walls)
Ditto (ceilings)
Floors
Windows and doors
Central heating
Game kitchen
Kitchen and bathroom

It seems too daunting. I quite simply don't know where or how to begin. I turn over the paper and write another list.

To buy:
Fungicide

I leave Freya with Tobias and drive down to the valley to look for a poisonous product to kill the lichen in the kitchen. The Astra has celebrated the coming of spring by developing a fault that prevents us from closing the hood. The rain runs down my forehead and into my eyes, half blinding me. Even with the headlights on I still don't see the hitchhiker standing in the middle of the road. I slam my foot on the brakes, the car skids forwards, time slows. Branded on my retina is a flash frame of the person I'm about to kill: tall, young, slim with a fine olive face and dark eyes. Smiling trustingly at me.

The car screams to a stop. And then – way before I've had time to recover – he's clambering in.

'British plates,' he says in English. His voice is melodious with a hint of an accent. 'And an open car. How nice, even in the rain.'

It's a ridiculous thing to say. I gape at him. He looks instantly stricken as if he's been caught out in a lapse of politesse. 'I mean *especially* in the rain. I love the feeling of rain on my face. In the wind, especially.'

'Don't you mind it trickling down the back of your neck?'

'Oh no, I particularly like that.'

'Your English is perfect.'

'I studied on your beautiful Isle of Wight. I like everything English. Even milk in my tea.'

'Where are you going?' I ask.

He laughs, a nervous laugh, surprisingly high-pitched. 'I'm not sure. My family are Algerian, they're strict and they didn't approve . . . we had a row. To tell the truth, they threw me out. I don't have anywhere to stay. I can do *bricolage*, odd jobs. I'm not bad at mechanics either.'

'Could you fix my car hood? It's been stuck down since the rain began.'

'Hood? Rain?' He looks utterly confused. 'Well, I expect I could.'

I brake sharply and pull into a passing place. He's staring at me.

'Right now?' I prompt.

'Oh. Of course.'

He produces a spanner and screwdriver from his backpack

and sets to work. I feel as though I'm watching some kind of magic act. Within five minutes, the hood's snugly shut. The windows immediately begin steaming up.

He flashes me a smile of extraordinary sweetness. 'It might be difficult to get it down again,' he says. 'I need to put some grease on it.'

'Thank you,' I say. 'Would you like a job?'

As we drive back to Les Rajons the corridor of jagged rock veers up around us and the Astra's worn tyres screech on the bend. He cries out in fear, and I'm getting to know him well enough by now to wonder how he'll recover.

'I meant . . . it's breathtaking,' he says. 'It's so . . . so *mineral*.'

—

Tobias is still sitting in the living room where I left him. Freya is, fortunately, fast asleep in her Moses basket beside him. He's refilled his coffee mug, has taken off his head-phones and is doing the sudoku from a two-day-old British newspaper.

'This is Kerim,' I say. 'He is coming to help us with some DIY.'

'What a beautiful room,' says Kerim. 'You just need to plane those beams a bit and put some linseed on. And patch the walls. What a lovely sideboard. Oh – what has happened to the nuts?'

My *Homes & Gardens* bowl of walnuts is still on the sideboard but, presumably having hungry little mouths of their own to feed, the mice have launched an operation. Neat holes have been punched in selected nuts and the contents removed. Only a light litter of shell fragments over the dresser and floor hints at the felony.

'Tobias!' I shout. 'Did you see what's happened to my nuts?'

'Er . . . nuts?' says Tobias.

'The little buggers must have run right past you. In the last *hour*.'

Kerim looks enquiring.

'Mice,' says Tobias.

'I really like mice,' says Kerim enthusiastically.

'They came from in here.' I storm into the kitchen. Lizzy still hasn't cleaned it. The lichen on the walls seems to have grown thicker and more vibrantly green in the hour I've been away.

'Kerim! I have a job for you. I need a mouseproof kitchen.'

'Oh,' says Kerim. 'Do you really want to keep the mice out? Well, of course I could try blocking up all the holes into the kitchen, but that probably wouldn't stop them completely. I could make you some cupboards. With mesh around them. But it's a big job. Just for some mice.'

'You could really make me cupboards? That they couldn't get into?'

'Well, sure.'

'Hey, man,' says Tobias, perking up. 'I wonder – could you help me build a studio?'

'A studio?'

'Well, yes, a recording studio. The only problem –' he looks at me – 'is that we haven't got much of a budget for it right now. But I've been looking at the barn. There's a place we could soundproof with egg boxes so I could get my kit into it.' He flashes me a triumphant look. 'Anna – Sally's execs really loved the track. You're looking at the composer of the *Madame Bovary* score. Of course, I won't get paid until the recording stage, and they're still sorting out a few funding details, so that may be a little while. But eventually it will be seriously good money. And it'll be a fantastic boost for my career.'

—

Kerim has made himself a nest in the room next to the winery. 'Don't worry about me – I'm living like a prince,' he keeps saying, although my memory of that room is of a sort of decaying garage. When I pop in to check he's OK, I'm amazed at how comfortable he's made it.

'Oh, I just reconnected the pot-bellied stove and repaired an old iron bedstead and mattress I found in one of the ruins,' he says. 'I hope you don't mind me borrowing them. And I swept and polished a bit, of course. You know, this is a lovely room – look at the old glass in the windows. I could easily fit it up into an apartment for you. You could rent it out and earn some money.'

'That would come in handy. We could really use some more income. Tobias is earning bits and pieces from documentaries but it's looking like his big job won't pay for a while. I'm trying to start a restaurant but the tourist season round here is only eight weeks long and the tourists are all down in the valley anyway. It's Tobias's idea really.'

'What do *you* like doing?'

'I love cooking. That's what I do. That's what I *am*, really. It's just trying to find a way to do it up here.'

'Anna – why don't you try and work with what this place can offer? Beautiful surroundings, tranquillity, the middle of nowhere.'

'Not so great for a restaurant.'

'What about some sort of residential thing? Teaching maybe?'

'A cookery school,' I say slowly. 'I could write to René – this chef I know in Provence – and ask him for advice.'

'I could do up this room as accommodation. And you're bound to have some suitable rooms in the house as well.'

'It's just . . . there's so much to do. I need a kitchen. Tobias needs a studio. Yvonne needs a *laboratoire* for her sausages. And now accommodation.'

'We'll do one job at a time. I can't guarantee how long I'll be able to stay, but I'll put you on the right track. You just have to decide what your priorities are.'

———

I've pinned Lizzy down to three regular hours of childcare a day between nine and midday, starting today.

I've spent yet more time painstakingly explaining how to change a nappy, how to give Freya a bottle of expressed milk, how to burp her. How to put your thumb at the back of her neck when you lift her because she can't support her neck. Through all of this explanation, Lizzy has stared at me with large, round, otter-like eyes.

'I'm going out for a walk,' I say grimly. 'If Freya has a fit, call Tobias.'

I walk around the hillside for half an hour. When I get back, there's no sign of Lizzy or Freya. The pram and the sling are still in the living room but the Moses basket is gone.

Tobias is still in the corner of the room. I tear off his head-phones, risking his wrath.

'Where's Freya?'

'Oh, I thought she was still here, with Lizzy,' he says.

I race to the shipping container, but Lizzy isn't there. By now I'm trying not to cry. I dash into the barn. Kerim's in there hammering away at Tobias's studio. Beside him is Freya in her Moses basket, swaddled as tightly in blankets as even I could wish. Despite the noise, she seems utterly content.

By now I can't talk. I just point at the Moses basket.

'Anna – I hope you don't mind. I didn't like to disturb Tobias but I didn't think Freya should stay in the living room while he was working, so I brought her here.'

'But where was Lizzy?'

'Lizzy said she needed to go out.' He flashes me a smile. 'She has to do a special dance every day, you know, to increase her body energy. It's important to her. So I said I'd look after Freya. I don't think she really knew what to do with her anyway.'

—

Kerim is unfailingly cheerful and obliging. To everyone. To a ludicrous degree. He disappears for hours on end and reappears saying:

'. . . That sweet old lady from Rieu needed a few things from the shop, so I ran into Aigues to get them for her. She reminds me of my mother . . .'

'. . . The postmistress was a bit late on her round, so I cycled over the hill to deliver the last few letters . . .'

'. . . Jean-Luc from the farm down the road has trouble with his lumbago, so I went to milk his goats for him . . .'

He's got to know all the neighbours, which means that so have we.

Yet, for all his friendliness, he has an air of mystery about him. He won't go into why he rowed with his parents, he just says that he feels it's irreconcilable. And he flatly refuses to take money for his work.

'After all,' he says when Tobias tackles him, 'you're putting me up and . . . I might have to leave in a hurry. I don't want to let you down.'

How could anyone really be that nice? If he were a politician he'd surely be president by now. And that's the crux of it: if he's really as good as he looks why on earth is he living hand-to-mouth, here, with us?

———

Tobias has talked me down from the mesh cupboards. Kerim is now devoting all his energies to building his recording studio.

Instead, I've decided to seal the mice hermetically out of my foodstuffs. The Tupperware boxes in which I packed my ready meals are perfect for the job. They have lids that lock shut with a satisfying snap. I've examined my shelves and made a record of the dimension of each vulnerable item and have spent three hours fitting a neat plastic case of exactly the right size around every packet of sugar, of flour, of nuts and pulses.

This work gives me an indescribable amount of satisfaction.

———

Neither Tobias nor I is sleeping. We have a nightly ritual.

I retire first and I try to smuggle Freya into our bed. She takes up hardly any room. I wrap my arm around her and she wedges her face into my armpit, presses the length of her body against mine and instantly composes herself to sleep. She looks so neat, so sweet, so self-contained.

Tobias never comes to bed on time. I turn out the light and pretend I'm alone.

When he comes upstairs, he snaps the light back on with a roar. 'Get her out of here! I can't sleep with her in the bed!'

'She's making no noise. She's an angel baby.'

'You know as well as I do that she'll start twitching in the night just as I've got off to sleep. Or wailing. Or snoring. I'm not having it.'

Sometimes he resorts to tenderness and pleads: 'I want to go to bed with *you*. The old Anna. What happened to romance?'

Usually he wins and she ends up in her cot on the other side of the room.

Then the invisible wire that joins me to her pulls me a dozen times a night. I wake at the lightest sound and race to her.

Most nights, at least once, comes a barely audible suffocated cry. A call to me? A warning? A presentiment? I'll never know. It means she's beginning a fit.

I stand in the cold bedroom and hold her through it. First, the scariest part, when she seems not to breathe at all. She goes blue around the mouth. I part her hair to look at the raspberry birthmark on her head. Gradually it turns from red to black as her blood deoxygenates. Beside me is the rectal Valium we've been given for emergencies. I'm frightened to use it. So far, thankfully, just as I've been poised to take it out of its daunting packaging, she's managed a tiny breath, a half-gasp almost too quiet to hear. The black patch on her head lightens immediately to a dark wine colour. It tells me that, this time, she's winning the battle for life.

I imagine her body as the rope in a tug of war. Breath is on one end. On the other end death pulls teasingly, jerking her limbs.

I count the rhythm of her breaths and spasms. At first, there are three or four double jerks to half a gasped breath. A huge struggle, a couple of breaths. She gives a weak cry. Then a punishing orgy of jerking.

Gradually the ratio of breaths to jerks grows better – three breaths, then two jerks. Four breaths to just one jerk. Then a backslide: six jerks in succession. Invisible jaws grab her around the throat, pressing the life from her. Finally her jerking subsides to an occasional spasm. Freya lies drained, eyes staring into the middle distance, hiccuping feebly.

And now the wailing begins, long-drawn-out and inconsolable. I hold her tight against my skin and wonder if she's crying because she's lost and confused and frightened or simply because she's swallowed air.

Tobias sleeps as lightly as a cat. He's usually been awake through most of this. 'Come to bed. For Christ's sake, leave her. It won't make any difference.'

But I can't endure the thought of the little jackknifed figure convulsing alone in her cot or her inconsolable wailing cries when she comes to.

Most mornings I wake at four o'clock, trembling with fury. I lie in bed, thinking of people at random, imagining them pitying me, trying to avoid Freya, jeering at my baby. I embellish their taunts, gearing myself up into a pitch of outrage. I imagine how I'll take them on, stamp them into the ground, put them in their place.

Then, with a cold shock, I remember: none of this is true. I've made it all up. There's nobody to blame.

April

B REAKFAST, THE LES RAJONS way. Freya has just thrown up her milk all over me. Now she's slumped in her bouncy chair, hiccuping and kicking, and I'm already deep in French paperwork, absently playing with her legs, tickling the firm flesh, holding the perfect little hands and arms. At times like this she feels chunky and real. Tobias is finishing his coffee; he takes hours over breakfast. Kerim is standing on a stepladder trailing wire mesh down to the floor. Lizzy is trying to scratch saltpetre off the wall in a demoralised way.

The front door slams, bringing with it a gust of lilac-scented air. And another smell, familiar, incongruous: Chanel.

'Hello, dear. Isn't it rather late to be in your pyjamas? And goodness me, has that baby been sick on you?'

'Mother, what are you doing here?'

'I took a taxi from the station. I didn't want to bother you.'

Didn't want me to stop her coming, more like.

'But why are you here?'

'Well, since your father died, I don't really need to stay at home. And I know that you have your hands full with that baby and this terrible place. So I came to help out.'

'Help out. You mean stay? For how long?'

'For as long as it takes, darling. You never had a scrap of common sense and Tobias is even worse. Now who is that charming young man?'

Kerim is already getting down off the ladder, smiling his dazzling smile.

'Are you Anna's mother?' he says. 'Allow me thank you for having such a wonderful daughter.'

Even for Kerim, I think, this is over the top. But my mother is becoming a fluttering teenager before my eyes. And whatever the DVLA's opinion on the subject, there seems to be nothing too badly wrong with her eyesight. I see her gaze move over Kerim's perfect white teeth, his large dark eyes, his soft lashes.

'Well, she *has* had a good upbringing,' she preens.

He beams back at her. 'Your daughter and Tobias took me in and gave me work to do when I had nowhere else to go.'

'Oh, he's the wonderful one,' I say. 'He's marvellous at all our odd jobs.'

'Odd jobs as well?' breathes my mother. 'You are *so* lucky,'

<hr />

I've persuaded Tobias to give Freya her bath. My mother and I stand by the stove watching. Freya is quiet, enraptured; she kicks her legs under the water with immense concentration. His curly dark head is bent over hers and I think how similar they look. I feel, too, that this baby shares with him a sybaritic love of physical sensation.

'Can she feel heat and cold?'

'Yes, Mother.'

'What else can she feel?'

132

'Well, she feels happy and comfortable, and angry and hungry –'

'Humph.'

'What do you mean, humph?'

My mother sounds cross. 'That's nothing to boast about. I suppose even a plant can feel all *those* things.'

My mother is an animist; she's invented her own religion based on ancestor worship and superstition. In her bedroom at Les Rajons she's constructed a small shrine. Beneath the picture of her own mother, who died when she was a girl, she's placed votive images: blurry portraits cut out from family photographs.

I'm there, of course, and her favourite cats. Freya is up on our level. A little further down is a picture of my father. Right at the bottom is a minuscule picture of Tobias. On the dressing table under the shrine, like some kind of totemic animal, sits my childhood teddy bear, the one she brought to the hospital and has evidently decided not to give to Freya after all. But I'm not complaining: I'm agreeably surprised that Freya has made it to the highest rank of postulants.

'This place is a complete shambles, dear. Who is that strange hippy girl? Is she supposed to be doing housework?'

'Lizzy is a bit of a free spirit. She just sort of came with the house.'

'Well, she's certainly not very good at cleaning. Even worse than you. They don't train you young girls any more. And you will all run around having careers, damaging your wombs. No wonder the baby . . .' Exaggerated pause. Hand clapped to mouth. My mother's tactfulness could shatter glass at a hundred paces. 'Anyway, dear, you'd better let me take charge on the domestic front.'

I didn't know it until she said them but those are exactly the words I've been longing to hear. It feels the way it did when I was ill as a child: a wave of relief sweeping over me, the realisation that if I liked I could take to my bed right now and let her bustle around me with fluid efficiency, run a cool hand over my brow, tuck me up between crisp linen sheets, bring me home-made broth and lemonade on a tray decorated with fresh flowers.

My mother isn't just any housewife. She's a graduate of the London College of Domestic Science, a severe establishment where she spent the flower of her youth learning how to cook, clean and generally slave for a man. She trained in an era that wasted nothing, repaired or recycled everything. 'I was top of my class, dear,' she likes to say, 'and I can tell you, in those days, the competition was pretty stiff.'

My childhood memories are peppered with the regimental discipline of my mother's domestic chores: the washing up, the hoovering, the methodical polishing of brass. My school clothes were always beautifully folded in my drawers; everything was pressed, even my socks. She knows the right way to scrub, cook and iron. And I'm pretty sure she knows a nifty trick or two about dealing with lichen growing on the walls.

'Now, where,' says my mother, 'is your linen cupboard? That's usually the place to start. I expect it's in a terrible mess.'

───

My mother has sorted out our cupboards, encroached on my kitchen and has taken possession of our laundry.

'Between you and your Tupperware boxes and your mother and her ironing, we could open a sanctuary for obsessive compulsives.'

134

'Tobias, you're forgetting what it was like around here before she arrived.'

'I'm sick of the grotesque way she flirts with Kerim.'

'She's not flirting. She just grew up in a different era.'

But Tobias has a point. My mother has taken to doing the ironing wearing Chanel perfume and Hermès scarves. She's finally found a man who never tires of fetching and carrying for her. Best of all, Kerim holds the office of Mother in all the reverence that even she could wish.

'Oh, don't carry that,' he says. 'Let me help. You are a Mother.' And she laps it up.

She has theories about what is and what isn't damaging to the womb. She'll get down on her hands and knees and scrub a flagstone floor but she won't hammer a nail into the wall. 'That's man's work. Kerim dear, would you mind?' And Kerim never minds in the least. Tobias's studio is long finished; for the past couple of weeks he's been working on the kitchen and the game larder, but much of his time is devoted to carrying out my mother's commands.

'Your mother-in-law is very glamorous,' he says to Tobias.

'Watch out, she's already overworked one man to death.'

'Oh, you're kidding. She's a nice lady. Like my mother.'

'How did a guy like you end up falling out with your mother?' asks Tobias, incredulous.

Kerim just looks sad. 'I don't know, but I miss her. A mother is the most precious person you have.'

Kerim and my mother sit together for hours in the evening after the rest of us have gone to bed.

'He's a simply charming young man. It's funny, I can say anything to him, anything. We really *talk*. It reminds me of when your father was young. Before we were married, of course. You don't talk after you get married and have children. I expect you're finding that with Tobias. Kerim is much younger than me but we have a real connection. I think he values my company. And company is the most important thing in any relationship.'

'Relationship? I thought you hated that word. You told me it was nasty and newfangled.'

My mother looks flustered. 'Well, Kerim does use it a lot, I suppose, when we talk about things. Somehow it doesn't sound too bad coming from him.'

'What on earth do you talk to him about? I've never exactly found Kerim chatty. Obliging, yes, talkative, no.'

'We have such wonderful conversations, dear. In many ways he's older than his years. He understands all sorts of things.'

'What sort of things?'

'I've told him all about your father.'

'And what does he have to say about that?'

'Well.' My mother looks hazy for a moment. 'Well, dear, he quite agrees with me in everything I say.'

Kerim has been even more active than my mother in taking our lives in hand.

He's gently removed Freya from Lizzy, whom we're still paying to look after her. He hammers away with her by his side, solicitously covering her Moses basket in sheets like a canary so she doesn't breathe in dust.

He's kept me to my promise to write to René, enquiring whether he might be able to help me set up a residential cookery school here at Les Rajons.

Best of all, he's given me back my sanctuary: my new kitchen is taking shape before my eyes.

He's blocked the holes in the kitchen wall as best he can to stop the mice getting in. He's kept the saltpetre at bay with a *doublage*, a double wall. He's stripped the quarry tiles with hydrochloric acid to reveal their beautiful terracotta colour. He's removed all trace of old soot from the bread oven and has miraculously got it working. He has tastefully installed modern stainless-steel sinks, a range cooker and an impressive array of work surfaces and shelving.

His improvements to the game kitchen are even more dramatic. He's fitted the archway with a solid oak door he found in the barn, turning it back into a separate room. He's plastered the walls and has pulled down the polystyrene false ceiling where we found the dead mouse. He's planed the oak beams, cleaned the flagstone floor and has brought the place into the twenty-first century with discreet wiring and plumbing.

His work has revealed a small room but an impressive one, clearly built before the rest of the house. It's got a medieval look; long and thin, tapering slightly on both sides. At its narrowest point is a square stone window frame with four panes above a shallow stone sink. The shape of the room has the effect of emphasising the window and the sink: all the lines incline towards them. Above the sink is the butcher's hook, thick and rusted. The ceiling is high enough to hang a heavy carcass on that hook. It's positioned so that the blood will run into the sink.

'Ugh – look at this hook,' says Lizzy. 'What's it for?'

'For hanging game,' says Ludovic, who uses his work in the potager as an excuse to pop up in the house whenever he feels like it. 'There was often a whole stag hanging from that hook. When I was a child.'

He's a hunter and a tough old bird, but he must have a soft spot somewhere; he's got tears in his eyes.

I've got a letter back from René saying that he'll be delighted to refer students to me. By which he means, of course, those who are beneath his contempt: the lightweight Brits who want a holiday with some cooking thrown in rather than a proper *formation* in a professional kitchen.

For once, I don't mind being a lightweight. Suddenly it seems more fun and interesting to offer experience as much as education: foraging for ingredients, cooking them up in the bread oven and on the range, and eating them together on trestle tables outside in the courtyard.

'Kerim, you're an angel. What would we do without you?'

'Don't say that, Anna, I don't deserve it.'

'You renovate our house and refuse to take any money, you build Tobias a studio, run my career and look after our child. What else can I call you, if not an angel?'

He looks moodily down at the ground. 'I'm a liar,' he says. 'I'm not what I seem.' And however much I probe, I can't get anything more out of him.

—

Kerim has invited my mother to lunch at Yvonne's.

'He asked me so formally. He was quite shy,' my mother says. 'It's quite innocent, of course, but do you think it's a *date?* I don't want him to get *ideas*. It would be quite wrong to encourage him. Tell me, what do you young people do nowadays? Can a man ask a woman to lunch without any ulterior motive? Perhaps you and Tobias had better come too, dear. As chaperones. Besides, I don't think he can have any money. Yes, I think Tobias should pay the bill.'

I feel the familiar rising tide of irrational anger. Tobias is so difficult these days. How can I possibly suggest lunch at Yvonne's with my mother?

I take refuge the coward's way. 'Oh, for God's sake, Mother, what century are you living in? Don't be so ridiculous, how could it possibly be a date? You're three times his age. And besides, doesn't it even occur to you to pay for yourself?'

'You young people can pay for your own meals if you like. *We* used to look pretty and have a nice young man pick up the bill.'

My mother's girlishness has evaporated. Part of me hisses at myself: 'Well, Anna, I hope you're proud. You did that.' But once it starts, my sarcasm is a steam train rolling downhill. I can't jump off.

'You mean you had sex for food,' I snap.

'Good heavens no, they didn't expect anything like that. They just wanted to be seen with a pretty girl on their arm.' But she looks hurt anyway.

'*I'd* be proud to be seen with you on my arm, Amelia.'

Kerim has come through the door without me noticing. I feel a slow blush rising up my face, but he just smiles his politician's smile and glides effortlessly to the rescue.

'Anna – Amelia and I are going to have lunch at Yvonne's. I was wondering if Tobias and you might come along? As my guests, of course. I've already asked Tobias and he says it's OK if you agree. Oh, please do come, Anna, it wouldn't be the same without you.'

———

Over a substantial lunch of charcuterie, my mother downs half a bottle of Faugères and holds forth.

139

'I was considered rather risqué at college for wearing capri pants. Grace Kelly looked so wonderful in them, and I couldn't rest until I had them too. Don't look at me like that, dear – it was 1957, the permissive society hadn't been invented yet. It was all day dresses and dirndl skirts. The other girls wore nylons of course. But I was eighteen and I thought nylons were so *boring*.'

I think how attractive she looks for her age. Kerim's dark eyes are full of admiration. She's blossoming.

'Yes, I was quite a live wire before I married your father. But you know how it is: you get married and the day the honeymoon is over he brings you piles of dirty laundry instead of flowers. The man you thought was your knight in shining armour suddenly becomes a gigantic baby. I've never told you this, Anna, but your father was a huge hypochondriac. I was always telling him there was nothing wrong with him – and then he went and died. He never would listen to me.'

I roll my eyes; she has, indeed, told me this, many times. Out of loyalty to my father, I always consider it my duty to block out her confidences. But Kerim makes a soft clucking noise and puts an arm round her. 'I don't suppose he could help it, Amelia dear,' he says.

'I put up with him for years because I thought that at least I'd have somebody to grow old with. He's stolen my old age. I think it was . . . unfair of him. I really do. Badly bred.'

'There, there, Amelia, don't cry,' says Kerim, and I see that her eyes are brimming.

'That stupid man,' hiccups my mother. 'Why couldn't he just listen to me when I *told* him there was nothing wrong with him?'

'I reckon your mother has a bit of a crush on Kerim,' says Tobias.

'Don't be silly. My mother's lonely, sure – she'd never have come here otherwise – but she can't be seriously interested in Kerim. He's forty years younger than her.'

'Well,' says Tobias, 'I'm not so sure Kerim isn't interested in her. She's a well-preserved woman, obviously quite a catch in her day. She's what, late sixties? That's not so old nowadays. A widow. Comfortably off. Why not?'

'Never! Not Kerim.'

'We don't know much about him. He's very charming, but why don't we ever hear anything about his family or friends? He might be after her money.'

'He won't even take payment for the work he does for us.'

'Perhaps he's after bigger game. He certainly spends long enough with her. He's down in the living room with her now.'

'That's foolish talk.'

'Creep down and see what they're up to. You know you want to.'

'I do not.'

'All right, turn the light out and let's sleep.'

I turn over in bed. 'Well, I might just nip quietly and check they're all right . . .'

It's past midnight. I inch down the oak staircase, avoiding the treads that creak.

Through the open doorway I can see my mother and Kerim on the sofa in front of the stove. I hear my mother's flirtatious giggle. The one that knocked them dead in 1957.

'Oh, you've made me a teeny bit drunk. I'll lose my thread. I never used to drink when my husband was alive but it *is* rather nice. Now where was I? Oh yes, sex.'

I freeze on the stair. Sex? My mother talking about sex? When I was ten, she thrashed me just for saying the word out loud.

'The trouble with the permissive society,' she continues, 'is that it's brought so much . . . so much *nastiness* into the open.'

Kerim makes a noise that she interprets as encouragement.

'Underage sex, for instance, and sex outside marriage. Of course, in my day, we knew it went on but we didn't need to *hear* about it all the time. It wasn't something people boasted about. And homosexuals. Gays, they call them now. That used to be such a *nice* word and now you can't use it for fear of being misunderstood. I knew some poofs, of course, but they wouldn't dream of making a fuss about it. I don't want to be made to think about what homosexuals do in bed. Nowadays you can't turn on the television without somebody or other talking about it. A vicar, it was, the other day, saying what they do is quite all right. Well, it's not. Not at teatime. Not on the television. I'm quite glad that they haven't got a box in this awful house. It's just too embarrassing.'

I tiptoe back up to Tobias. 'I don't think we need to worry,' I whisper. 'She's telling him some of her views. Even the most dedicated treasure-hunter would be put off.'

        —

We've bought Freya a silver helium balloon in the shape of a fish. Tobias has tied it to the baby gym next to her head. She turns her face towards it. I believe she's staring at it. When I put the string of the balloon into one tightly curled fist she seems to hold onto it. She moves her fist; the balloon bobs up and down.

'Accident,' says Tobias.

'Well, I think that maybe she's doing it deliberately.'

'Oh nonsense. You're projecting. You want her to be developing, so you see development.'

'What do you think, Julien?' These days, I find myself appealing to Julien's judgement more and more. He doesn't answer at once. We all watch the podgy fist and the balloon falling and rising for a few moments.

'I'm not sure she knows her hand is connected to the string,' he says finally, 'but I believe she realises that when she moves, the balloon moves as well.'

'There, Tobias, you see!'

Julien smiles. 'I came to invite you to a party,' he says. 'At my place. I don't think you've been there yet. It's a celebration of spring. And please bring Freya — after all, she belongs to us too now, you know.'

I'm absurdly touched. I lean over Freya and roll her towards me, her fist still clenched around the string. She lifts her arm and we're tangled together.

'Excuse me,' says Tobias. 'Let me just unravel my family.'

For a moment, as he tries to loosen the string, we're all three pulled into its circle, bound up in it together. I think with some wonder: we are a family.

———

Tonight, instead of going up to bed alone, I sit beside Tobias in his studio, watching his concentrated face as he listens to silent music through his headphones. It has transpired that nothing about the *Madame Bovary* film is certain. It's a co-production; they're running out of funding. They've finished shooting but need more money for post-production. Sally wants Tobias – as cheaply as possible – to write parts of a score so that they can show these scenes to potential funders.

'What are you doing here?' he asks.

'Waiting for you,' I say. 'Do you want to play me some?'

He takes off his headphones. 'It's not . . . ready yet. Not right. Later.'

He doesn't seem defensive, though. For once. I plunge in.

'Why are you so hard to reach these days? I've never seen you like this over a piece of music before.'

'This is the big one. It's really important to me.'

'That's not really it, is it?'

'I can't explain. You wouldn't understand.'

'Try me.'

'When I get into my studio these days, I have the feeling that I'm composing for my life. Literally my life. That I'm being gobbled up and devoured and that only if I can hang on in here and process this, work at it until it's done, will I have any chance. It's not coming easily. Half the time I'm scoring the same scene over and over, only to have Sally email me to say they've recut it yet again to suit some potential client. I feel as if I'm trying to swim through treacle. As if I'm . . . a ship that's been hit below the waterline and I'm struggling along towards land. But all the while I'm sinking, I just don't know it yet.'

He's slipped an arm around me and he's talking quietly against my hair. I can feel his breath brushing my forehead. 'Emma Bovary was entirely trapped. It didn't matter who she was, how talented or beautiful or flawed, her hopes and dreams, how much she rebelled. In those stifling surroundings, she was doomed. I feel like that. That feeling of suffocation, it's getting into my music.'

I can't follow him, but I make myself nod sympathetically.

'Anna, we're both fumbling along alone in the dark, trying to deal with Freya in our own ways. I know I'm being . . . unavailable . . . but I need to do this. I need to find some way to escape, even if it's just in my head. I'm so afraid – I'm frightened all the time.'

'What of?'

'Of lots of things. I'm afraid you're falling in love with her – and I don't dare come with you. Because the more we let ourselves love her, the more she's going to hurt us. I'm afraid of the future. Of going to visit a middle-aged Freya in some institution, covered in bedsores. I'm afraid of our lives vanishing in a . . . a vortex of misery over a child who'll never even know who we are. I feel more and more alone. You rush around doing things and I just sit here, twiddling with music that won't come and an endless growing feeling that unless I can crack this piece I'll disappear without a trace.'

'Shh,' I say, as if I'm calming a child. I tighten my hold on him and we hug for a long time. 'Oh, Tobias, I love you,' I whisper. 'I don't think I'd even be alive without you. I only rush about because my method of dealing with a crisis is to fix it. I spend all my time trying to . . . solve Freya. To square some sort of impossible circle – to work out how I can keep my baby, my husband, my sanity. How I can regain control of my life. I'm afraid all the time too. What if we don't love her?'

'Oh, Anna, you still don't get it.' Tobias tightens his arms around me and his frank blue eyes are wide. 'What if we *do*?'

Every day the balloon shrinks a little; the fish has become tipsy. Gradually, it's drowning. One day soon I'll have to throw it away. But I can't bring myself to do it yet.

I wake early and the rising sun entices me out of the house. I leave Freya asleep in her cot and Tobias snoring in our bed. Outside, everything is golden and wet with dew and the birds are singing with what seems to me to be a kind of contentment as if they know there are months of good weather stretching before them.

Every so often I think I really ought to go back to the house. But then I see something fresh and exciting just a little further along the piste: a wild narcissus, a black-and-yellow salamander, a hoopoe with its absurdly exotic crest and scimitar-curved beak.

As I approach the war memorial in the forest, I hear voices in the distance. I'm puzzled: it seems ridiculously early to find anybody else here.

Ahead of me, I see a tight knot of elderly men wearing some sort of dress uniform. Ludovic is among them, his chest covered in medals. It seems disrespectful to pass by yet I don't feel I have any right to intrude. I stand back from the group, watching them. The men seem frail, their medals futile in the face of history.

As the group breaks up, Ludovic spots me. 'Ah, *bonjour, la parisienne.*'

'What are you doing?' I ask.

'Remembering. On this day in 1944 there was a battle here. With the Boche.'

'You can't have been old enough to have fought in the war.' It's a stupid thing to say; it sounds patronising.

'In 1944 I was fifteen years old. I'd been running errands

for the Maquis, the French Resistance, from the age of thirteen.'

'Was it dangerous?'

Another stupid question. Ludovic ignores it.

'Are you walking home?' he asks. 'Me too.' After we've walked a while he adds: 'This was a very important area for the Maquis.'

'Were you in this battle? The one you're commemorating?'

He merely shakes his head.

'Look at this forest, how thick it is,' says Ludovic. 'In 1944 there were men camping here, between the pine trees, hiding like animals. No comforts, no sanitation. Oh, that smell – woodsmoke and shit. Every animal has its own smell. Us too. I'd use a special whistle with two notes, and the men would appear from nowhere. I'd bring food from the village – not much, a little butter, some bread, some cheese.'

We're leaving the track now, veering into the pine trees. Tobias and I always avoid this forest. It's too dark, too sterile. The trees grow close, blocking out the sunlight from even their own lower branches. Nothing grows between them. It's a gloomy place.

'Right here, under this tree, there's a big sack of explosives,' he says. 'Over here Benedict has brought a mahogany mirror. We tease him because he likes to shave every day. You can't blame him – he has a pretty young wife.'

'What happened?' I ask.

'Some bastard informer told the Boche about the camp. There was an operation. I wasn't there that day, so I survived.'

He shakes his head and I stand foolishly looking at his medals, glinting in the fresh sunshine as if they're newly minted. There doesn't seem to be anything I can say.

147

'I have been considering your trouble with the mice,' says Ludovic at last. 'Maybe it isn't the mice. Perhaps it's the *loirs*.' He mimes a scampering animal with his hands. 'The little beasts with the big eyes and the thick tails. Once I had the *loirs* in my attic. Finally I am obliged to take a concrete gun and spray it over all the walls and ceiling. It's the only way.'

'Oh, I really don't think we want to do that.'

'If it's the *loirs*, then that is the only way,' repeats Ludovic.

———

'Edible dormouse,' says Tobias, googling.

'What?'

'The *loir*. Edible dormouse. Look, here's a picture.' It seems to be the only part of Ludovic's story that interests him.

Despite Kerim's best efforts, every time I go into the kitchen fresh pellets of shit mock me. It's clear the rodents are still finding a way in.

'They look quite sweet.'

The edible dormouse is almost a chipmunk. A much better thing to have in the kitchen than mice.

'They grow twenty centimetres long. That might explain why the droppings are, well, a bit on the large side for mice,' says Tobias. 'Oh look: the edible dormouse was once considered a delicacy. The Romans kept them in large earthenware pots called *dolia* and fattened them up with a diet rich in walnuts. They were served as a dessert dipped in poppy seeds and honey.'

'Well, there's a recipe to teach my cookery students.'

'I wouldn't like,' says Tobias, 'to be any kind of animal with "edible" in my name.'

We laugh together for the first time, it seems, in ages. On a good day I have just enough spare capacity to be generous to Tobias, to let him soak in the bath while I feed Freya. On a good day I manage to stay up until he comes out of his studio and so we can go to bed at the same time. On a good day he's grateful and consequently nice to me in return. We're on a knife-edge, both of us, balanced at the limit of what we can endure.

—

Yvonne's begun working in the game kitchen. She comes and goes on her mysterious business with a minimum of fuss. From time to time tantalising smells emerge but her processes are shrouded in secrecy.

She and I are becoming friends. In contrast to the fluctuating and temperamental personalities in our household, she's a given constant – dependable, predictable and trustworthy. She's always ready to help with childcare and often goes about her work with Freya wedged blissfully against her voluptuous bosom.

'Did you mention that you wanted me to help out with the garden?' asks Julien shortly after her first visit. 'I find I could do with some sous after all. Of course, because of my particular situation, I have to work on the black.'

He names a price that displays a surprisingly precise knowledge of the going rate for labour in the modern world.

Make no mistake, I tell myself, he's here because Yvonne is working in our game kitchen. Finally, I have something he wants.

—

This morning there's a letter for Kerim sitting in the postbox. With a handwritten address. My mother eyes it as we wait for him to come to breakfast.

'Perhaps it's from his mother,' she says.

The minutes tick by. Kerim appears. 'Oh, Kerim dear, here you are,' trills my mother. 'You've got a letter. Do open it! We can't stand the suspense.'

Kerim looks at the envelope. A deep flush begins at his neck and rises up to his hairline. Then he rips it open and devours its contents.

'My fiancée is coming. And maybe a school friend as well. Oh, *putain*. Today. That's just like them. I need to run to the station right now. May I borrow the Astra?'

His whole face has lifted. We're used to his thousand-watt smile but this is different, as though a lamp has been lit behind his eyes.

'Of course, go!' I say.

'I'll bring them to meet you at Julien's party this afternoon.'

We sit, stunned, listening to the front door slam and the car start up. It's my mother who eventually breaks the silence.

'Well I never. The devil. I knew he was too good to be true.'

⌒

My mother's on tenterhooks. She's taken particular care with her toilette.

'Darling, do you think you could help me set my hair? And perhaps I could do yours too. I think we should make an effort for Kerim's young lady. She might think he's fallen among a bunch of ruffians.'

Tobias has got her completely wrong. Yes, she likes to flirt, but that's as far as it goes. She's genuinely, girlishly excited to meet Kerim's fiancée.

'I do hope she's a nice girl. I'd hate to see him throw himself away on just anyone. Anyway, we'll have to let her stay for a while. I do so want us to make a good impression. I wonder why he never mentioned her. Only his mother. I like that about him – he talks about his mother a lot.'

Just after noon we put Freya in her sling and we climb over the ridge of rock that joins our mountain with the next.

'I always think it's like a dragon's backbone,' says Lizzy.

'Don't be ridiculous,' says my mother, but Lizzy is right – that's exactly what it looks like. We pretend we're walking along the spine of a slumbering creature.

Halfway over, I ask: 'What's that amazing smell?'

We stop, trying to place the perfume, familiar, evocative: old ladies and childhood memories. Yet nothing to be seen except ragged rocks.

'Down there,' says Lizzy, pointing down the chasm.

When I last looked, the dragon's flanks were brown and mossy green. Now they're a startling purple.

'Violets!'

They're impossibly fragile, growing apparently straight out of the stone, their perfume both delicate and overpowering.

At the infinity pool Lizzy leads us up a steep track. We arrive at a great white oak tree with a slab of stone resting upon two other slabs at its base. A large grey cat with amber eyes is sitting on it staring owlishly at us.

'It's a dolmen!' says Tobias scrutinising the stone slab. 'Look – there are cup and ring patterns on it. Amazing – just think, that stone has been here for thousands of years.'

'A sacred place,' breathes Lizzy.

'It's a hearth,' I say. 'A kitchen. There are pots and pans on it and a place for a fire underneath.'

I spot a wooden stair with the thick trunk of a living vine for a banister spiralling up the tree trunk. I shade my eyes and look up. 'There's a house up there. Not a normal tree house. A real house. With windows. And wooden shingles instead of roof tiles. And a *veranda*.'

'No, no, dears,' says my mother. 'We're in the wrong place. The party is over *there*.'

She's pointing beyond the oak tree to a cherry orchard with a clear view over the mountains. There are trestle tables and benches set out under the trees.

The orchard is full. Full with dogs fighting each other, with children running around like bullets, with people smoking dope, with pagans dancing, with an orchestra of didgeridoos and other outlandish instruments. Full with copper pots of stew, with whole sheep roasting over fires and with plastic buckets of mead. Full to the brim with life.

In the very centre of things, where the biomass of humans and animals is densest, we spot Julien. He's clearly been sampling the mead all morning and is delighted to see us. 'I didn't think you'd make it all this way,' he keeps saying.

'Julien, how on earth did you end up here?' asks Tobias.

'I was born here. In a yurt. I built the tree house myself. Let me show you.'

He darts back towards the oak tree. I wonder if he'll make it up the stairs in his unbalanced condition but he's as deft as a mountain goat. The cat runs, doglike, behind him. We puff after them, clinging onto the vine-banister, tripping on the uneven wooden treads. Freya, in her sling, thumps against my chest as I run.

'Welcome to my home. It's got the best view in the mountains – possibly excepting your own.'

'Wow,' I say. 'It's . . . spectacular.' I mean the vine.

'It's *glycine*,' says Julien. 'Wisteria.'

It has no leaves yet, just the ghostlike wraiths of blossom to come, curling out of the dark wood like smoke. It looks like a giant's hand clutching the cabin with gnarled black claws.

'What a house,' says Tobias.

The cabin is nestled in a crook between the trunk and a branch. There are no straight lines: the walls are curved, even the windows are rounded with forked branches dividing the panes. A shingle roof curls down to join the wisteria veranda.

'We have all mod cons. A genuine oak front door – no need for a key, it's never locked.'

He swings open the door. Inside we glimpse a single room with a wood-burning stove. No furniture except a hanging wooden bed slung from a living branch somehow incorporated into the structure. Walls, floor, ceiling all made of wood.

'It's difficult to see where the room ends and the tree begins.'

'I built it *in* the tree and *of* the tree,' says Julien.

'Kitchen?' asks my mother sternly.

'Downstairs,' says Julien, ushering us back down to the dolmen.

'I knew it,' I say.

'Very practical,' says Julien. 'I don't damage the stones and I can cook any dish I want.'

'Bathroom?' demands my mother.

Julien points vaguely to the path. 'The infinity pool is my bathroom. A bit cold in winter but perhaps you'll agree the view compensates.'

'You're the original man of the hills,' says Tobias. 'Do come round to ours any time you want a hot shower.'

'Are you from this area, originally?' I ask.

He shakes his head. 'My parents came to Languedoc from Paris after 1968. I suppose you'd call them part of the hippy generation. There were a lot of people at that time trying to go back to the land. The old peasants were mistrustful at first.'

'That must have been tough,' says Tobias.

'A lot of people didn't make it and went home. My parents worked hard and stayed. They didn't believe in property owner-ship. An old man lent them this piece of land in exchange for picking the cherries. They put up a yurt and – eventually – I came along. No birth certificate, no registration, no taxation. My parents are dead now and so is the old man but his son lets me stay on the same terms.'

Over his shoulder, I catch sight of Yvonne picking her way through the mud in pink patent kitten heels, a white pencil skirt and scooped-neck top accentuating her curves, her flaxen hair tied up in a pert pink-spotted bandanna, her accessories – shiny plastic earrings, plastic necklace, lipstick, handbag – in the same shade of bubble-gum pink as her shoes.

I spot her before Julien does. He's deep in another anecdote.

'The local school was hell. The kids . . . well, it wasn't easy. One day I was herding my parents' sheep, I was eleven years old. One of the old *paysans* saw me. His son had been a few years ahead of me at the school – one of my worst tormentors. He'd just left for a job in the town. That day his father said: "Julien – how are you this morning?" Just that, nothing more. And I'll never forget that feeling – it was the first time any local had acknowledged me in eleven years. It made me feel warm all over.'

He laughs easily. When he's like this, relaxed, impervious to anything, he's difficult to resist. Then Yvonne walks into his field of view in her spotted bandanna and her pencil skirt and he loses track of what he is saying. Around her he becomes tongue-tied and stilted, he loses his charm and confidence.

In spite of her ridiculous outfit Yvonne is looking more beautiful than ever. Like a perfect painted china doll. And what an effort she's made. Surely it must mean she loves him too.

———

Julien goes off to fuss around Yvonne. The spell is broken.

A bearded hippy reels past us, puffing on a joint: 'Are you coming or going?' he asks.

'I'm going to read everybody's palms,' announces Lizzy. I watch as she gathers a little gaggle of would-be clients around her, their palms outstretched towards her.

I've oppressed poor Lizzy with my demands for housework. I've been so wrapped up in my own projects and frustrations that I've forgotten how free-spirited she really is, how blithe.

'I can't read all your hands at once.' She's laughing.

'Me next, me,' says Tobias although he doesn't believe in horoscopes.

She takes his hand, still laughing, and turns it over. 'I have to look at your nails,' she says, 'to see if you have a temper.'

He smiles. 'You should know that by now.'

'I don't prejudge. I just read what I can see in your hand.'

'So do I?'

'What?'

'Have a temper?'

155

'Look – right here is your mount of Venus. You're very passionate. And creative. And kind.'

'And irresistibly attractive?' he teases.

She scrutinises his hand. 'That's a matter of opinion. It won't be on your hand. Here's your head line.'

'Intelligent?'

'Lazy.'

She's a mere teenager but she's poised and confident. A man could easily fall in love with Lizzy. Tobias certainly seems to have a soft spot for her. And if she has a soft spot for him – well, my bad temper must be making things pretty easy for her.

Suddenly I'm desperate to get away from the fortune-telling. I pick up my mead and march across the orchard.

Yvonne is sitting hunched on a log, tugging her white pencil skirt up to her thighs to avoid the mud that is already spattered on her pink patent leather shoes. Julien has brought her a glass of mead but she's pushed it angrily away. The matching pink patent handbag, too obviously her best, lies beside her. Her pink-spotted bandanna droops on her lowered head like the banner of a vanquished army. She looks as if she's trying not to cry.

I sit down next to her. 'You look lovely,' I say.

She stares around at the bacchanalian scene. 'These are not . . . proper people. Julien is not . . . I thought once . . . but he will never be *correct*. It is his upbringing.'

'I've watched him,' I say. 'When he sees you he can't concentrate on anything else.'

For a moment I think I've gone too far. It's none of my business, after all. Then she erupts: 'My father would apprentice him. We could sort out his paperwork. In ten years he could be the village butcher. He would have status. We could buy a plot of land and build a nice villa on the edge of town. With a fitted kitchen and maybe even a swimming pool . . .'

'Oh, Yvonne, I don't think he'd ever be happy in a villa.'

She gives a kind of heart-roar that begins in a sob and ends in a wail: 'Well, how am *I* ever supposed to be happy, living with him here, in a *tree*?'

The sun sets, the hurricane lamps are lit, the wild band strikes up, the mead flows, the dogs and children howl and the mud churns into a foaming mess. My mother dances with the best of them. First Julien spins her round and round, then an old man with a long grey beard and finally a neo-Celt wearing a felt robe with a hunting horn slung on a chain around his waist.

'Darling! It's just like doing the twist,' she cries and I get a glimpse of her irresistible younger self, full of *joie de vivre*.

Then she's shouting: 'Kerim! Kerim! Oh darling, he's here! I can't see *her*, but there is his school friend. Kerim! Where are your manners, dear? Introduce us to your friend. And *where* is your fiancée?'

'Allow me to present you with Gustav.'

'Hello, Gustav. I'm so delighted to meet any friend of Kerim's.'

'My fiancé.'

It seems to me that the music comes at that moment to a crashing stop, that the dancers stand still in their tracks, and all is silent in the glade. That can't be true but certainly my mother's next words ring out clearly for everybody to hear.

'Oh my goodness,' she cries. 'Oh how awful. You *disgusting* boys.'

May

I T'S FROWNED UPON IN the valley to buy your vegetables during the summer. Even up here on the hillside, where the soil is thinner, the rule holds.

'A euro for a lettuce in the supermarket!' says Ludovic. 'Extravagance. You can grow a hundred from one packet of seeds.'

Down in the potager, Ludovic's vegetables are planted in razor-sharp lines. His beans are shackled to bamboo racks. His tomatoes are pricked out to within an inch of their lives. Ludovic advocates pesticides, slug death, flytraps. Down on the lower slopes, his fruit trees jangle with plastic bottles announcing that they've been sprayed with various poisons. There are no weeds beneath his immaculate vines, only the crinkled brown of dead grass.

'What? You weed by hand?' he says. 'I use an excellent preparation: Roundup *de* Monsanto. Put it on the leaves of the weeds as they come through and it will kill them all.'

Kerim and Tobias have been working on getting the *béal*, the irrigation channel, flowing. It's an extraordinary feat of peasant labour, a rudimentary aqueduct carved out of the bedrock, over a kilometre long, with a wooden sluice gate at the top. All this to divert a mean trickle of water out of the river and channel it to the vegetable plot.

'Ludovic,' I ask, 'does anybody mind us taking water from the river?'

'Not any more. Sixty years ago everybody had to take turns; you could only use the *béal* on certain days. But nowadays there's nobody left. It was different when my uncle owned Les Rajons.'

'What did your uncle do?'

'Him? *Maître d'école*, schoolteacher, like my mother. And *chef de résistance* of the Maquis in this area during the war.'

'And what was he like?'

'A strong character, courageous. As you can imagine, to allow his nephew and his sister to take such risks.'

'Rose was in the Resistance too?'

'Yes. Not as a combatant. As an *agent de liaison*. Dangerous work, but nobody could stop Rose. Not my father.'

'Did he try?'

'Oh yes. He hated war. He lost an arm fighting in the trenches, in the first war. "The Germans, the Maquis – they're all criminals," he'd say. But Rose – she wouldn't listen. She had this headscarf with roses on. A gift from my father. She wore it all the time – he didn't know she'd sewn a double hem into it for when she needed to carry coded messages.'

'He never found out?'

Ludovic's eyes flicker and he slides past the question.

'She had the perfect cover – schoolmistress at the hamlet way up along the piste, high in the chestnut forest next to the camp.'

'We found the village,' I say. 'It's all ruined and the forest has come up and covered it.'

162

He nods. 'The Boche burned it at the same time as they destroyed the Maquis camp. The villagers were suspected of helping the Resistance.'

He pauses for a moment, then says: 'On Fridays my father would go to collect Rose for the weekend. He had the first car in the area – a *gazogene*, the car that runs on wood gas. I can see him now: driving along the piste, around those bends, at high speed, honking his horn, his one arm on the steering wheel. Sheep running in front of him. An impressive sight.'

He leans on his fork and smiles at the memory. 'They were good times, when my uncle owned Les Rajons.'

'When did your uncle lose the farm?'

'After the war. He had a choice: keep the house and lose the vineyards, or sell the house. A simple choice. He kept the vines; now they belong to me. He sold the house to an outsider and built himself a bungalow in the village. My uncle was a sensible man.'

I'm trying to plant out our half of the potager. Julien's been helping me. While I struggle with my fork, his spade slices deftly into the earth, pulls out a clod as dark and dense as chocolate, turns it over and slices back in again. Sometimes I see beads of sweat on his shoulders, sometimes I hear him grunting in exertion, but that's about the limit of his communication.

At his instigation, a couple of hippies with a donkey cart have arrived with a load of horse manure, which now sits in a fuming, malodorous pile at the side of the plot.

'It's a bit fresh,' he says. 'We'll need to work it in well.'

'Must we?'

'The more manure we work in, the more vegetables we'll get. It's as simple as that.'

While we're digging, Freya lies on the edge of the plot, her Moses basket swathed with mosquito netting. She's almost completely static but she's become a focal point for the household: everybody congregates around her, watching us work.

I know that she loves it out here, but I don't know how I know it. She can't smile and her eyes don't focus properly. All I know is that when I put her basket under the apple tree next to the plot, she goes rapt and quiet, the way she does in the bath.

Julien stops his work for a moment to look at her. 'She's looking at the sky,' he says.

'Do you think so?'

'I know so. A couple of years ago I ate a bad mushroom. I couldn't move a muscle. I lay on the ground, under a tree, just like her. And I saw the sky, such a vivid blue, through the canopy of new leaves. All I could think was: what a lovely day to die.'

Sometimes Gustav helps us with the digging. He rarely speaks; it's not just that his English isn't up to much, he won't even be drawn out in French. All I know about him I know from Kerim: he's just finished an apprenticeship with a hairdresser in Toulouse and now Kerim has persuaded him to enrol in the same English-language school on the Isle of Wight that he attended. 'It would be great if you'd allow him to stay for a couple of weeks,' he says. 'Just until his course starts at the beginning of next month. He won't be any trouble.'

'Of course he can stay.'

Kerim's handsome features crinkle in worry. 'There's another thing. Anna, I ought to have told you. I couldn't stay with him at his student accommodation while he was in

Toulouse but I've promised to join him in Britain. It'll be too hard for him alone; he barely speaks any English. Besides, I need to work to support his studies. I've said I'll be there by the end of July.'

I can't imagine what we'll do without Kerim; he's become a part of our family. Despite his taciturnity I'm growing fond of Gustav too. Beneath his military-style number-one haircut and his khaki muscle shirts, I sense a gentle soul.

———

Lizzy is enthusiastic about the concept of living off the land. 'Spring is awesome!' she keeps saying. 'This is when I come alive.'

'I wonder if you could help with a bit of weeding?'

'Of *course* not. I've been reading this great book; weeds are good. You mustn't take them out. Just trust nature.'

Julien gives a snort. 'Lizzy, let me show you how to double-dig.'

'According to my horoscope,' says Lizzy with dignity, 'today is a day of dreams, not of action.'

'She does have a point,' says Tobias. 'It's a shame to waste this fabulous weather digging. Besides, a euro for a lettuce doesn't seem all that much to me.'

He sits down next to her in the long grass and before long the sound of their giggling drifts across to us. I frown and slam my fork harder than I intended into the earth. Julien looks at me. 'I've got some seedlings for you,' he says. 'I'm heading home now. Why don't you take a break and come and look at my potager? If you don't mind climbing up the hill.'

I nod. 'Tobias, you'll watch Freya, won't you?'

'Aw, sweetheart . . .'

'I'll only be gone for an hour. She doesn't even need feeding.'

'Don't worry,' says Lizzy brightly. 'I'll chant to her.'

Julien and I walk along the spine of rock to the next hillside. In spring nothing stays the same, there are always surprises. Today, when I peer down at the dragon's flanks I find them dotted with pink, white and purple. The perfume is different too.

'Cystus,' says Julien. 'And wild lavender.'

The lavender plants are small and scrubby but their flowers are more intensely blue than any I've seen before. Their smell is so powerful it's almost medicinal, as if both colour and fragrance have been heightened by hardship. I laugh, for sheer happiness.

'What?' asks Julien.

'Well, just this place, really. Whenever I feel a bit knocked back, I see something so amazing it takes my mind off it.'

We climb in silence until we reach the immense oak tree with Julien's house in it. 'Oh!' I exclaim. 'Your wisteria is out.'

The other day the flowers were just buds and now they're definitely blossom, deep and abundant as bunches of grapes.

'They look inviting,' I say. 'Like the entrance to another world.' I stop, afraid of sounding stupid.

He smiles. 'It *is* another world. My world.'

I stand for a moment admiring the tangle of flowers around the base of the tree – something between a wilderness and an English cottage garden.

'Your flower garden's charming. Where's your potager?'

'Look again.'

Among the tumbled mass of flowers I spot peas and beans and the delicate green fronds of carrot leaves between sturdy onion shoots. It couldn't be further from Ludovic's ordered approach.

'It's a complete muddle,' I say. 'In a good way, I mean. I didn't know you could do it like that. I didn't know it was *allowed.*'

'It's not random. Some plants grow better when you put them next to other plants. I've put onions next to carrots, because the carrots throw off the onion fly and the onions throw off the carrot fly. Try planting mint between the peas – it helps repel white fly and it's always good to have some mint close at hand to eat with your peas. And it's not obligatory to grow things in straight lines.'

'But you've got flowers and vegetables together in one garden.'

'The flowers are useful too. Those marigolds, for instance – they contain a natural insecticide. Lavender is strong-smelling and so it keeps pests off tomatoes. Nasturtiums are a great trap for blackfly. Geraniums discourage cabbage worms. Borage helps strawberries. Camomile is a soil tonic – it's good for almost everything. Chrysanthemums and dahlias repel nematodes.'

I want to savour the magic, not to learn how it's done. But Julien can be implacable when he wants to be. When I admire the prettiness of roses climbing up his apple trees, he retaliates: 'The roses need a support and in exchange they attract the bees to help the apple blossoms with pollination.' When I exclaim at the bright shoots coming out of the dark earth, he talks to me about soil preparation and double-digging.

'Oh, don't spoil it, Julien!'

'You think it happens like this on its own?' He seems almost angry. 'You think it's effortless? I can tell you, it's not. It takes *years* of effort. You plant potatoes one year, Colorado beetle comes along and you have to pick off every grub by hand or you lose your crop. So the next year you spend your time looking out for the beetle and instead clubroot wipes out your brassicas. Or wild boar come along and trample your raspberry canes. You need to keep a step ahead of nature and you never can, not completely. You need nature and you fear it, you work with it and around it. Above all, you respect it. You pay attention. Making things grow requires structure and discipline.'

Walking back home alone, I linger on the piste by the pine forest to properly decipher the inscription on the memorial to the fighters who died there.

Passant pour que tu vives libre, dans cette forêt le 17 avril 1944 dix-sept maquisards ont été tués au combat.

'Giving their lives so that you might live free, in this forest on 17 April 1944 seventeen resistance fighters were killed in combat.'

Beneath are the names of those who died on the day the Germans attacked the *maquisard* camp. At the very bottom is one I recognise: Rose Donnadieu.

———

My mother is avoiding Kerim. She has dark rings around her eyes. In fact, I can't help noticing she's much more devastated by what she learned about him at Julien's party than by my baby having brains like a badly made omelette.

For a start, she's stopped dressing up. She moves listlessly around the house, polishing, washing, ironing.

Kerim is making futile efforts to win back her friendship.

'Can I run you an errand?'

'No thank you.'

'Perhaps a nice cup of tea?'

'No, I'd prefer not.'

The more she rejects him, the more he courts her. It's pitiful to see.

Without Kerim to divert her attention, she's fallen back on goading me.

'Oh darling, you're not looking your best. You've begun to look so *old*. And your *toes*.'

'My toes? My *toes*? Of all the things you could possibly pick on, what's wrong with my toes?'

'Well, you've let the varnish on your toenails get awfully chipped, dear. You don't want to give off the wrong signals. In my day, only a *certain* kind of girl went around with chipped nail varnish.'

Infuriatingly, Kerim still springs to her defence.

'You shouldn't be too hard on your mother,' he says when he catches me alone in the kitchen, counting to ten. 'She really is an extraordinary woman. And she loves you very much.'

'I know all that. It's just she's constantly saying things that get on my nerves. More than that really – they're objectionable. Not just about you and Gustav. When she talks about Freya, she's positively offensive.'

'She doesn't mean it,' he says. 'She's had a hard time. Her husband is dead and she's trying to make sense of what has happened to Freya.'

'*I'm* trying to make sense of what's happened to Freya. But it doesn't make me a crypto-fascist. I'm so sorry, Kerim, for how she's behaving towards you.'

'No – it's all my fault. I should have been honest with her from the beginning. I'm a disappointment to her.'

'Don't be silly, Kerim. You're being impossibly hard on yourself. Anybody can see you're a lovely person.'

'Lovely.' His voice is full of bitterness. 'I'm not *lovely*.'

'You are so. You're lovely about my mother – and about your own mother too, for that matter.'

'My mother?' He lapses into moody silence, leaning forward and fiddling with the switch on the kettle. He flips it on and holds down the switch until the water begins to hiss. Then he flips it off. He repeats this a couple of times, seeing how quickly he can react to the sound. It's beginning to get on my nerves, this turning on and off of the kettle.

'My mother killed herself,' he says without looking at me. 'When I was nine.'

'Oh my God.'

'The funny thing was that I couldn't cry. Not even at her funeral. People kept saying how well I was taking it. But I felt terrible all of the time.'

I remember how, when Freya was first born, my tears were a release; they brought calmness.

'To this day I go round being so *nice* to people it makes me want to scream.' He's still not looking at me; his perfect lips are curled, as if at some vision of himself he detests. 'It's not *lovely*,' he says. 'I'm a coward. I don't dare stand up to anybody. I can't take the risk that anybody will reject me like that again. Ever.'

'This baby reacts to your voice, dear, when you come into the room,' says my mother. She's been holding Freya for a moment while I fetch the coffee things.

'Oh, nonsense.'

'Nonsense yourself. Of course she does. She doesn't need a brain for that, you silly girl. You are her Mother.'

It seems to be part of our relationship contract that I never agree with anything my mother says and she pays me the same compliment. So, as I take Freya from her and balance her on my shoulder, I don't mention that I too sometimes wonder if she's beginning to connect with me.

When she lies next to me in bed her arm negligently touches me. There's never a moment when I can say 'now she's putting out her hand to me'. But there's always some part of her body in contact with mine.

She stares into my eyes while I feed her. This morning I copied the face she makes: an upward inclination of her head, like a miniature Mussolini. After a few goes, she stopped sucking and stared at me transfixed. I'm sure the penny had dropped. I'm almost sure she moved her head whenever I moved mine: copying me, copying her.

My love for her is changing. It's less physical, less automatic, but it's deeper too.

Kerim, poking his head through the door of the living room, breaks my train of thought.

'We're having coffee,' I say. 'Come and sit down.'

He looks appealingly at the place next to Amelia, but she turns her head away and ostentatiously shuffles her body further from the empty chair.

'I'm all right, thanks,' he says, and leaves the room.

'Mother, you mustn't be like that to Kerim. It's really hurting him.'

'It's really hurting *me*. He listened to all my views and he seemed to agree. I trusted him. He's betrayed me.'

I wonder whether I'm authorised to repeat his confidence

about his mother. It would certainly provoke her sympathy. But the thought of her making some blundering attempt at tact is too awful to risk, so I merely say: 'If you look at it another way, he's trusted us with his private life and we're letting him down. He's still the same Kerim. Can't you see?'

'I can't, I can't. It's not the same. He's gone.' There's a trace of real tearfulness in her voice. And suddenly I realise that she's in mourning for him. She's lost the person she thought she knew.

Just at that moment, I feel the soft caress of Freya's arms curling round my neck. There is nothing informed or intentional about the way she does it. Coincidence? Contact? Can she really be trying to reach out to me?

Hammer blows have been resounding through the house all afternoon. Kerim, his shirt stripped off to reveal his magnificent torso, is in the back bedroom taking out his frustrations on the rotten floorboards like some Norse god of thunder. He obviously hopes to win back Amelia's affection through heroic acts of DIY.

From time to time, when she thinks he isn't looking, my mother takes a quick fascinated peek. I can practically read her thoughts in a bubble above her head: an attractive young man with a lump hammer at her beck and call is not an easy commodity to find.

Ludovic has begun encroaching on our land. He's put sheep in our field and has strung vicious electric fences everywhere.

He's attached chains with padlocks to the fence batteries so that we can't undo them.

'This place is full of *voleurs*. There are thieves everywhere nowadays. You must secure your possessions.'

'Tobias, did you give Ludovic permission to put up fences on our land?'

Tobias looks vague. 'Well, we had some kind of conversation about it. I think we'd better just let him get on with it. We ought to be on good terms with our neighbours.'

Tobias's French is coming on. Or rather, he's learning Occitan patois without any reference to formal written French. He has long conversations with Ludovic and with other incomprehensible *paysans*. He often seems to understand more of what they say than I do. But he still hasn't learned to say no in any language.

So Ludovic drives his tractor through our fields and snorts at our irrigation system and shakes his head at our half of the potager. Worst of all, when I went yesterday to look at our vines I found the flower-studded grass that used to surround them has dwindled to a frazzled brown.

'I've sprayed with Roundup *de* Monsanto. I had some spare in my *pulvérisateur*.'

'Oh, Ludovic, I'm not sure –'

'Nonsense. If your weeds go to seed, all your neighbours suffer. You must be strict with nature before it is strict with you. *Il faut empoisonner*.'

⁓

The hillside is covered in flowers.

When we go for walks we take baskets to pick up the treasure that litters the countryside: wild roses and delicate wild raspberries on the mountaintops, elderflower growing along the piste, blueberries in the woods, tiny wild strawberries in the fields. In my potager, the rhubarb is uncurling its delicate leaves. The first strawberries are appearing and the canes of raspberries, blackcurrants and redcurrants are bursting into life. It scarcely matters that we're amateur and flighty gardeners. The work of previous generations is bearing fruit, literally.

'Here, I brought you something,' says Ludovic when I see him in the potager. He hands me a slim notebook. 'Rose's recipe book,' he says. 'You are a chef – it may be useful for you.'

'Ludovic, this is precious. I don't know how to thank you.'

'That's OK. Besides, I'm still waiting for that wild boar stew.'

As soon as I have a moment alone, I sit down to look at it. On the torn blue paper cover there's a name in impeccable copperplate handwriting: Rose Donnadieu. The wartime paper is flimsy and squared.

The pages are covered with Rose's careful, schoolmistress's handwriting. Many of the recipes are for preserves, following the seasons and the local produce.

There are a couple of pages of observations on life in the remote mountain hamlet where Rose was teaching, perhaps drafts of letters. I can almost hear her brisk voice, slightly disapproving the backwardness of the people she's chosen to live among.

My students come to school in *sabots*. I have been obliged to severely rebuke some of the parents for keeping their children away from classes to tend the sheep.

To tell the truth life is hard. Winter nights are freezing. There's no running water, no electricity. The women wash their clothes in the river with ashes from the fire.

There are a few blank pages in the middle and then, starting from back to front, are her household accounts; page after page of meticulously kept records of how many francs she paid for bread, sugar, tea and fat.

There's nothing to suggest that she was living a double life as an *agent de liaison* for the Maquis.

———

Freya has started making new movements when she fits. Her legs do a grotesque doggy-paddle, her arms a boxer's right and left jab: extravagant, all-compassing twitches. Her muscles contract to their full extent every couple of seconds for minutes on end. I can't believe her little body can bear it.

'Tobias – she's off again. I've just fed her and she's been fitting every time she needs a burp. Please call Dr Fernandez and find out what to do.'

I sit with Freya, timing her convulsions with a stopwatch.

'The doctor is fairly laid-back,' reports Tobias. 'She doesn't want to increase the dose of pheno again. She says bring Freya in next time we're in London. And if a fit lasts more than five minutes, use the rectal Valium or call an ambulance.'

'That's four and a half minutes. I'm going to unwrap the Valium.'

'I think that fit is over. She's taking a few breaths.'

'But now she's off again.'

'Well, that's another fit – you start counting again from the beginning.'

'Do we?'

'Yes, of course.' After all these years, I'm still fooled by his confident tone.

'Wake up, sweetheart,' I say. 'Look at your mummy.' Freya's jerks gradually subside and she slips into her dazed post-fit state. In the morning, I'm wrung out, exhausted, empty. I pick up Rose's notebook.

Rosehips are rich in vitamin C, she says. *Remove the seeds carefully and boil the flesh into a cordial. To keep a child in health, give one glass every day diluted in three parts water.*

There's no harm in trying out a few recipes from her book. It doesn't take long to dash into the village to buy glass preserving jars and sugar.

—

This morning I wake up to a delicious fragrance. When I look out of the bedroom window my view is framed with pink roses. I can't wait to get to my preserving.

Wild strawberries should never be washed before preserving, it will alter their delicate flavour, advises Rose. *Boil three parts fruit to two parts sugar with a spoonful of lemon juice to promote gelling.*

I squirrel away my hoard of preserves in neat, trim jars with informative labels. I line them in perfect rows on my shelves. Already I've made jellies, syrups, relishes and more jam than we'll ever be able to eat.

'You need to pace yourself,' says Julien. 'The fruit season is only just beginning. You'll die of exhaustion by the autumn.'

I don't bother to answer. The kitchen is my artist's studio, my science lab. And now Rose presides over it.

As if to counter wartime austerity, she's noted down wistfully lavish recipes from before the war.

Preserving edible flowers requires patience but is not difficult and, when sugar can be obtained, is a local speciality.

Under her instruction, I've been experimenting with heavy red damask roses, boiling them down with sugar into a cloying pink preserve redolent of warm weather and Turkish delight. I've succeeded in capturing the colour and smell of violets by painting each delicate petal with a preservative mixture of egg white and sugar. I've reduced dandelion flowers to a thick yellow cordial.

'"Strawberry jam, batch two, forty per cent sugar,"' reads Julien. '"Dandelion cordial. Elderflower champagne." These labels are a bit dull.'

'Dull? What do you mean?'

'Well – if you're going to the trouble of preserving things you should preserve what they mean to you.'

He picks up a pair of scissors and begins to cut out long strips of paper. 'Give me a pen. I'll show you.'

I look over his shoulder as he writes.

'"This is the strawberry jam that was made on a beautiful morning in May when Anna was wearing her blue dress."'

I giggle. He hands me the pen.

'Your turn.'

'I don't know. What shall I put?'

'Anything – whatever's most important to you at precisely this moment.'

I pick up the pen and write: '*This is the dandelion cordial that Anna made on the day Freya first held onto her hair.*'

He smiles. 'See – you're getting the hang of it now.'

'I'm bottling memories,' I say. 'When we open this in six months' time, I'll remember what it's like to be me, here and now.'

~

'Today is VE Day,' says Ludovic. 'Perhaps you will come to the memorial.'

Tobias and I walk down into Aigues, taking Freya in her sling. We've come dressed in our wellies and work clothes but as soon as we see the crowd by the memorial we know we've made a mistake: they're all wearing dark suits and sombre dresses. Yvonne has decorated the memorial with flowers in red, white and blue – except she's used orange flowers for the red and turquoise for the blue.

'Bright colours are more exotic,' she whispers to me. 'Hold *la petite* up so she can see them.'

Almost every village in France has a memorial with a long list of those who died in the First World War. Aigues is no exception. Unusually, it also has a long list of resistance fighters who died in the Second World War.

Ludovic is already there, dressed up in his medals.

'He was a charmer, that one,' says Yvonne. 'He always had an eye on the ladies – and you can see that he still has.'

The mayor welcomes the crowd. 'This,' he says, 'is the sixty-third year we have celebrated our victory and it is our duty to continue to do so for as long as possible. Therefore, we should pass on to the younger generation the story of what happened . . .'

'The 8th of May 1945, I'm injured, in hospital in the

Ardennes,' Ludovic tells me in a confidential bellow. 'They come and find me and they carry me on their shoulders. I'm only sixteen but I've played my part. I'm a hero of the Resistance.'

The mayor's words come to an end and there's a brief pause as he fiddles with an antiquated cassette player.

'How did Rose die?' I ask him. 'I saw her name on the memorial in the forest.'

But Ludovic, usually so garrulous, ignores my question. 'Every year the cassette player breaks. It's a scandal,' he says. 'We must have a *loto* to raise money for a new player.'

The cassette cranks into life with a bugle call for the dead. The flags of France and of the Resistance are ceremoniously dipped.

The 'Marseillaise' blares out, followed by 'Le Chant des Partisans', the anthem of the Resistance. It is curiously moving, the flags waving gently in the breeze, the knot of locals dressed in their smart clothes, Ludovic looking just a little tearful, the cassette wavering as if the voice of the singer is cracking.

The mayor snaps off the cassette a moment before the song has ended. Deliberately, he unfolds a piece of paper and begins his address.

'During the Second World War the honour of France was upheld by a minority who became more numerous day by day. We must remember that France was the only country, along with Britain, to declare war on Germany after the invasion of Poland. After her occupation, her honour was upheld by the Resistance. It is important to recognise this and to tell our children.'

'Where was the mayor during the war?' Ludovic shouts in my ear. 'He wasn't in the Resistance although he is a year older than me.'

179

The mayor folds his piece of paper. 'This memorial is now at an end,' he says. 'As usual, the *mairie* would now like to invite everybody back to Yvonne's cafe for a toast.'

The knot of people begins to unravel and they drift across the square. Ludovic and I fall into step behind the mayor.

'My friend Roland, he's a very good woodworker,' says Ludovic. 'He makes miniature coffins for us. I slip out at night and post them through the doors of people who've talked a bit too much. With a note inside: "Keep your mouth shut, or else." It works very well. It's my first real job in the Maquis. Beautiful little coffins − but I don't suppose anybody who received one has kept hold of it.' He glares at the mayor's back. 'I sent one to his father once, you know.'

Inside the cafe, Yvonne pours everybody pastis and the atmosphere becomes congenial. Ludovic slaps the mayor on the back and congratulates him on his speech.

—

The potager has filled with eels. A plague of biblical proportions. In my state of heightened alarm it seems a warning that Freya's condition is worsening.

'They must have swum down the *béal* last night,' says Tobias.

'I think they're endangered.'

'Well, these ones are.'

We find one or two still alive and throw them back into the river. It's horrible to think of the poor things swimming down the *béal*, believing they are reaching the freedom of the wide sea and ending up here instead, imprisoned in our mud.

Freya's having two or three fits a night. I still go to her but I'm slowing down. I don't always pick her up. Sometimes

I just stand and watch her turning blue. I stare at her convulsing, willing her to catch her breath. I don't want her to live until we're old and she's middle-aged. Logically, that must mean I want her to die before I do.

But not now, not now: an involuntary prayer, torn from me.

Her hair is rubbed away at the back of her head from lying down all day. Sometimes I turn her onto her stomach; it's supposed to be good for her. She tries to coordinate her arms and legs in a pre-crawl but it doesn't work out. She keeps forgetting to use one arm, kicks her legs hopelessly behind her, struggles to raise her head and drops it back exhausted. She moans in frustration and anger.

Not now, not now.

I don't have time for her. Or rather, I *won't* make time for her. The cherries are ripening. There's such a short time between the fruit appearing and falling, useless and shrivelled, to the ground. I have to preserve it.

Cherry is my favourite jam, thick as treacle, dark as wine, with dense pieces of fruit to chew on. I've made it with petals of the pink rose outside my window, to Rose's recipe. Her instructions are precise, reassuringly pedantic. *Make sure you use a copper pan and a wooden spoon. If there is no sugar available you may use syrup made from boiled grapes. Add the rose petals exactly four and a half minutes before you finish boiling the cherries.*

When you toss the petals into the pan a marvellous cloud of fragrance envelops you. I imagine her doing the same thing in this same kitchen all those years ago. Gradually the smell of rose subsides, mingling with the lower note of cherry. It returns again when you open the jar, as if you are capturing summer.

The cherries keep on coming: an unstoppable onslaught, a barrage, a tour de force.

Kerim and Gustav have been picking them from our orchard by the box, by the barrow, by the shedload. They're ripening in waves, according to variety. First bright red ones, then huge deep black ones, then the local speciality, yellow-and-scarlet ones, like miniature apples.

I've bought a cherry stoner. I work at it for hours on end. Left to nature, cherries will rot in days. If I want to preserve them, I have to work fast.

My hands and arms are stained up to the elbow with cherry juice. My nails and cuticles are dyed black. With Rose as my guide, I've made crystallised cherries, cherries in rum, cherries in vinegar, dried cherries, cherry sorbet. And still they come. Nobody could eat this many cherries in a thousand lifetimes.

I keep telling myself that my bottling enterprise is part of our future. That one day I'll run courses in home-made preserving, or I'll sell my own preserves to clients. But really I'm oppressed by nature's wasted bounty. I'm hoarding.

Everywhere we go the abandoned cherry trees strew their treasures in front of us. They're ragged and half dead but the urge to reproduce is still in them.

In the middle of my preserving I make a discovery. The mice have gnawed right through the plastic lid of the Nutella. The jar, which was full when we moved in, has been licked clean. I find a neat disc of plastic lid lying in the bottom.

It raises an agonising question: does that mean they could potentially gnaw though my Tupperware boxes?

'Tobias, look what they've done. Do you think I should put everything into glass jars with sealable lids? They couldn't get into those, could they?'

Tobias, so calm, so humorous, the love of my life, is often driven to inexplicable fury these days.

'Just let it alone with your jars and boxes! I can't keep up with all your massive displacement schemes. Anna, for God's sake – can't you see? However many jars you fill with jam – however obsessed you get with this Rose woman and all that stuff from the past – our daughter will still be fucked. And if you don't pull out from her soon, then you will be too.'

———

I walk into the kitchen to discover that my mother has cornered Kerim and is lecturing him: 'You must understand, dear, you're not a homosexual. Not really.'

'Amelia,' says Kerim, 'I know this is difficult for you to understand but . . .'

I find that I'm biting my lip, willing him to stand up to her; to compel her, for once in her life, to see the world as it really is, not the way she wants it to be. He's so close, I feel, to mustering the courage to jolt her out of her state of permanent denial.

'I love Gustav,' he says, but his voice quavers so it seems to end on a question. She cuts him off with a cry of something close to panic. Tears well up in her eyes. And all at once he's backing down; his next words are muttered: 'We were at school together. We were best friends . . .'

She instantly pursues her advantage. 'Of course,' she soothes, 'that's quite natural. You were young and confused. You were experimenting. Possibly he led you on.'

She puts her hands on her trim hips and looks at him the way she used to look at me as an adolescent when she wanted to discuss what she called the Facts of Life. 'This silly falling-out with your mother,' she says. 'I'm guessing that it might be to do with her finding out about Gustav.'

There's a beat of silence; his eyes give the slightest suggestion of assent.

'You have to see it from her point of view, dear. She probably feels hurt and confused. You must remember that she still loves you. And it will be all right when she realises it's just been . . . growing pains.'

Time and again my mother has amazed me with her ability to ignore inconvenient facts. But in denying this huge reality in front of her eyes, she's surpassed herself.

'Why don't you give me her address?' she says. 'I'll write to her. If necessary, I'll visit her and explain it all to her. Anywhere. Even in Algeria. You know, dear, I'm sure she and I can sort this silly misunderstanding out, mother to mother.'

But not even Kerim can bring himself to agree to this one.

'I won't push you, dear,' she says. 'I'll just leave you to think it over for a while.'

As she goes out, she flashes me a triumphant look. I glance over at Kerim. He's sitting at the kitchen table where she's left him, entirely still, staring out of the window with fixed almond eyes.

⌒

Gustav must love Kerim very much. He dares to address my mother in his slow, curiously sweet English.

'Madame, one day please permit me to style your beautiful hair. I have done my *formation* at a top *salon de coiffure* in Toulouse.'

She's clearly torn for a moment. In another universe, one in which she got off her high horse, Kerim could run chores for her and Gustav could do her hair. I can see her wavering, repulsed yet attracted, like a planet in orbit around a sun.

~

It's the middle of the day. I'd planned to make a bouillabaisse but I haven't got round to beginning the stock, let alone simmering it for hours as René Lecomte taught me. So I've turned to Rose's notebook.

She has a recipe for *bourride*, from Sete on the Languedoc coast, a far simpler dish than bouillabaisse. Instead of a fish stock, it just requires a court bouillon of herbs and vegetables. Instead of four sorts of fish, just one: monkfish. Simply simmer the monkfish in the court bouillon, whip up an aioli in a bowl and emulsify it into the broth in which the fish has been cooked.

The simplicity of Rose's modest Languedoc dishes is liberating. In their throwing together of fresh ingredients, I can sense the origins of so many of the grand haute cuisine set pieces I've slaved over in the past. Cooking from Rose's book feels like I'm getting back to fundamentals.

I'm standing with a whisk over a steaming pot with Freya in her pram by my side. The whole household is already sitting at the kitchen table, drawn by the delicious smells wafting over from my *bourride*.

'Darling, Freya is fitting,' my mother, suddenly says.

'OK – give me a minute. This mustn't boil or it will curdle. It's beginning to thicken.'

'Is she breathing, dear?'

'She's fine,' I say shortly.

'Well, she looks rather blue.'

'She's not blue.' I don't even look at the pram.

'Well, you know best, dear,' she says. 'You are her mother. You'll always do what's best for her.'

And that's when I erupt.

'I'm sick of your fucking cult of motherhood. I'm not supernaturally endowed with a mystical ability to do what's best for my child. I haven't slept for a week. Have you any idea what it's like to watch her night after night? Not knowing whether she'll pull through?'

My mother looks at me narrowly. 'You look a bit peaky, dear. Let me feel your forehead.' She reaches out a hand.

'For God's sake, I haven't got flu – I've got a profoundly disabled daughter. I'm sick of people telling us we're doing fantastically or that she'll always be lovely to us. She's not always lovely and I'm not all right. I only carry on because I'm too tired to work out what else to do.'

'I don't think you really meant that, did you, dear?'

'You tell me then – go on and tell me. What's the point of her?'

My mother struggles visibly for an argument. 'Well, she feels hot and cold, happy and sad.' A thought seems to occur to her. 'And you never know. Perhaps it may be possible to train her.'

'Train her?'

She brightens. 'Yes, we'll certainly be able to train her. After all, you can even train a *slug*.'

'For Christ's sake,' I say. 'That's your suggestion?'

'It's just a tricky patch, darling, you'll see. All new mothers get them. You'll be all right. So will she.' There's a beat of a pause and I try not to notice her bottom lip quivering. Then she breaks out: 'You *have* to be all right, dear. I can't bear for you not to be.'

Since I was sixteen, my mother has been talking about, planning for and looking forward to the day when she would have a grandchild. Her suffocating desire for me to have a baby is possibly the real reason I left it so late. I've not troubled to ask her, but she must be grieving for Freya too.

I'm opening my mouth to try to make her feel better when Tobias launches in.

'Anna's right, Amelia,' he says. 'We have to be realistic. You never do get over something like this. You never can.'

'My daughter will get over it,' says my mother. 'That's an order, Anna.'

'No she won't,' says Tobias. 'By the mere fact of that baby's existence, our lives are destroyed. And the more we come to love her, the more destroyed our lives will be. I don't know why you're defending Freya, because that . . . Tamagotchi is ruining your daughter's life.'

My mother looks from Freya to me in something close to panic and I can read her thoughts as clearly as if she's spoken them. How can she possibly choose between us? For a second I glimpse past the make-up and the Hermès scarf and the whole edifice my mother's constructed around herself and it's like watching a train crash in slow motion, seeing the stricken faces of passengers in doomed carriages careering off the rails and knowing there's nothing, absolutely nothing, you can do.

And then Kerim steps straight onto the tracks. 'Tobias, you're talking nonsense,' he says. 'Your lives aren't destroyed.'

His voice is unrecognisable, full of confidence and calm

authority. All trace of nervousness is gone.

'I don't see,' says Tobias doggedly, 'what makes you think that.'

'Because,' says Kerim, 'I am not going to allow it.'

Tobias is staring at him belligerently, but Kerim holds his ground. He's always been good-looking but now he looks manly.

There's a beat of silence. Then, with a sort of gasp, Amelia collapses into Kerim's arms. Before she knows what's happening, Gustav is rushing towards them. For a fraction of a second, my mother looks as if she's contemplating doing her implacable statue act. Then the three of them are hugging in the kitchen

'I've been wondering,' she says, edging imperceptibly out of Gustav's embrace, 'now I've caught such a tan, whether my hair wouldn't be nicer just a shade lighter than this. Do you think we should try?'

⁓

Freya has a cold and a temperature. She's blocked up and having trouble breathing, which makes the oxygen-deprivation of her fits even worse.

I sit on the sofa, holding her on my lap, sponging down her boiling body as she slips into another fit. When she's like this, it's unbearable to be alone.

'Tobias!' I call.

Tobias doesn't answer. He's doing that thing of not hearing me again. It drives me mad, quite literally mad; I act irrationally. After I've called a couple of times I scream: 'Come quickly – she's not breathing!'

Tobias comes running. He looks at me in disgust. 'She's breathing fine.'

Her body is tensed, eyes up, head rolled to the right, one arm up, one leg down, rigid as a pointer dog. When I turn her round, she maintains that position. Then gradually she begins to come out of the fit, her mouth making a little clicking noise.

'I'm going to bed,' says Tobias. 'It's your *turn*. She had three fits at least as bad as that when I had her downstairs after you'd gone to bed last night and I didn't wake *you* up.'

Left alone, I give Freya a little kiss. She flashes me a smile, sudden and complicit. I'm sure it's a smile; it's different to her wind grimace and it's appropriate to the moment.

I give her a bath and the miracle happens again. She smiles: a secret, interior smile, shy and fleeting.

As I put her into her cot, I have a sudden sense of how easily she can be taken away – not just her life but her essence. Most of the time I can't conceive of this; my mind won't let me access that knowledge.

'Tobias.'

'Hmm.'

'Tobias, please wake up.'

But he snores on. I lie awake listening to her laboured breathing, holding my own breath every time hers stops, not daring to go back to sleep in case it doesn't start again.

—

Freya is at the centre of our many fights. I propose, he opposes. Should we try rectal Valium? What's the bloody use? Should we call the ambulance? The hospital is two hours away – I can't face another hospital stay. Will you call Dr Fernandez?

No, I called her last time. Well, I'm tired – I'm not calling her. So then, why should I?

So far, she's always come out of a fit. It's easier to leave her. It's become almost a point of honour to leave her. She's the ball in a dangerous game of brinkmanship. And there, at the back of our minds, is the fear – or the hope – that this time she will not pull through.

'Tobias, I saw Freya make, well, a flash, not quite, but, well, yes, I really think, a smile. A *pleased* look.'

'Nonsense,' says Tobias. 'She's not smiling. It's just wind.'

I think: he doesn't dare hope for a better prognosis.

———

The house is full of mosquitoes, flies and biting insects. It's driving me crazy. We need mesh screens on the windows. We need nets on our beds. I've lost track of all the things we need.

Freya's face is covered in bites but she doesn't notice – she's lying on the living-room sofa in the middle of a fit. She's having between six and eight of them a day. We never bother to time them any more.

Freya convulses and knocks a soft toy onto the floor. As I bend over to pick it up I notice a ragged hole in the skirting board with something just visible behind it. The skirting's loose anyway. I pull the edge. It resists, but there's a spring-like tension in it. I pull harder and the whole length of skirting comes away with a sound of wrenching nails.

I'm thrown backwards. An object sails in a parabola above me. I land on my back and the thing thuds onto my chest. Yellow, desiccated, long-toothed, bald, whiskered. It takes me a moment to realise it's the mummified body of a rodent. Far, far too big to be a mouse.

I hear myself yelling: 'Kerim! I must have those mesh cupboards. They're not mice! They're rats! No wonder they make so much noise. No wonder their shit is so big. No wonder there's such a funny smell.'

Kerim arrives at a run and picks me up gently from the floor. 'Oh, Anna. I didn't want to tell you. I'm so sorry.'

'Kerim, you have to make the cupboards now. And can you replace the skirting board? So they can't get in?'

He opens his mouth and then closes it. There is a moment's pause. I listen to the blood thudding in my temples. He opens his mouth again.

When he next speaks, the note of command is back in his voice.

'Anna, you've lost the ability to see what's right in front of your nose. You must stop this crazy mouseproofing and look after Freya. Call the emergency services. Do it now. I'm sorry to say it but you and Tobias are killing your baby.'

June

T HE THING ABOUT MAKING an emergency call is that it
fossilises a single moment into a point of crisis. For
weeks Tobias and I have argued about whether Freya is bad
enough to go to hospital. Now, from the moment I say 'baby'
and 'convulsions', we're in a different world.

'How old is she? How long has the fit lasted? We'll send a
fire ambulance – it will be faster and it has better breathing
apparatus.'

I begin packing an overnight bag for Freya and for myself.
The fire siren is blaring up the hill before I've finished.

'It's a real red fire engine,' says Tobias, who seems to
consider it necessary to appear detached. 'The breathing equipment is for smoke inhalation, of course. The French have a
very joined-up service.'

Six burly firemen rush Freya onto a stretcher and lay her in
the van. 'Jump in,' one of them says to me. Tobias loses all
his sangfroid, leaps up too and clambers into the van.

A minute ago I was fine but now I'm swept up in the drama
of the situation: the tiny figure laid out on the adult-sized
stretcher, the oxygen mask covering her face, the monitor
bleeping above her head. I cling on to Tobias and weep.

The fire ambulance roars down the hairpin bends to the valley. Through the small, high window in the back door I catch glimpses of the vineyards and immaculate allotments vanishing behind us and of the old folk still resting on their spades where they've stopped to watch us pass.

The Aigues river valley itself is in the High Languedoc. As we continue to descend the hills become softer and more rounded and then flatten out altogether. I crane forward to peer through the windscreen and get a glimpse of a wide plain shimmering in the heat with the glint of the Mediterranean beyond.

We drive at high speed through a baking yellow landscape. 'By the end of the summer everything will be dry as dust,' says the leader of the firemen. 'The trees will be ready to explode at the slightest spark. And if you should get a fire on a day there is a wind, well . . .' He makes a moue. He doesn't look like a hero. He's stocky and compact, probably one of the *chasseurs*. I can imagine him and his men strolling into the burning hell of a forest fire simply because somebody has to try to put it out. The Maquis must have been full of men like this.

At the A&E department of Montpellier General Hospital, we say goodbye. The leader of the firemen claps us on the backs and delivers an impromptu speech: '*De l'avant! Il faut toujours aller de l'avant! Bon courage!*' They take turns to shake our hands.

'Well,' says Tobias, 'you heard what the man says. We'd better go forward.'

At A&E we're told to wait; there has just been a motorway accident. What are we doing here, I wonder, among people with real injuries, real blood running down their faces? Then Freya begins to fit again.

I grab her off the stretcher and run to a nurse, holding her little rigid body up in two hands like an offering. The nurse snatches her from me. Doctors rush around, putting an oxygen mask over her face, trying to get a cannula into her. They can't find a good vein and have to stab at her again and again. She comes out of her fit and screams at the top of her lungs. The intern jabs a needle into her foot. Her blood gushes all over him.

She's whisked away down a corridor to have mysterious things done to her by people in white coats.

'She's becoming their creature again,' says Tobias. 'She belongs to them now.'

~

The hospital will only let one parent stay the night so we both check into a dingy hotel next door. The sheets seem clean, but during the night a warm animal smell creeps up from the mattress and gets into my dreams in the form of thick sweaty arms pulling me down into a swamp.

As I wake, the arms melt away but the sweaty smell persists. The hotel room is unbearably stuffy. At three in the morning I get up and dress quietly, telling myself I'm going out for a breath of fresh air.

I find myself walking through the deserted hospital reception and taking the lift up to Freya's floor. The night nurse seems neither surprised nor interested to see me. 'She's fitting every hour or so,' she says. 'As you're with her, you can note the time of each fit and how long it lasts. If a fit goes on for more than five minutes, I'll see it on the monitor and I'll come in.' She points towards a door. 'Go in quietly – there's another child in there.'

There are only two cots in Freya's room. Beside each is an adult-sized bed, one of which is clearly occupied. I find Freya lying propped up on pillows, sleeping deeply, her breath bubbling out of her in loud rasps. She's got a tube in her nose and another in her mouth.

I lie stiffly on my bed and watch the gleam of the monitor above her cot. Her heartbeat is a series of mountains. A thin green line climbs each one untiringly and slides down the other side. On the line below is her respiration, more ragged but just as deft – a spider's busy zigzag. Both lines reach the right side of the screen at precisely the same instant, fall off the edge and begin a new line again from the left without a moment's pause.

Freya gives a moan. The spidery line stops. An alarm bleeps.

I go over to the cot and see that her arm is making the familiar pumping motion. I note the time on a piece of paper by her cot: 3.45. I stroke her forehead and resist an urge to grab my baby and take her out of this place. The fit stops after three minutes; not long enough to alarm the nurse. The respiration monitor stops bleeping and resumes scribbling – implacable, uncurious.

All at once, I'm overcome by a need to have my child with me. I stand by her cot in the freezing hospital air conditioning wondering how to move her without setting off the alarm. I'm shivering. Eventually I notice a button that says 'Suppress alarm for two minutes'. Pressing it, I untangle the various lines and whip Freya into my bed. I fall asleep gazing into her snuffling face, feeling her soft breath on my own cheek.

The day nurses wake me at six. Opening my eyes is like having them sucked out through a hose. Nobody mentions the fact that Freya is in my bed.

The woman in the other bed gets up looking rumpled, her black hair in a mass around her shoulders. She twists it and the glorious mane disappears into a neat bun making her fine, thin face look instantly austere. She slips a headscarf over the bun.

'I'm Najla. Are you English? We are foreigners too, originally. Although now we are French, of course.'

There's a single cry from the cot next to her and she bends to pick up her child. 'This is Sami. He's nineteen months old.'

Sami is emaciated. His long sallow limbs are like sticks of bamboo, his joints stick out like knots. He stares at me with huge black eyes.

Najla looks apologetic. 'We've been trying to feed him but he won't take it,' she says, a world of sadness in her voice. 'He has convulsions, many of them; he's tired. We tried for a long time to feed him at home. Tomorrow they're going to teach us how to put a tube in his nose.'

At eight o'clock, Tobias appears with a cup of coffee for me.

'Oh,' says Najla. 'Your husband. My husband doesn't like to come so much. He's working and his mother is at home looking after my other children.'

Suddenly it seems as if Freya's isn't the worst case in history. 'You'll meet my husband tomorrow,' says Najla. 'They've told him he must be here to learn how to put in the nose tube.'

The ward round arrives. A consultant, young and professionally worried, introduces herself as 'Dr Dupont'. She wears a white lab coat with strappy silver sandals. Two white-coated interns carrying clipboards trail behind her. A flurry of nurses brings up the rear.

'Freya is heavily sedated,' says Dr Dupont in excellent English. 'She had several fits on admission and during the night. She's been given a high dose of phenobarbitone.'

'Will she be all right? Can you stabilise her?'

'There is a treatment we could try. With corticosteroids. Nobody knows how it works but it can improve seizures. It's not easy – for instance the child can be irritable, wakeful during the night and sleepy in the day, can cry a lot and can retain water. You must think carefully. You have a specialist in the UK who knows her. Your friends and family are there. You do not know the French system. It might be better for us to arrange for her to be sent home under medical supervision. To stay here on your own, and to undergo this treatment . . . well, you must be prepared for a very difficult time to come.'

We leave the hospital feeling unloved. Everybody seems to be trying to shunt us away. Tobias puts his arm around my shoulder. 'Hey, things aren't so bad,' he says. 'We have twenty-four-hour childcare. Let's try to treat this in the spirit of a city break.'

We spend what's left of the day wandering around Montpellier. It's a great city; every street seems to open out into yet another medieval square full of bars and restaurants. As dusk falls, students from the university come out to carouse. Music floats from open doors and windows. We sit down at a pavement cafe and eat delicious food of the type that in Britain you find only at the most luxurious establishments: fresh oysters, marrowbones in broth, salt cod. We down a bottle of chilled white wine between us.

'I don't want to go back to London,' says Tobias.

I feel just the same way. Right now London seems to

represent death and defeat. Life and hope are right here, in France.

'OK,' I say. 'Let's keep going. *De l'avant.*'

—

Sami's parents are being taught how to tube-feed him. For the past half-hour they've stood, helpless and silent, watching a nurse try to put a tube down his nose while he's screamed and screamed and screamed.

Sami's father is a busy, plump little man. Before this ordeal, he was expansive, arriving with an important air, making a point of formally introducing himself: 'I am enchanted to meet you. My name is Monsieur Hakim. You have already met my wife, Najla, and my youngest son, Sami. All children are a blessing from Allah. In our religion, children like Sami are especially blessed.'

Najla, I notice, defers to him in everything, asks his opinion on all sorts of things she must know better than he does: how Sami should be dressed for the nurse's visit, what he prefers to eat.

When the nurse arrives, he launches again into his speech about Allah and children like Sami.

'Watch me carefully,' interrupts the nurse. 'You're going to have to do this next.'

As soon as he sees the tube, Sami begins thrashing his emaciated limbs. With a gigantic effort, the nurse manages to get the tip of it into his nostril. She braces his skeletal frame against her and begins pushing the tube down. Sami gags loudly.

'If he gags, pause for a moment, then carry on,' says the

nurse. 'You must open his mouth to check that the tube isn't coiling up at the top of his palate. Look, I'm using a torch.'

She carries on pushing the tube down further than seems possible into his stomach. Sami's screams take on a desperate quality; now they are bubbly and muffled as they try to force themselves past the object that's being inserted into his windpipe.

I couldn't do this. Well, maybe I could but I *will* not.

'You must check that the tube is in the stomach and not in the lungs,' says the nurse. 'Inject a little air into the tube like this and listen for the sound with a stethoscope. Then pull on the plunger and draw up a bit of fluid – test the pH to check that it's stomach acid.' All the colour has drained out of Monsieur Hakim's face. He bows his head, fixing his eyes on a point just down and to the left of Sami's suffering form.

'It's all right, Sami,' Najla says, stroking his hand. Sami tries to push her away.

'They couldn't leave him at this age even if they wanted to,' Tobias hisses. 'He's too old. He'll get scared on his own. He knows them now, you see.'

The nurse pulls out the tube and turns to Monsieur Hakim. 'Now it's your turn,' she says. He backs away a step. 'No, no. My wife will do.'

'No,' insists the nurse, speaking slowly and distinctly, as if to an idiot. 'You must learn too. Perhaps your wife will be ill one day. It is very important that you both learn.'

Reluctantly, Monsieur Hakim takes hold of the tube.

'This is only a short-term solution,' encourages the nurse. 'If he doesn't start eating again we'll fit him with a stomach tube. It will be much easier.'

The feeding bag sits limply in Monsieur Hakim's hand. His

boy stares at him with his coal-black eyes. Then, as he realises he is about to be betrayed, his whole face scrunches up in a new bout of screaming.

'We will have to get shot of Freya,' says Tobias to me, 'while she's still young enough. You have to do it early or you get . . . attached. Things just keep getting worse and worse and by the time they're really awful it's too late. She'll have come to trust us. And we'll never be able to explain things to her. We'll be in it for life and then one day we'll die and she'll end up in an institution anyway. It'll be worse for her really, because she won't be used to it.'

Sami's father edges towards his son. 'I'll hold him,' says the nurse. It takes all her strength to pinion his frail limbs.

'French social services are brilliant,' wheedles Tobias. 'And don't be fooled – it's exactly the same deal here as in the UK. If we don't take her home, they'll *have* to find an option.'

I can't drag my eyes away from the boy, rigid in the nurse's grip. His head is jerked back as far from the tube as he can manage. With his long limbs and big black eyes, he looks like a panicked colt.

His father makes an ineffectual motion with the tube close to his nose. The boy can't thrash about any more but he utters a low, terrified moan.

The man abruptly throws down the tube. 'I go back to my shop,' he says. 'My wife will do it.'

The door shuts with a slam behind him. The nurse makes an exasperated noise and lets Sami go. She picks up the tube and gives it to his mother. 'OK. He can try later. Now it's your turn.' Najla looks at the closed door and opens her mouth. Then she shuts it again. She looks as though she wants to cry.

'Look,' says Tobias, 'caring for a child like Freya is a full-time job. A job for professionals. It's not fair to force parents to do it themselves.'

He holds out both his hands to me, fingers slightly splayed as if he's offering to pull me out of a swimming pool. He's always had lovely hands, musician's hands – long and squared and competent – I know those hands so well.

His face is pleading. 'I love you. I need you. I'm so sorry to put you on the spot, but you have to choose. Me or her. I'm going back to the hills.'

Do I really have a choice?

Wordlessly, I slip my hands into his and then we turn and leave.

———

It's green-fig season. *La fleur de figue* – the flower of the fig, Rose calls it. An early flourishing of fruit, less abundant than the main crop in autumn, but all the sweeter for it. A promise of largesse to come.

The hospital has called us, wondering acerbically where we are. I would come, my own little baby, I would come to you, but I have to put fruit into jars.

Picking figs is comforting work. The trees are open and generous. Their broad leaves are like outstretched palms offering food and shade. When you pull off a leaf it leaks sticky white milk. I know how that feels: I'm trying to dry up my breast milk. It makes me too dependent on Freya, too intertwined with her.

It's not an unreasonable thing to do. She's six months old now. Most professional London mothers do the same. Besides, she's getting hungrier; I've already begun supplementing her diet with formula.

When you're breastfeeding, your baby and your breasts form a strange alliance, they dictate to you. You have to be ready to put aside any other task at a moment's notice. Whatever anyone tells you, breastfeeding and holding down a proper job aren't usually compatible.

Of course, I don't have a proper job any more, but that's not to say I don't have commitments. *Figs must be picked*, writes Rose in her notebook, *at* 'le bon moment'.

I like this concept. Not a frantic deadline, not the last possible moment or the first, but the perfect one. That might depend on a whole range of factors: the weather, the slope of a valley, the position of a single fruit on its branch. Too soon and the fruit has no taste. Too late and it has shrivelled in the sun and solidified into jam.

'Rose sometimes used to send me out two or three times a day to pick figs,' says Ludovic, 'to make sure I got each fruit at exactly *le bon moment.*'

Adding a little red wine improves the taste and colour of a fig preserve, writes Rose. *Sugar is unnecessary, although honey may be added if you have a hive. The simplest method of preservation is to dry figs in the sun. Run a thread through their necks and hang them from a tree in strings. If marc is available it is worth the effort of putting it with the figs into a large, sealed crock.*

'I can't reach the fruit at the top of the tree,' I say.

'Cut them off with an empty tin can on a stick,' Ludovic advises. 'The fruit falls into the can. Or drag the branches down with a hook – fig trees are supple. I'll help you.'

We pick together for half an hour or so, Ludovic pulling

the branches down so that I can reach the fruit. I'm glad to accept offers of help from any direction. Tobias is permanently unavailable. My mother's busy ironing. Gustav left for his English college while we were at the hospital and Kerim is renovating bedrooms. Lizzy is busy doing whatever it is she does.

'How is *la petite*?' asks Ludovic.

I assume he's being a good, polite neighbour, so I answer non-committally that she's receiving excellent care in hospital. But he presses me: 'What was the emergency? Was it a convulsion? Or a chest infection? What hospital is she in? Will she recover? What do the doctors say? Who is her specialist?'

He's gone far further than general interest requires. Further than is polite. His questions are dragging me away from the fat ripe figs plopping into my basket, back to the sterile ward and its respiration monitors.

'You know a lot about the hospital,' I say, finally.

Slowly he lets go of a branch. We both watch it spring back, freed from the burden of its fruit.

'Thirty years ago Thérèse and I had a baby,' he says. 'A boy. We called him Thomas. It was months before we would finally admit that he had Down's syndrome. Thérèse was already old to be a mother – she couldn't have another child after that. She always loved him without question. But I . . . for me it wasn't so simple.'

I've never thought of Ludovic as a parent, even though he's hinted at it. 'To tell the truth,' he says, 'I wished he would disappear. But when he did eventually die, the strange thing is that I was grief-stricken.' He pauses and pulls another branch down for me. It bends almost double on itself, offering me its fruit. 'I think I must have loved him without knowing it,' he says, 'I must have loved him all along.'

—

The rats are busy making nests. They've pulled the wire wool out from Kerim's building materials, the fibreglass from the roof, the clothes from our cupboards.

'Ordinary traps won't work,' says Ludovic. 'Rats are sociable. They talk to each other. You must get dry plaster and mix it with Parmesan. Leave it in bowls around the house. One rat will eat the plaster and it will turn into a rock in his stomach. Then he will die slowly and he will utter the death cry of the rat. All the other rats will become afraid. They will flee your home and never come back.'

'For Christ's sake, this house is bad enough with the hissing ghost,' says Tobias. 'I don't want to live with the death cry of the rat as well.'

He's permanently on edge at the moment. He finds my mother's presence oppressive. And, if I'm honest, mine too. He spends his time in his egg-box recording studio – his agent has been throwing him a stream of documentary jobs and he doesn't dare turn them down because he has no idea when, if ever, he'll be paid for *Madame Bovary*.

'They always want it yesterday,' he grouses. 'I've just had a call from the director of a Discovery wildlife show. He wants music for sharks and bears by 6 p.m. today and tomorrow it'll be eels and badgers.'

When he's not working, he flees down to the river where Lizzy can usually be found.

The house is full of people demanding things from me. I

need him to be engaged. But trying to corner Tobias is like pinning down the sea. He doesn't oppose, he just flows through the gaps.

'Sweetheart, Kerim was wondering what we want him to do next. Could you just go and brief him? I'd do it myself but I'm so busy with the figs.'

'Sure,' says Tobias absently, helping himself to a spoonful of fig preserve. 'I think you put a bit too much sugar in this.'

'My mother says there's a rustling in her bedroom. I've told her it's just squirrels in the fig tree outside but I'm afraid it's you-know-what. Could you just sneak in and see if there are any places in the skirting board that rodents can get through?'

'Sure.'

'Julien's supposed to be dropping by for lunch. I'll have to make a chicken go round six. Coronation chicken, I think, with roast potatoes and home-grown salad greens. You did collect the chicken from Yvonne's father yesterday, didn't you?'

'Sure.'

'Where is it then?'

Tobias looks at me blankly.

'The chicken. From Yvonne's father.'

He slaps his forehead. 'Shit. I knew I forgot something.'

'Tobias,' I say, trying to keep the grating note out of my voice, 'could you please go and collect the chicken now, or there won't be any lunch – and God knows this bunch can eat.'

'Sure,' he says. 'I'll just make myself a coffee first. And have a shower.'

'It's twenty past eleven. The butcher's closes at twelve. You can have a coffee or a shower, but not both.'

Tobias looks at me with hurt blue eyes and puts the coffee pot on to boil. Then he wanders off to the bathroom. I hear the shower start.

'I feel like a harridan,' I complain to my mother. 'It's so unfair. Tobias *forces* me to nag him. I'm not a bossy person – not like you, anyway. I hate being like this.'

My mother looks astonished. 'But of *course* you must nag Tobias,' she says. 'How else is he supposed to know that you love him?'

'I'm going to stop. Right now. It's not worth it. I *won't* become a nagging wife.'

'I've been wondering, dear,' she says, 'if you're finding it too difficult to find time to visit Freya in hospital, whether I should go instead?'

'I don't think –'

'I can easily take the bus, and I believe they have some sort of camp bed on the ward. I'm sure a grandmother will be *nearly* as acceptable as a mother.'

'I really don't want –'

'I can tell them you've got other children at home to look after. Surely that's allowable. How could you leave other children?'

'Mother! No!'

I'm shouting at her again. Why do I always end up shouting?

'All right, all right, dear,' she says in her pretending-not-to-be-hurt voice. 'It was just an idea. Just in case it might be helpful. It doesn't matter to me whether I see Freya. Not at all. *You're* the one I came to France to visit.'

When I'm preserving fruits I like to think that I'm saving them from the otherwise inevitable process of ruin and decay. Without me, they'd only live for a matter of days. In my sealed jars they'll retain their perfect shapes for up to a year.

I imagine the figs in my jars hailing me as a saviour, the ones still on the tree begging me to pick them. I hate to miss any of them out. This afternoon I pack fifty half-litre jars with figs in marc.

'I didn't expect to find you here,' says Julien. 'I heard that Freya was in hospital.'

'That's right.'

'A fire ambulance. It's the talk of the valley. When did she get back?'

'She's still there. We . . . we needed to have a break.'

I instinctively look down while I say this. Suddenly I need to look him in the eye. He holds the gaze a moment longer than is comfortable. Then he smiles curtly.

'So you're preserving figs.'

I don't know why I feel defensive. 'Perhaps we can put labels on them and sell them to tourists. God knows, we could do with an income.'

'I'll write you some labels. Not for the tourists though. How many jars do you want to keep for yourself?'

'Oh, about twenty.'

We work together for a while. Neither of us chats; I like that about Julien, he isn't afraid to be silent. I listen to the scratching of his felt-tip pen as he writes out labels.

'I hope Freya is better soon.'

Before I turn round he's gone.

I don't finish until almost midnight. Carrying an armful of jars to the shelf, I read his labels for the first time.

These are the figs that were made while our little Freya was in hospital. When they are opened, may she be back with her mother where she belongs.

My breasts have begun to leak milk. I can't bear the thought of giving up Freya. Not ever.

———

At ten to six this morning I'm waiting for the bus to Montpellier. Tobias has flatly refused to come with me and he says he needs the car. He's made me promise to get the afternoon bus back.

I'm at the hospital by nine. The sight of Freya attached to monitors, tubes and electrodes no longer has any horror for me. I'm a step removed from her.

She's wired on steroids. Instead of curling her body up to mine, she lies rigid, bashing me spasmodically with her fists, uttering protesting cries. She has the champing jaw and wild-eyed look of a person on speed; she doesn't appear to sleep at all.

I hold her in my arms, give up my good resolutions and let her clamp her mouth to my nipple. She sucks rhythmically and without pleasure.

In the next cot, Sami is sleeping. Tear tracks have dried down his face. Najla is beside him, holding his hand.

'How's it going?' I ask.

She makes a delicate gesture of despair. 'He doesn't like it. Neither do I. But what can I do? I am his mother.'

———

This morning, I wake to the sun filtering through my own clean curtains. The branches of the fig tree wave me a lazy greeting. There's a wild cacophony coming from the tree – it's full of tiny birds, ripping at the figs with their beaks. Destroying every one. The end of *le bon moment*. I've missed a single day of fig-preserving and they're over.

But now I've discovered a place high up in the mountains where there's elderflower still in bloom. It has a heavy fragrance, like a drug. You can capture it, this spirit of early summer. You can bottle it with sugar and zest of lemon. After twenty-four hours it begins to fizz. It becomes the essence of itself.

I love this alchemy, this certainty. Ingredients conform to rules that are known and understood. They behave in a given way under given conditions. There are limits to my love. I must draw a line in the sand.

I shake Tobias awake. 'Tobias, you're right.'

'Huh?'

'I've decided. I'm not going through what that other family is going through. I can't. I just can't.'

'Right,' says Tobias. 'I'm with you. A hundred per cent of the way. So you're not going back to the hospital then?'

'Well, I didn't exactly say that. Actually, I'm not sure what I'm trying to say.'

'I think you're being pulled in two different directions,' he says. 'You've got the power of being a mother dragging you towards Freya, and an instinct for self-preservation dragging you away from her.'

'Maybe you're right,' I say. 'And they . . . cancel each other out. They just sort of jam me. I can't think, I can't even feel. All I can do is obsess about how to get everything under control.'

We kiss for a while, before I pull myself away with a sigh. 'We'd better go and see about breakfast for the masses.'

In the kitchen, I throw open the fridge. Instead of a welcome blast of cold, there's a breath of warm, swampy air against my face.

'I can't believe it,' I say, 'the fridge has broken. It's brand new.'

'Oh, it's probably just come out at the socket,' says Tobias.

Together we haul it away from the wall. Behind it, we find the corpse of a fat rat, its teeth still clamped onto the cable that electrocuted it.

~

This morning, Tobias lets me take the Astra to Montpellier. He sees me off and kisses me goodbye. But he won't come with me, however much I plead with him. Driving down the motorway, I feel a familiar empty, angry feeling in my stomach. A picture comes into my mind of myself as a yo-yo. No matter how much I bounce up and down, none of my efforts to hold my family together has any chance if he doesn't hang on to me to stop me unravelling.

When I get to the ward, I find the nurses pushing Freya around in a pram.

She, however, seems strange to me. Where is my pretty fragile elf? Who is this fat-faced ruddy child with piggy eyes? The steroids have done their work. I pick her up. She smells of the hospital. I understand why animals will abandon their young if you handle them too much. She even *feels* different – heavier, stiffer, with a new habit of arching her head back. I want to take her home and bathe her then cuddle up to her and make her mine again. Except for the part of me that wants to leave, right now, while I can, and never come back.

Sami has visitors. An old woman – presumably his grand-mother – and a little girl of about four or five.

'My husband's mother,' says Najla, 'and my youngest daughter, Amina.' The old woman begins to talk to me without invitation or interruption as if she's known me for years.

'Hospital again – and the weather is so hot. Still, it will pass. It will pass . . .'

—

When I finally stagger home I find Tobias and Lizzy in the living room, poring over his computer.

'I'm teaching Lizzy Internet research skills,' says Tobias. 'I think being more computer-literate will change her life.'

'I've discovered this wonderful new prophetic system,' says Lizzy. 'The Incas have put it all up on the Internet for free. Anna, can you remember the date and hour and minute of Freya's birth? I'm doing her horoscope.'

'Lizzy,' I say, 'perhaps another time. I'm so tired. And besides, didn't the Incas rip out people's hearts?'

'Oh, come on, Anna, it's just a bit of fun,' says Tobias. And Lizzy gazes at me with round, impassioned eyes. I think crossly: why is she still here? I must persuade Tobias that we need to sack her – *now*. But I'm too exhausted at the moment to face the row that this is bound to provoke.

'Come to think of it, just the date of birth will do,' says Lizzy. Her fingers fly over the keyboard and she scribbles frantically on a notepad. Suddenly she exclaims: 'But this explains everything!'

'Great,' I say.

Lizzy is undeterred by my sarcasm. 'Freya doesn't *do*, she

is,' she says triumphantly. 'She influences the lives of the people around her. She brings about change.'

'Lizzy!' I snap. 'Don't you ever presume to make up that kind of nonsense about my child.'

But Lizzy doesn't seem to hear me. With her long black hair streaming over her shoulders, she looks like some South American shaman.

'She's come to earth to evoke emotion, particularly love,' she says. 'That's what she's here for. To draw people to her, open them to love.'

～

Freya is due to be discharged today.

The steroids may have turned her into a miniature sumo warrior but they've at least brought her fits under control. They've also given her a ferocious appetite. Her newly chubby cheeks have roses in them. She looks robust.

I dress her in an outfit my mother has made for her – a blue-and-white cotton frock with hand-stitched smocking at the chest. She looks adorable in it. Better still, she looks like any other baby. It's easy to let hope come creeping back again.

Tobias still wants to leave her in the hospital. But I sense he's weakening. For all his dogmatic talk, he's a softie at heart. He's grudgingly agreed to come along and meet the consultant.

First, we go through endless briefings on medicines. Freya must take a daunting number of them: three different types of anticonvulsant, two drugs to protect her stomach from the side effects of the epilepsy drugs, plus a battery of vitamins and minerals. She needs to have her blood pressure and urine checked twice a day. And physiotherapy sessions three times a week. We've got appointments with an army of health workers and social services employees, not to mention referrals to half a dozen other specialists.

She's racked up hospital bills of thirty thousand euros.

Thankfully, under reciprocal agreements covering all EU countries, we'll eventually be able to claim back her medical costs. Unfortunately, we don't yet qualify for any childcare or disability benefit in France. In my sleep-deprived state the mere thought of dealing with UK and French bureaucracies on top of Freya's demanding care schedule is impossibly daunting.

'In France,' grouses Tobias, 'it's OK to have no brain, but you're stuffed if you've got no *carte d'identité*.'

To make matters worse, the well-meaning Dr Dupont launches into a lecture. 'You must both work very hard to help Freya achieve her potential,' she says.

'Why, exactly?' asks Tobias.

She fails to pick up the warning tone in his voice. 'It is natural that you should want to. You love her because you are her parents.'

'Actually,' says Tobias, 'we're seriously thinking about putting her into care. We don't appreciate being told how much and whether we love our daughter.'

Dr Dupont looks startled and changes tone. 'Of course it's hard. This is a thing that breaks up couples. What is important is that you stay together and that you love each other.'

'And if we don't take her home?' asks Tobias boldly.

'We will have to call in social services. But you know, in France there is a great deal of support for the families of disabled children. And there is always the possibility of *un établissement*, an institution, in four or five years' time.'

'We'd like to know what to expect medically over the next

few months,' says Tobias. 'So we can make an informed decision about her future.'

'Well, Freya is at a delicate period now. There's a very difficult time between four and eight months as the brain matures. Because the underlying structure of her brain is very abnormal, it is likely to affect this process. We will probably never be able to stop her fits entirely. All we can do is try to manage them with drugs. You need to do your bit too. It's a complicated regimen but it is of vital importance. You must keep to the drug schedule and never forget her medicines – withdrawal could trigger a massive fit which could in turn cause her to lose abilities she has already developed.'

'Which abilities?' I ask.

'She could lose the ability to suck or to breathe independently.'

I feel a sick lurch at the pit of my stomach.

'Can we take a moment?' asks Tobias.

When we leave the room, I realise he's crying. That his uncaring act is simply that – an act to cover up the fact that he's terrified.

I hang on to him, feeling his shoulders shake, comforting him.

'She's so sweet,' he weeps. 'And so fucked.'

'If the consultant could see you now,' I say. 'She thinks you're a horror. You were so . . . outspoken. People may think those things, but they don't say them.'

'Fuck the consultant. Fuck all the rest of them,' he says. 'I'd rather people thought I was a complete jerk than that they felt sorry for me. Look – I've already said the unsayable. I've done the hard bit. This might be our last chance to get out before it's too late.'

'It won't be,' I say. 'I meant it when I said I'm not going through the same shit as Sami's family. We'll make a pact – draw a line in the sand. So we both understand exactly how far we're prepared to go.'

'How far is that precisely? Just so I know.'

'How about this: tube-feeding. And ventilation. The first sign of either of those and we hand her straight over to social services. Deal?'

'Do you think you can do that? Because it's going to come, you know. The doctor as good as said so. Can you really take her home knowing it's just for a little while? Do you think you'll be . . . hard enough when the time comes?'

'Believe me, I'll be hard enough. I have to be.'

I mean it. I must never go through this again. I can't afford to love Freya unconditionally. I must hold something back.

July

I've decided to pack away Freya's good clothes. They're mostly presents from friends and family before they knew that Freya was a write-off. Plus a few extra-lavish ones from people after they heard the news.

My particular favourites: a woollen receiving blanket I bought when I was pregnant. The blue-and-white dress with hand-sewn smocking my mother made her. Indian batik tops from Martha. Embroidered cotton socks. Broderie anglaise knickers. Initialled linen cot sheets. What good are all these items for a seven-month-old who can't even support her neck? Maybe I'll be able to use them for another baby one day.

More and more often recently, I've been letting myself slip into a blissful daydream. I'm pregnant again. I've none of the sickness, discomfort and misery I had with Freya. It's twins this time: one spare in case the demons are chasing us still. I've finally learned detachment – perhaps that's what Freya was for. They arrive without difficulty and Tobias weeps when they're born as if it's the first time and we have our magical moment over again, this time with no nightmare following on its heels.

It's a crazy fantasy but I have to believe it will happen. I'm relying on my twins to keep me so busy I won't have time to worry when Freya's taken away from me. When they put her into an institution, I'll be hand-washing embroidered dresses for children who can walk and talk instead of agonising about whether she's lying all alone covered in her own vomit.

I look over to where Tobias is still asleep on the bed. Freya is lying next to him, and their two heads are pointing in the same direction. Each of them has one arm flung up. They are snoring. Two peas in a pod. So peaceful, so beautiful. Both of them. And before I can brace myself, love sneaks into me and turns the knife again.

I pull the piles of little clothes off their shelf and sort rapidly through them. I put back anything easily machine-washable: terry-towelling bodysuits, acrylic jumpers, cotton vests. Anything pure wool, frilly, embroidered or non-colour fast goes straight into an extra-heavy-duty sealable plastic bag. I put it high on the top shelf, ready for the day when my life is once more back on track.

⁓

Lizzy is full of strange energy. 'A new era is coming!' she keeps telling us. 'A time of abundance!'

In a way, I suppose she's got a point. Down in the valley, the allotments beside the river are flourishing. Dark red tomatoes drip off the vines; artichokes hold high their huge heads; and the neat rows are bright with runner beans, courgettes, peppers and aubergines.

Yvonne's sausages hang from the butcher's hook in the game larder in a glorious, riotous profusion.

'Wow,' I say, when I'm permitted a quick peek. 'They're a bit damp though.'

'It's part of the process,' she tells me. 'The water must drip out of them. Only the pure meat is left behind. The humidity helps wild yeasts to grow. Soon they'll be covered in white mould.'

'Lovely.'

'It's just like making a fine wine or cheese. They must be left exposed to the air in a cool place to age, slowly and with love.'

'What are you cooking over here?' I ask her.

'Fricandeau,' says Yvonne. 'It's made from some lean parts and some fat parts of the pork. And from *abats*, offal, of course. It must be cooked slowly in a *crépine de porc* – the fat that surrounds the pig's stomach. Delicious. Oh, Anna, maybe if I win this competition I can have my own *laboratoire* just like this.'

'You can have this one, Yvonne. You could give lessons to my students. I can't think of a better selling point for my cookery school than having my own in-house *charcutière*.'

'Especially if I win the *médaille d'or*,' says Yvonne dreamily. 'Perhaps I shall devote my life to my charcuterie instead of marrying. Since Julien doesn't care for me.'

'Oh, Yvonne, he does care for you.'

'If he cared for me, he would learn a proper trade. Butchery, for instance. He would marry me. He says he doesn't believe in marriage.' Her clear gaze falls on Freya, in her sling against my chest. 'I'm afraid I might miss my chance,' she says. 'To become *maman*.'

'You know how Julien loves parties,' I say. 'Perhaps if you agreed to have an unofficial marriage in his glade, he'd go for it.'

'I will not be his concubine,' says Yvonne. 'I will not be shamed in front of the whole valley.'

223

'Or maybe he'd go for an official marriage if you agreed to do it in the tree house.'

But Yvonne, usually so tractable, is entirely unmovable on this issue. 'I've always wanted a church wedding. With a white dress. Papa would pay for it.'

The only glimmer of hope I can see is that Julien has been appointed custodian of the *saucissons*. He alone is allowed unsupervised into the inner sanctum, he alone may witness the secret processes, and he alone has been entrusted with the key, which I notice he is carrying on a chain around his neck like some hierophantic emblem.

Yvonne, I suspect, hasn't entirely lost hope that some day he may be persuaded to apprentice himself to the butcher.

———

This morning, the sun floods into our bedroom at half past six. As the sunlight touches her, Freya goes 'waa!' and bats me with her fist. Her hand is wet from where she's sucked it. It hits my face and slides down my nose to my lips, leaving a warm, sticky trail.

I open my eyes and stare into hers. They're no longer slate grey. One is light hazel like mine and the other, the one with the paint-smear pupil, is blue like Tobias's. I lie looking at her, thinking how unusual and interesting it is to have a baby with eyes of two different colours.

Tobias wakes up and leans over her, smiling in spite of himself.

Freya – immediately and unequivocally – smiles back at him.

'Wow,' breathes Tobias.

He's gazing at Freya in a way I've never seen him look at her before. Raptly, as if he's just witnessed the birth of a new planet.

And I think: it's happening, it's happening at last. He's smitten. Whatever magical chemistry babies possess to ensnare their fathers as well as their mothers has finally kicked into action.

'Her very first smile,' says Tobias. 'And for me – her daddy.'

Moments pass. The world shrinks down to just the three of us. The bed cradles us together as softly and infinitely as the sea. Tobias and I are Freya's devoted slaves. She looks from one of us to the other and gives a lopsided smile. She lies between us and kicks us both simultaneously, froggy-style. She looks at her outstretched hand and, with infinite concentration, succeeds in bringing it back to her face. After a try or two, she manages to get the back of her knuckle into her mouth. She crows, as if seeking recognition for this clever act.

'She's cut a tooth,' Tobias tells me. 'Look – the front bottom. So tiny. Isn't it sweet?'

We coo over her tooth together, revelling in being an ordinary family, proud of her progress, taking delight in normal things. 'This calls for a celebration,' I say. 'I'll bring us coffee in bed.'

I go down to the kitchen and cover a tray with a linen cloth, placing a rose in a cut-glass vase on it along with the best coffee service. I put a baby bottle into a bain marie and carry the whole lot upstairs.

'Come on,' I say, handing him a coffee. 'It may be a red-letter day, but we have chores to do.'

Tobias puts his coffee down on the bedside table, moves

Freya onto a sheepskin on the floor, then takes my cup out of my hand and pulls me down onto the bed beside him. His embrace is part passionate, part playful. I laugh out of sheer happiness and think: it's all been a blip. It's just taken us a while to find our feet. Everything is going to be all right.

People, particularly women, are always telling me how attractive Tobias is – how broad his shoulders, how blue his eyes, how thick his dark hair – but I love him for other things. Even when he's serious, his eyes have creases at the edges that make them seem to hover permanently on the brink of laughter. His jaw has a tiny dip in the middle that drives him crazy when he's shaving. He has no idea he's handsome.

He makes a quick, self-deprecating face at me and I grimace back. We're both as shy as strangers, circling warily, reaching towards each other, tasting each other again, as if we've been a long time apart and have crossed a huge distance to be together again.

Afterwards, we lie in each other's arms and drift in and out of a sensual semi-sleep. We feel the day rise and the room heat up.

The sound of chanting comes to us from the living room.

'Lizzy,' I say. 'I'm really, really fed up with her.'

Tobias looks at me innocently, as if this is news to him.

'Having no personal space,' I press on. 'Paying her, even if it *is* a pittance. Providing full board and lodging. Not to mention dragging her along to social engagements to be as mad as she likes. For that, an au pair would do five hours' work a day. Tobias, please, we really must sack her.'

'Humph,' says Tobias, suddenly huffy. 'Damn this heat. It would drive anybody round the bend.'

He springs up and rummages around in the wardrobe.

I lie back on the bed and close my eyes. 'All right – I'm sorry.

It's absolutely the wrong time to bring that up. Can I have the sexy Tobias back please?' But the moment has evaporated.

'My music equipment's not coping well with this heat,' he says, still rummaging. 'Although, frankly, the funding's stalled again for *Madame Bovary* and there are no docs to be had at the moment. I might as well take a break. I'm going to go and sit by the river. I'll take Freya if you like.'

'It's OK. I think it's a bit hot for her outside.'

'It's better outside than here, in this oven.'

'There are mosquitoes by the river. I'll keep her with me.'

'Suit yourself.'

The heat always makes Tobias grumpy. He thumps out of the house, leaving me wondering why on earth I wanted to move to a hot country in the first place.

The bedroom is stifling. Freya stares at the white ceiling, making snuffling noises of protest. I try sponging her down but her cross red face is a mirror of Tobias's own. I go to the wardrobe to get a lighter bodysuit and stop dead, staring at the shelf.

All Freya's nice clothes are back, neatly stacked in piles. Tobias. It must have been him. There's no trace of my impermeable plastic bag.

—

Since Freya has been discharged my days are filled with meetings. An army of health and social workers has demanded to see us, horrified that she's been allowed to slip under the radar for so long.

In the beginning I was filled with relief. How could I have failed to realise there's a safety net expressly for cases like ours?

227

But gradually I've become exhausted and deadened by the ordeal of recounting the long, awful story of Freya's history over and over again.

Tobias always seems to manage to absent himself from these meetings. 'Your French is so much better than mine,' he says, as he rushes off to work on his score. 'And besides, you always blub – it makes it all *so* much more powerful.'

It doesn't help that he's right about the blubbing. I only have to start telling the story of Freya's birth to dissolve into great racking unstable sobs – just when I'm trying to show how balanced and reasonable I am. The officials look at me knowingly, jot notes in our formidable case-history files and make reassuring promises of home help and childcare.

But first, each official adds to the daunting documents in French that I have no idea how to fill in, and which will take a minimum of six months to be processed by the proper authorities in two countries. This teetering mountain of paperwork already takes up half of the space on the living-room table, dwarfing even the pile of documentation required to start a residential cookery school.

Until it's processed, months from now, the very same people who've just told me my case is top priority, say: '*Mais vous n'avez pas le droit . . .*' And off they go.

'You don't have the right to . . .' has taken its place alongside '*mal fait*' as the most terrifying phrase in the French language.

Tobias and I both wake in the early hours, worrying.

'I can *hear* the rats gnawing the beams,' I whisper.

'Why are you whispering?' Tobias whispers back to me.

'Shh! Can't you hear them? A sort of regular munching noise. I'm afraid they're going to bring the roof down.'

'Well, I don't know what to do about it.'

I sigh. 'I know. It's just . . .' I stop.

'Just what?'

'I know it's not fair to expect you to be able to do those kinds of things. But it does feel like, well, *man's* work. At least, everybody around here thinks so.'

'Oh God – not that again. Nothing's stopping *you* doing anything about the rats in the beams.'

'But I don't know how. Anyway, I feel as if I'm already doing enough drudgery. It's five in the morning and in two hours I've got to mix up Freya's morning medicine. Then try to set up her ophthalmic appointment – I can't get past the hospital switchboard. Not to mention spending another miserable day in meetings and trying to tackle her paperwork again. Couldn't we have some sort of rota and share the chores between us?'

'Don't start on me again! You sound like a primary-school teacher – instead of saying "Damn well do something!" you say "Let's have a rule for this . . ." Well, I'm sick of it!'

'She's got to have follow-up appointments for everything from her diet to her genetic make-up. Most of them are in Montpellier – that's nearly two hours away, by the way. And it's always me that takes her.'

'And, come to think of it, what's all this got to do with the rats?'

'Not to mention mixing up five different kinds of drugs. Tapering doses up and down. Taking her blood pressure twice a day in case she's having an abreaction. Testing her urine. It's a huge responsibility.'

'Why do these discussions always have to take place in the middle of the night?'

'Tobias – I need you to understand. Every day, I feel as if

I'm on . . . a tightrope. I'm wobbling with Freya along a tight-rope of drugs. Too much, and her liver and God knows what other organs fail – not enough and she goes into convulsions. It's an incredibly delicate balancing act. And it's working; it's stabilising her fits. That's what's allowing her to express her personality. That's why she's started smiling at us. So I have to carry on. If we fail . . . can't you see that I'm terrified of getting it wrong?'

Tobias relents. 'OK – what's the chore you're dreading the most?'

'Well, I suppose all the paperwork to try to get the NHS to reimburse her French medical bills. We're spending two hundred pounds a month on drugs at the moment. Not to mention what we owe the hospital. We can't afford it. Our credit cards are maxed out. I'm so anxious about money. All the time.'

'Let me get a little more sleep and I'll help you with it this morning. I promise.'

I look at him suspiciously. 'Really? Without fail?'

'Scout's honour.'

'What time?'

'Anna – always one for nailing things down. Let's say nine thirty.'

'Oh, Tobias, that's such a relief.'

We cuddle and I think of the love flowing between us. I need to hold on to that.

—

I fall in and out of sleep. Dawn breaks. At seven I blearily give Freya her medicine and tuck her into bed next to me for a moment's more sleep. She snuggles up to me, lodged under my armpit, nudging me to the edge of the bed. Seemingly minutes later, it's nine o'clock. Tobias's place in the bed is already empty.

I jump up and race downstairs. Lizzy is in the living room, tapping at Tobias's laptop computer.

'Lizzy, what are you doing?' I ask.

'I'm doing both of your Incan horoscopes.'

'We don't believe in that stuff, do we, Tobias?'

'It was Tobias that asked me to,' says Lizzy innocently. 'Didn't you, Tobias?'

Tobias has the grace to look embarrassed. 'Harmless really,' he mumbles, although I know full well he thinks Lizzy's ideas are idiotic. She has our birthdays written on a piece of paper, I notice, in Tobias's handwriting.

'Tobias is a white serpent – to do with physical things. You are a red dog, Anna – your life is about finding a balance between heart and head.'

'Lizzy . . .'

'Your unexpected power,' says Lizzy, 'comes through play.'

'I'm fed up with this nonsense.'

'Your relationship is the golden eagle.'

'Never mind our relationship.'

'The golden eagle is important. It means that together you and Tobias can see things clearly.'

'Tobias – do you want a cup of coffee before we start the French paperwork?'

'Oh, yes please,' says Tobias.

But before the water has even boiled, Lizzy says: 'So do you still want to come on that walk then?' and Tobias says: 'Of course I do.'

'He can't come – we're doing paperwork this morning.'

'We have to go – today is a blue galactic gale day,' says Lizzy. 'It's all about liberating energy and giving it back to the cosmos.'

'Why don't you come too?' says Tobias.

'I can't – this paperwork needs doing. You promised to help . . .'

'Well – it's galactic activation day, Anna,' says Tobias. 'Didn't you hear?'

I feel a rising rage. Bring it on, I think grimly: make it as bad as you can, because then I can feel furious and powerless, which I'm addicted to.

'It's all right,' I snarl. 'I'll stay and do it by myself then. As usual.'

'Remember, Anna,' Lizzy calls behind her as they leave, 'do it in a spirit of play.'

~

There's no doubt that Freya is becoming a daddy's girl. She smiles her biggest and best smiles for Tobias and gazes adoringly into his eyes. He gazes back, shell-shocked.

This morning she's been staring at our stripy pillow.

'You're absolutely delighted, aren't you?' says Tobias. 'You thought that you'd have to wait for hours before we got up.' Freya stretches out her hand – not just a fist, an open hand – and gently touches the pillow.

'This is your favourite time of day, isn't it?' I hear Tobias saying as I go to make the coffee. 'Your daddy and your stripy pillow. It's a party.'

I stop in the doorway of our bedroom and watch them

together. Tobias puts the stripy pillow on his head and begins pulling faces at Freya from underneath it, trying to make her smile. He stops as soon as he sees me watching.

———

The wild lavender has already shrivelled; the flowers slip away quickly in the first heat of the summer. But it's tenacious – you can't walk on the hillside without its dried-out leaves leaving traces of aromatic oil on your hands and clothes.

Now it's the turn of the cultivated lavender to flower. The bees are contentedly droning in the pots of it I've put all along the covered wooden bridge that forms a balcony beside our bedroom. When we first looked round Les Rajons, this was the only place that didn't seem threatening. I imagined it as my private retreat and I put two chairs up here in the hope that Tobias and I would sit together in the evenings.

But Tobias has turned it into his summer headquarters and he needs both chairs for his Internet lessons with Lizzy. From the sound of their laughter, the lessons are amusing.

'You have to keep an eye on your husband,' my mother tells me. 'Men are all fools. And that hippy girl is a fast piece, anybody can see that.'

'Tobias has always been a bit of a flirt,' I say, 'but I trust him implicitly.'

We're sitting in the cool of the living room. My mother is sewing and I'm trying to feed Freya. A particularly long gale of giggling comes from the balcony, accompanied by the sound of thumping.

My mother springs to her feet and grabs hold of a broom. 'I'm going up there to launch a raid,' she says.

I struggle with myself for all of three seconds before I desert Freya in her bouncy seat and race upstairs after her.

Tobias and Lizzy are on their hands and knees, staring at the balcony floor.

'An invasion of giant ants!' exclaims Tobias. 'Look at that one! It must be nearly an inch long.'

A train of enormous ants is marching from the balcony to our bedroom. My mother produces a spray can of insecticide from the pocket of her apron. 'When I pray,' she says, 'and promise that I will be kind to all living creatures, I exclude the ants. I say "*nearly* all living things".' She gives them a few sharp blasts. 'I'm not too fond of wasps, either.'

Tobias watches sadly as the ants stagger off to die.

'Have you nothing to do, the pair of you?' demands my mother. 'Tobias, is this how you support my daughter and granddaughter? Or are you hoping, young man, that *they* will support *you*?'

'I'm giving Lizzy a computer lesson,' says Tobias. 'I think it's time somebody gave her a break. The poor kid's had almost no education.'

My mother puts her hands on her hips. 'The poor kid is being paid to do a bit of work around here. Lizzy, there are plums ripe in the orchard – will you go and pick them right now please? I'm going to make a tart.'

Tobias opens his mouth to protest but Lizzy stops him. 'That's all right,' she says brightly. 'I'll do a plum-picking meditation.'

My mother superintends her downstairs. Tobias and I are left alone on the balcony. I sit down next to him. For a few minutes, neither of us speaks. We watch the bees gorging themselves in the lavender.

Tobias breaks the silence. 'Look at that one, Anna,' he says. 'It looks just like a hummingbird, hovering over the flower. But it's an insect. See its proboscis. Shall we call it a humming-bee?'

'You wouldn't have an affair with her, would you?' I say. 'You wouldn't fall in love with her? Because if you did, it would break my heart.'

He's about to fob me off, I can tell. I've spoken without thinking, but now I picture what life would be like without Tobias. Unbearable. I make what I mean to be an ironic, sophisticated little moue, but it comes out wrong and I find that my lips are trembling.

'Anna, what can I say? It's just nice to sit up here in the sunshine and have a giggle for once, without worrying about whether I've done all the chores on your list or whether our baby has a brain.'

'It's not my fault,' I bridle, 'that there are things that need to be done. The house is falling down – literally.'

'That's just what I'm talking about,' he bursts out. 'I didn't marry your mother, you know. It's bad enough having *her* living here on an apparently permanent basis, without you turning into her mini-me. All that stuff. The routine, the duty, the drudgery. It feels like my life is over. Lizzy's just a kid and her notions are crazy, to say the least. But she's *fun*. She's full of – energy and enthusiasm. And that seems important right at the moment.'

'So do you . . . like her?'

'Don't be ridiculous.' I wonder whether or not he's answered too quickly. He's looking directly at me, with a plea in his eyes. 'Haven't you ever had the feeling of wanting to feel alive – whatever it costs?'

'Tobias,' I say, 'in so many ways you're my opposite. I have to work for every single thing; you're effortlessly gifted. Your music, even when you're doing some lousy documentary, is so beautiful and moving. But your sheer talent makes you think you can get away with being lazy. You can't. Not round here. It takes so much energy just to tread water up here. Nobody can afford a free ride.'

I expect a fight back. But he offers sudden and total capitulation instead.

'I know, I'm sorry. The truth is, I'm just hiding up here. I feel as if I'm the wrong person for this place.'

'You're not the wrong person,' I say. 'Perhaps it's the wrong place.'

Tobias looks round at the lavender in pots and the guzzling bees, and shakes his head. 'No – I love this place. I always have, ever since we first saw it. It's worse than that: I feel as if I'm the wrong person in the *right* place. The rats in the beams, the house falling down . . . I can't do any of the things that need doing.'

'I feel the same,' I admit. 'Helpless and powerless. We have the wrong skill sets for this environment.'

'Kerim's leaving at the end of the month and then it'll be worse than ever. We'll be living alone here with your mother.'

I reach out from where I'm sitting and give him an awkward sideways hug. 'I promise I'll ask my mother to leave. Soon, anyway. I really will.'

'All the men around here can build their own houses, plant their own fields and look after animals,' says Tobias. 'All I can do is compose music and give great dinner parties.'

'I wouldn't trade anything for your blue eyes or your sharp wit.' As we walk downstairs together, I wonder if this is strictly true.

Julien is waiting for us.

'Hi, Tobias,' he says.

'Hey, Julien,' says Tobias. I see his body stiffen. He looks big and awkward next to Julien's wiry frame.

'I came to remind you about your drinking water,' says Julien. 'It's stopped raining for the summer now. You need to check your cistern.'

'The water cistern. Yeah.'

'I can help you look it over if you like.'

'Sorry, I can't stop. I have to run along and work on my score. They've done yet another recut. I've got a deadline.'

Julien and I watch his retreating back.

'Julien, this is really kind of you,' I say. 'I'm around, if you want to show me what to do.'

Julien smiles his enigmatic smile. 'Well, the first thing we need to do is to make sure there are no leaks – in the tank or the plumbing in the house. A dripping tap can lose you thousands of litres of water.' He stops and looks at me seriously. I notice, absurdly, the flecks of grey in his eyes.

'Anna, you know it's possible that it might not rain properly now for another two months. Three months in a drought year. Your tank holds ten thousand litres. You have to hoard every drop of water from now on. No running taps, no baths, wash down in the river whenever you can. Are you sure Tobias realises how serious this is?'

'Oh yes, I'm sure he does. It's just – he has a lot of work. Somebody has to pay the bills.'

'Well, we should lag the cistern. If there's a chink of light or it gets too warm your water will spoil. You need to make sure that no mosquito larvae can get in either. Do you have a filter?'

'Er, no. Tobias hasn't quite got round to ordering one. I've been boiling water for myself and Freya.'

'You need to boil it for at least twenty minutes from now on. And use boiled water to wash fruit and salads until you have a filter fitted.'

We spend the day doing exactly as he's said. I watch his sure, thin hands tinkering with our plumbing, plugging every leak, stopping every running tap, making things watertight.

He says nothing, but I sense his disapproval that Tobias isn't doing this for himself. It's easier for me, as a woman, to fit in here. I can learn to make preserves and grow vegetables. But Tobias is expected to be able to undertake a huge range of manly tasks. No wonder he's intimidated.

Lizzy reappears from the orchard with a meagre handful of plums.

'Is that all there were?' I ask.

'I really think we should share the rest of them with the worms and the birds,' she says.

'Lizzy needs some more friends,' I say to Julien when she's gone. 'Couldn't you introduce her to some of the hippies? You know, the pagans and suchlike who were at your party? She could play around with them, surely.'

'The hippies round here work very hard,' says Julien severely. 'They till the land, work with animals, make handicrafts to sell to tourists, grow dope and bring up children. Lizzy just talks nonsense and surfs the Internet.'

His words echo Tobias's self-deprecating description of himself. Perhaps that's what he sees in her. They're both struggling here, looking for a place to fit in.

'Be careful,' Julien says as he leaves. 'Until it rains again water is precious. Irrigate your potager.' He looks down at

Freya asleep in her bouncy seat. 'Remember: everything you neglect will die.'

I'm shifting her seat into the coolest part of the living room when I hear Ludovic's distinctive hammering on the front door.

'Ludovic, have you come to work in your potager? Would you like a coffee?'

Ludovic's face is raw; he's choking back tears. He doesn't come into the living room as usual. Instead he takes off his hunting hat and stands on the threshold wringing it in his hands. 'Ludovic? What's wrong?'

'Thérèse. She collapsed this morning. She's unconscious. The doctors say it's an aneurysm.'

I don't know what to say. I get an insight into the utter discomfort people feel when we tell them – nowadays with almost sadistic brutality – about Freya.

'Oh, Ludovic. Is there anything we can do to help? Won't you come in and sit down for a while?'

He stands in the doorway, looking lost. Finally he shakes his head. 'I must get back to the hospital. I just wanted to inform you. You are my neighbours, after all.'

＊

Yvonne telephones us to say that Thérèse died in the early hours of yesterday morning.

'It's the custom,' she says, 'to go and pay one's respects to the body before the funeral. I thought we could go together. I'll meet you in front of Ludovic's bungalow in half an hour.'

I walk down the hill with Freya in her sling and together we file through Ludovic's concrete front garden, through his PVC door, into his orange breeze-block bungalow.

239

'It's a lovely house,' Yvonne whispers to me. 'He built it all himself, you know, everything *comme il faut.*'

The inside of Ludovic's house is as immaculate and sterile as his potager. Every surface is shiny and wiped clean. The sofas are shrink-wrapped in transparent plastic. A microwave has pride of place in the kitchen; a vast television dominates in the living room.

We find Ludovic sitting hunched on the very edge of a sofa. A couple of mourners are on their way out, embracing him with simple formality, making offers of practical help. It's not so bad being old in a village, I reflect. People may squabble, but when somebody suffers a real loss, they pull together.

Thérèse's body is lying in state in an open coffin lined with electric-blue satin. She's heavily made up: the undertaker has tried to improve on nature by drawing over her eyebrows with a thick black pencil and colouring her cheeks with rouge. She's dressed in a pink polyester skirt and jacket. I've no idea when she would ever have had a chance to wear that outfit during her lifetime of drudgery. Perhaps it's been bought specially for the occasion.

I feel desperate to escape from this sterile environment, but Ludovic says: 'Sit down for a minute,' in a tone that contains so much of a raw plea that Yvonne and I squeeze awkwardly on either side of him on the plastic-covered sofa. His shoulders begin to shake silently.

'*Pauvre*,' murmurs Yvonne putting her arm around him.

'Everybody is gone,' says Ludovic. 'My father, Rose, my son. And now Thérèse. I'm alone.'

'Don't say that!' says Yvonne. 'We're here – your friends are here.'

'My friends are dead,' Ludovic bursts out. 'Seventeen of

my friends from the Maquis were shot in one day. All my contemporaries. We should have grown up together. They should have been here with me today, mourning with me.'

He pushes his fist into his mouth as if he can physically prevent the grief from rushing out. There's a long silence. I listen to the steady tick-tock of the plastic clock above the television, watching its white minute hand clack around its orange face, trying not to feel Ludovic's body beside me shuddering from the effort of restraining his tears.

He looks at Freya on my lap. 'Thérèse always wanted another child,' he says and his hands make an involuntary movement towards her.

I offer her to him and he takes her from me and cradles her; it seems to comfort him. I keep making to take her back, but he hangs on to her for what seems an age, crying for his lost child.

———

Julien and I are up in the attic, looking at where the rats have gnawed a beam.

'Look — there's the nest here. Rats don't systematically destroy beams. They were just making a way inside.'

'What if they bring the roof down on Freya?'

'Pass me an Accro.'

I hand him the metal reinforcing rod and he twists it deftly into place.

'Well, it's safe now. The Accro will hold the roof up until you can get it properly mended. But most of the gnawing you've been hearing isn't rats anyway.'

'Not rats? Thank goodness for that. What is it?'

'Woodworm.' He smiles at my shocked face. 'Don't worry – they can't get through massive beams like this. Termites are the ones to watch. They'll eat away the structure from the inside without leaving a trace until your house falls down.'

'Good God! Not another thing to worry about.'

'Anna, you already worry too much,' says Julien. 'You need to relax.'

I wipe a strand of damp hair off my forehead. 'I wish it wasn't so hot. I can't believe it's the same place. Everything's just frazzled up.'

His touch on my bare shoulder is cool and confident. 'It's going to get worse,' he says. 'It'll become a second winter. That's why plants grow so fast in the spring – in the summer everything dies. You know Freud had a theory that there are two conflicting drives, which he named after Greek gods: Eros and Thanatos. Love and Death. Living in this area, it seems to me that we spend our lives crossing between them – at any one time, we're in the domain of either one or the other. Spring is Eros, certainly. But summer – well, summer here is Thanatos.'

'How do you think up all this stuff?'

'Anna – it seems to me you've had a shock. All that organising, mouseproofing, putting up barriers to life – it's Thanatos. You need to move back into the domain of life.'

I put Freya into the Astra and take her to her neurological follow-up appointment in Montpellier. Dr Dupont looks grave and worried as usual.

I say: 'She's put on weight,' and she shakes her head and says: 'It's the steroids.'

I say: 'She's having fewer fits,' but Dr Dupont asks: 'Is she always that sleepy?'

She wants to know every detail of Freya's fits – are they different? longer? more on one side than another? As I describe them, I feel my optimism falling away.

'Do you feel that she's making progress, developmentally?'

'Oh yes,' I say. 'She's smiling and looking at her hands.'

'Hmmm,' says Dr Dupont. 'Let's go through some developmental milestones. Is she beginning to crawl?'

'No.'

'Does she recognise her name?'

'No.'

'Is she able to sit?'

'Oh no.'

'Can she pass you objects?'

'Well – no.'

'Grasp objects?'

'No.'

'Does she jabber or combine syllables?'

'No.'

'Does she imitate sounds like "baba" or "dada"?'

'Oh goodness, no.'

'Does she turn her head towards loud noises?'

'No.'

'Bear her weight on her legs when you hold her up?'

'No.'

'Roll over?'

'No.'

'Support her own head?'

'No.'

Dr Dupont sighs. 'I'm afraid that this is consistent with the prognosis that we expect from her,' she says, scribbling a note. 'There is a residential care home in Montpellier that takes children from two years old. If we are going to arrange a place for her, we need to start doing the paperwork now.'

So now I know the worst: an institution in Montpellier is where she'll probably end up.

—

Back home, I go upstairs, draw the curtains against the glare and lie down in bed with Freya next to me.

Nobody will lie in bed with her in Montpellier. What will she make of it? Will she feel confused, deserted? Should I get her used to the life she'll have to live? Leave her in her own bed? Touch her merely professionally, briskly? Or should I try to charge her up with a whole lifetime's worth of cuddles, hug her for hours while I have the chance? Let the love flow between us like an electrical current?

She throws her head back to look at me and smiles her lopsided smile. I clutch her to me and whisper: 'I'll never send you away. Never.' For a moment it helps. But I know that if her condition worsens we may have to send her to Montpellier anyway. That any promise I make to myself or to her is conditional only and hence worthless.

I need to get back to my chores. As I'm carrying her downstairs, Freya begins to cry. If she cries in Montpellier, will they come and comfort her? Better to get her used to it.

I put her down in her pram and begin to reorganise the kitchen shelves, trying to blot out her enraged wails and the sight of her little face, scrunched up and purple.

'My goodness, dear, why don't you pick up that baby?'

My mother sweeps up Freya, who hiccups to a standstill as if somebody has pressed an off switch.

'Do you need a hand, dear? Organising things? Or with Freya?'

'No – I'm quite all right, thank you, Mother.'

'It's just that you're always so busy. I can see you have such a lot to do. I'm pretty good at organising shelves myself, you know. I'd like to feel I'm being of use.'

I shake my head.

'I'm your mother, dear. I know my little girl. She pretends to be tough, but really she's so fragile.'

'I'm not fragile. I can't afford to be.'

My mother sighs. 'I'm worried about Gustav and Kerim,' she says. 'They've had a tiff. It's about us, I'm afraid: Kerim was trying to stay and help out here for a bit longer. Most unfair of him, I thought. After all, he's forced Gustav to the Isle of Wight and *promised* he'd join him.'

She pauses for my reply; I continue ostentatiously with my work.

'Anyway, what I'm saying, dear, is that I'd love to stay here with you, but only if you *needed* me.'

I think about my promise to Tobias. This is the moment to make clear to her that she can't stay.

'I can manage on my own,' I say.

She sighs again. 'Well . . . if you really don't need me here *at all*, I think I'll take the opportunity to travel back to England with Kerim. Perhaps I can stay with Gustav and Kerim for a week or so just to keep an eye on them.' Her voice descends to a piercing whisper: 'Between you and me I think poor Gustav is henpecked.' When it resumes its usual volume it is, if anything, firmer and more decided than ever: 'But after that

245

– I've come to a decision. My proper place is in my own home; I need to get used to being alone.'

I look up, finally, from my organising. I'm not even close to being able to tell her how bereft I suddenly feel at the thought of her leaving.

—

I've decided that I'm going to make sure Lizzy does the babysitting she's supposed to. It's part of some elaborate game I'm playing with Tobias; I need him involved. And if that means pushing things to a crisis, then so be it.

'Lizzy,' I say, 'can you come away from the computer and look after Freya?'

She shakes her head convulsively and bends down over Tobias's laptop as if she's protecting it from harm.

'You know the white trails after airplanes?' she says. 'They're called chemical trails and the CIA is poisoning them.'

'I don't see why that gets you out of babysitting,' I say. 'I need to go into Aigues.'

'I can easily mind Freya,' says Kerim. 'I usually do –'

'No, I need you to come with me and help load the car. I've found a great old butcher's block in the *brocante* and I'm not sure how we're going to get it into the Astra.'

'But Freya's hungry,' says Kerim. 'I'm not sure whether Lizzy's ever –'

'Well then, Lizzy can learn,' I say, adding cruelly: 'You're not going to be here for much longer, Kerim – we've got to stop relying on you for everything.'

I fetch a fresh bottle of feed and stand behind Lizzy's chair, shaking it at her. 'It's your *job*,' I say. Lizzy continues fiddling at the computer, apparently deaf. 'What are you doing anyway? Saving the world?'

'Well, yes,' says Lizzy. 'At least, I've taken a few steps towards saving the world.' But she moves away from the computer and takes the bottle from me.

Kerim gestures me into the kitchen. 'Do you think she's having some sort of psychotic episode?' he whispers.

'I don't know how we'd possibly tell.'

But I can see there's something wrong with her. Her eyes are bright with repressed energy and she's got deep bags under them, as if she's not sleeping properly. I'm sure she's losing weight.

In the living room. Lizzy has begun feeding Freya. She's got her at the wrong angle: her head is bent too far back and the slope of the bottle is too steep. Freya's hungry, she's gulping the formula down too fast; at the same time her little body is writhing, she's trying ineffectually to bat the bottle away with her hands, arching backwards as far from it as she can get.

I'm launching in to take over, but Lizzy just hunches closer to Freya, mute and deaf, and the bottle glugs faster and faster and suddenly an uncontrollable wave of rage overwhelms me. Why's it me who has to babysit everybody all the time?

'Come on,' I say grimly to Kerim. 'Let's go into town.'

We're gone about an hour. As we arrive back outside the front door with a butcher's block upended in the back of the car, I hear Freya wailing.

Freya doesn't cry as often as other babies; often not even for food. She never uses tears as an instrument to get her own way; she never plays mind games. A cynic might say this is because she doesn't have a mind as such, but I prefer to believe that she is stoical. Now I hear her making a sound I associate with pain. A sort of long drawn-out 'oww, oww, oww'.

'It's all right,' says Kerim, catching my alarmed look. 'If she's still crying she's OK.' His voice is grim.

'It's colic,' I say. 'She's taken in air with her bottle and she can't get rid of it.'

We dash into the living room. Lizzy is back at the computer, headphones clamped to her head, presumably to block out the noise of Freya howling beside her.

Freya is writhing with wind. She can't roll herself over into a better position to relieve the pain. I rush to snatch her up, but Kerim has beaten me to it, and is throwing her over his shoulder with her tummy pressed against his shoulder blade and her head hanging down behind him, rubbing her back, trying for a burp.

'Anna!' he bursts out, exasperated. 'I wish I could stay here to look after you, but I can't . . . Gustav needs me – and I can't risk losing him. I'm so sorry but I have to go, don't you see?'

I nod at him, chastened. Freya gives a great burp: loud, satisfied, relieved.

'Look,' he says. 'I understand why you sometimes close your eyes to things regarding her care or her future. I know it's painful for you to think about them. But you're going to have to try, Anna. I won't be here to watch over you.'

I don't know what to say; there's nothing I can say. I feel unfit to be a mother. It's the lowest feeling in the world, as if I've been reduced to zero. I nod and mumble something about dinner. Then, leaving Freya in his arms, I take refuge in my kitchen.

I'm busy chopping onions as a cover for my tears, when

Julien throws open the door. He doesn't bother to say hello. He does not, apparently, notice my red eyes or my streaming nose. He begins speaking as soon as he sees me.

'Do you know what she's done? She's issued me with an ultimatum. If I love her, I have to marry her. Properly. In a church. And get what she calls a real job. Just tell me, how am I expected to live in a modern villa in the town and work for her father? I'd rather be dead in my grave.'

'Julien,' I say, 'why don't you marry her? It's just a piece of paper. Then maybe she'll get off your back on some of the other issues.'

But Julien, always so ready with advice about what's best for me, seems to have a blind spot in his own case.

'It'll never work,' he huffs. 'I've told her so and we've ended everything. I am no longer attached. I have chosen not to be a slave.'

He strides up and down the kitchen. 'It comes down to this: I need to be free more than I need love. *That's* the most important thing to me.'

—

It's the end of the month and my mother and Kerim are packing their bags into the Astra. To my surprise, there's no sign of Tobias, or Lizzy either, for that matter.

'It's all right, Anna. They've already said their goodbyes,' says Kerim in a voice that instantly makes me suspect he's making excuses for them. 'Can you believe they were actually going to delay their walk until after we left? Luckily I managed to persuade them not to be so silly.'

'I'm a bit surprised they're not coming to see you off.'

'There wouldn't have been room in the car,' says Kerim. 'No, no, Amelia, let *me* sit in the back.'

He's right — about the space, anyway. He jams himself in between Freya's car seat and a huge suitcase of my mother's, and we set off for the station.

There's the usual stilted wait on the platform.

'Well, goodbye, darling,' says my mother. She's looking at Freya, but she's speaking to me. Or perhaps to both of us. Gingerly, she leans over and gives Freya a kiss, and then another one.

'So the doctor says she's definitely not going to develop?' she asks.

'I'm afraid so.'

'She'll never walk or talk?'

'No.'

'She'll always stay a baby?'

'Yes.'

'She'll never leave home and go away?'

'No.'

'She'll need and depend on you for the rest of her life?'

'Yes.'

My mother looks serious, as if she's processing something important.

'In many ways,' she says slowly, 'she's the perfect baby. You can be a mother forever.'

She reaches into her handbag. 'Anyway, I wanted her to have this. I tried to give it to her once before but it wasn't a good moment and it seems to have slipped my mind after that.'

The train rolls into the platform. 'Oh well, I must go.' She pushes something into my hand. She doesn't try to kiss me: trains panic her. She's already hurrying down the platform.

Kerim gives me a brief hug, whispering 'you'll be all right, you'll see' and 'remember what I said' in my ear. Then he dashes to help my mother onto the train.

I'm left standing on the platform, holding my teddy. I turn him over in my hands. Bernie the bear. Cherished companion of my childhood. He's lost an eye; his neck droops as badly as Freya's; his fur is worn smooth with loving.

My mother waves frantically and blows me kisses from the doorway of the train. She disappears and pops up again a moment later waving again through the window of the carriage. I hold Bernie above my head and wave back with him. I'm still waving long after the train has drawn out of the station and has become a speck in the distance, long after they can no longer see me. I've often longed to be rid of my mother, but now that she's gone I feel an overwhelming sense of being alone.

—

When I get back to the house, there's still no sign of Tobias or Lizzy. I find Yvonne in the game kitchen.

'Have you seen Tobias?' I ask, adding in a softer voice: 'Or Lizzy?'

'You just missed them – they came back but they've gone straight out again. They were heading for *le col des treize vents*,' she says.

'I'd better go and find them,' I say. 'I need to talk to him.'

She gives me an understanding look.

'Do you want me to look after Freya? I'm around the whole afternoon. You and Tobias could take some time together perhaps . . .'

'Oh, Yvonne,' I say, 'that would be so lovely of you. There are a couple of bottles of feed for her made up in the fridge.'

'Don't hurry back. I know how to look after this *petite puce*. I'm sure you can find Tobias if you go right now.'

When I walk out onto the hillside I discover that I'm not looking for Tobias at all. All I can think of is Eros and Thanatos and about wanting to feel alive, whatever it costs.

I'm walking, almost running, across the dragon's spine, past the infinity pool, to the glade and to Julien's tree house.

I'm racing up the spiral staircase, barely noticing that every last trace of blossom on the wisteria has gone or that its leaves have lost their ethereal quality and are dense and tough.

I'm hammering on his door so loudly that he flings it open in alarm.

When I kiss him, his lips feel thin and hard and they taste of woodsmoke. His eyes slide away from me. For a moment, I think: he won't do it. And the thought of him backing away from me is like a kind of shrivelled-up death. I wind my arms around his neck as tightly as ivy.

I feel him waver. And then he's pulling me deep inside the heart of the tree. I can hear the subtle creak of it as we move and the secret whispering of its leaves.

Inside there's nothing except the sound of the branches, of the breeze, of the owl, of the tree. Nothing but the touch of its living wood and of his hanging bed rocking us in its embrace.

August

THE WEATHER IS SCORCHING. One perfect, sunny day succeeds another. As Julien predicted, it's like a second winter. Anything we don't water dies.

Julien doesn't stop here on his way down into the village any more. I think he's avoiding me. I have no idea why I did what I did, or even how I feel about him. If only I could simply have a long cry over him – or at least could feel the emotion I'm supposed to be feeling, instead of this strange sense of being removed from it all that occasionally spills over into undirected rage and confusion.

There's a dark box in my mind and into it I've become adept at pushing anything that might do me damage. The single episode with Julien is in there. Tucked away beside any unwanted thought about Freya's future.

I'm missing my mother, and Kerim. And not just because my two most reliable sources of childcare have vanished. It's as though they've both been benevolent influences watching over us – unnoticed and unthanked – for months.

Now that the weather is so perfect, it seems that almost everybody we know in England happens to be passing by and is wondering whether we can put them up for a few days.

Tobias is delighted to be spending the summer as an unpaid tour guide. He collects groups of friends from the airport and organises parties by the river, by the lake, by any pool of open water.

I've spent the past two weeks throwing together picnic hampers. I make salads of wild purslane and sorrel tossed with our own tender lettuce leaves, or of broad beans and artichokes from the potager drizzled with thick local olive oil and a hint of garlic and lemon juice. I fill Thermos jugs with gazpacho pressed from our own tomatoes or with *velouté de concombre*. I pack wicker baskets with succulent slabs of Yvonne's ham and her pâté studded with chestnuts; with *tielles sétoises*, a local pasty filled with octopus; with iced oysters fresh from the *étangs*, to be prised open with a penknife and gulped down with Tabasco and a dash of lemon; with apricot tarts; with blackberry and apple crumbles; with quiches made from our own butter-softened leeks and trout from our river; with ratatouille of vegetables I've picked an hour before; with my home-made *confiture d'oignons doux*, to be spooned decadently onto crusty French bread. All of which we wash down with quantities of chilled Picpoul de Pinet, the local white wine.

Mysteriously, Tobias and I are being nicer to each other.

'Your cookery is changing, Anna,' he says, as he crams his mouth with *caviar d'aubergine*.

I'm surprised, and a bit alarmed. 'Don't you like it?'

'I love it.' There's a curiously intent look in his eyes. 'It's just . . . I've often thought that there are two sorts of chefs – ones like Nicolas who train and follow rules. They're in it for perfection. Then there are those who take risks – who throw ingredients together – because what they love is the providing of food to others, the pleasure it brings. Don't get me wrong, your cooking has always been sublime, but it's always been very much under control. Suddenly you're daring to let go.'

I stare back at him, amazed that he's has given any thought to my cookery, let alone constructed such an elaborate theory about it.

'Must be Rose's notebook,' I say. But a small voice in my mind asks whether this change could be also linked to Julien.

Lizzy's *joie de vivre* is evaporating before our eyes. For a start, she's definitely losing weight.

'Delicious,' says Tobias, as we tuck into *seiche à la rouille*, the cuttlefish in tomato sauce that is a famous dish from Sète on the Languedoc coast. Like so many of my new dishes, the recipe is from Rose's book. 'Lizzy, let me give you some *seiche*.'

'No thank you.'

'Come on. You'll fade away. Time to start eating.'

'I've become a vegetarian.'

'OK, then have some pudding.'

'Becoming a vegetarian is just the first step,' she says. 'I've found a website where you can have your DNA changed so you can live on light.'

'Light?' says Tobias. 'Nothing but light?'

Lizzy looks sulky. 'Or light foods,' she says.

I'm becoming genuinely worried about her. I look at Tobias and mouth 'Internet' and 'your fault' at him, but he merely shrugs.

'Lizzy, you don't really believe it all, do you?' I say. 'That stuff you read on the Internet?'

To my surprise, her defiant little nod wavers under my gaze. 'Anna, I don't know why you're so threatened. It's just a little bit of community, that's all. After all, I don't have anybody else. Of my own.'

She gets up hurriedly and leaves the table; the front door slams behind her.

'I'm going after her,' I say.

Outside, I'm in time to see her crossing the courtyard, walking quickly away from me in the direction of her shipping container. From behind I have a clear view of how skinny she's getting. When I call to her, her shoulders jerk as if my voice has struck her a physical blow. For a moment I think she'll just carry on walking away from me, but abruptly, angrily, she turns to face me and I see that there are tears running down her cheeks.

I take a cautious pace towards her. She doesn't back away, so I carry on until I catch up with her.

'Lizzy,' I say, 'what's the matter? Please tell me.'

'You wouldn't understand.' She sounds like the teenager she is.

'Try me,' I say, as gently as I can.

'Yeah. Now you're being *understanding*. Which is all I need. Which is, in fact, what I came to Europe to avoid. People being understanding.'

'OK,' I say. But just to keep the conversation going. I haven't a clue what I'm supposed to say.

'You *can't* understand. Because you've never been shat on. By life.'

I can't believe she's said that. She's succeeded in needling me, in spite of my good intentions. 'You're forgetting,' I say, 'that my daughter is profoundly disabled.'

I'm not prepared for the force of her contempt at this. 'Yeah. You're pretty sorry for yourself. So your daughter has disabilities. Big deal.'

I open my mouth to retort, but she's already speaking again.

'At least she loves you. And so does *he*. You bitch about your mom but at least you've *got* one.'

Her teenage sarcasm is melting; she sounds like a small child. 'My mom had me put into care. Now even *he* thinks I'm becoming a drag. I know he does. I can see it in his eyes.'

I think, in sudden surprise: she's not just fooling around — she's in love with him.

It makes total sense. Nobody's ever been kind to her before.

'He thinks I'm just a kid,' she's saying. 'He loves *you*.'

She's not crying in the usual sense: there are no sobs, just silent tears running down her cheeks. And without thinking I've stepped forward and have done what I now realise is the one thing — besides slapping her — that I've wanted to do to Lizzy for weeks. I've grabbed hold of her and I'm hugging her as tightly as I can.

'Don't tell him. Please, I couldn't bear it,' she says.

'Of course I won't.' I mean it; I can't see any point in humiliating her.

'Oh Christ,' I say. 'What a mess.'

———

Martha arrives in Aigues on the afternoon train. I spot her getting out of her carriage, looking slim and about a decade younger than me. I've been looking forward to her stay for weeks. But I'm nervous too. We used to tell each other everything. I'm aware that this is my chance to try to get back some of the closeness we've lost since Freya was born.

She's looking at me with a reproachful expression. 'Anna,

I'm glad to see you're *alive*. I've been worried stiff about you, to be honest. You've barely been answering my emails, and when you do answer them, you never *tell* me anything.'

'You've got news about city life,' I say, already defensive, 'I've got nothing in return except how many dirty nappies I've changed.'

She purses her lips and hugs me, hard. I still feel the rebuke in the hug.

Later, we put Freya to bed together. 'Here, darling, a present,' says Martha. 'I thought it would be interesting for her because she isn't very mobile. You strap it to the side of the cot.'

It's a box that projects coloured pictures onto the ceiling and plays the *Winnie-the-Pooh* tune. It has a motion sensor that switches it on whenever Freya moves. I find myself inexplicably fighting back tears. The reassuring pictures of Winnie and his friends, the comforting tune all belong in the world of normal children with happy futures ahead of them. Here in Freya's room they seem like a hypocrisy.

'What's the matter?' asks Martha.

We've always been able to explain things to each other. I blurt: 'Oh, Martha, it's just . . . It doesn't feel as if she's a *real* baby. I cuddle her, immerse myself in her – but somewhere deep inside I feel like a fraud. As if I'm not a real mother at all and everybody's just indulging me in a strange wish-fulfilment fantasy. As if the entire world except me can see that she's . . . make-believe. Like some kind of toy.'

'Don't be silly,' she says.

'Of course,' I joke bitterly, 'we'd have preferred the model with real gripping hands.'

'Whatever you say to shock me, I know that if it came down to it, you'd take a bullet to protect your child.'

I can feel my sadness dissolving into furious rage. This flipping of emotions keeps happening to me.

'No I wouldn't!' I almost shout. 'I can't afford to. I can't love Freya unconditionally because I don't dare to. All I can manage is a . . . different sort of love. Day by day. The amount of love you can give to a child that doesn't behave like a child and that might be taken away at any moment.'

For dinner I make *travers de porc aux navets noirs de Pardailhan* from Rose's book. Nobody eats it. I'm feeling sick. Tobias isn't hungry. Lizzy seems to have given up eating. Martha has gone to bed early with a headache.

Alone in my room, I look at myself the mirror. Since having Freya, I usually swell up by the end of the day, and tonight my stomach looks enormous.

There's a light knock, and the door swings open.

'I've been thinking about what you said,' says Martha. 'I can't pretend to understand what this must be like for you. I shouldn't have taken offence.'

It's an olive branch. I don't know why I can't accept it with grace. Instead I smile stiffly at our reflections in the mirror.

'How ironic, to constantly *look* pregnant,' I say.

'Have you done a test?' she asks.

'Oh, don't be silly.'

'Well, are you late?'

'A couple of weeks. I lose track.'

'Have you been using contraception?'

'No.'

'Then do a test.'

Feeling slightly stupid, I find a pregnancy test left over from the months of hoping for Freya and take it into the bathroom. And watch in amazement as a second blue line joins the first.

I rush back into the bedroom and wave it in front of Martha's eyes. She grabs it from me, shrieking. 'Let's rush and tell Tobias. He'll be so pleased.'

'I don't want to tell him just yet,' I say. 'It's complicated.'

She looks at me narrowly. 'Complicated?'

'I had a sort of affair. Less than that. A one-night stand. A weird one. With Julien.'

'A weird one-night stand?'

'It didn't mean anything. At least, I think it meant s*omething* – but about Freya, about being alive. Not about Julien. Or Tobias.'

'God, I can't believe I'm hearing this.'

'It's *got* to be Tobias's. If I'm more than two weeks gone, it has to be his.' I add slowly: 'But it's not impossible that it belongs to Julien.'

'That's what you're worrying about?'

'I definitely can't tell Tobias. Or Julien either.'

'And how are you feeling?' asks Martha.

'Fine,' I say. I'm thinking: it'll be my secret, a seed growing in my womb.

Like dynamite on a long fuse, Martha explodes. 'You had an affair? Without telling me. Without discussing it with me! And you're pregnant? And I have no idea how you feel?'

As she says this, I can feel the sides of the dark box in my brain buckling, thudding against my skull. If it blows open, my head will explode, I swear.

'I can't allow myself those kinds of feelings,' I say. 'Not about Julien, or Freya or anything. Feelings are all connected – like grass roots. They all join up under the soil. If I let go of one, they'll all go . . . flying about. I have to keep them under control.'

'Under control? It's too late for that. You're totally *out* of control. I don't know you any more. Not since Freya was born.'

She peters, for a moment, to a stop, but she's worked herself up again in a second.

'I'm thirty-eight and I'm single. I may never have a baby of my own. I thought – I may have been presumptuous but I *assumed* – that you might make me Freya's godmother . . .'

'We were going to,' I say miserably. 'It's just, with Freya the way she is . . . we thought you might not want –'

'At least you should have let me choose! Anna – during that last bit of your pregnancy we were on the phone to each other every day. Sometimes twice a day. Tobias didn't want to know about baby kit – it was me who came to look at Moses baskets with you. We were making decisions about *breast pads*, for God's sake. And then – the minute she was born – it just stopped. I went through hell when you were in the hospital. Then you ran away to France and took her with you. You didn't even give me a chance to get to know her.'

I know she's right. But I'm barely holding myself together. I can't afford to let go.

'I'm sorry,' I say. 'I just did what I had to do. To survive.'

She shakes her head, rejecting any apology that doesn't come from the heart.

'This isn't you, Anna. You're not mean to your friends. And you're not the kind of woman who doesn't know the father of her child.'

———

This morning, when I go to look at Freya in her cot, I see to my amazement that she's noticed her *Winnie-the-Pooh* box and

263

is fascinated by it. She hasn't quite worked out that she can make it play by bashing it with her fist but when the music stops she says 'wah!' in a loud and, I believe, indignant tone, staring at the empty ceiling as if she's looking for the coloured lights.

I rush downstairs to recount all this to Martha over breakfast, hoping it will help repair things from last night. She has, at least, agreed not to mention my pregnancy to Tobias.

'I didn't sleep a wink,' she says. 'Too much scurrying around in the ceiling. What would that have been, do you think?'

'Squirrels probably,' I say. 'We have red ones round here, you know.'

Tobias comes downstairs.

'Did you sleep OK, Martha? That room Anna's put you in is rat central,' he says. 'And be careful in the corner of the kitchen – there's a rat trap.'

Martha gives me a look, and then abruptly, almost against her will, cracks her old smile.

'This house has a bad energy,' says Lizzy. 'Even when I was on my own, I never spent a night here. Give me a shipping container over this place any day.'

She looks so solemn that Martha catches my eye and, in spite of myself, I start trying not to giggle. I feel bad about poor Lizzy, but it's so good to have somebody to share a joke with again.

⁓

After breakfast we go into the market at Aigues. Summer visitors have descended on the place like flocks of exotic birds, to coo over its medieval buildings and the picturesque poverty of the *paysan*. The race is on to make money out of them before they desert the valley in September.

The village market-stall keepers have jettisoned their winter stock of old saucepans and second-hand clothes in favour of local delicacies: vintage wines, goat's cheeses rolled in ashes, dried sausages flavoured with mountain herbs, cuttlefish from the Mediterranean, fragrant honey from the *garrigue* and black truffles from hidden places in the forests of green oaks. Not to mention gaudy handicrafts made by the hard-working hippies during the long winter months.

Under the plane trees, Yvonne has laid out tables and chairs with red-and-white-checked tablecloths. Ludovic is sitting at one of the tables with his napkin tied around his neck, tucking with gusto into a glutinous meal.

'Do you want to eat today?' Yvonne asks us. 'The *plat de jour* is pig's trotters with bread.'

'No thanks,' says Martha hastily.

An enormous open-air stage is being constructed in the square. I notice Julien standing beside it but he doesn't see me.

'It's Aigues' fete on the last day of the month,' Yvonne says. 'You must come. There will be a laser disco light show with over thirty professional dancers. There'll be an orchestra playing *chansons*. And a singer who's just like Kylie Minogue is coming all the way from Toulouse.'

But Ludovic pauses in his meal and shakes his head at us. 'It's all right for Yvonne to go to the Aigues fete,' he says solemnly, 'because she is of the valley. But you should come to the fete at Rieu. You are of the hills.'

Martha leads us to a stall laden with the sharp green local olives called *Lucqes*. As we stand in the queue, a small boy ahead of us bends his head deep into a bowl of them and sniffs offensively. Then he starts putting his fists in and pulling great handfuls out to eat.

The waiting customers utter a collective mutter of disapproval. To make matters worse, the boy's parents are staring straight ahead, blatantly pretending not to notice what's going on. His elder brother squirms with embarrassment. '*C'est juste pour goûter pas pour manger!*' he says.

The kid puts his fist back into the bowl and I, along with all the rest of the customers, notice at precisely that moment that he has Down's syndrome.

Instantly, everybody in the crowd looks away – except me. I watch him, mesmerised; if the doctors are right, this boy will be a genius compared to Freya. And he's long-sighted, just like her.

The boy carries on putting his fists in all the plates of olives. The stallholder beams, trying to make it all right. '*Mais ce n'est qu'un enfant,*' he says to the boy's brother. '*Ce n'est pas grave . . .*' There's a polite ripple of agreement from the customers, now determined to find him cute.

People are just beginning to behave that way with Freya. Babies are sweet, but when people realise she's got disabilities, Freya becomes the sweetest baby that ever lived. If they can't get away with just ignoring her, that is.

—

There's a hint of corruption in the air. Or maybe it's only the smell creeping up from the hillside where the septic tank should

266

be. The orchard is full of overripe fruit. The wasps and gigantic hornets are eating it up. They devour the plums from the inside, leaving just the skins, empty husks in the shape of fruit. Even I can see there's no point in preserving any more.

My potager has an overblown, past-its-best look. Everything is going subtly wrong. The yellow courgettes are turning brown. The tomatoes have blossom-end rot. The peppers are black inside. The cabbages have mildew. The fennel has bolted. I'm not at all sure we've got out more potatoes than we put into the ground and, curled cosily inside each tuber, is a soft white grub. The carrots are tiny, intensely flavoured and twisted from the effort of forcing their way through the stony soil.

There's a plague of bugs. Some are red with black stripes, some are brown and some look like Green Shield stamps. They're sluggish; everything about them is second-rate. If you touch them, they let out a moderately nasty smell, like cheap 1970s aftershave. They can fly if they want but they don't bother. They don't run and they don't hide. Their safety is in their massive numbers; you can never pick them all off. They don't kill vegetables outright, but suck the juice from them, imbuing them with their mediocrity. Everything they've touched has a jaded, pre-chewed look.

If Freya's problems are due to a recessive gene that the doctors haven't yet spotted, there's a one in four chance of the baby I'm carrying being born with the same defect.

I must push these thoughts away. They too need to go into the dark box in my mind. I wonder how infinitely extensible it is, this box. And whether, deprived of light and air, all these unwanted thoughts will rot.

Yvonne's sausages are covered in a fine, white mould. Tobias, Lizzy and I all troop in to inspect them.

'They're putrefying,' says Lizzy in disgust. 'Ugh. A bunch of suppurating pig guts.'

'Don't be silly,' I say quickly, in case she hurts Yvonne's feelings.

But Yvonne is unperturbed. 'Oh, decay is part of the process,' she says.

I'm being less natural than I was with Yvonne, trying to spare her even imagined pain. Even though her relationship with Julien has ended, I feel as if I've betrayed my friendship with her. Julien was a willing participant, and Tobias is certainly guilty of bad behaviour, but Yvonne is wholly innocent: she's never been anything but good-hearted and true.

'There's a box built under the window on the outside of this room,' says Tobias. 'The drain hole of the sink goes into it. We wondered what it was for.'

Yvonne takes a look. 'It's for foie gras. You put the goose in the box and pull its neck through the hole in the stone sink when you want to feed it. Soon it becomes so fat it can't move. Its liver can grow up to ten times its normal size. And then you kill it. My grandmother used to make it like that, but not many people do it at home any more.'

'That,' says Lizzy, turning pale, 'is a horrible thing to do to any creature.'

'Oh, do you think so?' asked Yvonne. 'As a matter of fact, I'd like to start keeping foie gras geese. Because I am very fond of animals.'

'How do you kill a goose?' asks Tobias.

'It's difficult. If you're strong enough, they say, you can swing it round your head until the neck snaps. Then you strike it a blow on the back of the neck to loosen the feathers for plucking.'

'This place is evil, it's making me feel ill,' says Lizzy.

'Don't be silly,' says Tobias. 'It's just the smell of the linseed in here.'

She looks stricken, as if he's slapped her, and darts a look at me. Since our conversation a few days ago, Lizzy seems to be turning me into some kind of a replacement mother. She seems to want to please me; she's even been making an effort to learn how to look after Freya. I've decided it's a good idea to encourage her and have been spending time with her, patiently overseeing her bottle-feeding technique and showing her again and again how to change a nappy. But I've not so far trusted her again to mind Freya on her own.

—

It's one in the morning. Freya can't breathe. Her chest sucks up and down and she makes alarming rasping noises in her battle for air.

I shake Tobias awake.

'Mmph?'

'She's choking – it's not a fit. She just can't breathe. I don't know what to do. I'm calling the ambulance.'

For once, Tobias doesn't tell me I'm just fussing. 'God, Anna, she sounds awful. Shit – it sounds like she might die. Hurry up.'

I dial the emergency number and the operator puts me on to a doctor who listens to her breathing over the phone.

'Take her to the duty doctor in Aigues,' he says. 'I'll warn him you're coming.'

We bundle her into the car and race down the hill. I drive and Tobias tries to keep her airway clear.

Just outside the duty doctor's house, Freya gives an enormous sneeze. Her breathing and colour return entirely to normal.

The doctor takes it in his stride. He says she's got nothing on her lungs but she does have an ear infection. He gives us a bottle of antibiotics two years out of date, a prescription for a huge list of medicines to pick up when the pharmacy opens, and charges us seventy euros.

—

Tobias and I oversleep. When I wake up, Freya is peaceful and the night's adventure has receded like a bad dream.

'I should run and pick up her medicines,' I say sleepily. 'The pharmacy's only open in the morning today.'

'It's OK,' says Tobias. 'We'll take Martha out somewhere this morning. We can collect the medicines on the way.'

I leave him snoozing and go down to the kitchen where Martha is already at the breakfast table.

'Toast?' I ask. But then I discover that the rats have broken into the bread bin and have eaten a rat-shaped hole out of our nice brown loaf.

'Never mind,' I say, and Martha gives me another one of her odd looks. 'Why don't I do us pancakes? We can pop into Aigues and get some more bread later this morning. I have to go to the pharmacy anyway.'

Tobias joins us, and Martha and I giggle and chat and scoff pancakes like kids.

Lizzy shows up late for breakfast, her hair tousled.

'Hey, you,' says Tobias. 'Just out of bed? Did the spooks mess up your hair for you?'

But, if he hopes for some banter, he's disappointed. She won't engage with him.

'Who ate my shoe?' asks Martha. And sure enough, there's a neat hole, the size of a tennis ball, in the rubber sole of her flip-flop, which she left by the kitchen door overnight. 'Anna, about these rats –' she begins.

'Where shall we go today?' asks Tobias. 'Anna – you choose. Anywhere you like.'

'Let's go to the *étang*,' I say. 'There are flamingos.'

'What about taking a picnic for later?' asks Tobias.

I glance at the clock: almost midday. 'There's no time,' I say. 'I have to get to the pharmacy before it closes.'

'Anna, I'm on holiday,' says Martha. 'And your rats have eaten my shoe, so you're going to have to wait while I change, if nothing else.'

'Go on, Anna – knock us up one of your picnic specials,' wheedles Tobias.

I feel a surge of desperation. I find myself shouting far too loudly: 'No! We need to leave *now*!'

Martha stares at me.

'We had to take Freya to the doctor as an emergency last night,' I explain. 'She couldn't breathe. The pharmacy closes at noon. I need to pick up her medicines right now!'

There's a moment's stunned silence. Martha looks horrified and quite angry. 'Anna – what's wrong with you? Why didn't you tell me? You cooked breakfast! You joked with me! You suggested a *jaunt*! We can't go anywhere with a sick baby. You should have just rushed to the chemist as soon as it opened.'

She's talking complete sense. And, just like that, Freya has built another barrier around me. Martha will never understand that Tobias and I normalise things because we have to. We don't go around telling people Freya is ill – because Freya is *always* ill. We're always teetering on the brink of emergency.

Every moment of time is divided from every other, as if somebody has wrapped each individual segment in cling film. It feels like being a very young child. Like when I was being teased at kindergarten and could never tell an adult because the moments when I was strong enough to explain were cut off irrevocably from the moments when I was being bullied. This, I suppose, is what New Age types like Lizzy call 'living in the now'. But I'm actually doing it, and I can't recommend it at all.

———

The thermometer is still rising. It feels as if the whole of the natural world is holding its breath. The air is getting heavier as if each individual molecule is becoming saturated with water, and sooner or later will have to burst.

Now we understand the value of the *béal*; it allows us to provide a constant stream of water from the river to the potager. It's turned the horse-manure-enriched soil a rich dark brown. Melons and squash are growing luxuriantly out of the putrefaction.

Ludovic is giving me a lesson in making compost. 'It's just like cookery,' he says, 'you need the right balance of ingredients, mixed the right way, heated to the right temperature for the correct amount of time. Come closer and look. Never mind the smell.'

I smile at the image of the filth-encrusted Ludovic having a place in my kitchen, but he's deadly serious.

'Decomposition is a natural phenomenon. You're just helping it along a bit.'

Like everything else in his potager, Ludovic's compost is strictly under control, in three smart plastic bins. 'You can get them for free, from the *mairie*,' he says. 'Plastic is much better than wood. It doesn't rot. Otherwise I make it exactly the way my father taught me.'

He picks up his three-pronged pitchfork and starts forking material from one of his plastic bins into another.

'Fetch me some of those dead potato plants, will you? Put them in here. You need a balance of brown ingredients – dead plants, twigs, shredded dried leaves, straw – and green ones – grass cuttings, young weeds, rotting fruit and vegetable peelings from the kitchen. Too much green, it goes slimy. Too much brown, it doesn't do anything.'

He stirs the rank mixture enthusiastically with his fork. 'If you get the mix wrong, it gets off balance, goes sour.'

'It's disgusting. It really stinks.'

'It's not disgusting – it's just in the process of transition. There's decay and decay. If you get the composition just right, it's the beginning of something new. Here, crush up those eggshells and put them in. They'll encourage the worms to breed. It's the worms and the friendly bacteria that will break it down for you.'

Ludovic turns over the compost again and again.

'You need air to get through it. Turn it with a pitchfork regularly – at least twice a month. I do it every week. The more you turn it, the more quickly it will change.'

When he's turned it to his satisfaction, he covers it with a straw cap, looking up at the blazing sky. 'And of course, you have to give it just the right amount of water. You mustn't let it get too dry – but if you leave it uncovered during a thunderstorm, it can get waterlogged. You must irrigate it gently.'

As I'm leaving with an armful of lettuce I turn round and catch Ludovic, flies undone, irrigating his compost in the traditional manner. If he's discomforted, he hides it with an insouciant shrug.

'Some people have newfangled ideas about composting. But the old-fashioned way is good enough for me. You need to break things down to create something new. I told you – just like in the kitchen.'

⌒

The food around here is getting stranger and stranger. I thought it might encourage Lizzy to eat if I asked her to do some cooking but it's been a disaster.

'Oh no,' I groan quietly to Tobias, 'not caterpillar stew again.'

'*Cauliflower* stew,' he says. 'Remember she's a vegetarian.'

'Perhaps that's why she doesn't touch it herself,' I whisper, looking down into its three-day-old depths and thinking of all the caterpillars not removed by the demoralised labour force.

Lizzy is still full of the pent-up energy I've been noticing in her more and more. She won't laugh or flirt with Tobias any more and she speaks constantly of an evil presence in the house, particularly the game kitchen. She's moved her collection of magic crystals in there along with a huge number of figurines of Catholic saints. Yvonne is *croyante*, so on balance she's happy to share her *laboratoire* with the saints, but I can't for the life of me see how they fit in with Lizzy's extraordinary spectrum of other beliefs.

⌒

The weather continues oppressive and sultry. There's a giant tempest brewing, but for the moment we're cut off from it. Everything is still parched and dry.

Freya has come out in a heat rash. Martha and I are bathing her suffering little form with cotton wool soaked in rose water when Tobias comes to find us.

'Let's go up to the infinity pool. Please,' he urges. 'I have to swim.'

'It's going to rain soon – it has to,' I say.

'And you know what it's like around here when it rains. It could pour down for weeks. This might be our very last chance to swim. We haven't even shown Martha the pool yet.'

'I can't,' I say. 'It's too hot to take Freya with us, and Yvonne's not around today. Now that my mother and Kerim have gone, childcare's not quite as easy to sort out as it was.'

'Ask Lizzy then,' says Tobias.

'I don't think it's advisable to ask her to babysit alone.'

'Don't be silly,' he says. 'Lizzy may be just a little bit cracked but she's devoted to Freya.'

'She's got so much better at looking after her now,' says Martha. 'I think it might be good for her self-esteem if you trusted her alone for a couple of hours.'

When I seek her out, lurking in her broiling shipping container, I'm shocked at how wan she looks. She's a million miles from the confident, energetic girl of a few weeks ago. At the mention of babysitting, her eyes light up. She seems so pleased about it, so enthusiastic.

I think: Tobias and Martha are right, Lizzy means no harm – giving her responsibility, showing that we trust her, may be just what she needs. And I try to pretend that there's no small voice somewhere deep inside me telling me that I can afford to take chances with Freya because now there's another child growing in my womb.

Martha, Tobias and I walk up to the infinity pool. The path takes us close to Julien's tree house and Tobias insists on running ahead to see if he'd like to join us. He comes back shaking his head and I wonder again if Julien is avoiding me.

'I've invited him to join us for the meal at the Rieu fete on Saturday,' says Tobias. 'Our treat.'

The clear mountain water at the pool is a delicious relief. I plunge into it as if into a baptism, thinking: I am pregnant, everything is different now. And sure enough I can feel my worries and preoccupations washing away and my reborn self filling with optimism. We splash under the natural waterfall that gushes straight out from the rock, gasping at its icy chill. Afterwards swimming in the mere ordinary coldness of the pool feels like luxuriating in tepid bathwater.

Some village children who are swimming in the pool give a great shout and rush to look over its stone lip. We join them and see that four adolescent wild boars are drinking in the river just below us. With the stubbornness of youth they ignore us. Then they run across the shallow water, their tails straight behind them, their long snouts wobbling: wild, prehistoric and free.

Tobias and I catch each other's eyes and smile. On impulse I squeeze his hand and whisper in his ear: 'I'm pregnant.'

His blue eyes open in surprise. Then he reaches out to hug me and we share a secret laugh from the sheer happiness of the thing. I have a moment of epiphany. This baby is a gift. I'm going to enjoy my pregnancy, and trust.

The joyous feeling lasts on the walk back. Tobias says: 'Let's cut down round to Rieu and walk back up to Les Rajons that way. Martha will get a good view of the house through the vines below.'

Ludovic's vines are luxuriant with leaves and thick with darkening fruit, full of bacchanalian promise.

'No wonder they're better than ours. He's irrigating them,' I say. 'Look, the rows are running with water.' At this time of year, we're used to the dusty dry stone of the furrows but these are glistening wet.

'How would he get water up here? It's above his house. And it's not the whole vineyard, just a couple of rows in the middle,' says Tobias, adding: 'It looks more like a flood.' We stare at each other for a moment in growing alarm.

'Our cistern,' says Tobias.

'Freya,' I say, my voice tight with fear.

We start to run up the hill, through the vines, following the line of water.

Les Rajons comes into view but we have no time to enjoy the sight. We can hear a sort of keening coming from the courtyard.

The lid of the cistern is open, leaving an ugly dark hole like a newly dug grave in the courtyard. Freya's pram is next to it, shrouded in muslin. Silent as death.

My throat is so tight it's strangling me, like one of those dreams where you try to speak and the words won't come. 'Freya! Freya!' I manage. 'Oh God, Freya, what have I done?' My legs won't work properly. I stagger to the pram and tear off the muslin.

Freya is lying underneath, peacefully asleep. I rip her out and squeeze her to me. She wakes and flails her arms and legs in rage at being disturbed.

Tobias is looking morosely at the cistern. 'It's empty,' he says. 'The drain hole has been opened.'

'Tobias,' Martha says quietly, 'there's somebody up on the balcony. Standing on the handrail.'

It's Lizzy, her long black hair spread wildly. She's swaying on the handrail, as if daring herself to jump.

Tobias swears and runs for the house.

'He'll be too late!' sobs Martha.

I run under the balcony and look up at her, absurdly pale and small, teetering on the edge of the rail.

'Lizzy!' I shout. 'Stay where you are! Don't move! Tobias is coming to get you!'

Her face is wet with tears. She's mouthing 'Tobias' and, as she raises both arms above her head, she seems to sway further towards me.

Then Tobias appears behind her, catches her in two strong arms and pulls her back towards him.

When we reach them, he's cradling her in his arms, making the noises you use to hush a child. Lizzy is weeping. It's the first appropriate emotion I've seen from her for days.

'I failed,' she keeps saying. 'I should have had the courage to jump.'

———

It occurs to me that Tobias and I both have our means of escape. These are our routes:

Me: Mouseproofing. Cooking. Gardening. Putting things in jars.

Tobias: Going into his recording studio. Composing his
music. Until recently, flirting with Lizzy.

Both of us together: Black humour. Pretending to
ourselves that there is nothing wrong with our child.
Letting the madness in.

I wonder whether Freya's fits, too, are a form of escape. I've
often noticed them getting worse when she's stressed or
overloaded – perhaps they act like a safety valve, allowing her
brain to shut out when it can't take any more.

The fire ambulance has come calling for a second time this
summer. For Lizzy this time. At first I was worried they
wouldn't take our call seriously. But, having spoken to her on
the phone to assess her, French emergency services snapped
into action once again.

Along with the paramedics came a duty social worker, a
motherly woman with whom Lizzy seemed instantly to bond.
She told us Lizzy had been assessed as a high suicide risk and
that she'd now receive appropriate residential care at a
specialised unit attached to Montpellier General Hospital.

My last glimpse was of her wrapped in a foil blanket, clinging
on to the social worker as, between sobs, she tried to explain
why she emptied the cistern. It was pretty incoherent stuff –
something about making a sacrifice – but it all seemed to add
up to a simple cry for help. She'd never had any intention of
harming Freya.

'She must have *somebody*. Friends, if not family,' Martha
says, ever-practical. 'Anna, we really must check through her
things.'

'It seems like an invasion of privacy,' I say. We've lived
with her for months but we know nothing about Lizzy. I'm

amazed, with hindsight, that we never realised it, never saw past the smoke and mirrors of her flaky, deceptively transparent persona.

So Martha and I pick our way guiltily round her shipping container, rooting through incense sticks, magic crystals, prayer beads and packets of Himalayan mountain salt. But there's not so much as a family photograph, let alone an address.

Tobias does only slightly better with a trawl through her mail – coming up with a letter from a fostering agency in the US asking her to get in touch. After much discussion, we've sent a brief reply, stating which hospital she's in.

'I should have gone with her in the ambulance,' I say. 'It sort of proves her point about having nobody who cares about her.'

'Don't even think about it,' says Martha. 'You can't take responsibility for every waif and stray,'

'At least I ought to go and visit her. But I can't bear the thought of another series of commutes between here and Montpellier.'

'If I'm brutally honest, you're having enough trouble coping with life as it is,' says Martha. 'Besides, Freya needs you here.'

It's unbelievably difficult surviving in the middle of August in this place with no running water. Martha is a trouper; she takes the dirty dishes down to the river to wash them up and pretends she doesn't mind not being able to wash her hair properly. I'm afraid of carrying heavy weights while pregnant so Tobias bears the brunt of filling twenty-litre canisters with drinking water from the communal tap at Rieu. We all bathe in the river every day and I give Freya frequent sponge baths with our precious drinking water, for fear that the river will give her a cold or a tummy upset. We're desperate for the rain to come and liberate us.

———

It's the day of the fete at Rieu. The hottest and heaviest day of the year so far, stifling and almost unbearable. The sky isn't blue any more; it's a parched, angry white. The storm is on its way but it feels as if it will never break.

Down in the potager, I can't resist a quick peek at the compost. Gingerly, with one prong of the fork, I lift its straw cap and thousands and thousands of maggots come teeming out. New life has already been born out of Ludovic's decaying matter, but I don't like the look of it.

We gather at the front door of the house just as the swallows are coming out to swoop for insects in the early-evening air. Swallows love the midges so I suppose we have our bug life to thank for this aeronautics display.

We walk down to where you can see Rieu clinging to the side of the hill, stopping for a moment to admire the red-gold glint of its stone houses catching the dying sun. The lengthening shadows in the valley below look like black fingers stretching up towards them.

By the time we arrive, the shadows have already engulfed Rieu. Now the village is bright with coloured lights. In the square, an accordion player in a beret and with a red kerchief tied round his neck is playing traditional *chansons*. A few couples are dancing together under the trees. Two men are using a shovel to stir a huge iron container of *moules* roasting over an open fire. A whole pig is turning on a spit while a gaggle of men sip pastis and stand about watching and offering advice.

We stand for a moment, shyly, beside the barbecue.

'That's odd. No sign of Julien,' says Tobias. 'Nor Ludovic either.'

I feel a stab of disappointment. Not about Julien, I tell myself.

We don't see anybody else we know. The men ignore us and we feel like tourists.

'Do you think it's by invitation only?' I ask Tobias. 'Was Ludovic inviting us specially? I'm not sure we should be here – it seems very intimate.'

'Look,' he says. 'They're selling tickets.'

I go over and brashly ask for three adults. 'But who are you?' they ask us. 'Where are you from?'

'Les Rajons,' I say and they all gather round to kiss us and make us welcome – so it is a special invitation after all.

Then Ludovic appears, properly washed for once and wearing clean clothes. He's beaming to see us here. 'Ah, so you chose to come and be with the people of the hills,' he says. 'You resisted the dancing girls in the valley.'

'I haven't seen Julien,' says Tobias.

Ludovic smiles. 'Julien had his celebration in May. Not many of the *soixante-huitards* or their children come to this fete – it's organised by the *paysans*, the families who've been here for generations.'

We take our places at long trestle tables, where we've been seated next to a handful of other foreigners. Course after course is brought to us so rapidly and in such enormous portions it seems to me that perhaps we're getting special attention. First they fill and refill our plates with roasted *moules* until we feel we'll die if we ever see another mussel again, then they bring hunks of bread smeared thickly with pâté, then great wedges of roast pork with white beans swimming in lard.

I've been put next to the accordion player, a friendly middle-aged man with a twinkle in his eye who turns out to be German.

'When did you move here?' I ask him.

'Oh,' he says, 'way back in the seventies. It was only supposed to be for a month but I fell in love with a girl and wrote to my employer, handing in my notice.'

'What happened to the girl?'

'She's married to a banker in the north,' he says. We all laugh and he makes a mock-wry face and toasts us with rough red wine. On my other side, a young woman who's recently moved here from the Netherlands starts complaining about her life. She has a little girl of seven – she feels tied down by her. She wants to go to Goa for the winter months, but the girl is in school. I look from her fretful expression to the cheerful one of the jilted German and I'm amazed that human beings are sometimes so resilient, sometimes so easily overturned.

My thoughts dart back to poor Lizzy, to her saying that I've never been shat on by life. What she meant, I'm now sure, was that I've always been loved – by my mother if by nobody else. Love is the earth holding our roots in place. Without it, there's nothing to keep us from falling over.

The storm breaks and lightning forks across the sky. But the old *paysans* sit in the drenching rain and finish their meals rather than dash for cover and waste their fifteen euros.

'Wow,' I say, peering at the far hills, as the water runs down into our plates. 'Aigues have paid a lot for their fireworks.'

'How can they afford all that?' asks Tobias.

'My God,' I say, 'it's not fireworks – it's lightning.'

The storm rebounds across the hills. Lightning forks down to earth and what appear to be balls of fire shoot across the sky. A signal that we're heading into autumn and from there we'll move into winter, and all the things that are growing so profligately now will die back. But out of winter comes spring, and when things are broken down new things grow.

We all drink thick black coffee and *digestifs* in the warm summer rain. Freya, whom I've swaddled up in a raincoat, is passed from hand to knotted hand, cooed over and made a fuss of.

Everyone is interested to know about the time we called the ambulance for her. They all recount where they were when the *sapeurs-pompiers* came to our hills, as people are supposed to be able to do about the shooting of JFK. And I realise that our lives are starting to intertwine with theirs – little shoots of lives tangling together like vines.

September

THE STORM'S BROUGHT COOLER weather. A cleansing coolness, inviting us to take stock, to get on with our lives, to roll back from the sheer craziness of the last weeks.

First thing this morning, I set to work harvesting the pumpkins that have grown in the potager. The rain has pumped them up overnight to a size and weight so enormous I've had to use a wheelbarrow to transport them.

I'm suddenly overcome by a wave of nausea. I dash into the bathroom and throw up. I have a weird metallic taste in my mouth; my breasts are sore; I feel utterly wiped. But this is very minor stuff compared to my last pregnancy, when it seemed as though somebody had turned the volume up on all physical sensations. I hang on to the edge of the sink and worry: am I feeling sick enough?

The interior of a pumpkin is a succulent deep orange; slicing through it is like cutting through some creature's flesh. When you sink your knife into its guts, the juices gush out and stain the blade. A wonderful smell, something between cucumber and melon, assails you. They'll keep us going all winter if I can only find a way to preserve them.

Sterilising low-acid vegetables, such as pumpkins, is trickier than the highly acidic fruits I've tried so far. They carry a special hazard: they may harbour botulism, a lethal microbe able to multiply in the airless environment of my glass jars. To be really safe, you need a pressure canner, a piece of equipment unavailable in France.

I've spent the morning in the kitchen, reading, and considering. Two strains of botulism are destroyed only at enormous temperatures: above 121 degrees centigrade. However, these strains produce a bad smell. Two strains can kill you without smell or taste, but simple boiling destroys them. Therefore, if I boil my preserving jars normally and discard anything with a bad smell on opening, there should – in theory – be little danger.

But the moment you're pregnant, everything changes. You can't afford to take risks. I hate the thought that germs may be multiplying invisibly inside my jars. I'd feel safer if I could only know for certain that every single one has been eradicated.

I tell myself I ought to trust nature. If the embryo is good, nature will protect it. If it's no good, there's nothing I can do about it. In pregnancy, as in preserving, there are no guarantees.

This afternoon, I find a drop of blood. The pregnancy test is still positive. I had a little drop with Freya too but I'm taking no chances. I phone the doctor in Aigues, who is sympathetic.

'False positives are very rare. Do you feel pregnant? Go to bed now and I'll arrange a scan for tomorrow afternoon.'

———

I wake up thinking about the scan. Tobias brings me coffee in bed. 'I'd prefer green tea, there's less caffeine,' I say.

'Don't be ridiculous.'

Then we have a proper shouting row – me crying: 'Why can't I have the drink I want?' and Tobias yelling: 'We've got another bloody nine months of this madness?'

Eventually I take a deep breath and say: 'They never excluded the possibility that it's a faulty gene both of us are carrying – if it is then the baby will have a one in four chance of being born the same as Freya. Tobias, can't you see I'm petrified?'

His anger clears. 'It's not a faulty gene. They couldn't find one. And even if it is, there's a seventy-five per cent chance of the baby being fine. Look, Anna, when something awful happens it's normal to go around trying to find out what went wrong and why. But sometimes you have to accept that it happened for no reason, or that you'll never know the cause. Dealing with uncertainty is the hardest thing.'

I spend the whole morning finishing my formal application for permission to start a residential cookery school at Les Rajons, an impressively thick dossier that has been sitting half completed on the living-room table for weeks. Finally getting it done is my little bung to karma to make the scan all right.

We've agreed to take Freya to the scan rather than leave her with Martha and to treat ourselves to lunch in Aigues on the way.

'I'll drop my application off at the *mairie* before it closes for lunch,' I'm in the middle of saying, when Ludovic accosts us in the square. He's carrying a bunch of carnations. There's a new spring in his step, he seems cleaner and his hunter's hat looks suspiciously as if it's been brushed.

'I'm on my way to Yvonne's cafe,' he says. 'I'm hoping that she will be *gentille*.'

'Ludovic . . . you surely don't mean . . . ?'

'I've written her a letter. I may be old, but I am a soldier. I know how to carry out a campaign.'

'Come on,' says Tobias to me, 'you can hand your dossier in later. Right now the most important thing in our lives is, clearly, to find out what he's written in that letter.'

We follow Ludovic into Yvonne's. He presents his carnations with a bow and then settles himself at Julien's old table, the one closest to the bar.

'The special today is *museau de porc*. The nose of the pig,' says Yvonne, looking harassed.

Just then, Julien walks in. He looks at me and hesitates, as if he's going to walk straight out again. But when he spots Ludovic he clearly changes his mind. He sits down as far from us as possible. Yvonne ignores him.

'Yvonne,' says Julien, 'could you please come over here and serve me?'

'I've received a letter from an admirer,' she says brazenly to us. 'I'll read it to you: "You are a good cook. You are very beautiful. We are both alone. I wish to offer you marriage, my vines and a home."' Ludovic smirks and raises his hat. 'Well,' says Yvonne, 'it may not be in perfect style, but he does get to the point. Unlike some.'

Over our meal, Tobias and I start squabbling again. The scan is at Montpellier General Hospital and I want to visit Lizzy while we're there.

I feel guilty about not telling Tobias about Lizzy's crush earlier, about doing nothing tangible to help her. I believe it's our clear duty to support her. But, to my huge surprise and anger, Tobias is against visiting. I can't pin down his reasons. He's strangely sheepish about her, as if she's pulled something over on him.

290

By the time coffee arrives, we've bickered ourselves to a standstill. I stare fretfully out of the window and see the mayor striding across the square. The town hall has closed for lunch but if I run I'll be able to give him my dossier in person. I catch up with him by the war memorial.

'Ah, the English who are breathing life back into Les Rajons,' he says to me. 'Have you enough water now?'

I nod and smile self-consciously, wondering exactly what gossip has reached him about the goings-on at Les Rajons.

'I hear you're starting a cookery school. Rose would have liked that. She was such an excellent cook.'

I start. 'You knew . . . Rose?'

'Of course. Everybody of my age knew her. She was my teacher when I was in the *maternelle*.'

We both glance instinctively at the memorial. Rose's name is here as well. It has a line to itself, just below the list of *maquisards* who died in the German attack. 'Rose Donnadieu, heroine of the Resistance. 1944.'

'You mustn't believe all the legends about the Maquis,' says the mayor. 'Of course, through the filter of time, things become idealised. But, since you are a foreigner, I can tell you plainly that at the end it all got very messy. All sorts of riff-raff joined at the last minute: they wanted to prove they'd been on the right side during the war. There were informers, denunciations. There were incidents . . .'

'Incidents?'

'There was a guy from Aigues, a bit of a *bavard*. He let slip to the Germans that there was a Maquis in the area. I don't think he did any harm, but somebody overheard him. The Maquis got hold of him, took him to the forest and hammered slivers of bamboo under his fingernails.'

'Oh God – did Rose have anything to do with that?'

I don't realise that I'm holding my breath until he says: 'Oh no, not at all. She was an extraordinary woman,' and I hear myself exhale in a rush. 'Better than her son,' he adds.

'But Ludovic was a hero of the Resistance too, wasn't he? At least, he's got medals.'

'They're from when he went north to fight, in late 1944. After –' The mayor breaks off and his expression becomes inscrutable. 'But I don't like to speak of unsavoury things. Down here there are rumours. Next time you see him, ask how his mother died.'

And probe as I might, I can't get another word out of him.

'I've brought you the dossier for the school,' I say. 'But I have to admit I'm a bit worried that they won't grant permission. Because we don't have mains water.'

'Around here,' he says, 'we try to keep our local affairs local. If the planning department doesn't ask about the water, we're not obliged to bring it to their attention. I'll add a personal note saying that I think a cookery school will promote tourism. It will be good for the area.'

———

On the road to Montpellier Tobias and I renew the argument about Lizzy. It lasts us, in a half-hearted, circular fashion, until the motorway tollgate, where a thin, slightly hunched young woman approaches us. I assume she's begging but instead she asks: 'Can you take me to Montpellier?'

'Of course,' says Tobias without hesitation. 'We'd love to give you a lift. What takes you there?'

'My grandmother. She's in a home. I want to visit her.'

She seems consumed with nervousness. There's the same slight weirdness to her that you find in people trying to score money for drugs: they really are anxious, just not for the reason they're telling you. But she hasn't asked us for any money.

I offer her the front seat while I hunch in the back next to Freya, gripping a wine bottle for a weapon. Tobias, on the other hand, is calm and relaxed and soon gets her telling us her life story.

'I work in an office for the handicapped,' she says. 'To tell the truth, I'm handicapped too. I have difficulties. It's just, my brain, it doesn't work like other people's.'

Perhaps France is a good place for people with disabilities, I reflect. This girl has a job and a life. In England she could easily be living on the streets.

Tobias is smiling his encouraging smile and I can sense his charm snapping into action. She's unfolding before our eyes, opening up to us.

'Did I tell you that I'm a widow?' she says. 'My husband was handicapped too. I met him through my work. He died eight weeks ago.' Without transition, she begins to cry. Tobias reaches out and pats her hand.

We let her out at an old people's home in the centre of Montpellier. Tobias and I watch her crooked figure stumble up to the door.

'Poor little thing,' I say.

'Look,' he says wearily, 'if you want to visit Lizzy after the scan, go ahead. You're right. We have a responsibility towards her. But I'm not sure it's a great idea I go along with you. As a matter of fact, I've been thinking and worrying about my . . . behaviour.'

'It was pretty bad,' I break in. 'OK, so she flirted with you

293

– big deal. She's just a kid. But you should never have flirted back. What on earth possessed you?'

'It's hard to explain,' he says. 'You know when you're cooking – do you ever get the feeling that you're doing the thing you're best at in the whole world? You're totally on the top of your game and it all seems to flow?'

I nod, reluctantly.

'I used to get it from composing music. But recently, the music has been stuck. The only other skill I have is making people like me; I did it just now with that woman. I got a kick out of helping her come out of her shell.'

I've lived for years with the consequences of Tobias's effortless charm. In a sense, I'm a victim of it. But he seems genuinely shaken by his experience with Lizzy.

'I thought Lizzy and I were just having a laugh, but now looking back it's clear she was in a terrible state. I thought I was helping her, but now I feel as if I used that poor girl. I wasn't a good friend to her.' There's a second's pause. 'I'm afraid of seeing her again. I'm afraid the sight of me might make her suicidal again, or something terrible like that.'

'Don't be silly,' I tell him. But he shakes his head.

'You go and see her alone. I'll mind Freya and wait for you in the cafeteria.'

⌒

The doctor who's going to do my scan is interested in Freya. He looks grave when we say that the ultrasound in England didn't pick up her disabilities while I was pregnant. 'I have always spotted an absence of a corpus callosum. Perhaps I've just been lucky,' he says. He shows us the picture on the front cover of his textbook. 'That's an absence of a corpus callosum.'

'How can we be sure it's not a recessive gene? That the same thing won't happen to my new baby?'

'I'm afraid we'll not be able to tell for sure until late in your pregnancy. I'll refer you to a geneticist and you'll be very carefully scanned. You'll probably be offered a foetal MRI around the twenty-sixth week or so. However, given the fact that they didn't manage to locate a gene in the UK, on balance it's unlikely to be a recurring problem. My best advice to you is to relax and enjoy your pregnancy.'

Then it's time for the scan. Straight away he says: 'There!' And there, indeed, is a little blob. Just one, but in the right place. We see a sort of pulsing – slight and flickering – and he makes a pleased noise and says: 'The heartbeat.'

'What . . . would be the latest date of conception? Just in case I've got it wrong,' I ask as casually as I can. 'It's possible it was just under five weeks ago, not seven . . .'

'Oh, sweetheart,' says Tobias. 'You're getting all mixed up.'

I feel myself flushing; perhaps I'm imagining the doctor looking narrowly at me.

'At this stage it's possible to date very precisely,' he says. 'Judging from this heartbeat it's at least seven weeks from conception. It can't be less than that.'

The baby belongs to Tobias. I feel an unreasoning flush of joy. My life is coming back on track after all.

———

Lizzy's in a special unit for young people with psychiatric problems in the grounds of Montpellier General Hospital. The corridors are lined with giant pictures of Arctic scenes. I walk past polar bears and icebergs. The patients all have their own rooms, each with a name badge on the door in the shape of a different animal. Lizzy's has a penguin. I knock and, after a moment's hesitation, a muffled voice says: '*Entrez*.'

She looks worse than I've ever seen her, worse than I could ever have imagined: skin stretched over bones; the angles of her skull showing under her cheeks; dark shadows engulfing her eyes. Her shivering has become a tremor that permeates her frame, her voice, the way she moves.

At first she doesn't seem to recognise me. When she does, silent tears start to roll down her gaunt cheeks and I'm filled with pity for this girl who should be blooming and who, I'm now convinced, we've all treated more harshly than she deserved.

'Anna,' she says brokenly. 'You came.' The stick arms stretch out towards me and I move forward and hug her, gently, because I'm afraid I'll snap something inside her. My stomach lurches with misery, pain and remorse. She's a child. She has absolutely nobody of her own. We may not have chosen it, but Tobias and I are *in loco parentis*. There's no suffering of our own, no personal problem that could ever excuse us for not having had the decency to be here for her.

'I'm sorry,' I say. 'Lizzy, I'm so sorry. I should have come before.'

The muffled voice echoes me. 'I'm sorry, I'm so sorry . . .' and the tears pick up silently where the voice trails off. When she speaks again, her voice is so quiet I can barely hear her. 'I didn't try to kill myself, you know.'

I have no idea whether or not this is true. 'Hush,' I say. 'I know.'

296

'I just . . . needed something to *happen*. Something to change in my life.'

'Of course you did, darling.' I find myself slipping back into my own mother's vernacular. I have a template for this, from my own childhood: holding on to her, smoothing her hair, making hushing noises and ineffectual comments, giving her time for the tears to flow, letting her ramble on.

'The fostering agency wrote,' she's saying. 'My birth mother wants to be back in touch but . . . I'm just too fragile right now. It wouldn't be a good idea.'

'Your mother?'

The flatness in her voice has resolved into heaving sobs. 'Why couldn't she have let me stay with her? What was so wrong with me?'

If I put Freya into an institution, she'd never be able to articulate this. She'd not even be able to think it – certainly not in words. But would she be able to *feel* it, this sense of having been abandoned? Would it damage her the way it's damaged poor Lizzy?

'I'm sure there were reasons,' I say inadequately. 'I'm sure she had very powerful reasons that might have been . . . wrong, but that at the time seemed overwhelming to her. Lizzy, please get in touch with your mother. At least try to find out what really happened.'

'But what if it was because of *me*?' There's no trace of the otter left in her eyes, nothing joyful or blithe. Just a look of complete, unfeigned terror.

'Of course it's nothing to do with *you*. Lizzy, loads of people love you. We . . . Tobias and I . . . we're both awfully fond of you.'

'Really? Both of you?'

'Of course we are,' I say. 'And you'd better hurry up and get better so that you can come back to us. Freya misses you, you know.'

'She does?'

'Of *course* she does. And so does Tobias.' I take a deep breath. 'Lizzy, your mother has spent every single day since you last saw her missing you and thinking about you and worrying about whether you're all right.'

'Do you really think so?'

'I *know* so. Get in touch with her, and you'll know it too.'

'How can I risk it?'

'Lizzy, maybe this is an opportunity. You know, like fate or something. To get back in touch with your mother.'

She seems to waver for a moment. Her reed-like body physically sways. Then she tenses and I can tell I've lost her again. 'I don't have a mother,' she says.

—

When we get back, Martha is waiting for me. Her eyes roll significantly towards the door. With elaborate casualness we stroll out into the courtyard to talk.

'It belongs to Tobias,' I say.

Martha hugs me.

'It's more than you deserve, you dirty stop-out,' she half laughs, half scolds.

And now that I have every reason to be glad, I discover that I'm crying after all. Because, however wonderful my new baby turns out to be, there will always be loss. Of Julien, who will never again treat me as a friend. Of his baby, who will never exist. Of Freya, who will never be the person she was supposed to be.

'Oh God, Martha, I've been such a fool,' I sob. 'I've hurt people I love. It feels so bad.'

And she holds on to me and pats my hair and keeps saying 'there, there' until I understand that, in all this loss and confusion, I've somehow managed to hang on to my best friend.

'I think I'm quite enjoying the new Anna,' says Martha when my hiccuping subsides. 'She's a bit flakier than the old one, but she's a hell of a lot more entertaining.'

'Would you like to be godmother?' I ask. 'Of the new baby?'

'I'll be Freya's godmother, thank you,' she says. 'I was more involved with her. At the beginning.'

⁓

I can't believe this is the final day of Martha's visit. She, Tobias and I have been squandering the last precious hours of it discussing what to do about Lizzy. Tobias is utterly adamant it's not in her best interests to come back here. I'm equally adamant that we have no choice but to take her. Martha is backing me because she's my friend. But I can see she really thinks my own mental condition too fragile to take on another needy person.

We agree to shelve the subject. I've laid a trestle table under a tree in the courtyard for Martha's goodbye lunch. We feast on fresh bread, Lacaune mountain cheese and salad made with the last of the season's succulent tomatoes – as good as a steak – washed down by a glass of St Chinian. Freya sleeps in my arms throughout the meal. She looks so sweet that I can't resist kissing her dimpled hands and she wakes up smiling at me, such a happy baby, so pleased to be alive.

I squeeze Tobias's hand and think of the normal child

growing safely in my womb. The normal child that will finally enable me to accept Freya for what she is.

After our meal, we all go down to Aigues station and once again I wave goodbye to somebody I love. Then we're driving up the hill, to settle back into a home where, for the first time, Tobias, Freya and I are living on our own.

Yvonne still comes and goes during the day, of course. And wherever she is, her inconvenient admirers follow. Ludovic is around all the time nowadays; I can't stop him because he has the right to cultivate his half of the potager until the end of the year. Julien works assiduously in our half, and the pair of them glower at each other over their spades.

Ludovic's *pulvérisateur* of Roundup slips in his hand and sprays a row of courgettes that Julien has been coaxing back from the mildew. When I go down to pick lettuce for lunch I catch Julien throwing snails over onto Ludovic's side.

Yvonne basks innocently in this rivalry.

—

I've bought a little rubber toothbrush for Freya's new tooth. It's silly, but I feel excited about brushing her tooth for the first time. I've got no idea if she'll like it, whether she'll even open her mouth. I've never tried to brush a baby's teeth before.

I take her into the bedroom and lay her on a towel on the bed. I put a tiny splodge of baby toothpaste on the brush and foam it with a dab of water. Gingerly, I nudge it to her lips. She smiles and her mouth opens for me. She seems interested in the taste of the toothpaste. I think, in some wonder: this is the first time she's ever tasted mint. She clenches the rubber brush in her jaws, gumming it avidly, and I realise that she must have more teeth on the way.

The thing parents of normal babies always say is how miraculous it is that every day there's some new development. But with Freya, the extraordinary thing is how everything stays the same. We've become attuned to minute degrees of change. Any new discovery is a precious nugget to be stored away like treasure.

I brush her single tooth with care and then pull out the toothbrush. She gives me a full, gummy smile. For a moment we stay there, smiling at each other. Then she gives a moan; the noise she makes just before a fit. The familiar rhythm of jerking and gasping begins. Her jaw clamps down and her tongue slices into her new tooth. She begins to bleed.

I stare at her. Her jaw is locked. I lay her on her side to help her breathe. The blood runs from her mouth onto the towel. I wedge her onto the bed with a cushion. She gives one ragged gasp. For an instant she half regains consciousness and moans.

She's in pain and there's nothing I can do to help.

I think quite suddenly and distinctly: I can't bear this.

I move out of the room and onto the covered walkway, closing the door quietly behind me. I walk across the bridge, all the way across, into the long building that houses the barn. I need to be sure I'm out of earshot, in case she moans again.

I'm in the little room with straw on the floor where we saw the barn owl when we first looked around the house. Maybe the owl has babies of its own by now. Moving quietly, so as not to disturb its nest, I stare through the small opening at the vastness of the barn. Will it ever be done up and full of clients, laughter and normality? Or will we be freaks living in a ruin forever?

It seems to me very important to concentrate minutely on

details. To engross myself so entirely in my physical surroundings that there's no room in my mind for a single unwanted thought. I study a piece of timber in front of me. It's a rudimentary winch that must have been used for moving hay bales. At some point in its history it has clearly snapped and has been fixed with a piece of grubby, coloured cloth. I'm able to make out the pattern beneath the dirt. A rose.

Slowly it dawns on me that I'm looking at a scrap of Rose's favourite headscarf. Recycled and turned to another use by people who couldn't afford to cling on to sentimental things.

Abruptly my anger turns on myself. How could I leave Freya in the middle of a fit? How dare I decide there's anything concerning my baby that I can't bear?

I hurry back to the bedroom where Freya is lying in her dazed post-fit state. The blood runs in two long trails from her mouth down her white bodysuit. It's begun to dry on her chin. As I get close to her, she moans. I scoop her into my arms and hold her to my chest. She gives a low, quavering wail. Gently, I carry her downstairs and lay her on her mat on the table.

She's bitten a neat triangular nick out of her tongue just where her tooth has come through. I'm overwhelmed by the pity of it. She'll have the scar forever now.

Only Tobias can comfort me. I pick her up again, still in her blooded bodysuit, and stumble with her into his recording studio.

He's slumped on his keyboard with his head in his hands.

'What's going on?' I ask.

'Another potential funder has just pulled out. If we don't find somebody to pick up the tab for this soon, they're going to sack me, I know they are. I've been watching those damn scenes again and again for months – no sooner do I write some music than they get shuffled about, or cut out altogether. It was stupid of me to believe that I could do this. It's way beyond me. I'm letting Sally and everybody else down.'

'You're a wonderful musician,' I say. 'You've just lost perspective, that's all. You're getting burnt out.'

He looks at me hopelessly. 'Anna, could I play you something? I've been wanting to for a long time. I've just been too scared to, or something.'

I nod, hardly daring to breathe in case he changes his mind. He shuffles around with his equipment and music fills the tiny recording studio.

I've always known that Tobias is good at evoking a particular mood. That's why documentary directors like him. He can take the most banal piece of footage and write something that will make it seem anything from menacing to comic.

But I can tell that this piece is more than that. The melody is full of yearning, and I know that it's been wrung from him.

'It's the saddest thing I've ever heard,' I say.

'I told you my feeling of suffocation was making its way into my music,' says Tobias.

'You said that your music might help you escape,' I remind him.

'You know, when Freya was tiny,' he says, 'I'd put her in the sling and walk around pretending she was normal. Now she's getting older, there's still a sort of parallel child in my head who's developing normally, doing the things she should be doing. Most of the time I kind of superimpose one on top of the other, and pretend. The real Freya's situation is the same as ever; she isn't going anywhere; there's absolutely no hope of normality or progress in the usual sense. It's only my feelings that have changed. It has the effect of making my whole life seem unreal.'

I reach out and squeeze his hand. 'We're having another baby,' I say. 'This one is going to be normal. I can feel it. This one will rescue us.'

'Oh, Anna, don't you see? I look into her eyes and I think: there is nothing, absolutely nothing, that I wouldn't do for you. It doesn't matter a damn whether the next one is normal or not. Nobody can rescue us. We're fucked.'

———

Tobias puts Freya in the sling and we all go for a long walk. It's hunt day, but we know the hunters now. We've learned the rules.

The clouds are lying warm and thick on the hills. A cosy, closed-in feel. 'Like being in a cloud forest,' I say.

'Or a British summer,' says Tobias.

We walk across the dragon's spine, enjoying tiny details in the rock under our feet that we've never noticed before: usually the wild open view is too distracting.

'I was reading that this path dates from Neolithic times,' says Tobias. 'In the Middle Ages it was packed with mules and lined with stalls and people bartering their wares.'

'A magical place,' I say and then hope I don't sound like Lizzy.

The clouds swirl, giving us glimpses of intense blue sky behind them. We enjoy the view of the mountains appearing and disappearing, and we find secret places where huge parasol mushrooms are growing, and fairy rings of field mushrooms. The river is beautiful at this time of year: swift, wide and very bright. We hug each other and remember why we're here.

On the way back, Tobias says: 'Come and look at this.'

I follow him, expecting to see some new loveliness. But it's a wild boar lying on its side, an adolescent – about half the size of an adult, already out of its baby spotted coat – not quite dead. I see that the glazed eye is half open, its flank rising and falling. Flies are already gathering in its mouth and around its eyes.

Tobias pokes it with a stick and the poor thing staggers up on unsteady legs and takes a pace, wobbly and infinitely slow. There's something sickening about this slow-motion walk. Its muzzle drags on the ground; clearly it doesn't have the strength to lift it and so a grotesque little pile of hay forms around its snout as it inches forward. All the time it leans crazily as if it's going to fall again. It makes me feel low and sick and desperate.

'Its jaw is broken,' says Tobias. And I notice the unnatural angle of its mouth, yawning open far too wide.

'The poor creature must be in absolute agony.'

'It's very thin,' says Tobias. 'It might have been wandering round like this for days. We've got to find somebody to finish it off.'

'I'll go and find Julien,' I say. 'We're right next to his place.'

Julien is in his garden. I feel a pang of embarrassment. His glance slides off me, as if he wishes that he can slide after it. 'Julien! We need you – it's an emergency – there's a dying boar. It's suffering terribly. We need somebody to kill it.'

'Anna, killing isn't really my thing.'

'But what can we do about it? We can't let it suffer like this.'

'A wounded boar. It could be dangerous. Better leave it alone. Never tamper with nature.' He turns away, a beat too fast.

I'm suddenly furious. I instinctively feel that we ought to intervene. He just doesn't have the guts for it; he doesn't even have the courage to look me in the eye.

'I have something to tell you,' I say spitefully. 'I'm pregnant.'

He half turns back to me, his thin shoulders hunching slightly forward, as if he's bracing himself against a gale.

'Say something then. At least say something!'

Again his eyes flicker away from mine. 'You know, Anna,' he says, 'this isn't a time for confrontation. I need some space for myself right now. I hope you understand.'

I watch the thin figure turn away from me. How could I have thought him any better or wiser than anybody else? How could I have imagined that he had any answers for me? My absurd crush is over.

I can hear the *chasse* in the distance. I hurry on until I find Ludovic with his hunting gun.

'A boar – it's hurt! It's suffering!'

After all that he's seen of human misery, I assume he'll consider the suffering of a mere boar as nothing serious. But as soon as he gets my drift, Ludovic comes hurrying along with me.

'Don't worry, Anna. I'll put it out of its misery.'

We walk on in silence for a few moments.

As we reach the boar, in a single practised motion, without pausing in his stride, Ludovic points his gun at its head and fires. Its back legs convulse forward in a final kick, its whole body bucks and then it's still.

'A young male,' says Ludovic. 'One of the hunters must have hit it poorly. Not all of us are excellent shots.'

'Ludovic,' I blurt, 'how *did* Rose die?'

'*La drôle de guerre*,' he says, and shrugs.

306

I'm not going to let him blank me out again, like he did at the VE Day memorial. 'What exactly does that mean?'

We stare each other down for a moment. Finally he says: 'She went to warn the men about the German operation on the camp. But she was too late. She couldn't get through the cordon. A sniper picked her off as she was heading home. I told you: *la drôle de guerre.*'

I imagine Rose bravely charging up to the camp to try to warn the men; losing her life through the stupid accident of being in the wrong place at the wrong time; dying in the knowledge that she's failed to save anybody by her heroism.

Ludovic hesitates for a fraction of a second. When he speaks again, it's in a different tone. 'I shouldn't have let her go up there. I have lived with . . . guilt . . . for over sixty years. For many years I convinced myself that poor Thomas was my punishment.'

I start to shake my head, but he silences me.

'Since Thérèse died I've started to see things differently. We thought we would never have a child at all. Perhaps Thomas wasn't a punishment. Perhaps between us we did just enough good to earn us a miracle – a *small* miracle.'

The boar's mouth still gapes open. Inside, I can see the beginning of the long tooth that would have become his proud tusk upon maturity. Just a little shoot of a tooth.

'Could it be the same with *la petite*?' asks Ludovic. 'Could she be a *small* miracle?'

My good mood is over. I have a hammering headache. I feel exhausted, bone-achingly so, and low.

307

'Tobias – slow down. I'm tired all the time at the moment.'

'Sit down then, I need to walk a bit. I'll come back for you.'

I sit down on the heather. This was a field once. Nature is taking it back, just the way Ludovic told us. First comes the heather, the broom and the brambles. They choke out the smaller plants and form an impenetrable thicket. Even animals can't get in. The saplings get a chance to grow. After a few years, there are tall thin trees; they choke out the brambles in turn. After thirty or forty years you have new, unmanaged forest. Where the soil is too thin for that you have scrubland, called *maquis* on schist and *garrigue* on limestone.

I look down. There are splashes of red blood on the purple heather. Mine.

Everything that lives chokes out something else. Everything that dies makes way for new life.

There might still be a chance for this baby. I know I should sit still and wait for Tobias and be calm and think good thoughts. But I can't – I need him with me too much.

I get up and start to run.

'Tobias!'

He turns round and waves at me, cheerful again.

I shout: 'I'm bleeding!' At first he doesn't understand. Then he begins to stride towards me, Freya bouncing against him in her sling.

'Too many bad things have happened,' I weep. 'I can't survive this.'

Wordlessly, he holds on to me for a moment, as if he can keep me from falling apart by the sheer strength of his arms. Then he snaps into action: getting us back to the house, packing Freya's anticonvulsants and her pram, loading us both into the car and driving to A&E in Montpellier.

Even at top speed it takes an hour and a half. I see the sea, churning in an un-Mediterranean way. Blood flows, at the speed of a dribbling tap. I have pins and needles down my arms. I wonder idly how long it will take for all my blood to run out.

～

Tobias parks outside the hospital, dashes inside, comes back with a wheelchair, half lifts me into it and somehow manages to push me and to pull Freya along in the pram.

In A&E an officious nurse makes us queue after a belligerent woman and her daughter, both of whom can stand and who are therefore better off than me.

When the nurse finally notices that a huge red pool has formed around me, she visibly flinches. She grabs the wheelchair and pushes me past people lying on trolleys in corridors. Her sense of panic panics me.

The first doctor she finds dismisses us without looking at me, saying: 'I'm not on duty.'

A young female intern takes a look at me, hastily says: 'Excuse me,' and goes and finds the doctor who sent us away a few seconds before. The world begins to look fuzzy and strange. A crash team arrives and hooks me up to all sorts of machines.

I hear a doctor saying to a colleague: 'This woman came into A&E and they didn't even take a blood count or put her on a drip.' Then I'm taken into theatre and put out cold.

～

I wake up with Tobias smiling down at me. I'm still attached to two drips, shivering with cold under my blanket. Tobias puts Freya into bed with me and I feel the warmth of her body like a furnace beside me, banishing the cold. Tobias puts up the chrome bed rail and she stares at it transfixed. After a few minutes she reaches out her arm and tries to touch it with her hand.

Too soon, it's time for them to leave. When Tobias goes to pick her up, Freya begins to roar.

I look at her furious, scrunched-up face and burst into tears of my own.

'Freya,' I weep, 'you've broken my heart.'

Tobias lifts her out of my bed and, as her warm little body leaves me, the cold comes back in a rush.

October

I'M SUFFERING AN AWFUL kind of ennui. We've made a horrible mistake in coming here. I long for sparkling blue seas and citrus groves and no wind and interesting happy-go-lucky locals – not bolshy French people with their dire bureaucracy and boorish insistence that their ways are the only ways. I feel guilty, too, about Lizzy. I haven't been back to visit her, and I've tacitly let drop the question of her coming back to live with us when she gets out of hospital.

This morning I have a brief burst of energy and get dressed and then I rearrange furniture in the living room. I do this on my own because I know Tobias will object to any change but will be too lazy to do anything about it. It involves hauling around the heavy sideboard and other massive items. My stomach aches. But the baby's dead; what harm can it do now?

There's nothing in the potager except cauliflowers. I bring one up to the kitchen and spend half an hour picking out tiny caterpillars wedged into the crevices between the florets. There are over fifty of them. I have to break the cauliflower into tiny pieces to winkle them out. From this labour of love, I make cauliflower soufflé.

There's no sign of Tobias. From somewhere outside I can hear the sound of banging.

'Come and eat!' I shout out of the front door. 'It's a soufflé.'

'Of course I will,' he says, but of course he does not.

'Come and eat, you bastard!' I find myself yelling at him. 'Come right NOW!'

This time there's no answer at all. I stand, watching my soufflé deflate, imagining the mess it would make if I dared to hurl it against the wall.

It's fully five minutes before Tobias appears. I launch straight into him. 'You don't give a toss about a damn thing I say, do you?'

It's then I notice that Tobias is pale and his hand is bleeding. 'Where have you been, anyway?'

'Up a ladder. Trying to fix the guttering. Like you asked me to two days ago. I told you this morning I'd do it.' He can't resist adding: 'But you obviously weren't listening.'

Somehow it makes me even more furious, this feeling that he's grabbed the moral high ground from under my feet. 'Maybe I've just got used to you putting off your chores,' I snarl.

'You're determined to do me down,' says Tobias sadly. 'What kind of world would it be if I jumped every time you told me to? How long would it be before you got fed up with me?'

For a brief moment I see myself through his eyes: chivvying and bullying him, getting madder and madder.

Afterwards Tobias comes to the kitchen (where I'm doing the washing-up again) and I say: 'I'm sorry, I'm sorry, I'm sorry. I love you so much,' and of course he says it's all right. But I know it's not really all right and that my anger will bubble up again. And eventually it will ruin us.

314

It used to be that when somebody was awful to me and I couldn't do anything about it I would say: 'Well, at least I don't have to *be* that person.' But I don't say that any more. Because I *have* become that person. I'm trapped inside an awful person, and it's a kind of hell.

———

Having managed to spin out her stay with Kerim and Gustav for nearly a month, my mother is back home on her own. She's started bombarding me with ridiculous phone calls again.

'Darling.'

'Yes, Mother.'

'I believe there's a thing called a television watchdog. Is that correct?'

'Well, yes, there is.'

'Oh good. Listen, dear, could you just give them a ring and tell them my picture is getting fuzzy?'

'You'd better get a repairman. It must be your telly.'

'No, it's not that. I've had one of them round already and he says there's nothing wrong with my box. I think it's a disgrace.'

I slam down the phone. 'I'm fed up with her madness,' I storm. 'It's *wilful*. Delinquent. Attention-grabbing. She has absolutely no sense of anybody other than herself.'

'And you have?' asks Tobias.

'What's that supposed to mean?'

'You didn't used to be like this – so absorbed in your own misery that you don't give a toss for the people around you. Listen to what she's *not* saying.'

'Such as? Seeing as you're so empathetic suddenly.'

"'I'm terrified about you living in France with a disabled daughter," for a start. Not to mention: "I need to find a way through to you but I'm too proud to ask."'

Deep down, of course, I know that he's right; she wants some emotional response from me. But the years we've spent not talking to each other are like a frozen wasteland. I can't cross it. I don't even want to try.

This morning, a fat white envelope plops through the door. I open it and discover that I'm now officially entitled to establish a residential cookery school on my premises.

I ought to give a cheer. I look over at Freya, lying on her baby mat, and burst into tears instead.

I've been looking forward to this day for months. Planning for it. Hoping it would be a milestone. Every time I've thought I couldn't carry on, I've told myself that, when this letter comes through, somehow our lives will get better. Now that it's here, I understand they won't. They can't.

I keep on making myself little goals but every time I achieve one of them I'm forced to face up to the fact that nothing has changed. The thing that is wrong is still wrong and always will be. But that's too difficult to face so all I can do is to pick another goal and start again.

—

Outside, the chestnut trees have turned gold. Their burrs have split open and all at once there's another lavish feast on the roads. The ripe nuts are glossy, smooth and a deep chocolate brown, as alluring as treasure.

In Rose's day chestnuts were the main crop of the year, the difference between plenty and starvation. Ludovic has explained

316

to me how the *paysans* used to dry them in *seccadous*, special stone buildings that still litter the countryside. Chestnuts are the reason Rose's remote mountain hamlet existed at all.

The land up here is too poor for wheat, she writes. *People rely on chestnuts to keep alive. Every night, after the harvest, they sort them out by candlelight. They remove the skins and grind them into flour.*

We should be gathering them up. I ought to make *marrons glacés* and *purée de châtaigne*. But Julien's prediction in the spring has come true: I've worn myself out.

Just feeding the baby is exhausting. I'm often too demoralised even to try breastfeeding. Every bottle is a struggle. More often than not Freya doesn't finish her meal, and if she does, she throws it up. I jump when she shows any sign of hunger but usually by the time I've mixed up a bottle or shown her the breast she's fallen asleep again. Two hours per bottle, four bottles a day. That's eight hours a day spent feeding her. Not to mention the time it takes to clean up when she vomits.

The chestnuts will have to wait. I haven't the energy for any more preserving. Even if I could persuade Tobias to help me collect them.

We're having some of the best weather of the year. The odd rain shower has conjured up wild flowers and soft emerald grass out of the scorched brown earth. It's like a second chance, a new beginning. I prefer this gentle loveliness to the frantic growth of spring; it's more measured, as if the world is taking stock, considering its next move.

I feed Freya too quickly at lunch. She vomits all over me. I've read that a baby her age needs thirteen hundred calories a day. We're lucky if we get seven hundred into her. She's getting thin. I think it's still OK for the moment, but she has no more weight to lose.

Every creature planning to survive the winter is putting aside food. High in the walnut trees, I glimpse red squirrels harvesting the walnuts the day before we do. The attic is full of little caches of chestnuts; the rats too are getting in their supplies.

It's still warm enough to want to be in the fresh air but there's a *fin de siècle* feel about the lovely weather. Half of the natural world is beating a path to our open door in pursuit of a place to overwinter.

A huge hornet buzzes in and lands beside Freya, waggling her bum in a peculiar dance. I'm too frightened to try swiping her in case she attacks.

'Tobias!' I call. 'Tobias – can you come and help with this hornet?'

But Tobias is back in his usual position in the living room: at his computer, oblivious to anything I say.

Four or five of the hornet's followers are circling outside; she's a queen, trying to persuade them to follow her in. I grab a broom and slash at her. She buzzes wildly and flies back out of the door.

Freya vomits her bottle this evening as well. The nights are full of moths again, the cupboards with cicadas, singing their final songs.

—

'Oh hello, dear, I just thought I'd give you a call.'

'Mother, are you all right? It's five a.m.'

'Really? It doesn't seem that late. I must have dozed off again.'

'Five *in the morning*.'

'Yes, dear. I heard. I'm not deaf. What are you up to?'

318

'I was asleep. Mother, what's going on? Aren't you sleeping?'

'Of course not. I've already been for my walk. There was a lovely moon.'

'Your walk?'

'Well, yes, I always like a walk after my lunch.'

'What time did you have your lunch?'

'At midnight, dear.'

'But – you mean to say you went all day without having your lunch?'

'Oh, don't be silly, dear, it was *tomorrow's* lunch.'

'Mother, please don't let this mean I'm going to have to worry about you too.'

'It's all right dear, it's perfectly simple. I've decided to have lunch as my main meal. When you're alone the evening is the bit that's really horrid. Having your main meal in the middle of the day makes it a bit less horrid.'

'In the middle of the night, you mean.'

'Night, day,' says my mother, 'they've all got mixed up somehow.'

I can't get back to sleep after her phone call. Beside me, Freya stirs and begins to hiccup.

I shake Tobias. He mumbles, only half awake. 'I need to get her a bottle,' I say. 'Will you keep her awake while I go and make it up?'

In the kitchen I enjoy a moment of peace by myself. Is this why my mother has become nocturnal? It's an attenuated happiness, this appreciation of trivial things under control, running the way they should. The regular tick-tock of the kitchen clock. The hum of the refrigerator. The sparkling cleanness of the quarry tiles on the kitchen floor. My glass jars lined up on their shelves.

319

As I make up the bottle, I fret about a question that's circled in my mind since Freya was born. What makes me a mother? Is it going down and making up her bottle when she needs it? Is it always, obsessively, remembering her medicines? Is it fulfilling her needs, however tired or resentful I feel?

When I go back upstairs, Tobias and Freya are both fast asleep, wrapped in each other's arms. I pull her gently out of his embrace and try her on the bottle. She won't take it. Instead she arches her body backwards and pushes her tongue up to the roof of her mouth the way she used to when she was newly born. Every time she catches sight of me, her face contorts in reproach and she opens her mouth and howls.

Tobias wakes up again.

'Let me take her,' he says. 'Do you need a burp? Burpetty-burp.'

Freya, daddy's girl that she is, stops screaming and smiles at him.

'You know, Anna,' he says. 'I wouldn't have missed this experience for anything. We don't want the silly old bottle, do we, Freya? Try her on the breast again.'

Her lips pinch the tip of my breast and I feel her inconsequential pull. It feels lovely to me and, I presume, to her. But it's not enough to anchor her to life.

These days, Tobias talks to Freya when she fits.

'Oh, sweetheart, no! no! Oh please don't . . .'

He never seems to get used to it, he always reacts as if it's the first time, as if he believes that – if he can find the right words – he'll be able to cut off the fit before it begins. I don't know if talking to her helps, but it seems to. Tobias always holds her hand and he says that helps too, but God knows.

My mind slips away from the sight of her body convulsing.

There are so many other things to worry about. What, for instance, if the rats manage to scurry along the shelves and send my glass jars crashing to the ground?

Tomorrow I'll go into Aigues and buy some lengths of dowelling. I'll stick them along the edge of the shelves, locking the glass jars in place. Then my system will be complete.

—

The only thing that makes life bearable is thinking about my twins. Sometimes they're a girl and a boy; sometimes they're both girls. A fair amount of the time they look just like Freya. Vibrant, sparky versions of Freya. Unlike her, they're developing. I decide what their first words will be and what they prefer to eat. I make up names for them and menus for their meals and I try to imagine what a normal baby – one with the correct muscle tone – would feel like in my arms.

It seems necessary, to me, to pin down the people I love most in the world.

'Tobias, I've been thinking. Who would you like in your bed?'

A slow smile spreads over Tobias's face. 'Anna – are you coming on to me?'

'That's not what I mean. Imagine it's the perfect Sunday morning. You've got tea in a silver pot, wholemeal toast and home-made jam and the newspapers. So, if you could have just the people you really love lazing around with you – who would you have in your bed?'

'Well, you and Freya of course, and also – it's a party, right? Well then, I guess I'd like my friends from London. And all the people we've met here – Yvonne, Julien and Kerim – even poor old Ludovic has a lot of good in him. Perhaps not Lizzy, although I definitely think you ought to go and visit her in hospital again soon. And my pals from college, I haven't seen some of them for a while. And my family, of course. It's such a shame my mum lives so far away. Hey, possibly even your mum.'

And that's the fundamental difference between us. Tobias would like all the world in bed with him. And when all the world is there in your inner circle there's room – of course there's room – for one little duff baby.

But me, I just want him, and my perfectly normal twins.

$$\sim$$

'You didn't call to wish me happy birthday.'

My mother is actually crying down the phone.

'Oh God, I'm sorry,' I say.

'I waited in all day. Don't you love me any more?'

'I'm sorry – I forgot, we've been having all sorts of problems.'

'What sort of problems? What could be so important that you forgot me?'

The raw pain in her voice makes her sound like a little girl. I'm used to her demanding my attention in all sorts of indirect ways but this time I'm disarmed by her frankness.

Since adolescence, I've had a hard and fast rule: I don't let my mother into my interior world. However much she goads me, I don't upset her in return by telling her how I feel.

I take a deep breath. 'I had a miscarriage a couple of weeks ago,' I say. 'It seems to have . . . hit me in some vital organ. It's had a weird effect on me.'

So we have a real conversation and of course it doesn't hurt her so much, the truth that I claim I keep from her in order to protect her, but that really I hide in order to protect myself and to punish her.

~

It's a beautiful day. I step out of the front door and look around the courtyard. Sometimes I find the flower-studded grass and our eccentric collection of stone buildings picturesque. But today all I can see is that a fresh chunk of masonry has fallen, that there's a pile of rubbish needing to be taken to the dump and that the outbuildings contain thousands of rat runs leading directly to my house. We'll never, in a million lifetimes, succeed in keeping the rats out of our home.

I think: my world is out of control. I can't manage my husband or do the huge structural repairs we need. I don't even know how long I'll able to look after my child.

The thought sends me back into the one tiny corner of my life where I'm winning the battle against chaos: my kitchen.

My glass jars have been safely secured with dowelling rods. For all I care, the rats can run all around them, gazing at them. They can't be touched any more than you could touch the exhibits at the British Museum. I like the image of a world from which I've screened out all the untidiness, filth and disorder. It makes me the curator.

Tobias comes into the kitchen and surveys my handiwork with a disgust I find inexplicable: after all, it's perfectly reasonable to have a system in place against the rats.

'You and your glass jars!' he splutters. 'I feel as if *I'm* about to be put away in a jar.'

I stand at the sink, chipping a patch of congealed egg off a saucepan and imagine myself gazing benevolently through the glass at a perfect Tobias and Freya, safely bottled inside one of my jars.

Freya's barely taken any feed today. I forget my principles and spoon sugar into her bottle. At first she gulps it down greedily but soon she starts writhing and crying and about an hour later she vomits the whole lot. Along with all her medicines, presumably.

If she vomits her medicines she's in danger of having a severe fit. But if I give her more medicine she could overdose.

I pick up the bottle and feed her all over again. It takes two hours. Then I give her another half-dose of medicine and put her to bed.

It's four in the morning. I wake up and lie worrying. Tobias is ignoring me more and more these days. He's deaf to me, and I dread the long winter of his deafness and my shouting louder and louder, heckling in order to be heard. I have night-mares of him, headphones clamped to his head, in a cavern so deep that, however loud I shout, my voice can't penetrate to him. Him gone forever, and me unable to reach him.

Instead of lying awake for hours, I get up. I find Freya asleep in her cot, soaking wet; she's been lying in a pool of vomit all night. She must have thrown up most of her second evening feed as well.

I clean her up without waking her. Then I tidy Tobias's recording studio, file his papers and leave the things he has to do in a neat pile on his keyboard. I make a list of our finances and work out how many more days we can possibly afford to carry on here.

When Freya wakes up I feed her extremely carefully. She vomits about half an hour later.

—

Freya has screamed solidly for eight hours. Screamed through an entire night. At seven in the morning I too have a screaming fit, one of those bad ones where you listen to what comes out of your mouth and wonder if it's really you saying those things or not.

'I can't bear it. I can't bear this life. I wish I was dead. Please, please let me get cancer so I can die. I can't commit suicide because I can't let you down – so let me just die. I'm so fucking miserable.'

This is all addressed to Tobias, but he carries on sleeping; he's wearing earplugs.

At eight, he stirs and calls weakly from bed: 'Sweetheart – would you mind making me a coffee?'

On the fridge door is a picture of Freya taken three months ago. I glance at it as I flip the switch on the kettle. It's shocking how much weight she's lost.

I pull down a mug, tip coffee powder and milk into it, wait until the kettle has boiled and top the whole thing up with hot water.

'It's ready,' I shout.

'Oh good – could you bring it here for me?'

'No – you can bloody well come down. I'm making breakfast.'

Tobias appears a full ten minutes later, wiping sleep from his eyes.

I plonk his coffee down in front of him. He sips it and looks up at me reproachfully. 'Instant? Oh, Anna.'

'If I make you a bottle up, will you feed the baby?'

'Look, sorry, Anna. I've got a few emails to send. About the score. It's possible the funding is really coming through this time. Any chance of some real coffee?'

I put bread in the toaster, lay the breakfast table, go back into the kitchen, stack the dirty supper plates in the sink and do the washing-up. I wipe down all the work surfaces, scour out the sink and polish the taps. I mix up the baby's medicines, add a spoonful of honey to them and draw them into a syringe. I get down a tray and arrange the medicines and a blood pressure monitor on it. I make up a bottle of formula and put that down on the tray as well.

I'm about to head into the living room for yet another unrewarding session trying to feed Freya, when Tobias comes into the kitchen and dumps his coffee cup in the sink.

'What's wrong with washing up after yourself?'

'Sorry.' He leaves the cup in the sink, wanders over to the toaster, pulls out the cold toast and makes a face. Then he inspects my glass jars and pulls one down. He takes off the lid and shakes the jar so that home-made biscuits tumble onto the worktop. He helps himself and begins loping out of the door again, leaving the open jar lying on its side in the pile of biscuits.

'Tobias!' My voice is sharp enough to scratch the surface of his attention.

'Mmm?'

'I'm fed up with you not pulling your weight. You're up for the fun stuff but you don't put the hours in struggling to feed Freya. You never mix up her medicines and make sure she gets them on time. You never share any of the *drudgery*. Every morning I force myself to get up and try and try but I get no support – you're shifting sand, although actually you're a bit like a concrete block as well, but anyway you're not a rock, which is what I need. I'm fed up with never being able to count on you. I'm fed up of living this life. I don't *want* to leave you, it's just that I don't think I can stay here and stay sane.'

This is Tobias's cue to hug me and to calm me down.

Instead, he grabs a cup off the shelf – I notice it's a chipped one – and slams it against the wall.

'Anna! Enough of your nagging! Look at yourself! Where does all this drudgery come from? You've devoted your life to it – you're creating it. And then you blame me because you aren't having any fun.'

I give a great yell, from some pent-up source of fury I'm barely aware of. As if I'm standing aside and witnessing something inside me rushing uncontrollably out.

I yell and yell. Sometimes there are words, sometimes not. I can listen in on them but I have no control over them. 'Just go and sit on a rock with your friends the lizards, for all I care. I'm cutting loose. I don't want to do this any more.'

I begin smashing things. I've been fantasising about doing this for months, but the reality is much better. It goes on for some time; I watch Tobias grow from chastened, through amused to almost frightened. The sensation is pleasurable. I give into it, and scream wordlessly for a while.

Tobias tries to get between me and the things I'm breaking. But I'm too quick for him. I keep ducking out of his arms.

'For Christ's sake, Anna! Have you gone mad?'

I look round for something else to smash. All the crockery is gone. I begin to pull my precious jars down from their shelves and hurl them onto the floor. They bounce on the quarry tiles and shatter in an orgy of broken glass, Italian 00 flour, muscovado sugar, puy lentils, blanched almonds and Valrhona cocoa.

It's scary, this force from within me yet divided from me. At my core is a deep well of anger. A pool of seething magma with the power to burst up and destroy anything I've built.

'I'm going out!' I shout.

'No you can't: *I'm* going out – you can't leave the baby alone,' jeers Tobias.

And suddenly I know that I bloody well can.

'I couldn't care less about the damn baby. I hope the baby dies!'

I march off without looking back.

—

Outside, the world is quiet the way it is when a real storm is coming. As though all the air has been sucked out of it, ready to be blown back at terminal velocity.

I walk automatically over the dragon's backbone to the next hill. Today its flanks are bare and I can see that it's made of different stone than the rest of the hills. Harder. The river wore the gorge away over millions of years but not this bit. Would there have been any way to tell, all those years ago, which rock would crumble under pressure and which would endure?

I pass the memorial to the Maquis, past the hunters' hides. Sometimes I weep, sometimes I'm calm. I must have been walking for hours.

The wind begins to pick up. I stand on the top of a hill and watch it approaching, ripping at the trees in the forest. It roars up close and pummels me. Then it passes by. Gust after gust comes rushing past.

When the rain begins I shelter under the pine trees. How could the men of the Maquis bear it, living out here in the cold and wet for years? Did Rose ever come up here in a storm? I can imagine her marching up the hill, brisk and unafraid, her hair tied tightly in her rose-patterned headscarf, a loaf of bread under her arm, country butter in a greasy piece of paper in her basket.

I remember: oh God, I forgot to give Freya her medicine this morning.

Maybe Tobias did it. More likely it's still lying on the tray in the kitchen where I left it.

I tell myself that I ought to go home. Her vomiting means Freya's had less medicine than she needs for days. If she misses a whole dose now, she could have a huge fit. But I can't go; my legs won't take me there.

Freya is still a part of me, but I feel as if she's a sort of scab, glued to my skin. The edge is lifting. If I rip it off, it'll hurt like hell but it will be gone.

The rain stops but the wind picks up. The pines groan. I huddle under a tree trunk, trying to find shelter that doesn't exist. A wind like this can snap pine trees like matchsticks. As soon as it drops, I begin to move again.

I can't find my way out of the forest. I crash through wet trees and slip down a muddy bank. Then I stumble into the clearing with Julien's tree house. I have a moment to notice the tattered yellow leaves of his wisteria, and then I'm panting up his staircase and hammering on his door. It opens a crack.

'Anna!' He looks shocked to see me.

'Can I come in?'

'Look Anna, I love the fact you come and find me like this. I think you're great. You're a really great woman. It's just I don't feel it would be right...'

'Julien. I don't want to shag you, you fool. I need shelter from the storm!'

But Julien isn't listening; he's too wrapped up in what he's trying to say.

'Oh hell Anna, I owe you a huge apology. A few weeks ago I led you on. I gave you false hopes and dreams – I had no right to do it. I was free, sure, but at the same time, I wasn't free. Since then, I've been trying to make it up to you by keeping out of your way. I know there have been . . . unintended consequences . . . and I feel terrible about that. It's taken a woman like you – your spontaneity, your freedom, your coming here to me like this in the middle of a storm – to make me see that I've been deluding myself. What's the point of living in my tree? Of having my precious so-called independence if it costs me the one person . . .? What I'm trying to say is that I need to make compromises. And sacrifices. I need to go and do anything it takes to . . .' The opening in the doorway is getting smaller as he speaks. 'Oh Anna, you're brave, you're smart, you're beautiful – but you're not *her*. Isn't it obvious? I'm in love with somebody else.'

His hobbit-like door closes in my face. I stand looking at it in exasperated revelation.

'So am I,' I whisper. 'So am I.'

The door reopens. 'Anna – I'm being ridiculous,' he says. 'There's a storm. Come in.'

But suddenly I know that I must get back and apologise to Tobias and give Freya her medicine and toil for both of them uncomplainingly for the rest of my life before it's too late.

'No,' I say, 'I have to go.' I turn and run down the *piste*.

In a clearing in the forest, a group of hunters is sheltering under a tarpaulin, singeing the hair off the carcass of a wild boar with cigarette lighters. I'd forgotten it's a hunt day. Ludovic motions to me to join them but I don't want them to see me like this. I shake my head and carry on at a half walk, half run.

'Anna. What's the matter?' He's come after me. 'You're crying. What's happened?'

I can't answer, I just shake my head. He puts an arm round my shoulder. The wind is getting worse again; he can barely hear me anyway. Its roaring brings a kind of freedom to say what I like.

'Oh, Ludovic – it's been torturing me,' I burst out. 'Am I unnatural? As a mother? What would Rose have done?'

I don't expect an answer; I'm thinking aloud really. My feet are taking me homewards at last. We push against the wind at first, then we dip into the lee of our own mountain and the roaring gets fainter.

Ludovic is looking at me with a particular intensity. 'Anna, I think you have heard some rumour . . . I know that people talk, but it's difficult for me . . .'

I look at him blankly.

'I was a kid – I was fifteen. I couldn't resist boasting. I was proud of the Maquis. It's so easy to give information away by accident. The long and short of it is that the Germans got to hear about the existence of the camp near the chestnut village. Straight away there was an operation. Rose knew that if the Maquis realised what I'd done they'd . . . well, it was a rough time. Bad things had happened. That's why she wouldn't let me go to warn them. That's why she went in my place. That's why she died and why, when my comrades were being killed in battle, I was hiding exactly where she'd put me – in the game kitchen.'

We reach the top of the hill above our house and step onto the *col des treize vents*. The wind comes at us like an animal, vast and invisible – we see the trees moving down the hill and the roaring of it growing closer. Then it passes us and turns round. Something in the turning of the wind, in the speed of it, in the uncanny physicality of its movement sets off a sound unlike anything I've ever heard. A three-dimensional wailing, coming from everywhere, from the rocks themselves, from the earth and the sky.

'I've not heard that since I was a boy,' says Ludovic. 'It's said to be an omen.'

A cold terror claws at me.

'Freya's medicines,' I say. 'Ludovic, I've done a stupid thing. I have to get back quickly.'

We run down the hill. The wailing follows us as if the wind has found its voice and its voice is a lament.

I see the fire ambulance racing up the hill below us. Its blue light is flashing; its siren is lost in the wail of the wind. It stops by the house. We put on speed, shouting at it not to leave without me. The wind wails louder than we could ever shout. The ambulance turns and heads back down the hill.

—

When I finally get to the hospital, I find Freya lying in a cot, her lovely curls all covered in goo. She's wearing a pink plastic bonnet with hundreds of electrodes attached to it. From the electrodes run wires leading to a monitor. Her thought waves are scribbles across the screen. A cipher. If I could find the key, I could get inside her world. But I never will. I'm locked out.

Tobias is sitting at her bedside. He doesn't get up. We don't hug.

'It was my fault,' I say. 'I forgot her medicine.'

He nods and bends his head back to Freya. So I know that he blames me for all of this.

We sit together for a while in silence, listening to Freya's breath bubbling in her throat.

'I'm exhausted,' says Tobias. 'Stay here with her. I need to take a break.'

As he walks out, Freya makes a horrible choking noise deep in her lungs. The oxygen-saturation alarm begins to flash. A nurse comes in and switches it off. 'I'll send in the physiotherapist to aspirate her,' she says.

'Can you tell anything about her brainwaves?' I ask. 'From the machine?'

She looks at the chart. 'It says here there are abnormal alpha waves failing to develop.'

What do abnormal alpha waves failing to develop *feel* like? The concept is too strange. I can't imagine it.

Freya wakes and looks at me, almost alertly. Then her eyes roll up. Her head flops back. A trail of drool runs out of the side of her mouth. The image of the mentally handicapped, from whom – before she was born – I used to guiltily recoil.

Where does love stop? If I love Freya when her eyes are open and seem to be looking at me, can I stop loving her because her eyes roll up and lose focus? If I love her when her mouth is closed, will I stop loving her because it lolls open and drools? Is love like a mineral, to be chipped away with every new problem or deficiency? Do we make an internal calculation when a baby is no longer a good bet?

The physiotherapist comes in.

'I'm going to put a tube down her nose and suck out the fluid from her lungs,' she says. 'It's better if you watch, then you'll be able to do it next time.'

I make an instinctive motion of denial.

'You have to learn.'

'Why?'

'Because Freya is your daughter. I won't be here every time to do it for you.'

'Then I don't want her as my daughter.'

The physiotherapist wags her forefinger at me from side to side like a metronome, making a tutting noise with her tongue against her teeth. An irritating French gesture of rebuke.

'It's all right for you,' I say. 'I expect your children are normal.'

'You daughter's life is just as valuable as any other child's. Look, it's easy, you put the tube in here.'

'No – I won't learn. *Je refuse! Je refuse!*'

The physiotherapist is angry. She jerks the tube into Freya's nose. Freya gives a weak, bubbling cry of pain. I think: she hurt her deliberately, because she's cross. She isn't any better than me.

Tobias comes and goes. Only one parent can stay the night with Freya. Nobody asks which of us it will be. It's the automatic right and duty of the mother.

Freya's been unhooked from the EEG machine but they're still monitoring her heart, respiration and oxygen saturation. Her hair's still full of goo.

The nurses are unfriendly. Perhaps the physiotherapist has told them of my unnatural attitude.

'It's good for her to know you're here,' one of them says.

I want to roar: 'She does NOT know! It makes no difference if I'm here or not.'

But what I fear, what I also hope, is that it does make a

difference. That I'll have a real bond with her; that it will be the best thing in my life; that it will hold me prisoner, chained to her forever.

The nurse puts her into my arms to feed. As soon as I hold her, she becomes real again. My little Freya is under the lines and tubes.

'Your husband says she's been having difficulty feeding. Is that right?'

'Well, yes. She's always hard to feed but she's been getting much worse. For the past couple of weeks.'

'What do you usually feed her? Is she on any solids yet?'

'Oh, no – she doesn't really know what to do with a spoon. We give her an enriched formula in the bottle or else the breast.'

'We're going to run a tube through her nose and hook her up to a bag of feed for the moment so that she doesn't get weak. Don't worry, we'll keep letting you try to feed her.'

I try to sleep, not very successfully because the oxygen-saturation alarm keeps going off. The feed-flow alarm buzzes too. I assume it means the feed is finished so I turn it off. Sometime later, the night nurse comes in with her torch.

'Did you turn off the alarm? Why?'

I stumble to explain in sleepy French.

'It wasn't finished. We are already behind with her feeds because of these . . . attempts to have her suck.' She fiddles angrily with the bag and leaves, slamming the door behind her.

I've got the beginnings of a deep unease.

Eventually, I doze off under the blinking monitors. In my dream the Nazis come back to the area. They round up all the children. Then they ask us which child we wish, as a group, to sacrifice. The nurses and doctors and social workers try to persuade me that Freya is the obvious victim to save their normal children. In my dream, it seems terribly important to oppose them. 'She's my child!' I shout. 'You told me her life was worth as much as any other baby's. You *told* me so!'

—

Morning comes and Freya is gazing at me from her cot, quite awake. I say hello to her. A sweet moment, just for us.

Then the door is thrown open. The bath is brought and apparently it takes two care assistants to fuss around while I fill it.

I undress Freya, trying to have some quiet time as they rampage through the room, cleaning. I take out the electrodes, three on her chest to measure her heart and the oxygen-saturation monitor on her foot. I have to hold the tube in her nose up against her head as I bathe her. She kicks her legs a couple of times and opens her eyes. Then I massage her in oil and dress her. The assistant puts back the electrodes.

The ward round arrives before Tobias. It's reassuring to see Dr Dupont again.

'How has Freya been overnight?' she asks.

'She's a bit more awake this morning,' I say. 'Less snuffly.'

She breaks in: 'Has she sucked yet?'

'No – not yet.'

'And it was just the last couple of weeks before she was admitted that she has had problems sucking?'

I mentioned that only in passing, to a nurse, but it's been relayed to the specialist. It's clearly important. My unease is growing.

'She's too sleepy to suck,' I say.

'Indeed. Part of the sleepiness could be due to the medication,' says Dr Dupont. 'We gave her a large dose of phenobarbitone on admission, and now we've started her on Sabril, another medication which causes sleepiness. It could take up to a week for things to balance out. So we shouldn't worry yet.'

'Yet?'

'I must be honest with you. She has had a major seizure. Her brain was starved of oxygen for a prolonged period. We need to find out how much damage was done.'

Tobias arrives and we go out for breakfast. We don't talk, except to agree that we can't face going to visit Lizzy just at this moment.

When I get back, Freya is worse. She sucks weakly on my finger but doesn't make any attempt to swallow her own saliva, which is choking her. The nurse tells me the physiotherapist has just aspirated her.

'You mean she's going to aspirate her?'

'No, it's just been done, and it has to be done again right away.'

This time a student does it. It takes ages. I don't watch. The phrase *'Je n'accepte pas de faire ça'* runs round my head.

If she can't swallow, she's likely to inhale her saliva and get chest infections. If she can't suck, she'll need to be fed through a tube.

I've decided that, whatever happens, I won't help aspirate her – and I'll honour my agreement with Tobias and tell them we won't take her home if we have to either aspirate or tube-feed. Both are horrific.

It's silly how quickly one slips back into the hospital routine. The door flinging open at 6 a.m. The cup of instant coffee and the stale croissant. The clattering of the 8 a.m. ward round in the corridor outside. Tobias, appearing unshaven, out of breath and five minutes ahead of the doctors. Dr Dupont, professionally worried, with her white coat and fashionable shoes. Two interns with clipboards. Three or four nurses and hangers-on.

Dr Dupont usually begins by asking me questions. How has the night been? How many fits has Freya been having?

But not today. She frowns at Freya's chart and speaks so quickly that I've missed the beginning of what she says before I realise it's important.

'. . . For what it's worth, I doubt it was because of the seizure. Babies lose their tongue-thrust reflex at about six months. This is when they take over conscious control of their feeding and begin to learn to chew and swallow.'

'Excuse me, what are you saying?'

'Inserting a stomach tube is a very minor operation. Not at all significant.'

'*Je refuse.*'

'Very well. Some parents don't want to hear the words "stomach tube". That's all right. There are other things we can do. If you refuse a stomach tube, we can give her a nasogastric tube – to feed her through the nose.'

I look at Tobias. Up until now, whenever anything unpleasant has had to be said about Freya to authority, he's done it. But when I catch his eye, I can see he's going to flunk this.

'When will she be allowed home?' he asks.

'Now, don't get your hopes up for an early discharge. We need to monitor what other function she has lost. But in the

338

meantime, we think it won't hurt to begin giving you lessons in tube-feeding.'

I take a deep breath.

'We've already discussed this, as a couple,' I say. 'We've made up our minds, so it's no good trying to change them. We've drawn a line in the sand. We've agreed that we aren't able to cope with tube-feeding. We want her taken into care right away until she's old enough for a residential institution.'

A hush falls.

'I don't mind tube-feeding,' says Tobias.

I look at him in disbelief. At that moment the pain of his betrayal is so strong it is like being punched in the stomach. I can't catch my breath.

'But . . . we had an agreement,' I manage to whisper.

Tobias turns on me, furious. 'You don't understand. I'm not like you. I can't give and withdraw my love on a . . . whim. I didn't want to love her – and now I do love her, I'm trapped.'

The world, my world, is a long way away.

'This is an opportunity,' I hear myself saying, 'to leave her.'

But Tobias isn't listening. He's locked in discussions with the ward round about feeding tubes.

He doesn't even see me go. I'm walking out of the lobby of the hospital, through the grounds and towards the airport bus. The fresh air on my cheeks is invigorating. The pain's gone away. I've broken free. I feel detached. Detached, at last, and dissociated.

November

I HALF EXPECT TOBIAS to be here at the airport to stop me. He must guess where I'm headed. He has the car after all; he could have beaten me to it.

I don't know what I'll do if he's here. My mind bounces off the concept. But there's no familiar tall figure waiting for me.

I feel a brief pang. Then I'm numb again, propelled onwards, choiceless.

I buy a ticket but by the time I reach the gate the flight's already boarded. I watch myself pleading with the stuffy assistant to let me pass. Perhaps she won't – usually they won't. Then I'll be forced to stop and think. And if I do that, I'll go back. What I'm doing now can only be done unthinkingly.

I hear myself sob: '*Mon bébé, l'hôpital* . . .' My tears are real. The assistant gives way, talking quickly into her radio. A dash across the tarmac. I'm the last to board.

There's an empty seat in the middle of the first row. I throw myself down on it. The plane taxies. I can't get off now even if I want to. It's done.

'You cut that a bit fine,' says my neighbour.

'Somewhat,' I gasp. The plane begins to move. Dusty fields

343

flash by and then we're up in the air. I crane over my neighbour to watch my old life disappear. He's an elderly man, born in an age of chivalry. Instead of taking offence, he smiles and leans back so that I can look. The smooth patchwork of the plain becomes wrinkled and ruched as the land gets steeper. I catch one brief glimpse of my own hills, where somewhere down below is Les Rajons and everyone in it is living their lives without me.

Long after it's disappeared, I remain with my head wedged past my neighbour, watching the land fall away below us. Then we're in the clouds and there's no point looking any more.

'Do you live here?' asks my neighbour.

'I . . . er . . .' I have not the faintest idea how to answer that question. 'Sort of.'

'Ah – you're just in the process of moving?'

'Yes, that's right.'

'It took me a long time too. My wife and I used to come for holidays, but we never could decide whether to live here full-time. She would have liked to, I think. But it seemed like such a big step. And then, when she died, all of a sudden it seemed the natural thing to do. Ironic really. Where is your place?'

'We just passed over it. In the Avants-Monts.'

'Have you got family?'

'A baby girl.'

'Your first? How old is she?'

'Nearly a year now.'

'Annabel – my wife – and I went to our grandson's first birthday just before she died. And he took his first steps, right there around the tea table, in front of all his grandparents. It was a wonderful moment.'

344

His face is wrinkled and kind, tanned nut brown. He looks like the perfect grandfather, active enough for rough games, sympathetic with cut knees. I miss my father. I wish he was here to see Freya. To love her, to guide me.

'It goes so fast,' he says. 'It seems like yesterday I was carrying around his mother – my youngest daughter. We did that for a long time – she was born with a hip missing. She had to have an operation and after that she was in a plaster cast for fourteen months. I used to lug her around everywhere in a backpack. We went on walking holidays and everything. Then one day she had the plaster off and before we knew it she was walking on her own – and I felt quite bereft.'

I don't answer.

'Is your daughter walking yet?' he asks.

'No, not yet.'

'She'll be pulling herself up then.'

'Well . . . er . . . no.'

'Oh, don't worry about it. It takes some of them longer than others, but they all get there in the end.' He smiles at me reassuringly. I open my mouth and all at once it's impossible to stop talking.

'She won't get there, I'm afraid. She was born with profound disabilities. We found out just after she was born. At the beginning of the week the doctors said she might be a bit long-sighted – by the end they were telling us to mark her notes "Do not resuscitate".'

'And how is she now? What is she like?'

'Well, she's sweet really. She can't support her head or roll over or say anything but "wah" – but she does smile, and she's, well, she's floppy and that makes her very cuddly, and if you pick her up she curls into your body and lays her head on your

345

shoulder and at night she swims towards you in bed and presses up to you. She loves people, she loves . . . well, she just loves loving and being loved. That's all she does really. The future is scary. The future is ventilators and stomach-feeding and hoists. And I got along fine without looking at the future for a while, but now it's coming to meet us. They think she's forgotten how to feed on her own. And I'm afraid that will be the thin edge of the wedge. Because I can't bear the day when I smile at her and she's forgotten how to smile. And if we'd just left her in the hospital when she was born it would have been easier really – because we know her better now, you see.'

He smiles. 'You know, I always loved my youngest daughter best because I had to carry her around for fourteen months. That's what her disability taught me: the way love grows. You'll have other children, I'm sure – but you'll always, secretly, love her the best. Because you've had to do so much more for her than for the others. Do you have a picture of her?'

I reach into my wallet and take out a picture of Freya in Tobias's arms.

'She's lovely,' he says. 'Perfect.'

I say goodbye to him at the terminal. We don't swap addresses.

—

I don't have a base in London any more. I call my mother and ask if I can come and stay with her in Sevenoaks. I don't tell her why.

'Oh, but darling – the house isn't ready. Your room isn't aired. I haven't even been grocery shopping.'

'I'll go shopping. It's fine.'

She sounds flustered. I realise that she's getting older, slowing down. 'Well,' she says, 'why don't you wait until the weekend, at least? Spend a few days in London and stay with Martha.'

I can't face Martha or any of my friends with their normal, well-regulated lives. I check into a hotel.

My room is tiny. The hotel has provided a miniature plastic kettle, a thick china mug, sachets of fake milk and stale tea bags with strings in paper wrappers. The hairdryer is chained to the wall. This minuscule space is costing me an arm and a leg.

I have absolutely nothing to do.

It's remarkable how little I'm missing Freya. She's already receded into a shadow. Is this what it would be like if I gave her away? Or is it a deception, because really I know she's safe with Tobias and whenever I like I could let her little fern-like hands curl around my neck and pull me in again?

There's a constant muffled roar of traffic. People in London are pedestrians, not human beings. They scuttle through the streets carrying umbrellas. They hail taxis or wait at bus stops.

I sit for a long time with my nose pressed against the double-glazed window, watching how raindrops roll down a pane. Sometimes they plough their little crooked paths alone; sometimes they turn inexplicably and join other raindrops. They all end up at the bottom of the glass.

The numbness is wearing off; misery is starting to seep back. I pick up the phone and begin to set up appointments. I can't make myself be happy but I can at least try to organise things.

—

347

At 9 a.m. sharp I walk out onto the rainy street and hail a black cab.

We're heading into central London, past wet parks, bedraggled pigeons, drenched Victorian statues. I get out by a tall Regency building with black wrought-iron railings and a discreet brass plate.

Yesterday I set up a meeting with a family rights lawyer. She's sharp-suited, sharp-eyed and businesslike. At three hundred pounds an hour, I suppose, you can't afford to take your eye off the ball.

'Your marriage has broken down and you can't look after your disabled child? What exactly would you like us to do for you?'

'I definitely can't keep her. But I . . . I don't want to lose track of her. In the system. I need to know my parental rights, under the law.'

'Putting your child into care is a very big step,' she says. 'Initially, a foster family will be found. However, foster care is not considered a permanent solution. Social services will make every effort to reconcile you with your child but, once it is accepted that the relationship has irretrievably broken down, they will put her up for adoption.'

I begin to cry, softly. She pushes a box of Kleenex towards me and carries on.

'It's considered a more stable environment, and besides, it's simple pragmatism – the authorities have to pay for a foster family, adoption is free. If an adoptive family is found you'll no longer be your daughter's legal parent. While you will have the right to visit her, you must understand that she could be sent anywhere in the country.'

'There must be something else. She's very ill. She needs specialist care. By professionals,' I say.

She shakes her head. 'If you're talking about residential care then I have to tell you that nowadays there are very few homes for children and even fewer for babies in Britain. They're not usually considered in the best interests of the child.'

'Well, how am *I* in her best interests? We couldn't cope with her when we were together and I certainly can't cope with her on my own. Besides, I need to work. I'm a chef. I'm self-employed.'

'It's sadly a situation we see quite often. The father walks out, the mother is left to pick up the pieces. Where is the child right now?'

I pause. 'She's with her father. In France. I can't imagine he wants to keep her, though.'

The lawyer gives me a piercing look. 'But if you don't have custody at present and if she isn't even in this country, I don't think there's anything we can do. You would have to bring her back with you, establish residence here with her, and then we could reconsider your situation.'

I've been assuming that once I got back to England I could solve things. But it's even worse over here.

The lawyer relents. 'Look, this isn't a legal opinion but my guess is that you're exhausted and confused. It's a terrible time to be making long-term decisions about your daughter's future. If you like, I can make a call to a local hospice. Pop over to get an idea of what support they can give you. Then talk to your husband and ask what he wants to do — he may surprise you.'

———

The hospice is only a few blocks away. I walk there, keeping my eyes down on the wet paving slabs as I used to do when I was a small girl. Back then it was because I was afraid of walking on the cracks. Right now I just can't see any point in looking higher.

The nurse who answers the door greets me kindly. Perhaps they're used to tearful parents arriving with incoherent requests.

'We're a centre for children with life-threatening or life-limiting conditions. From what I've heard about Freya, she would qualify if you were living in our catchment area. Look, I know things must be daunting right now. We're here to help. Let me show you around.'

We go into a room that is bright and full of toys. There is only one child there, sitting in a wheelchair. His age is impossible to guess; he's as bald and wizened as an old man of eighty. A nurse is encouraging him to play with finger paint. He looks hesitantly at the open jars of colour. She takes his thin hand and gently dips it in a gaudy blue. He pinches his fingers together and stares at them for a moment. Suddenly he lunges at her, daubing paint on her nose. She catches his eye. They both laugh. His mouth and teeth loom huge in his shrivelled face.

I feel like crying again.

'It's quiet here,' I say.

'Yes, it's term time. We don't have educational facilities so we're not allowed children of school age here during the school term. Unless they're terminal, of course.'

'Do you have a lot of terminal cases?'

'Some. But most are children like Freya – they have very complex needs. They might be tube-fed, for instance, and the tube operated by a pump. Or they might have an oxygen cylinder. They're usually in a wheelchair. And, of course, all of them are on a cocktail of drugs. The first thing we have to do is to learn from the parents how to perform their routines.'

I'm glimpsing Freya's future. 'It's so exhausting,' I say. 'How do their families manage?'

'They all react differently. We can tell, of course, that some of them are desperate to dump their kids and flee. But others can't bear to be separated from their disabled children, even during their holidays. We have rooms where they can stay and we do the heavy work while they just chill out for a change. We're very flexible.'

'Could you take Freya? Permanently?' I haven't meant my question to sound so abrupt.

There's a second's pause. 'I'm not sure I've made it completely clear,' she says. 'We only do respite care. So that families can take a holiday.'

'Isn't there anywhere that could take her full-time?'

'The best full-time environment for these children is within a family,' she says, as if reciting from a manual.

'But I'm a single mother.'

'So are many of our clients. And they usually have more than one child to look after.'

I stare at her helplessly for a moment. She softens and smiles. 'But everybody deserves a break now and again,' she says. 'Freya would be entitled to two weeks' respite care a year.'

———

My last meeting is in Harley Street. I've got no idea how I'll ever be able to afford this but I can't bear to be separated from Freya without a replacement. I need my twins. I have to make them real.

I've tried getting pregnant naturally and it's been a disaster.

I've become convinced that Freya's problems and my miscarriage were caused by a faulty gene that Tobias and I are both carrying.

I tell myself I'm here because I've no chance of getting back with Tobias, but really it's because I don't trust nature. This time, I need everything regulated, under control.

Another Regency building. Another brass plate. I walk up the steps to the imposing front door and am bleeped into a private IVF clinic.

The other patients in the waiting room are all women: professional, well dressed, slightly older than you'd expect a mother to be. Staring down at us from framed collages on the walls are the photographs of thousands of babies conceived at this clinic. We sit together under the eyes of all those babies in the kind of unbreakable silence you get in libraries. I look around for a friendly face. Nobody smiles back.

I expect some kind of implicit moral judgement from the consultant, particularly as I've filled in my relationship status as single and without partner. But IVF, it seems, is more a business transaction than a medical one.

'We can put you on the list for sperm donation,' he says. 'Using a different partner will, of course, virtually eliminate any risk if your daughter's condition was caused by a recessive gene carried by both you and your ex-husband.

'Legally, you'll need to have an HIV and hep C screening test. It's probably a good idea to get a baseline FSH – that will tell us how well you are ovulating. Ovarian reserve permitting, I suggest we start with IUI – intrauterine insemination. We simply inject the sperm into your uterus. It's cheaper and less invasive. If that doesn't work, the next step is full *in vitro* insemination. And, of

352

course, if there's any concern that your egg quality contributed to your miscarriage we can consider egg donation.' He glances at his thin gold watch. 'You can get the blood tests done now. The nurses will give you some forms to fill in. We'll call you in a few days with the results.'

———

I've finally broken down and called Martha. She's got a big deadline but she's going to rush and meet me in Shoreditch, near the architect's practice where she works.

The waitress seats me next to two young girls in designer outfits. The eighties are back again, or maybe it's just a fad among the youth. These girls are barely out of their teens. Maybe they were at school together, like Martha and I were, and now here they are meeting up for the first time in the big city.

This is how it begins: caring how they dress, how they look, full of insecurities and petty embarrassments. Then life knocks them for six a few times and some of their friends peel off – but some of them will make it through together. Until they're battered and bashed and have wrinkles and scars both physical and metaphorical. Until they don't pretend any more. I've got friends I've known for nearly all my thirty-nine years – and if I make it to eighty I suppose I'll have friends I've known for nearly eighty years.

Martha arrives and gives me a hug.

'You look so smart,' I say. 'You've got a fringe. It suits you.'

Along with her new hairstyle, she's wearing a pink woollen dress, black leather boots and a black leather biker jacket. City clothes.

'It's such a fantastic surprise to see you here,' she says. 'Have you come to shop or something? What's going on in your life?'

'You first.'

Martha can sometimes be tactful when the occasion requires. 'Working too hard, as usual,' she says slowly. 'Seen a couple of good films. Still haven't met any prospective life partners. Been on a date or two I thought might be promising, but no luck. Men around here are so . . . well, selfish really. Self-absorbed. There are too many great women in London scrambling around after too few good men. It makes them complacent. The men, I mean. To be honest, now I hear myself, I could do with a more interesting life. Your turn.'

I try to keep my voice on the same casual note as hers.

'Well . . . it's finally become clear to me that we can't keep Freya at home with us. Tobias doesn't seem to agree at present. So I've come here to put her into care. And to have IVF so I can get my twins. Different partner, obviously. Sperm bank.'

Martha gives me one of her penetrating looks. 'When I said I wanted a more interesting life,' she says, 'I didn't mean I want a life as interesting as *yours*.' She pauses for a second. 'Anna, have you gone utterly, stark raving mad?'

'No, not at all. It's all true. Freya's in hospital. Tobias won't leave her. So I've left them both. It's for the best really. I'm sure of it now.'

'Are you kidding? You've left your child?'

'Martha — it had to come sooner or later. I've been hiding my head in the sand for too long. There's no point in pretending things are going to be OK, because they're not. I had a sudden reality check. And thank God I did. It was almost too late as it was.'

'And your husband? Tobias?'

'To be honest, Martha, that relationship has been barely functioning for months.'

'Now I really know you've lost it. If you must know, you and Tobias are probably the reason I haven't met Mr Right. I couldn't settle for anything that was less . . . passionate and fun and caring. Not to mention all the impossible things you two do effortlessly.'

'Oh, it's not effortless. I've finally got permission to start my cookery school but somehow everything seems to get in the way – there's the baby and Tobias and the land and the house falling down and the soft fruit to preserve and the place overrun with rats. Not to mention the weather – hurricane-force winds, or drought, or floods, or sub-zero temperatures, or baking heat. And so many bizarre characters, doing their thing in a way that's quite frankly out of control. And messy. I can't achieve anything. There are too many distractions. Life just gets in the way.'

'You know, Anna,' says Martha, 'I have a pretty good job. A career that keeps me busy all hours. Anyone can work until they die. Life is the bit I *want*.'

———

Since my father's death, I've avoided returning to the house I grew up in. It's exactly the same. The short walk up the garden path. The neatly painted front door, the brass knocker. The umbrella stand and the smell of wax polish in the hall. My mother's fur and my father's woollen coats hanging on their hooks. The living room with its bay window and comfortable armchairs covered in the same Liberty fabric as the curtains. The oak occasional tables. The tasteful blue-and-white vase full of fresh flowers. The framed prints of horses. All these things are as familiar to me as my own face. Every single one of them calls up some childhood memory.

It's only eleven in the morning, but my mother meets me at the door wearing a sleek black dress, full make-up and a pearl necklace. She's had her hair done; I can't help suspecting it's for me.

'You must be starving, dear. Sit down in the living room. We can have an early lunch.'

'I'll come and give you a hand.'

Her fridge is stacked with a ludicrous quantity of food.

'Mother – you shouldn't have. I'm not even sure how long I'll be staying.'

'I so wanted this visit to be a success,' she says with heart-breaking honesty. 'Food-wise, at least.'

We eat in the kitchen. My mother's delicious vegetable soup, smoked salmon with black pepper and slices of lemon, fresh brown bread and salad.

'I thought we might take a little walk,' she says.

We walk for ten minutes up the hill to the windswept corner with a view of rolling Kentish fields.

'I'll tell you what I have to say when we turn back,' says my mother. So, of course, we do turn back.

'I don't want any argument with this,' she says. 'Last November – before my granddaughter was born – I realised that since your father died I'd been compulsively spending money. So I started economising and without making any effort at all I began to save. When Freya was born, I wanted a goal, a reason to economise, so I put the money aside for her. Now I want to open a proper trust fund for her – and I need the parents' permission for that.'

'That's not necessary.'

My mother rounds on me with a ferocity unusual even for her. 'She's not just *yours*, you know, she belongs to all of us – to me, Tobias, your father, Martha, even Kerim and Gustav and that hippy girl who hangs around so much. I don't want you being possessive about her.'

'I'm very touched,' I say, 'but –'

'Touched! Touched? How *dare* you be touched!' shouts my mother. 'We're a family!'

—

The house of my childhood isn't as intact as I first thought. I'm beginning to notice that, although outwardly spotless, under the surface it's a mess. The knives and forks are stuffed anyhow into the kitchen drawers; the linen cupboard is overflowing. I open a cupboard and discover that my spick and span mother is hoarding old newspapers.

'Why do you need them?' I ask.

She looks petulant. 'I just do.'

The chest of drawers in my bedroom is full of moths, crawling blindly around among my teenage clothes like maggots. Eating the gussets of my woollen tights.

I scoop the whole lot up, launder what I can save and put everything into sealed plastic bags. Over the next days, I move on to the other cupboards in the house.

In the bottom of my mother's wardrobe I find a portfolio full of her old paintings from school.

'Mum – these are beautiful,' I say.

'It was my application for art college,' she says. 'The Slade School. I got a place there, you know.'

357

'Why didn't you ever tell me? What happened?'

'I was expected to settle down respectably, get married and have children. My parents thought domestic science was far more appropriate. And of course I'd met your father by then.'

'Why didn't you ever paint after that? Just for your own pleasure, I mean.'

'I suppose it was fear, dear. Once you've put something down on paper you're categorisable. Until then, you just might be an undiscovered genius. I spent years thinking: one day I'll show the world I'm a great artist, and then one day I was old and realised that I never would be.'

She puts the pictures carefully back into the portfolio. 'You know, I'm so proud of you for having a career. I'm a good cook, but you – you're a professional. In a way, you're the artist I never was.'

So I cook for her.

I spread the kitchen table with a white linen cloth and use her best crockery and cutlery. She protests, but faintly. She likes it really.

I make filet mignon with black pepper sauce, my father's favourite. Despite her objections, I open a very good bottle of burgundy.

'When I first became a mother,' she says, 'I was afraid I wouldn't be able to cope. Your father hired one of those maternity nurses. She was a complete nightmare – always whipping the baby away from me. Said it should be put on a schedule. Didn't approve of the breast. Oh, the hours I spent in tears because the baby was crying for hunger in the next room and I wasn't allowed to go to her. Finally I couldn't bear it – I crept in. Sister Poe was snoring away, fast asleep. I sneaked the baby back to my bed. I put it to my breast and it sucked and sucked. That's when I fell in love with you. Your eyes were so lovely – like pools, so deep you could plunge into them. Just like Freya's. I'd never felt such a love in my life. I never will. I got up the courage to fire the nurse the next day.'

We clink glasses. 'You were my only one,' she says. 'I knew every single thing about you. That's why I wanted you to know how wonderful it is to be a mother.'

'Oh, Mum,' I say, 'it's not wonderful. I'm not a good mother and trying to be is ruining my life. I'm fed up and angry and . . . resentful. Everybody else seems to have come to terms with what's happened to Freya except me. Even Tobias. But I can't. I see little girls with their mothers on the street and I just feel a . . . longing that I can't describe. I've had somebody taken away from me who I don't even know. It's worse than bereavement – I haven't even got any memories. She's not what she ought to be and she never will be. And it's not going to get better – I can tell it's not. Because I'm joined to her. I'm going to suffer everything she suffers. She'll never let me go. But she's incomplete.'

My mother is holding me, as tightly as she used to when I was a child. And I'm crying in the same uncontrollable gulps. I fight for words.

'Babies are supposed to be little . . . capsules . . . of hopes and dreams. You look at them and wonder . . . you sort of overlay . . . their first day at school, at college, their wedding. They keep you up all night and it's OK because you think, perhaps they'll be better at life than me. You look at that little screaming face and you see . . . a future prime minister, or just a happy human being. They make the sleep-deprivation, the anxiety, the backache and the heartache bearable; because they're the hope, they're the future. Freya's very sweet, but

359

she's just the present. She's not going anywhere – except possibly backwards. I don't think I'm a real mother. I don't even think I love her.'

'Now look, you ridiculous child. Don't worry about *that*.' My mother's hold on me is like a vice. 'Your love for that baby shines through everything you say, everything you do. I'm so proud of you for what you've done with her. You get out of babies what you put in, you know. That's what being a mother is – not getting things right all the time, not being a bloody saint.'

She pushes me back, arms extended, holding on to my shoulders, taking me in. 'I don't think I did too badly on that score either, you know.'

In grainy super 8, I slip back into a childhood memory. I'm sitting at this kitchen table. My mother is a young and pretty version of herself, standing at the cooker over a frying pan.

'Oh no, not fish cakes . . .' I'm whining. 'I don't like them.'

'All right then. You can get your money back at the door.'

I'm puzzled. 'But . . . I haven't *paid* anything!'

My mother does a triumphant double flip with her spatula. '*That*, my darling, is exactly my point. Now take what you're given and shut up.'

Where did my mother and I go so wrong? What did she ever do to me to make me resent her so? She loved me claustrophobically. She occasionally yelled. She did her best. Nothing compared to what I'm contemplating: giving up my child. If there are booby prizes for the worst mother in history, I have to be a candidate. Here I am with the daughter I've always wanted and I want my money back at the door.

Tobias can't even boil an egg on his own. And what about my little Freya, alone in hospital? God knows how bad her condition is by now.

'I have to go back,' I say.

———

I'm at the airport, waiting for my plane back to Montpellier. I've avoided the burger bar and am having a coffee in a concession that's part of a trendy chain. It has world music posters on the walls and tables made of retro moulded plastic.

All around me are the same kind of well-dressed professional women I saw the other day in the IVF clinic, except these ones are spooning home-made purée into infants, or trying to stop their three-year-olds from running wildly around the place. But for the way Freya turned out, this would have been me.

Even at this early hour, these women are wearing designer clothes and eyeshadow. They're still worried by what people think of them. They've never been knocked down to their foundations or challenged to their core until they're forced to understand what their core is made of.

I sit staring at the women sipping their cappuccinos and chatting about trivialities as they wait for their holiday flights. Their lives seem superficial and dull; their normal, healthy babies grotesque and lumbering.

My life and my child are both extraordinary.

My mobile phone rings. It's the IVF clinic. 'Your results are through,' says a nurse. 'You can come in tomorrow to discuss how to proceed with treatment.'

'That's all right thank you,' I say. 'I don't need a baby after all. I find I've already got one.'

—

The lobby of Montpellier General Hospital. A Pavlovian feeling of foreboding, like the first day at school. I know very well the way to the children's ward. You turn right here and go up in the lift. But what state will Freya be in? Unconscious, perhaps. No sound but the sucking of the ventilator keeping her alive. And Tobias, angry and still blaming me.

At the last moment, I realise that I'm going to bottle out again. I hate myself for it.

I turn round and walk out of the hospital.

I can't bear to face whatever there is to be faced. But I can't bring myself to leave either.

For a while I wander around the manicured gardens, across coarse, drought-resistant grass, past borders of over-bright succulent flowers.

Somehow I've arrived at the entrance of Lizzy's psychiatric unit. During my last stay here I managed to visit her a couple of times. She seemed to be doing a bit better; she mentioned wanting to visit Freya.

I walk up the three low steps to the door of the unit and through its Arctic corridors. Knocking timidly, I hear Lizzy's familiar voice say: 'Come on in.'

As I enter, a small woman, her dark hair streaked with grey, passes me on her way out. Lizzy's sitting in a chair by the window. We hug for a long time. She's pale but otherwise she seems more robust. I sit down opposite her and hold her hand.

'Lizzy – you're so much better,' I say.

She smiles at me, shyly. 'I've got important things to say to you,' she says. 'First of all, I know what I did was stupid. At least, everybody keeps telling me so.'

'Is that what you really think?' I ask.

'I think . . . it feels as if what happened to me was *for* something. As soon as I accepted that, funny things began to happen around me.'

Despite my worries, it makes me smile to see the old Lizzy flickering back to life again.

'It's no joke, Anna,' she says earnestly. 'I was finally allowed to visit Freya and while I was there she took a bottle – she began to suck. It was a kind of miracle.'

'Freya – she doesn't need tube-feeding after all?'

'No, no, that's what I was telling you. That was one miracle.'

'Lizzy – are you sure? It's very important to me.'

'Of course, that's the *small* miracle. But the *big* miracle is that I've been in touch with my mom.'

'You have?' The radiance in her face gives me confidence to add: 'I thought you didn't have a mother.'

'Oh, Anna, *everybody* has a mother. I thought mine hated me. But somehow I was finally able to get on the phone to her. She's got her life together much better now.'

Right on cue, the door swings open and the dark-haired woman returns with two cups of herbal tea.

'Hi there,' she says with a bright smile revealing perfect Californian teeth. 'I'm Barbie. You must be Anna. Lizzy has told me all about you.'

'My mom came straight out to France,' says Lizzy ecstatically. 'All the way. On a plane. For me.'

I look from Lizzy's pale, radiant face to Barbie's too-perfect teeth, and I'm filled with foreboding. Lizzy is so terribly fragile. Another desertion could be the end of her.

'I'm sticking around this time,' says Barbie, addressing me, as if she's read the doubt in my face. 'I thought I'd screwed up. I thought I'd lost my daughter forever. No way am I letting that happen again.'

For a moment, her round, impassioned eyes gaze straight into mine. Then the perfect smile returns and the mask is back. 'When we get out of here,' she says brightly, 'we're going to connect with a 13/28 natural time community.'

'Natural time?' I ask.

Lizzy gives a little laugh. 'Oh, Anna. Time isn't linear. It's fractal and multidimensional. Our calendar is completely unnatural.'

Barbie nods. 'In all spiritual systems twelve is the number of perfection, of completion – and thirteen is the Fibonacci sequence, it takes you to a new dimension. Besides, most intentional communities make you pay to become a member but these people let you in for free.'

'I have to go,' I say. 'I just popped by on my way up to the paediatric neurology ward to see Freya. Is, er, Tobias with her today?'

Lizzy and her mother are staring at me.

Finally Lizzy says: 'That's what I was telling you. It's a miracle. Tobias has left. Freya has been discharged.'

———

I suspected Tobias of having an affair, but it's I who betrayed him.

364

I blamed him for not committing to Freya, but it's I who walked out.

It feels as if we've been apart for months and years, instead of a week. I'm nervous to see him again, a butterfly-flutter in my stomach, like a first date.

I take the bus from Montpellier. I don't phone ahead in case he tells me not to come.

He's sitting in the living room next to the range. Freya is asleep on his chest, an empty baby bottle beside them. He looks more serious than I remember him. He still has the smile lines around his eyes, but there are other lines too now, lines of sadness, of worry. He's tired, of course, but it's more than that. Something has shifted in his face. He's taken responsibility.

'Hello there.'

He smiles to see me, and for an instant the old carefree Tobias is back. 'So you came back after all.'

'I've been to visit Lizzy in the hospital. I thought I'd drop by and see how you're doing.'

His face closes again. 'Oh, you know me – as you can see I've been sitting sunning myself on the rocks with the lizards.'

There we teeter, for an instant, on the edge of another row, another misunderstanding. And this, I realise, is our very last chance. Right here and now our love is going to tip off the precipice and shatter into irreparable fragments, unless I can dive and save it. And at the same moment, I know that my love – for Tobias and for my daughter – is the most precious thing I have. Beyond pride, beyond happiness, beyond hopes and fears. It can't be compared to anything else in my life. It transcends everything.

I dive. My words rush out:

'That's not why I came. I couldn't stay away. My family is here. I was . . . wrong . . . to go away. I'm sorry. I was confused . . .'

Once I've started, it's easier.

'I missed you. I missed you – both – so much. It was like being dead and numb and not able to feel anything at all. I mean . . . I *thought* I was numb for a long time here before I went, but when I'd actually parted from you both, it was as if the sun had gone out – as if it had been shining invisibly on me all the time – and that now I'd turned my back on it and shut it out once and for all. I couldn't bear it. I don't want another baby. I just want her and you.'

Very carefully, because he's holding Freya, Tobias stands up and comes towards me. Without putting Freya down, he enfolds me in an awkward, one-handed embrace. I put one arm around him and the other around her. The three of us stay like that for what seems a long time, until I feel our breaths synchronise.

'You don't have to apologise,' he whispers. 'We both behaved pretty abominably. We stopped talking to each other. We were both in separate bubbles of misery, thinking of ourselves.'

'I was worse. I ran out on my own daughter. All the time I thought I held the moral high ground, and I blamed you for not pulling your weight – and yet it was I who failed in the end.'

Tobias says: 'You didn't fail. You kept us going for weeks and months and I did nothing to support you. So no wonder you got exhausted.'

Gently, he detaches from me and puts Freya in my arms. I hold her so tightly that her face goes all red and gets pressure marks from my shoulder. She snuggles into my body and I can hear her snuffling against me. When I crane my head round I have an out-of-focus image of her ear and her little mouth, half open.

'She feels like the only real thing in the world.'

'In the beginning I was scared to love her in case I got hurt,' says Tobias. 'But the funny thing is that not loving her was worse. Now I love her so much, it's almost impossible to bear – because I know she'll break our hearts one day. But at least it makes me feel connected to life. It feels as if we're in the midst of things. This isn't easy, but it is the real deal.'

'I love you,' I say. 'I'm so lucky to have you both. I nearly lost you. Now I'm going to hang on to you.'

'Guess what,' he says. '*Madame Bovary* finally got funded. Sally's execs reckon my music helped swing it so I'm the golden boy. I'm going to wait for a fine cut before I even think of carrying on with the score. But it should all go relatively fast now – I ought to be able to go to London next month to start recording and then I'll be paid.'

He grins. The old Tobias is still here; he hasn't disappeared under all his worries.

'I bet you haven't bothered to cook a thing while I've been away,' I say. 'In fact, I'm going to make you a meal right now.'

'Ah,' says Tobias. 'Actually, Anna, could you just not . . .'

It's too late. I've already gone into the kitchen. Quickly enough to catch a glimpse of three or four familiar dark shapes dashing across the room.

'God, I'm sorry, Anna, I've only been back for a minute . . . well, for a couple of days anyway. I didn't have time to clean up.'

The smashed jars are still where I threw them. My kitchen is a desolate wasteland of broken glass, baking beans, cornflour, squid-ink pasta, Manuka honey.

The rats have had days to trample through the wreckage,

to shit everywhere, to build nests from torn-up cardboard. One rat has taken possession of a jar of Nutella. Instead of running away with the rest, he pulls himself up onto his back legs and bares his fangs at me. I freeze, unable to move or speak.

Tobias begins to gabble. 'Anna – I know I should have cleaned up. I'm really truly sorry – and you won't believe this but I actually coped really well with Freya on my own. She got all her bottles on time. And her medicine. I didn't mess up. I just didn't quite get round to tidying . . . but we can rebuild it. I'll get hold of some more glass jars and we'll redo the whole thing. Your system works. They can't get through the glass. Please don't go away again.'

The rat guarding the Nutella raises his nose into the air and begins to squeak in a series of shrill angry sounds.

My eyes fill with tears again. I double up, helpless with laughter.

'It's all right,' I say. 'I surrender. Just think of names for them all and we'll keep them as pets.'

Tobias starts laughing too. I suspect from sheer relief. 'Hey,' he gasps, 'if we don't manage to have any more kids, let's have a menagerie instead.'

We begin to move through the kitchen, clearing up the debris.

'You know, Anna, you're completely mad but you have worked some kind of magic,' he says. 'Not letting us give up and die. Bringing us out here. Making our life so complicated, so – well, I suppose you could call it rich.'

'It's not me,' I say, 'it's this place. I noticed it when I went back to London. People there are more . . . homogenous. Everybody over here's an individual. There's more room for oddness of one sort or other. A disabled baby just slips into the background.'

As I lob pieces of broken glass into a cardboard box that Tobias is holding out for me, I think: we've had our ups and downs but we bring out the best in each other; we're a hell of a good team.

Maybe we'll be able to cope with Freya, maybe we won't – but here we are on the road, and it's better just to cling more tightly to Tobias's hand and not look ahead.

Notes and Acknowledgements

THE WRITING OF THIS book took place at a time of almost no sleep. It gradually grew into a parallel world where I escaped to subvert a real-life existence that sometimes seemed unbearable.

None of the characters on these pages bears the least similarity to anyone living or dead. However, as a – very – few of the elements in this book are based on personal experience, perhaps it is useful to state which these are.

The medical symptoms and prognoses at the beginning of the book and throughout are those of my daughter, Ailsa. She has been hospitalised on various occasions, both in the UK and in France, including as an emergency – albeit never so dramatically as Freya. Needless to say, my partner's and my actions have never in the least resembled those of Anna and Tobias, who very soon confounded me by taking on a life of their own and behaving in the most outrageous ways imaginable.

The Natural Regional Park of the High Languedoc in France does exist, and we are lucky enough to spend a good deal of time there. I have tried to be true to the spirit of this wonderful area, but Les Rajons, the hamlet of Rieu and the river and village of Aigues are all fictional, as is Montpellier General Hospital.

In return for the liberties nature has taken with us in real life, I have taken an occasional one of my own – sometimes allowing plants to fruit and flower a little earlier or later than the norm. My rule has been to ensure that nothing is utterly *impossible*, although keen students of Mediterranean horticulture may entertain themselves with discussions of the 'in a year when mountain violets are still around at the end of April, would the first figs really be ripe in June?' variety. To these experts: please remember that the narrative takes place about thirty miles inland, at altitudes between about two hundred and a thousand metres – and be kind!

After all these disclaimers, explanations and excuses, on to thanks.

Many generous friends have bent over backwards to make space – both literal and metaphorical – for my writing. I owe a huge debt of thanks to Alex MacGillivray, Lilli Matson, Megan and Alba for loaning me their lovely house – and for not minding that I frequently dozed off in their living room instead of working. I must also offer heartfelt thanks to Bernie Kramer for turning up one day and quietly building me a beautiful writing cabin.

Kri Centofanti tirelessly kept French bureaucracy at bay and every now and then took us in hand: spring-cleaning our house, weeding our garden and cooking us a square meal. My sister Safia, my brother Tahir and numerous friends, who know who they are, offered love and practical support in person, by email and down the telephone.

Frederique Beaufumé not only became an oasis of loving calm for Ailsa but also corrected the French in my manuscript – pointing out errors in my English grammar into the bargain.

Charlie Mole cast a critical eye over my wild imaginings of the life of a freelance composer and his insights have, hopefully, helped make Tobias's work and earning capacity a little more plausible. My musical friends Mathew Priest and Dan Edge also assisted in this.

My wonderful agent Patrick Walsh and his team deserve particular thanks for their dedication, enthusiasm and hard work – not to mention their thoroughly entertaining parties.

Special thanks are due to the legendary Rebecca Carter, formerly at Harvill Secker, now at Janklow and Nesbit, for believing in me, for acquiring a first draft and for brilliant editorial comments that at times resembled a 101 in novel writing.

Thanks too to Liz Foley, Michal Shavit and everybody else at Harvill Secker for publishing this work in the UK, and to Emily Bestler at Atria for doing the same in the US. Their editorial input has helped make it what it is.

All errors, inconsistencies and idiocies are, of course, my own.

I hope that the dedication in the front of this book makes clear my three biggest debts.

The first is to my mother, by force of whose indomitable will I've been more or less required to survive various trials that life has presented. She bears no resemblance to any of the mothers in this book, but I confess to having occasionally purloined her bon mots.

The second is to my partner, Scott, who uncomplainingly cooked delicious meals and performed heroic acts of childcare to give me space to write about a woman who spends her time cooking and drudging for her husband and child. His support, love and encouragement have never wavered.

The third and greatest debt is, of course, to our beautiful daughter, Ailsa, who is a source of such joy to us. She has taught me everything I know about what it means to be a mother.